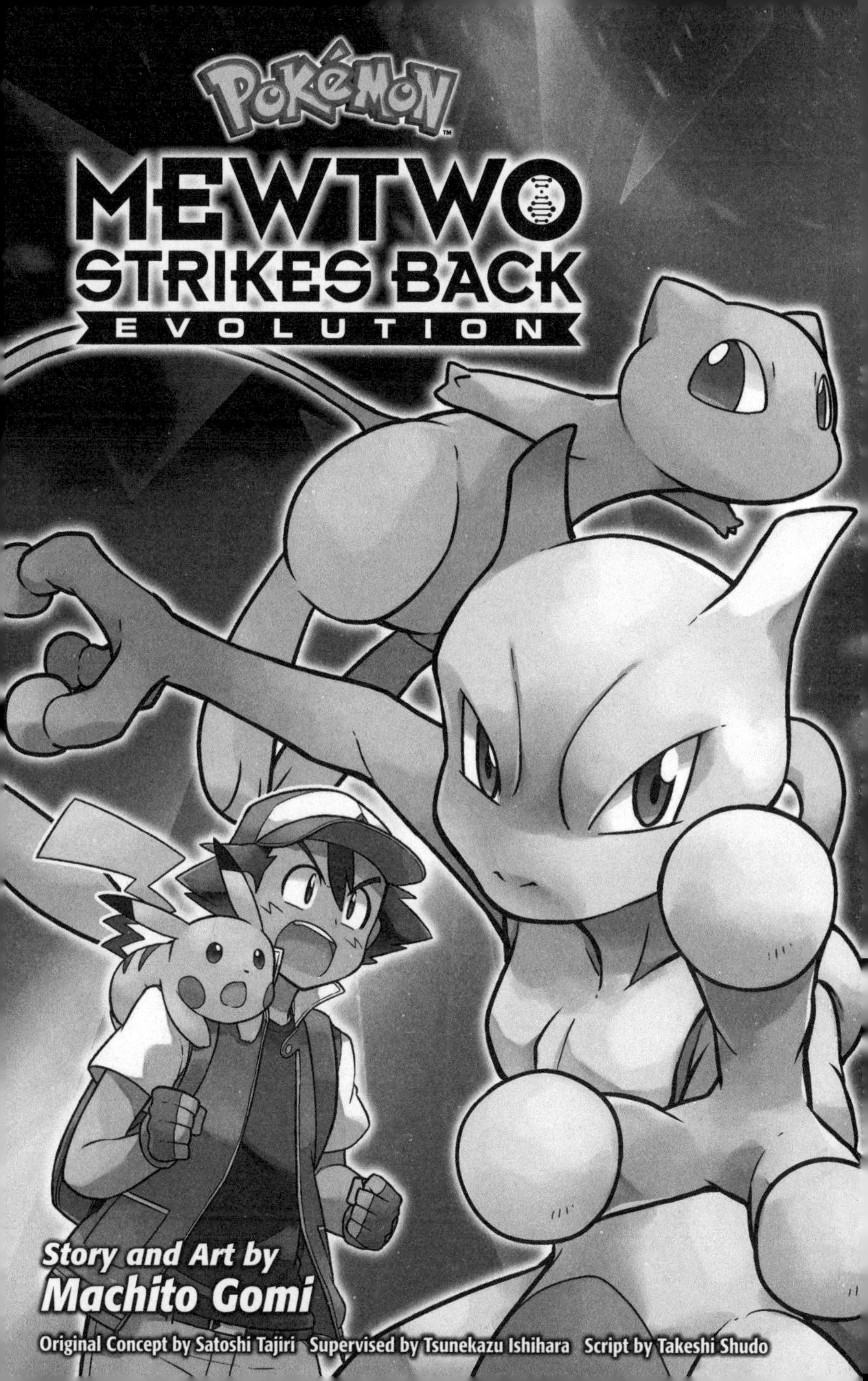

POKéMON

MEWTWO STRIKES BACK
EVOLUTION

Story and Art by
Machito Gomi

Original Concept by Satoshi Tajiri Supervised by Tsunekazu Ishihara Script by Takeshi Shudo

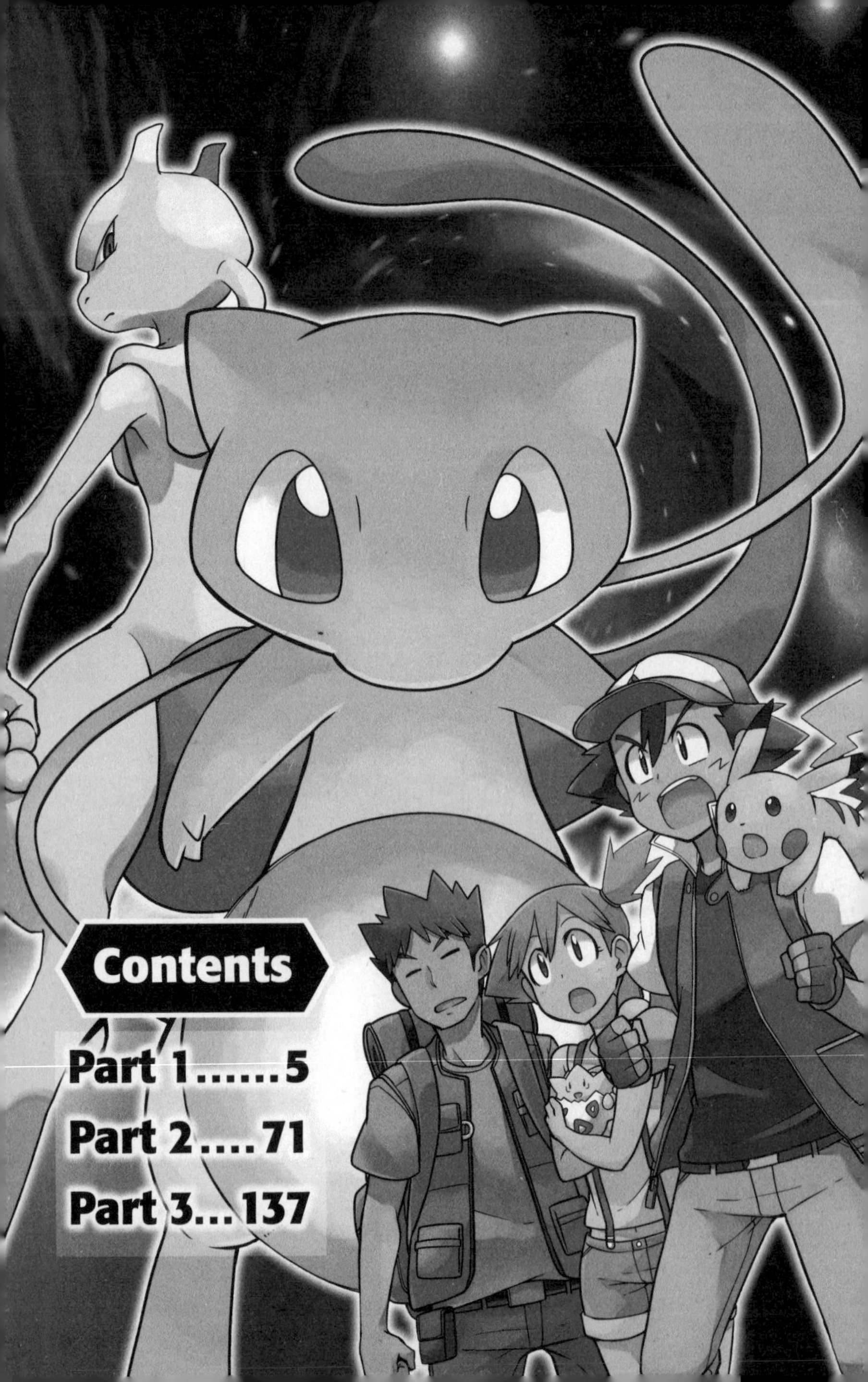

Contents

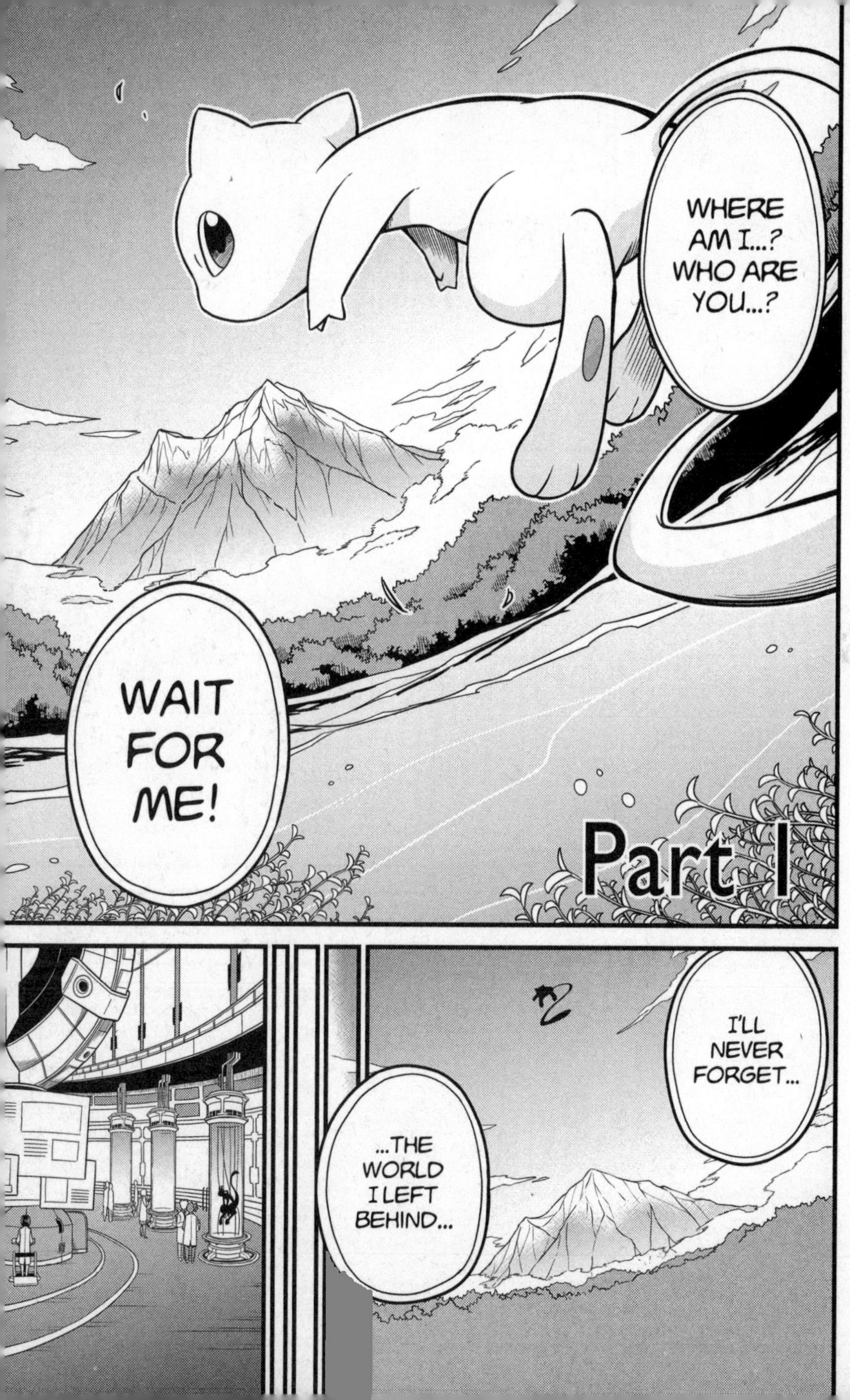
WHERE AM I...? WHO ARE YOU...?
WAIT FOR ME!
Part I
I'LL NEVER FORGET...
...THE WORLD I LEFT BEHIND...

IT'S READY TO COME TO LIFE!

FINISHED!

GLUB GLUB

GLUB

GLUB

THE WORLD'S STRONGEST...

...POKÉMON!

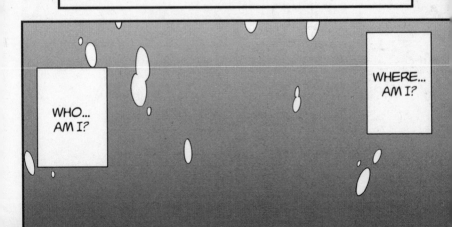

WHO... AM I?

WHERE... AM I?

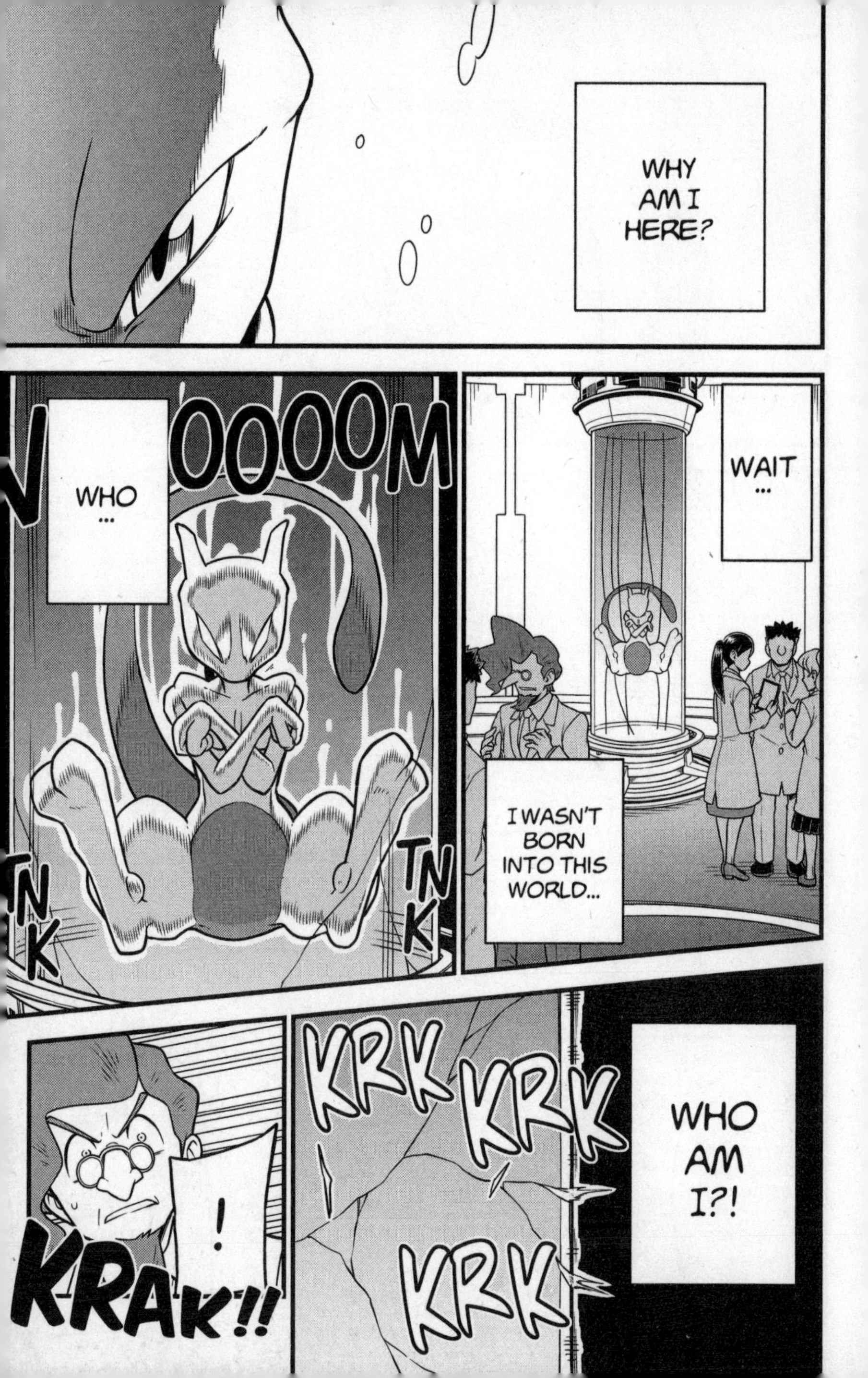
WHY AM I HERE?
WAIT ...
I WASN'T BORN INTO THIS WORLD...
WHO ...
OOOOOM
TNK
TNK
WHO AM I?!
KRK
KRK
KRK
!
KRAK!!

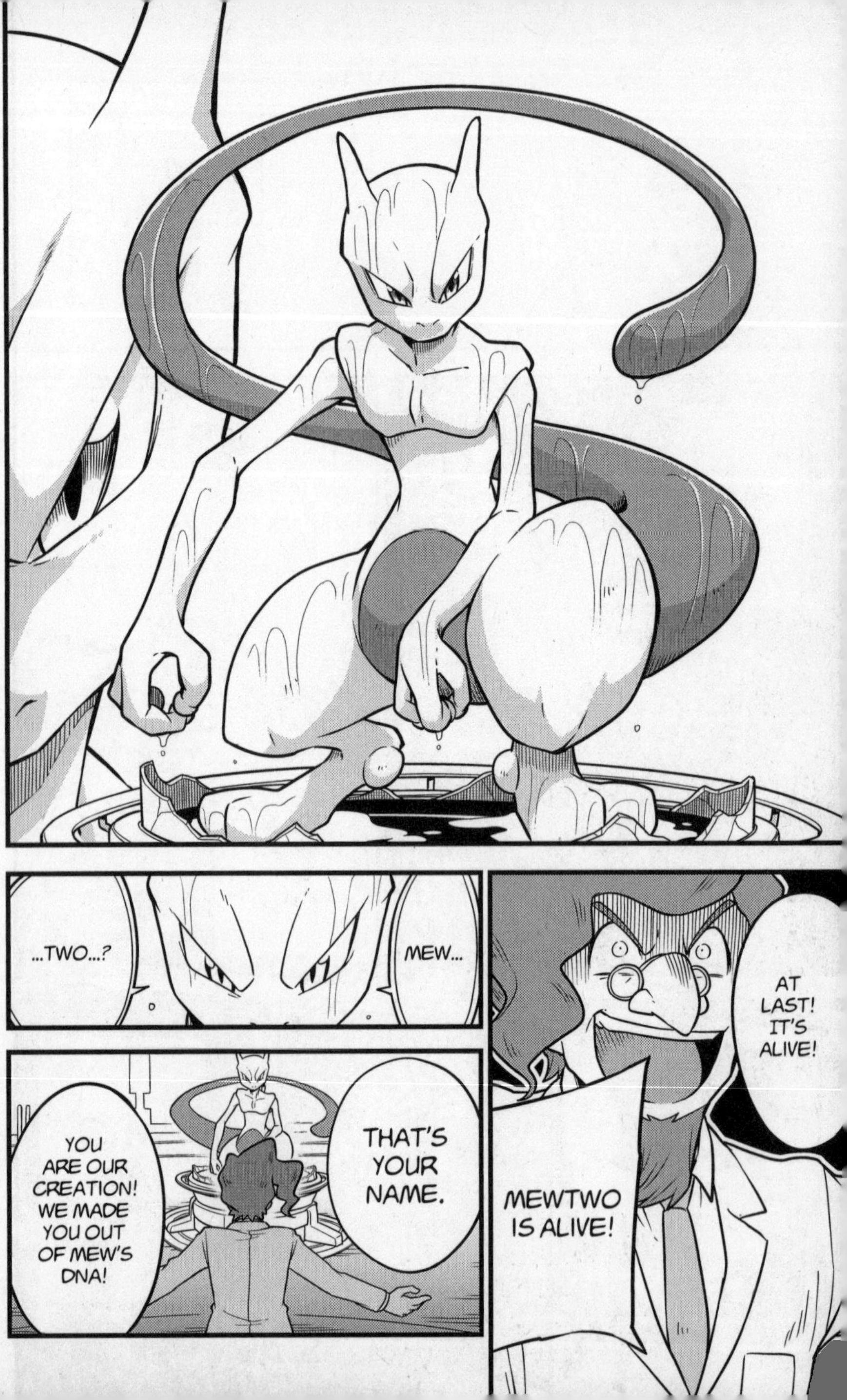
AT LAST! IT'S ALIVE!
MEWTWO IS ALIVE!
MEW...
...TWO...?
THAT'S YOUR NAME.
YOU ARE OUR CREATION! WE MADE YOU OUT OF MEW'S DNA!

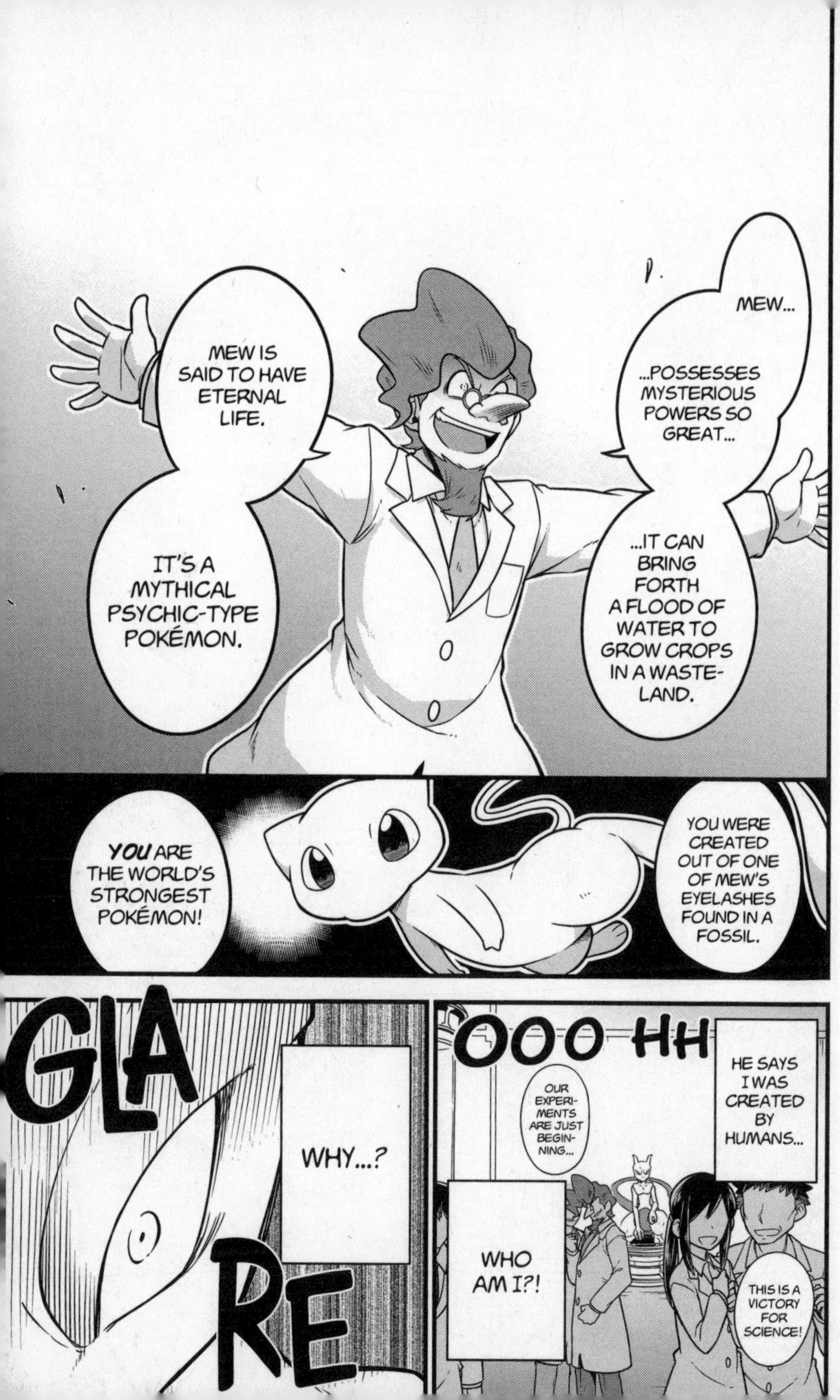
MEW...
...POSSESSES MYSTERIOUS POWERS SO GREAT...
...IT CAN BRING FORTH A FLOOD OF WATER TO GROW CROPS IN A WASTE-LAND.
MEW IS SAID TO HAVE ETERNAL LIFE.
IT'S A MYTHICAL PSYCHIC-TYPE POKÉMON.
YOU WERE CREATED OUT OF ONE OF MEW'S EYELASHES FOUND IN A FOSSIL.
YOU ARE THE WORLD'S STRONGEST POKÉMON!
OOOHH
HE SAYS I WAS CREATED BY HUMANS...
OUR EXPERI-MENTS ARE JUST BEGIN-NING...
THIS IS A VICTORY FOR SCIENCE!
WHO AM I?!
GLARE
WHY...?

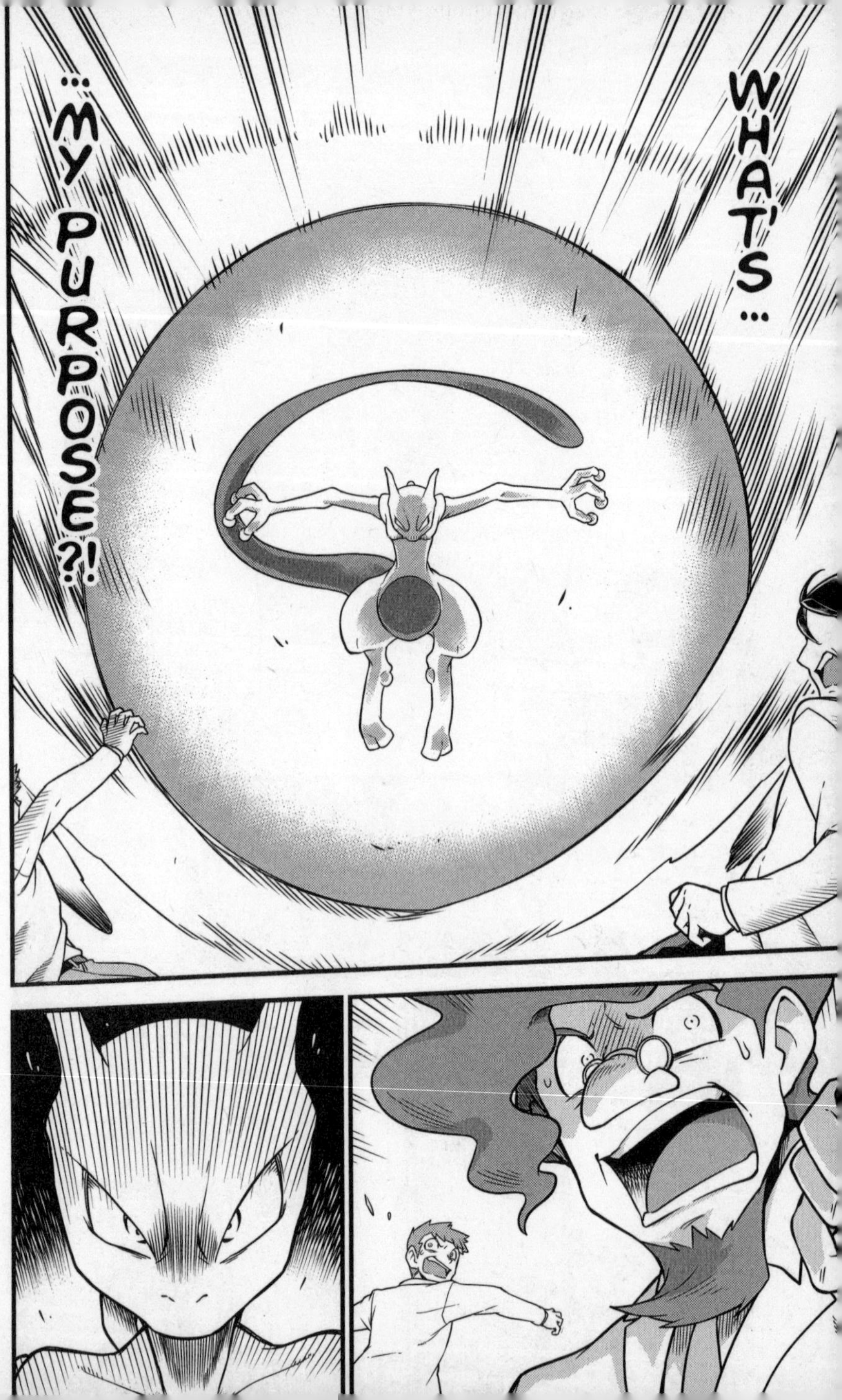
WHAT'S...
...MY PURPOSE?!

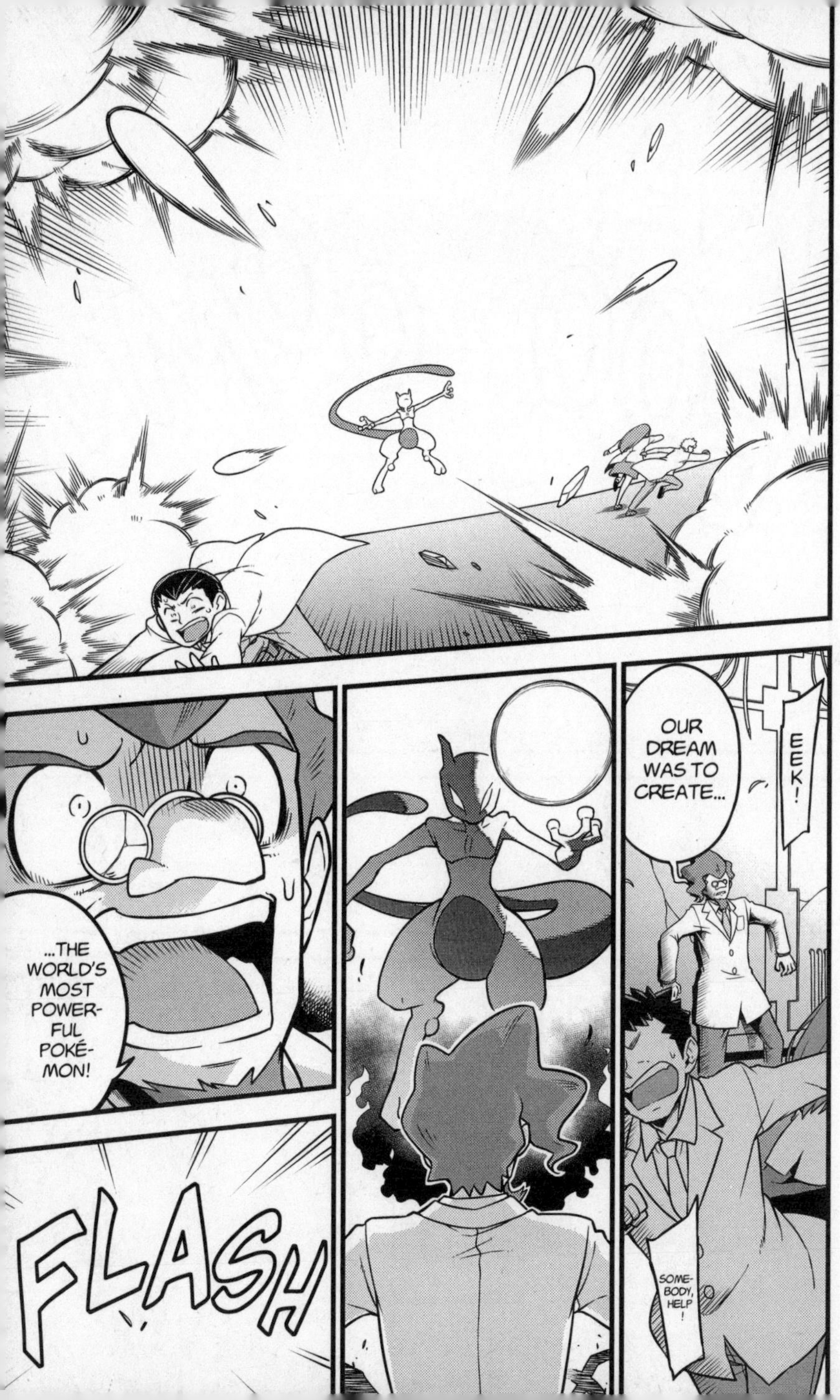

EEK!
OUR DREAM WAS TO CREATE...
SOMEBODY, HELP!
...THE WORLD'S MOST POWERFUL POKÉMON!
FLASH

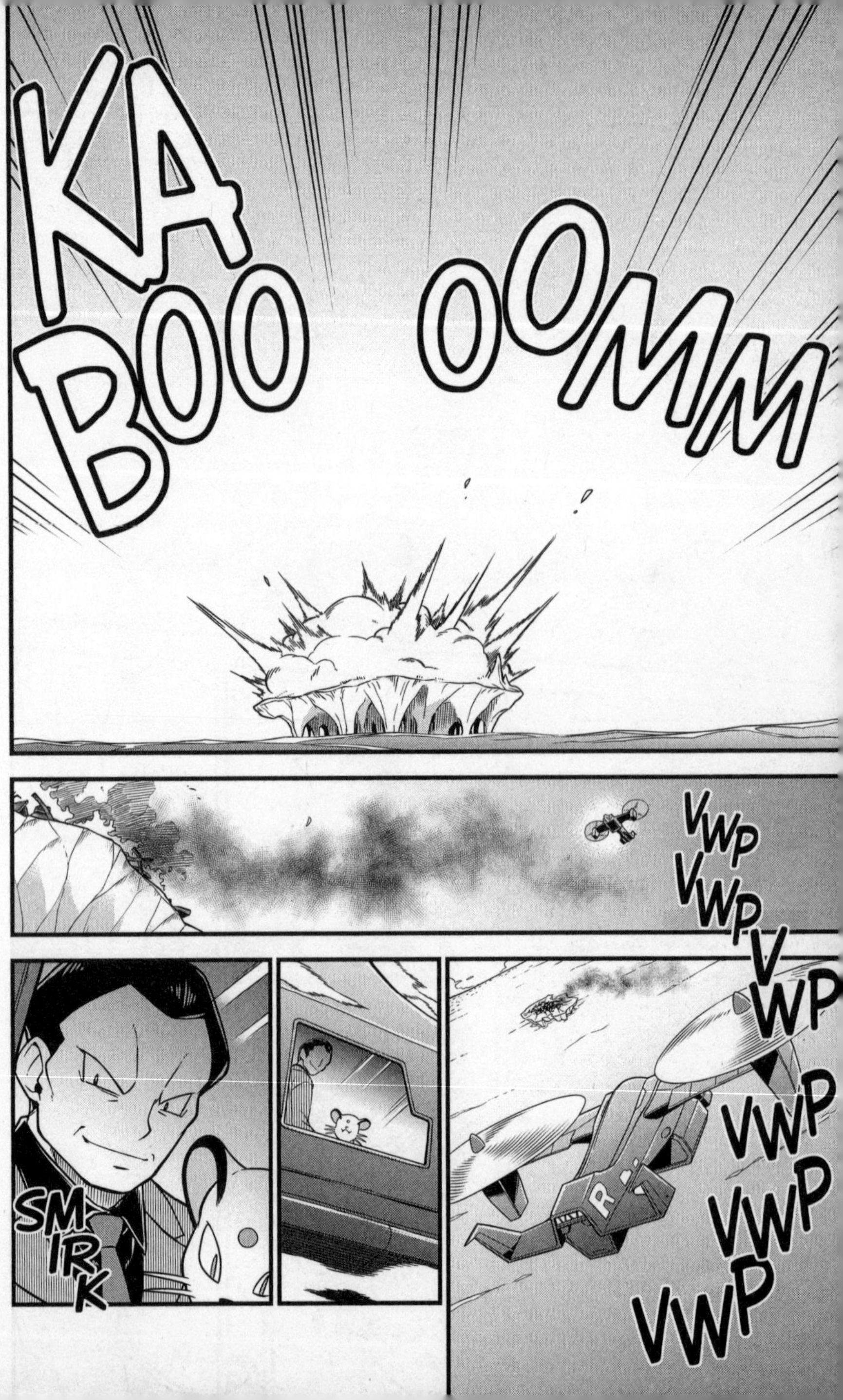
KA BOO OOMM
VWP VWP
VWP
VWP VWP VWP
SMIRK

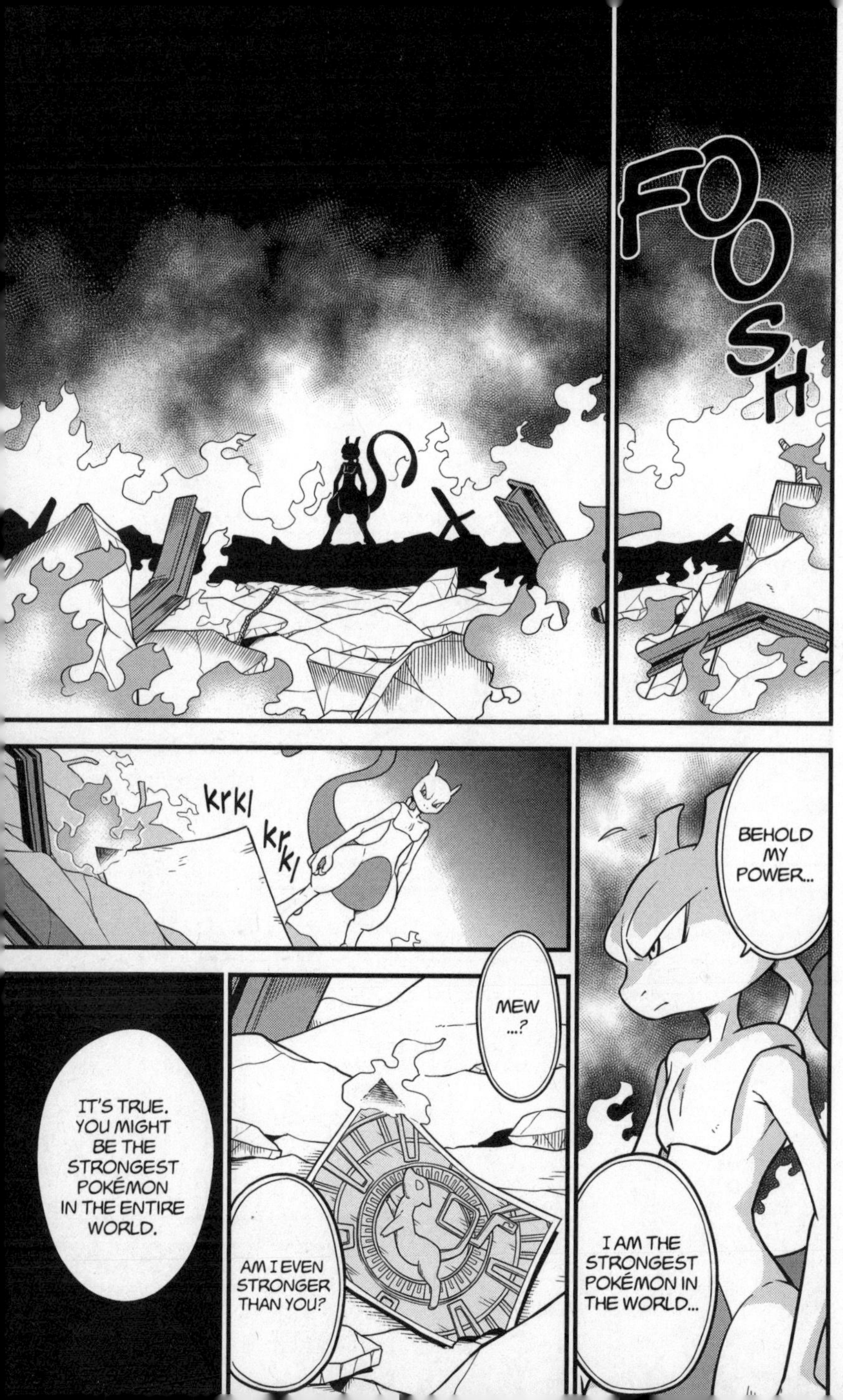
FOOSH
BEHOLD MY POWER...
I AM THE STRONGEST POKÉMON IN THE WORLD...
krkl
krkl
MEW ...?
AM I EVEN STRONGER THAN YOU?
IT'S TRUE. YOU MIGHT BE THE STRONGEST POKÉMON IN THE ENTIRE WORLD.

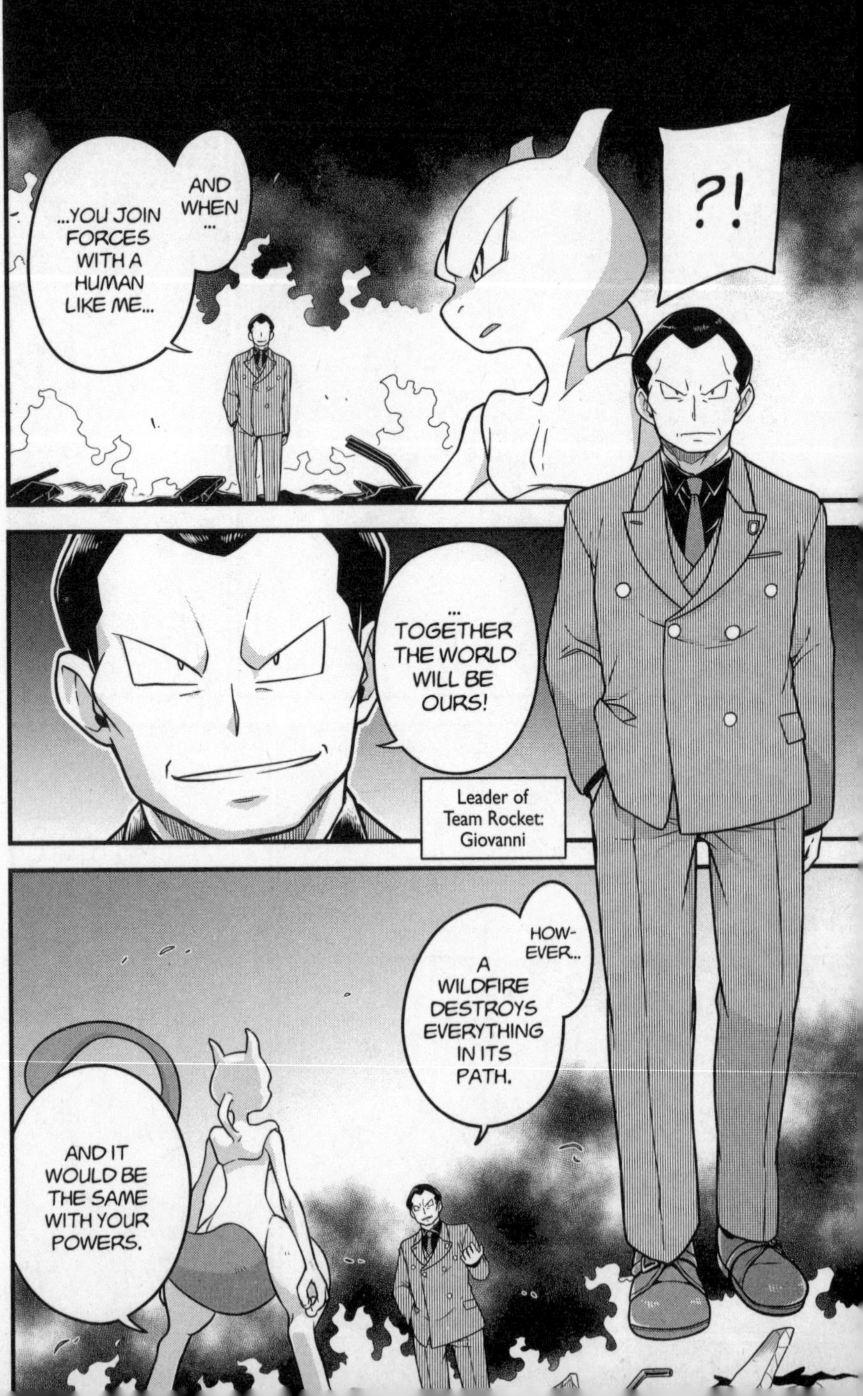
?!
AND WHEN ...
...YOU JOIN FORCES WITH A HUMAN LIKE ME...
... TOGETHER THE WORLD WILL BE OURS!
Leader of Team Rocket: Giovanni
HOW-EVER..
A WILDFIRE DESTROYS EVERYTHING IN ITS PATH.
AND IT WOULD BE THE SAME WITH YOUR POWERS.

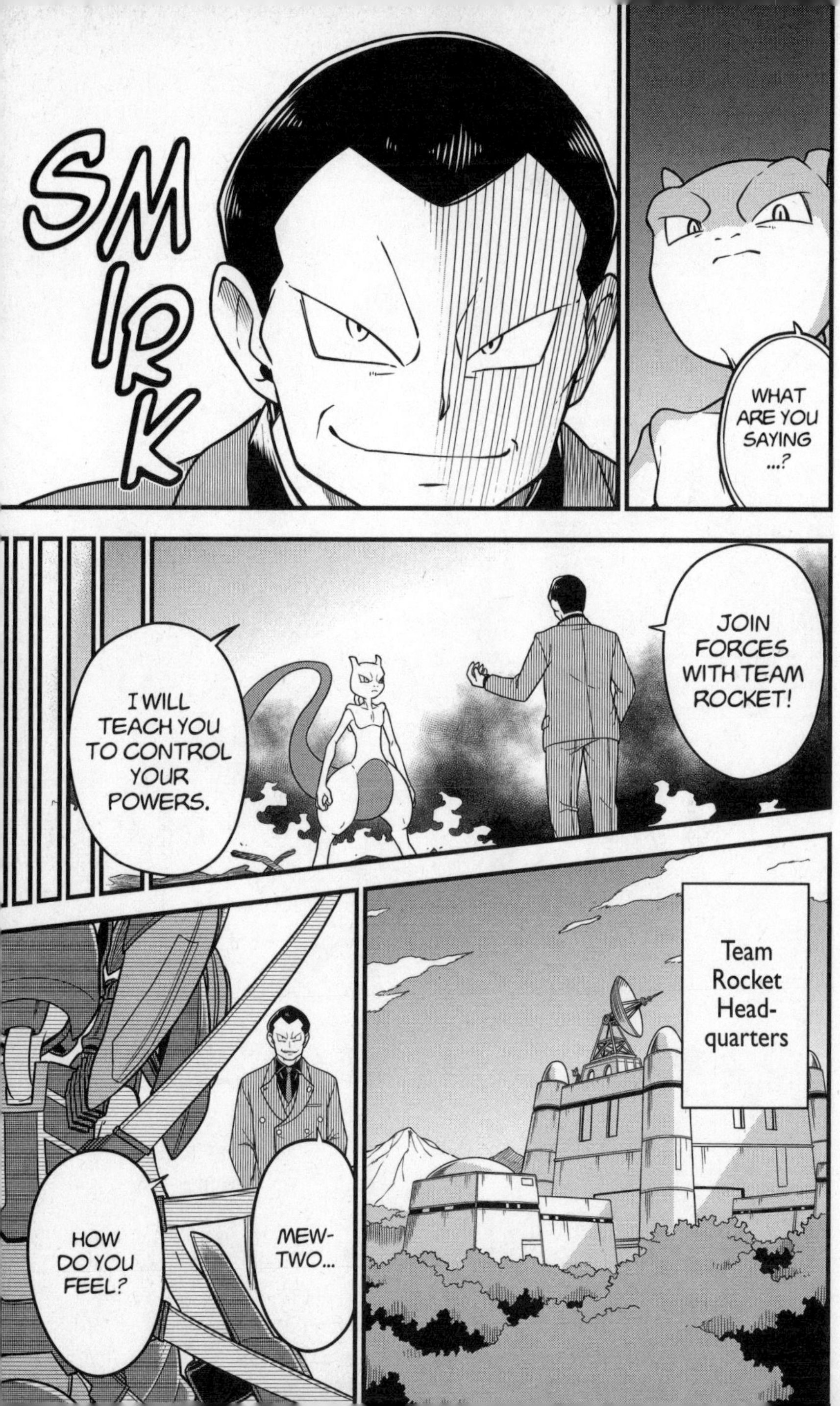
WHAT ARE YOU SAYING ...?
SMIRK
JOIN FORCES WITH TEAM ROCKET!
I WILL TEACH YOU TO CONTROL YOUR POWERS.
Team Rocket Head-quarters
MEW-TWO...
HOW DO YOU FEEL?

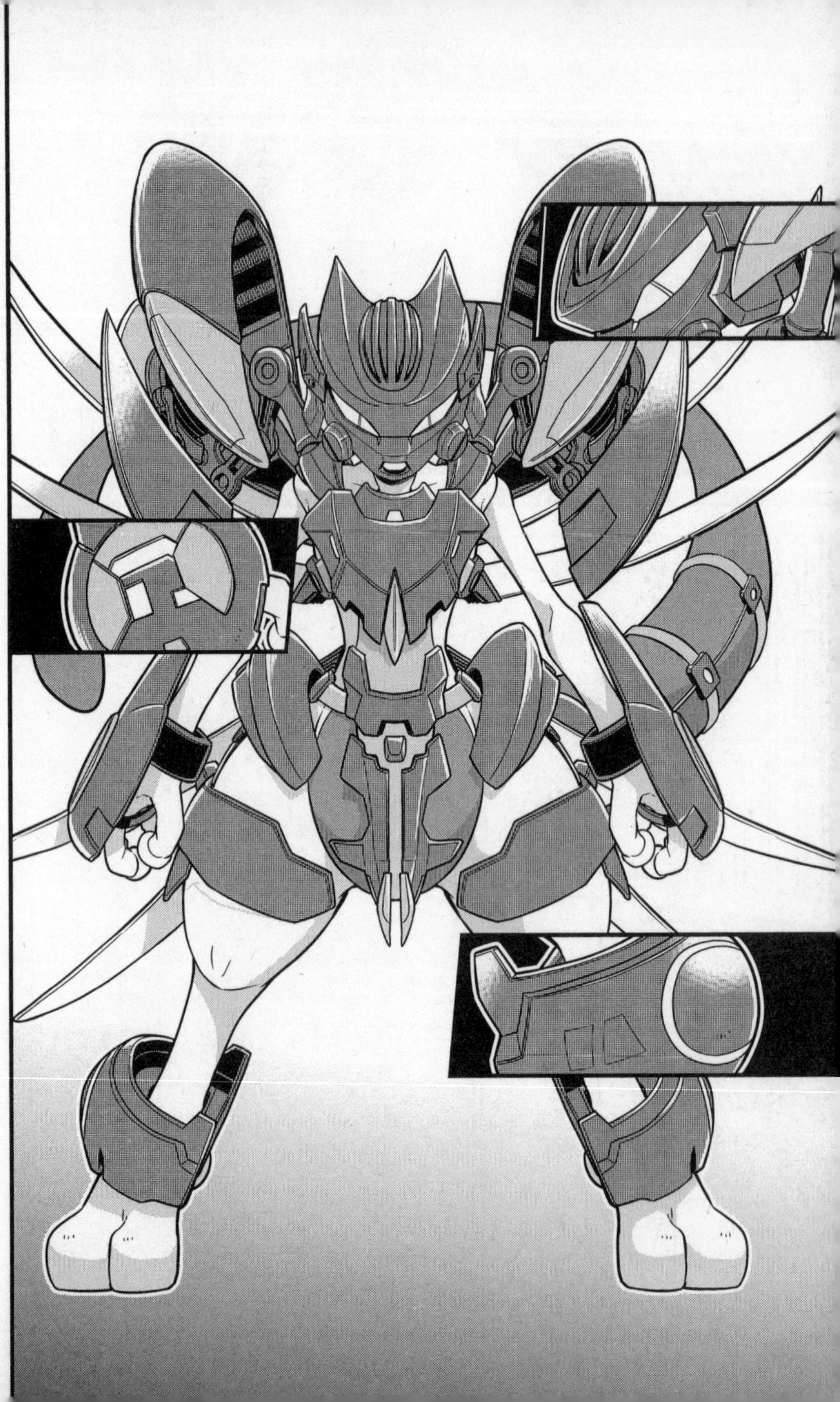

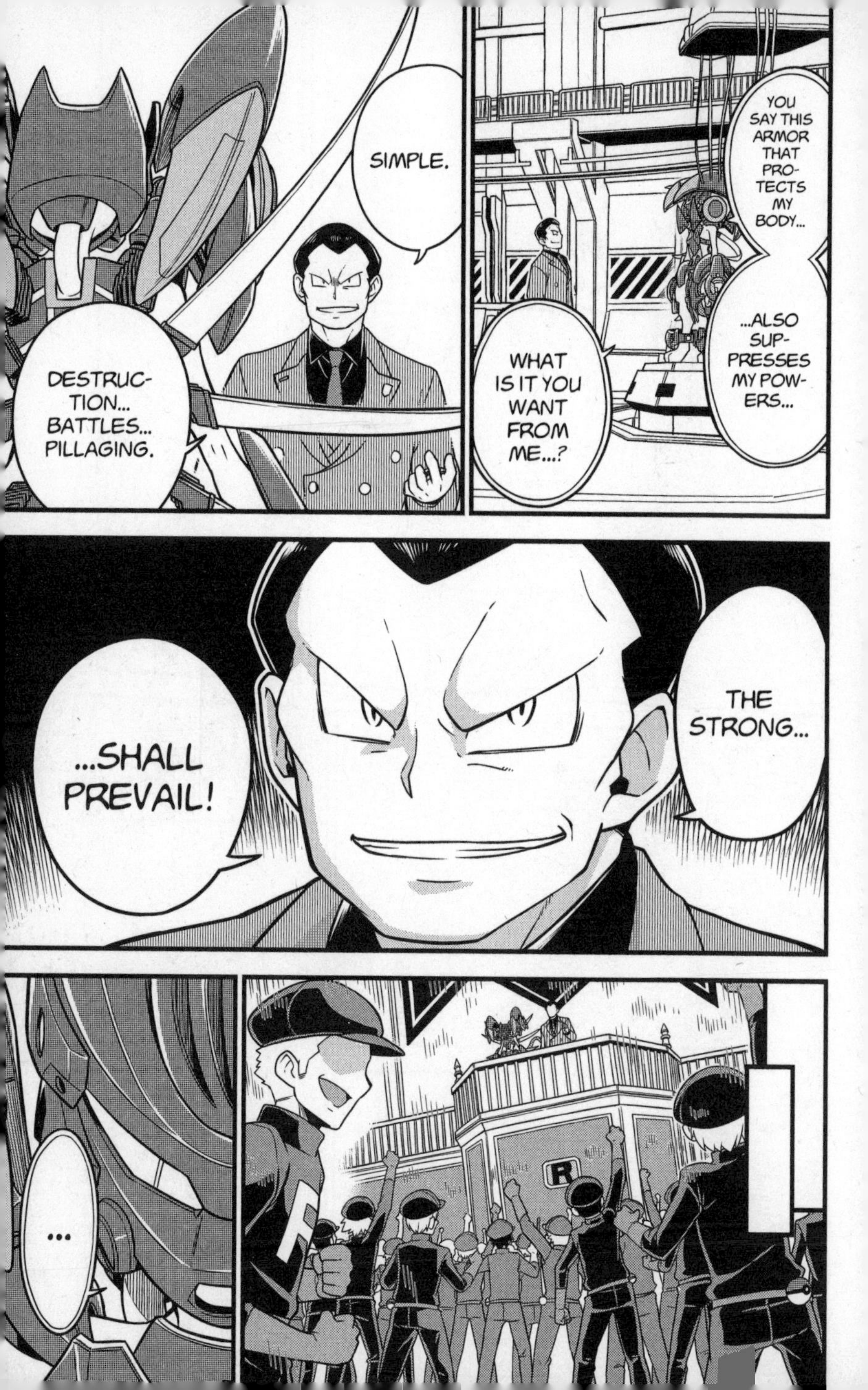
YOU SAY THIS ARMOR THAT PRO-TECTS MY BODY...
...ALSO SUP-PRESSES MY POW-ERS...
WHAT IS IT YOU WANT FROM ME...?
SIMPLE.
DESTRUC-TION... BATTLES... PILLAGING.
THE STRONG...
...SHALL PREVAIL!
R
...

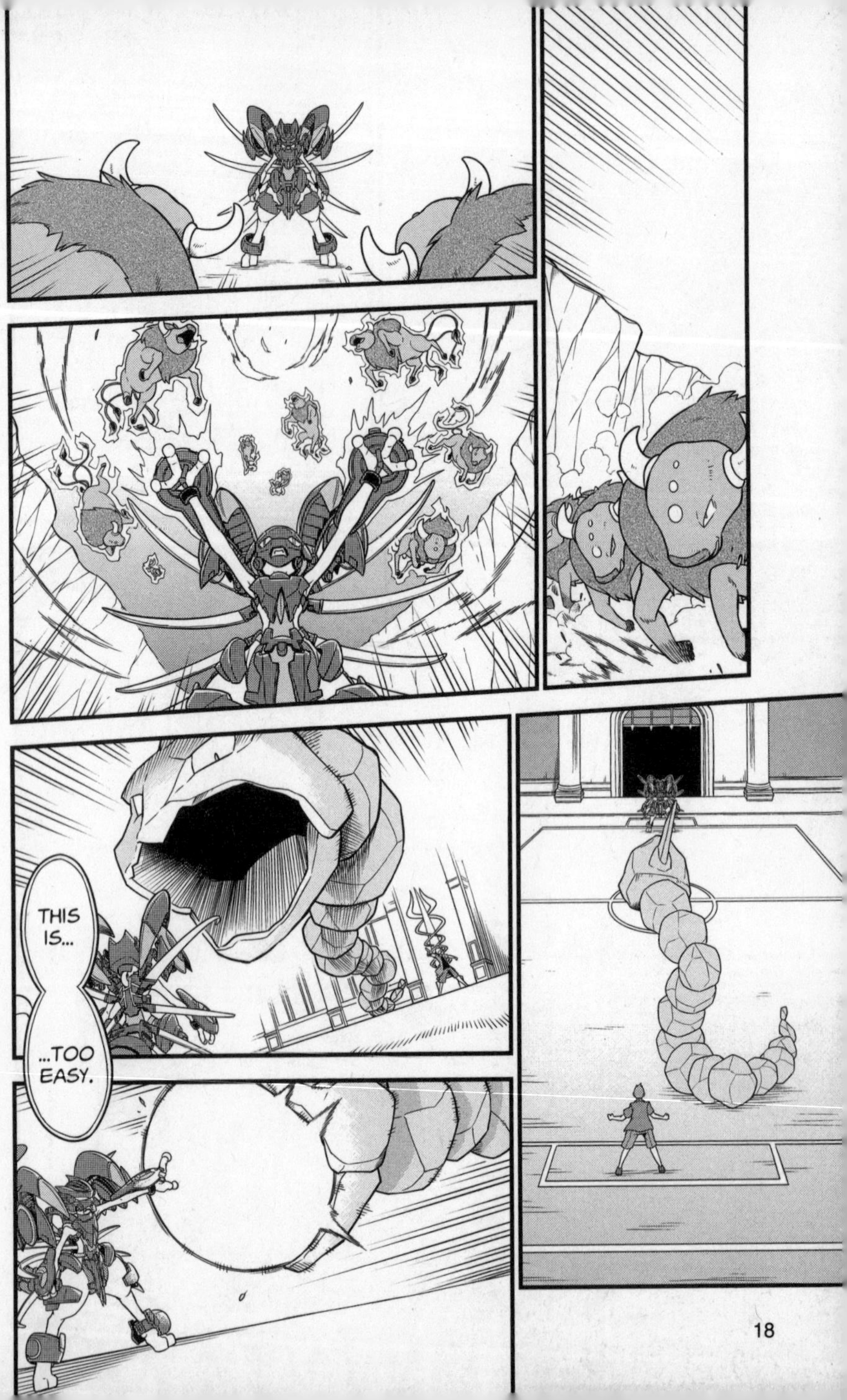
THIS IS...
...TOO EASY.

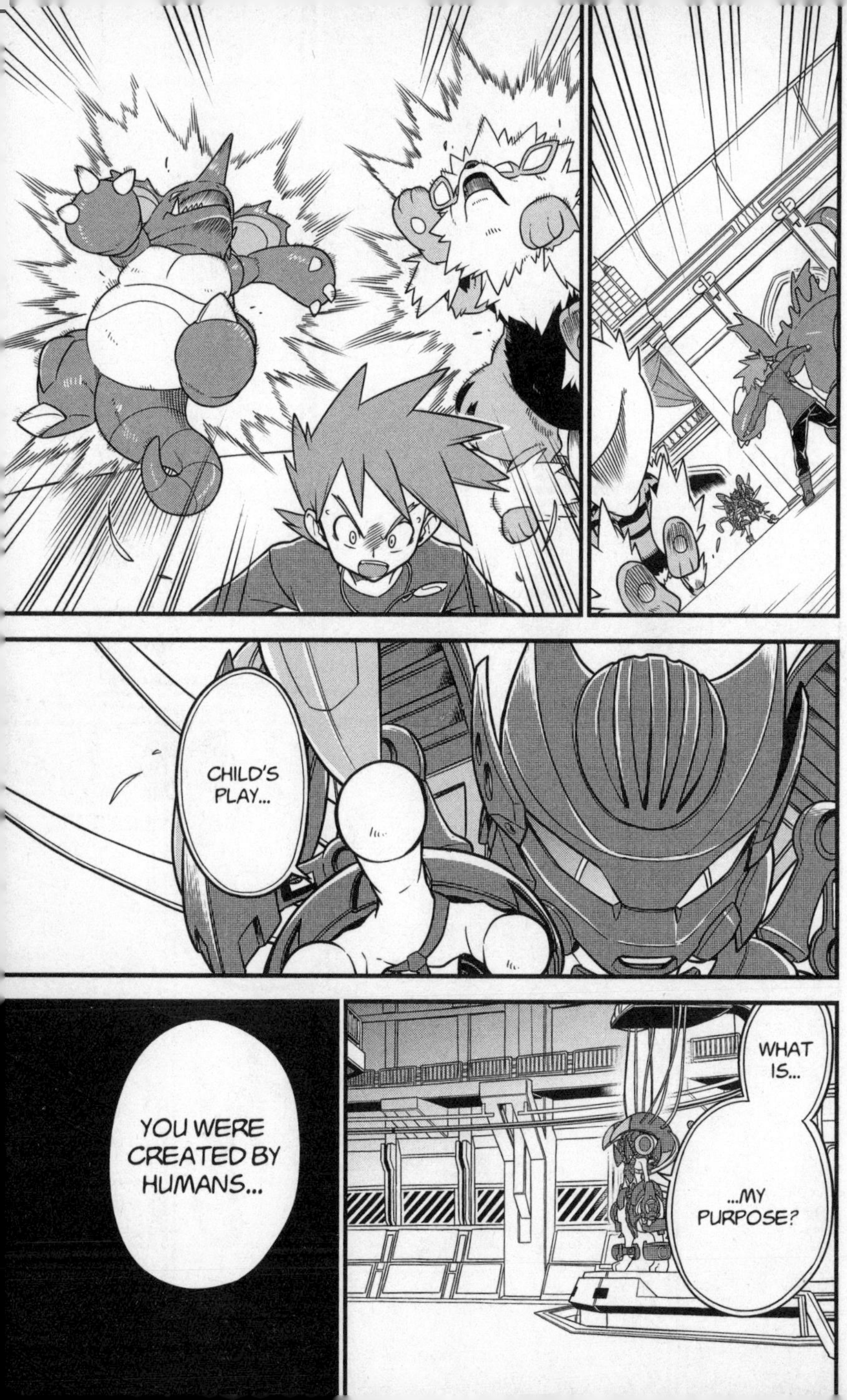
CHILD'S PLAY...
WHAT IS...
...MY PURPOSE?
YOU WERE CREATED BY HUMANS...

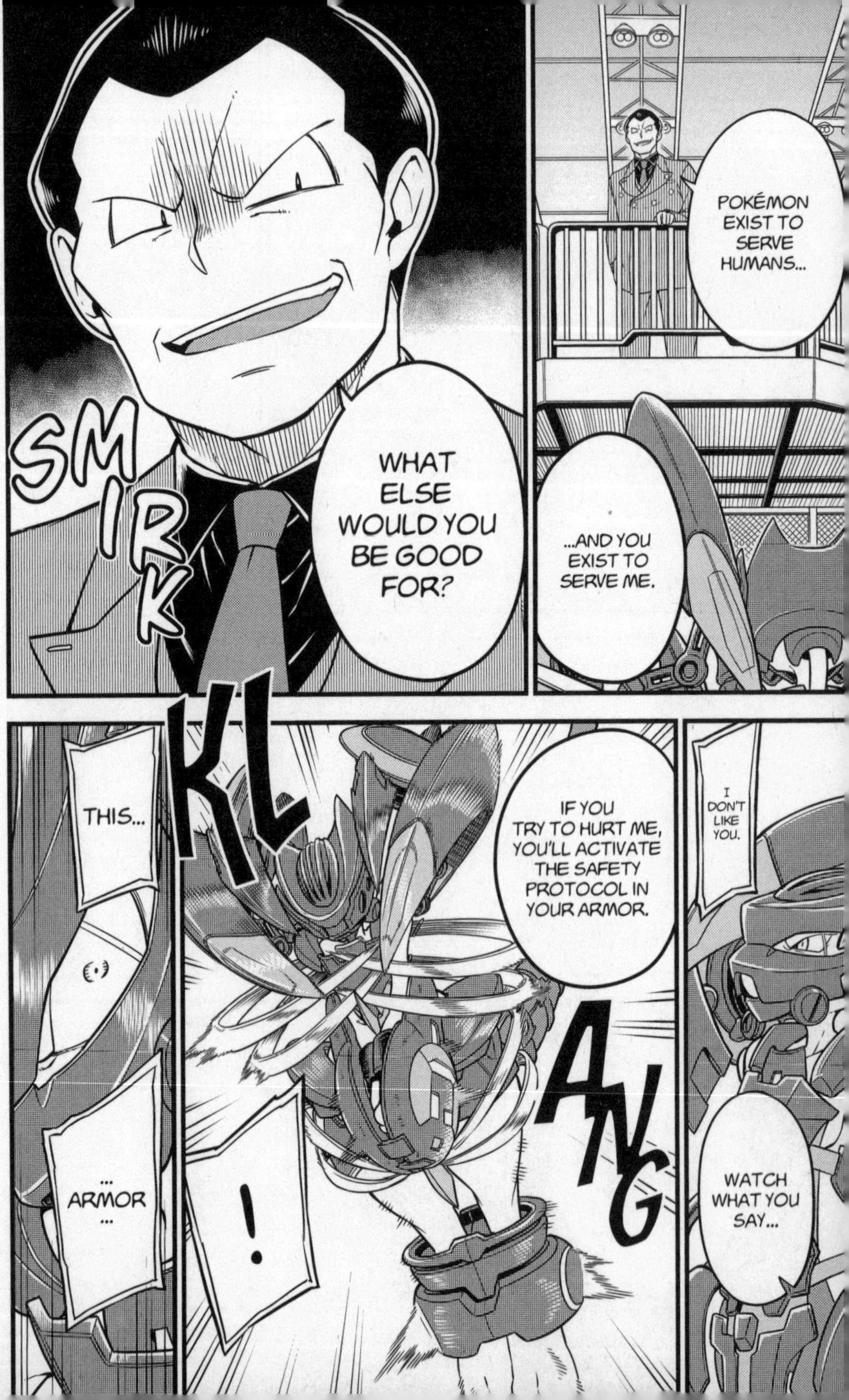
POKÉMON EXIST TO SERVE HUMANS...
...AND YOU EXIST TO SERVE ME.
SMIRK
WHAT ELSE WOULD YOU BE GOOD FOR?
I DON'T LIKE YOU.
WATCH WHAT YOU SAY...
IF YOU TRY TO HURT ME, YOU'LL ACTIVATE THE SAFETY PROTOCOL IN YOUR ARMOR.
KL
ANG
!
THIS...
...ARMOR...

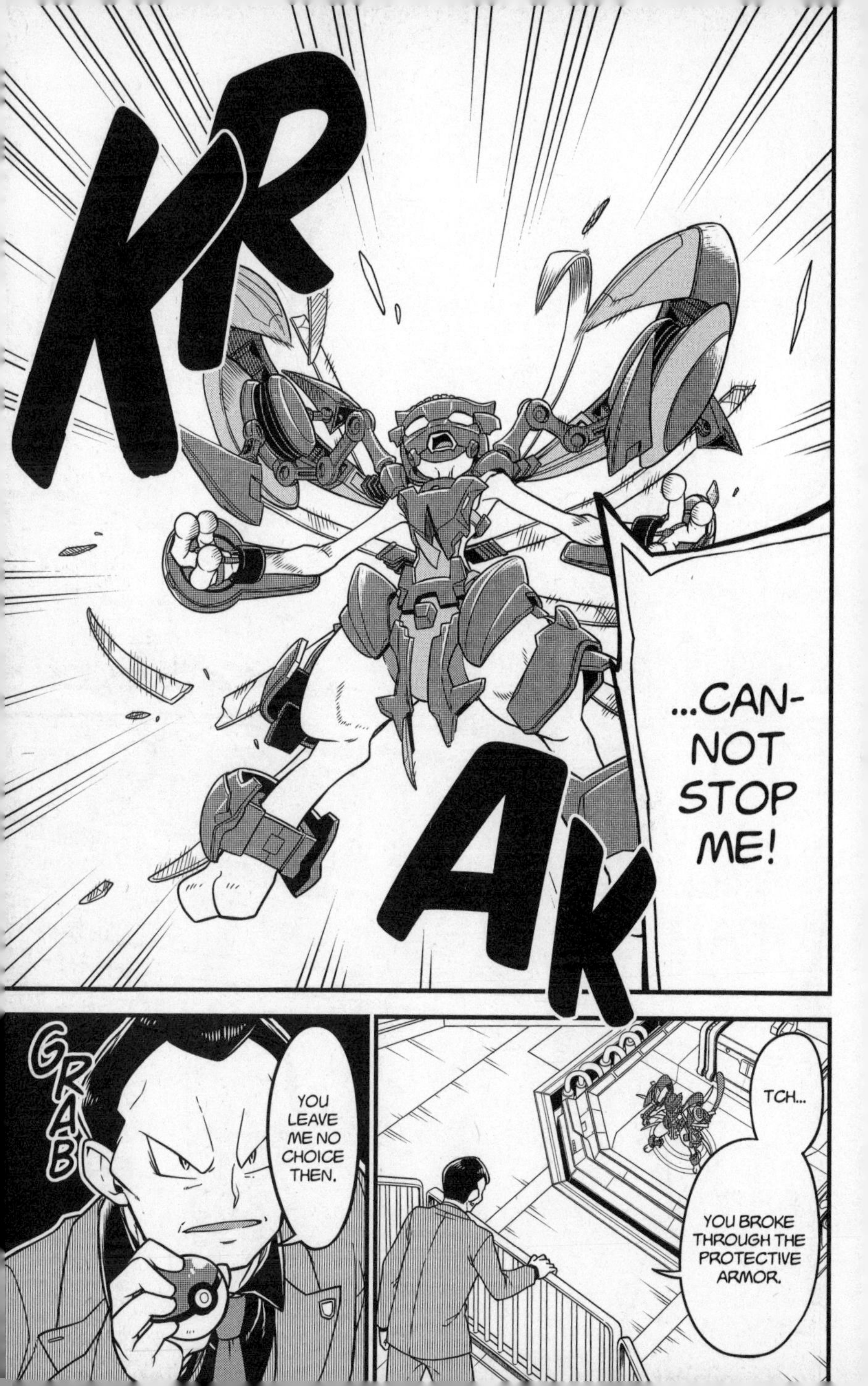
KR
...CAN-NOT STOP ME!
AK
TCH...
YOU BROKE THROUGH THE PROTECTIVE ARMOR.
YOU LEAVE ME NO CHOICE THEN.
GRAB

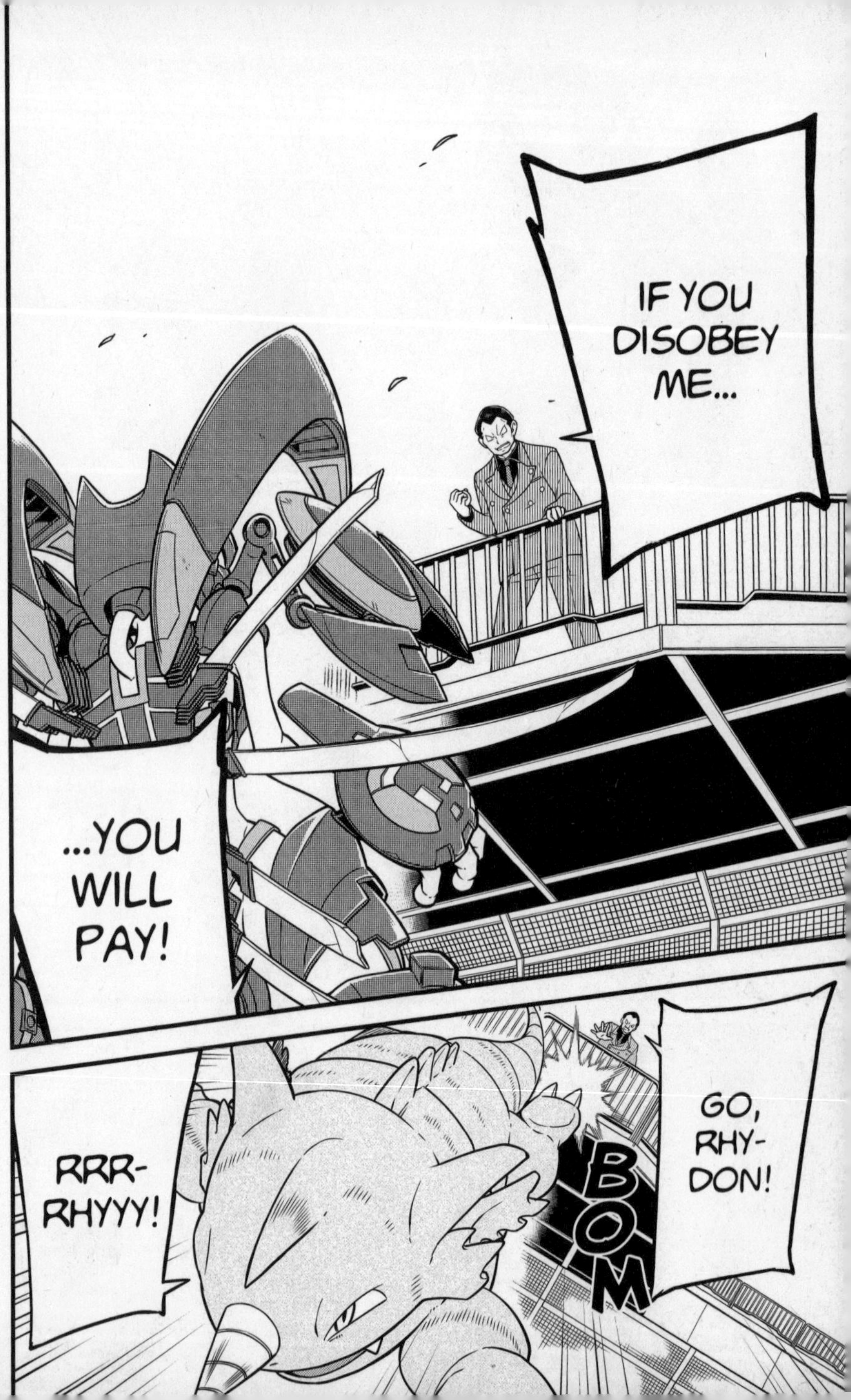
IF YOU DISOBEY ME...
...YOU WILL PAY!
GO, RHY-DON!
BOM
RRR-RHYYY!

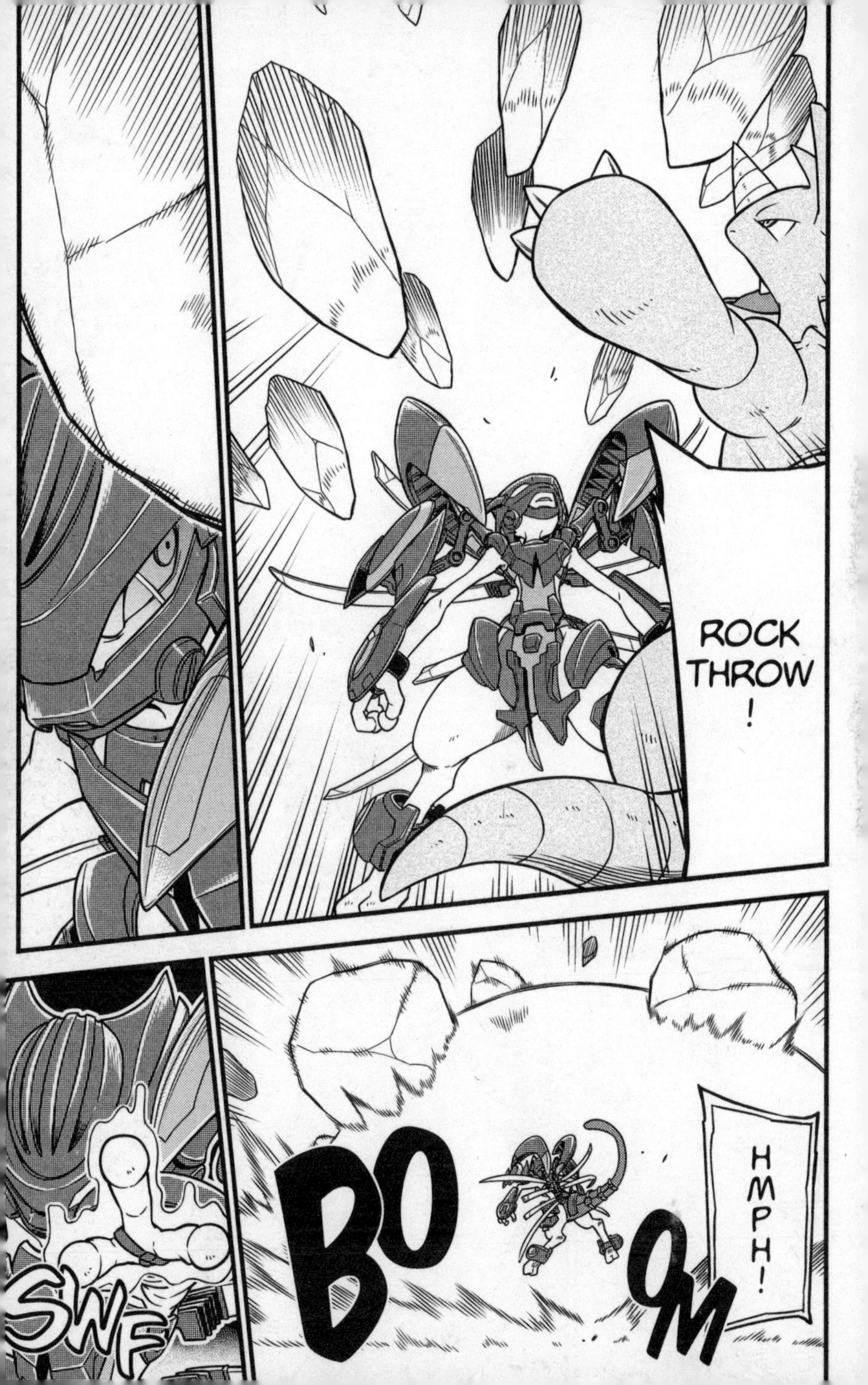
ROCK THROW!
HMPH!
BOOM
SWF

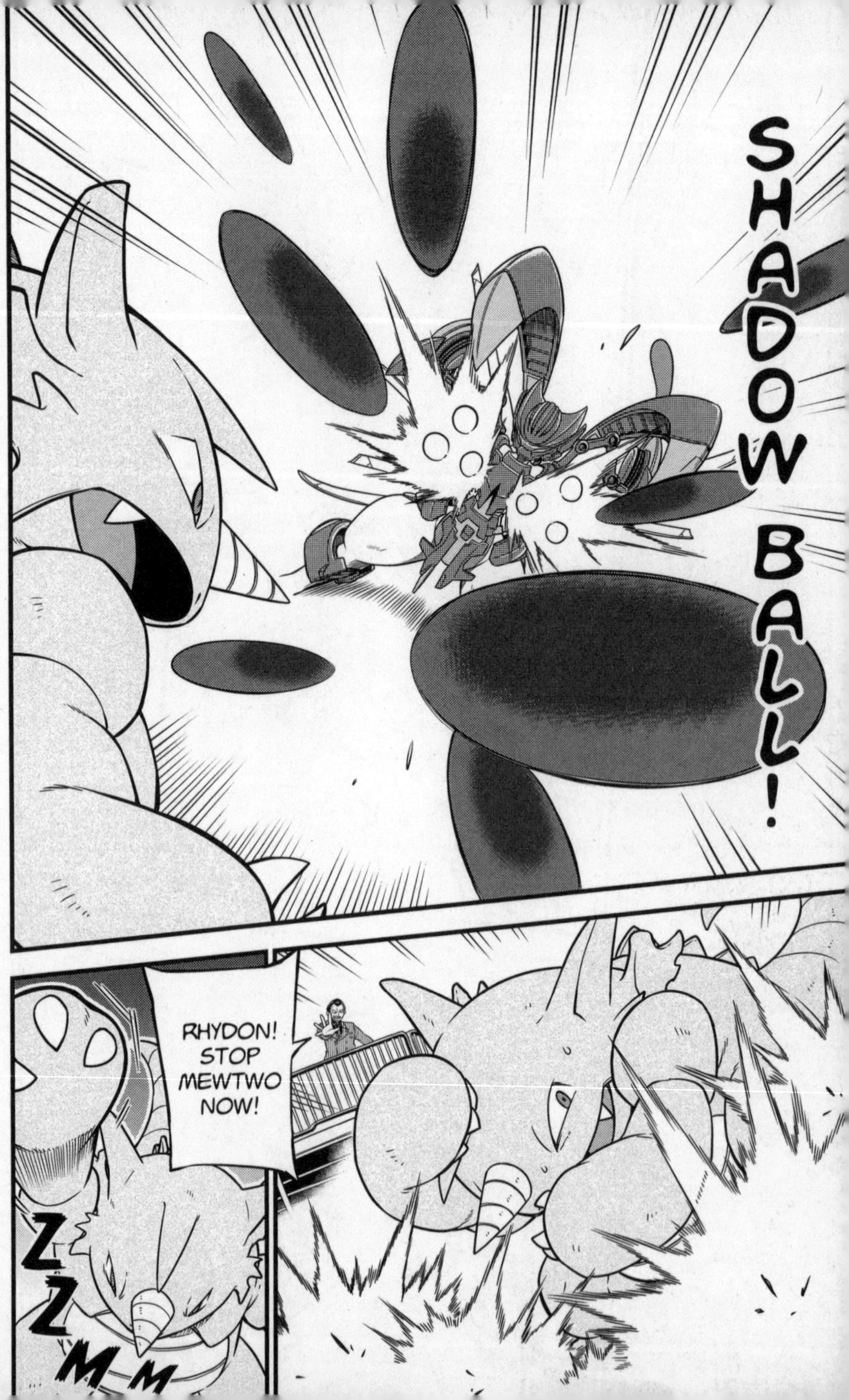
SHADOW BALL!
RHYDON! STOP MEWTWO NOW!
ZZZMMM

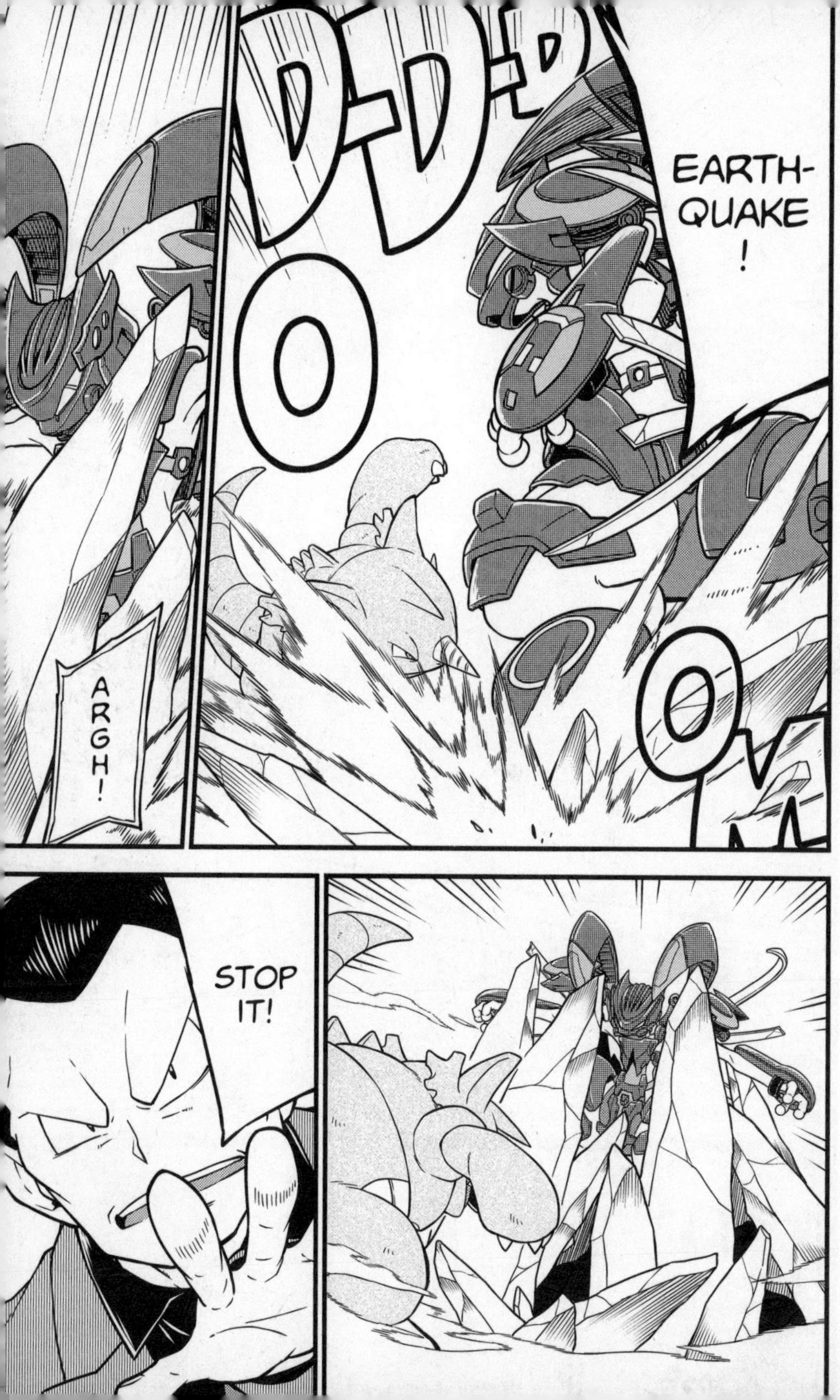
D-D-D-DOOM
EARTHQUAKE!
ARGH!
STOP IT!

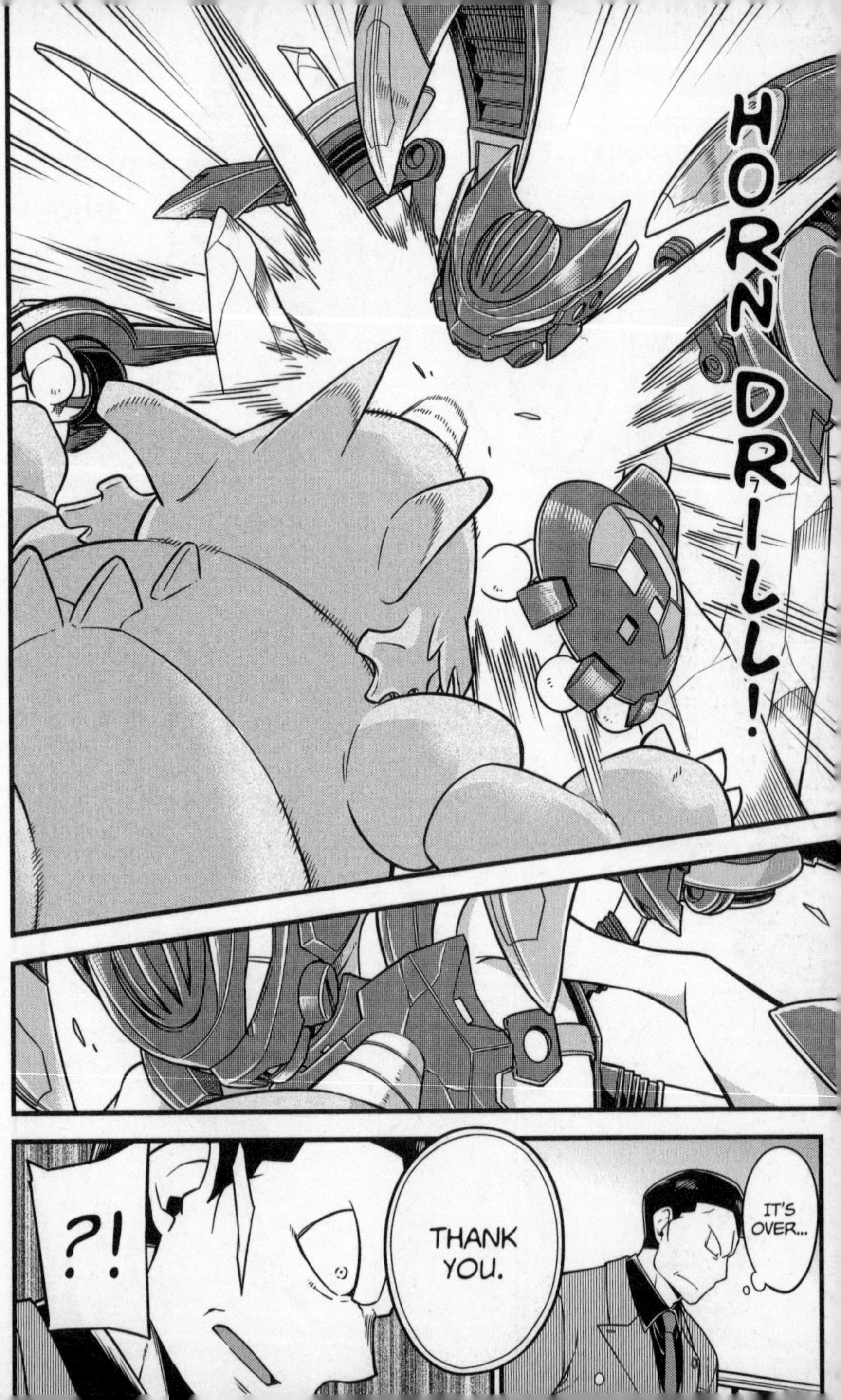
HORN DRILL!
IT'S OVER...
THANK YOU.
?!

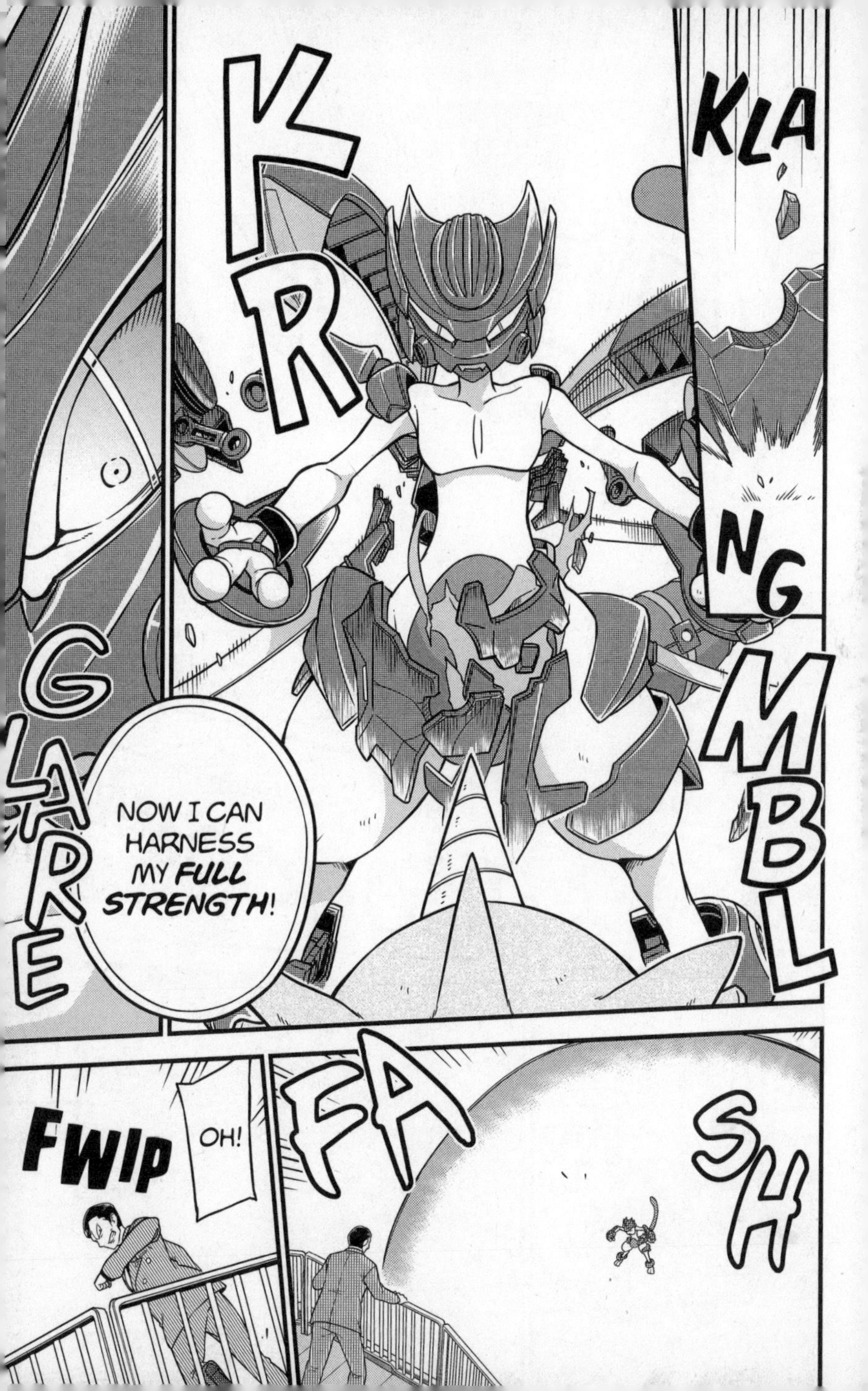
KLA
NG
KR
MBL
NOW I CAN HARNESS MY **FULL STRENGTH!**
GLARE
FA
SH
OH!
FWIP

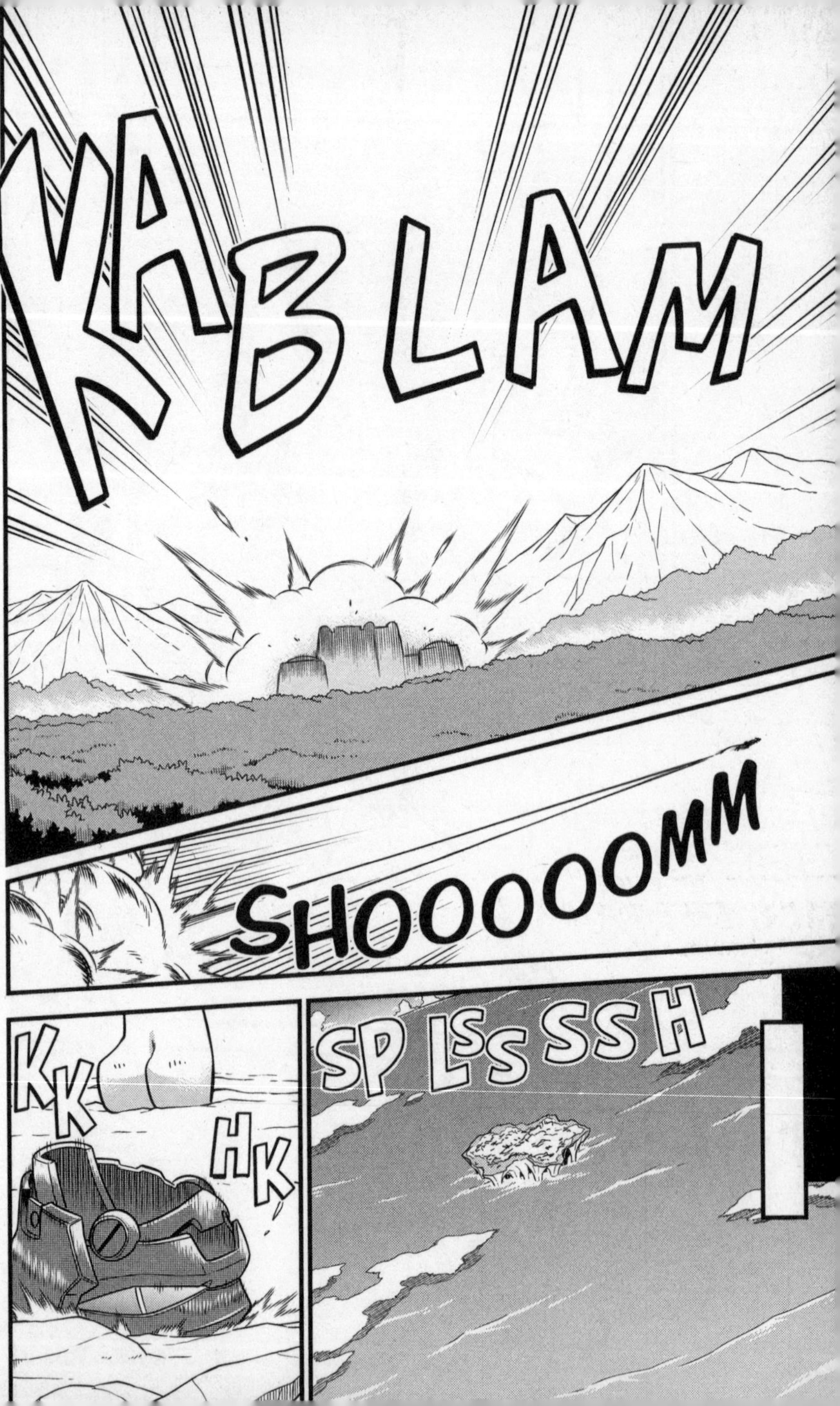
KABLAM
SHOOOOOMM
SPLSSSSH
KKK
HK

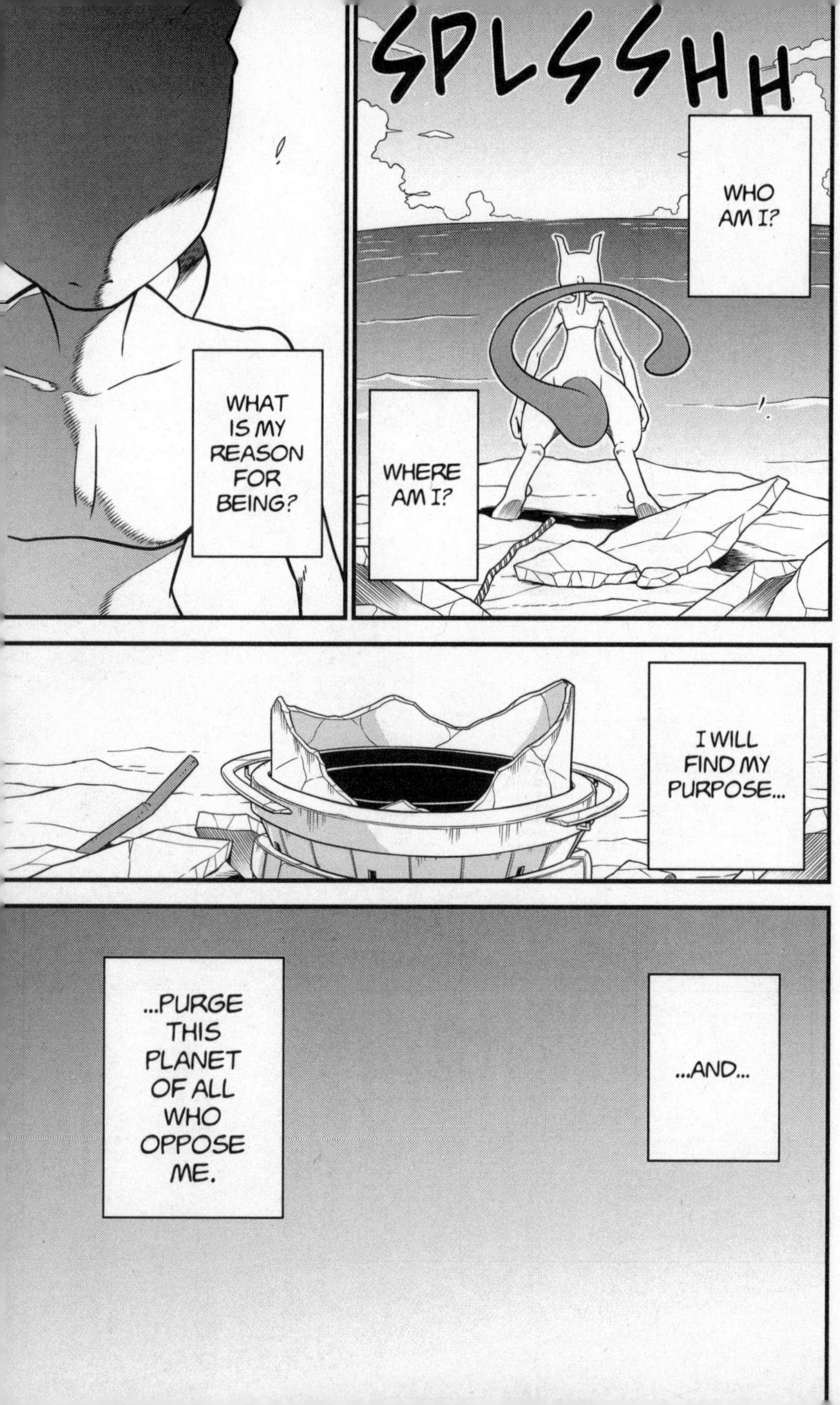
SPLSSHH
WHO AM I?
WHERE AM I?
WHAT IS MY REASON FOR BEING?
I WILL FIND MY PURPOSE...
...AND...
...PURGE THIS PLANET OF ALL WHO OPPOSE ME.

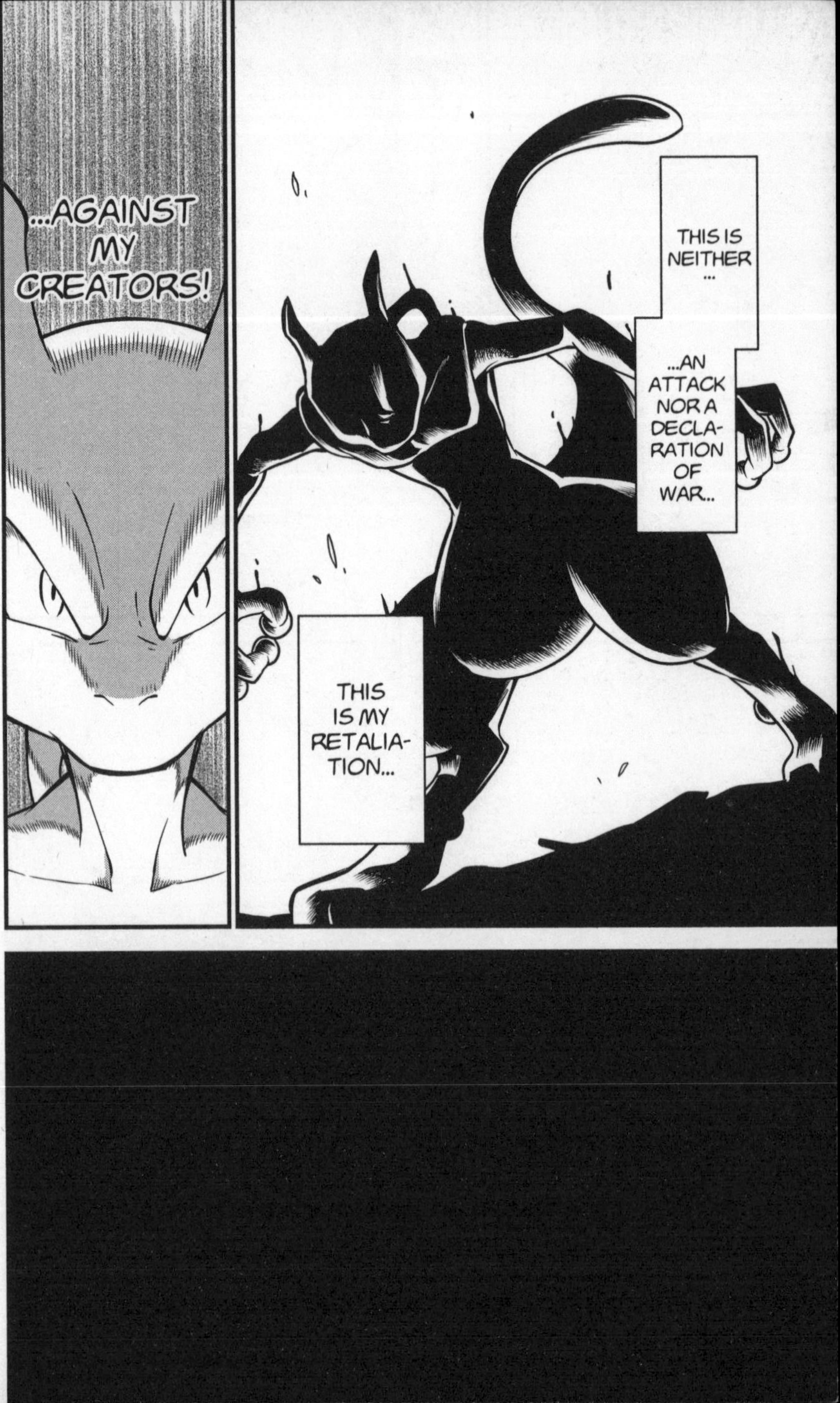
THIS IS NEITHER ...
...AN ATTACK NOR A DECLARATION OF WAR...
THIS IS MY RETALIATION...
...AGAINST MY CREATORS!

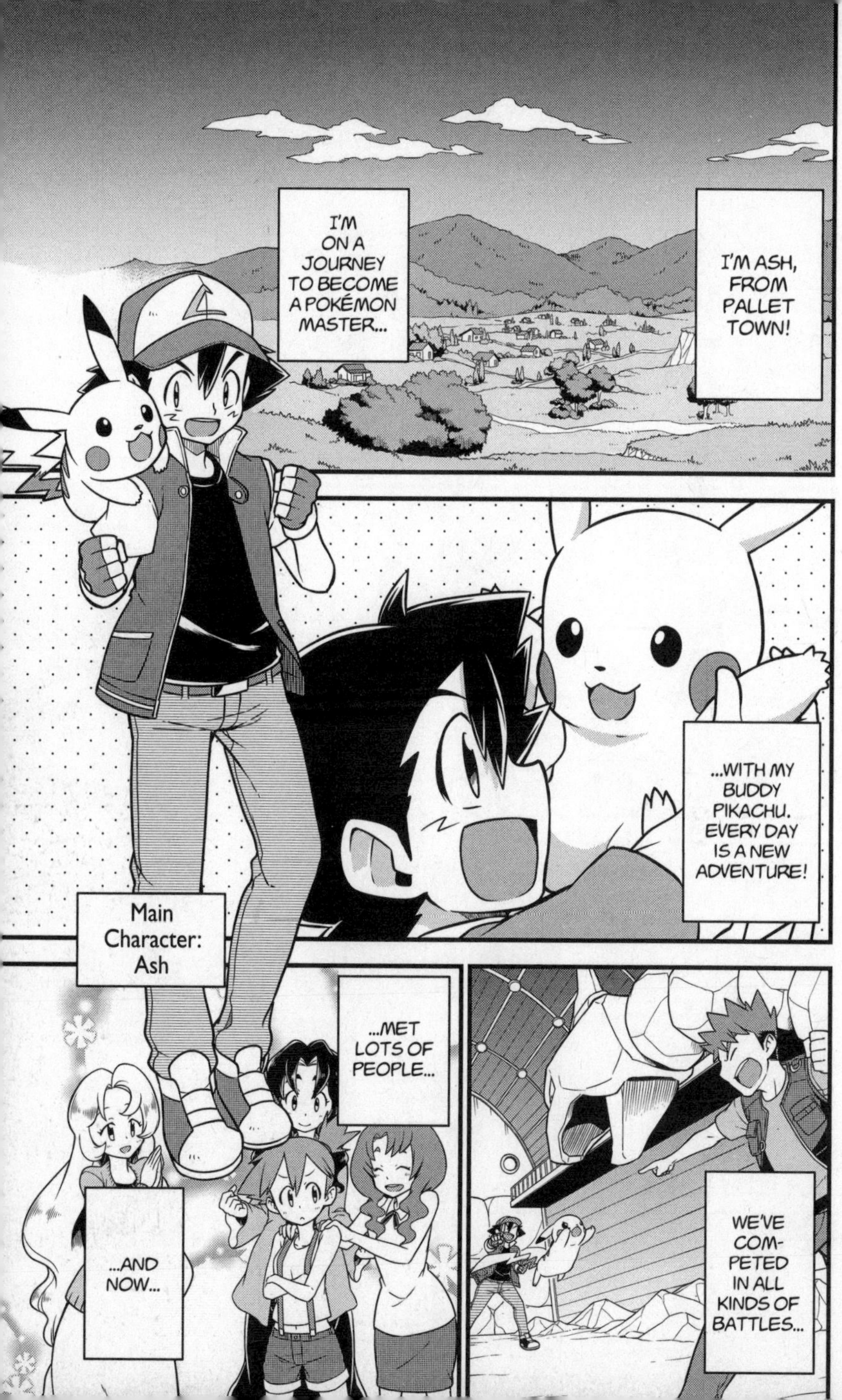
I'M ASH, FROM PALLET TOWN!
I'M ON A JOURNEY TO BECOME A POKÉMON MASTER...
...WITH MY BUDDY PIKACHU. EVERY DAY IS A NEW ADVENTURE!
Main Character: Ash
WE'VE COM- PETED IN ALL KINDS OF BATTLES...
...MET LOTS OF PEOPLE...
...AND NOW...

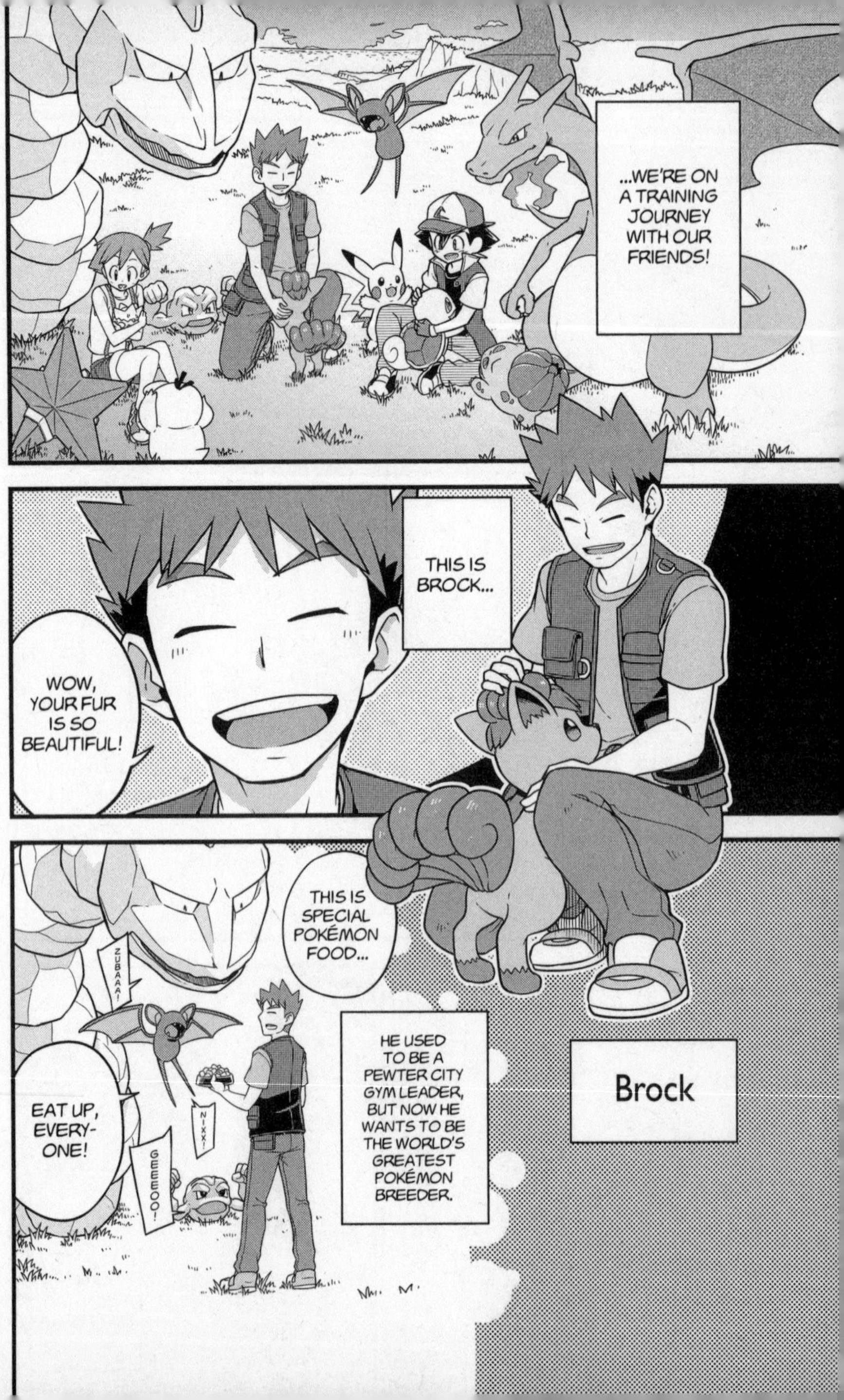
...WE'RE ON A TRAINING JOURNEY WITH OUR FRIENDS!
THIS IS BROCK...
WOW, YOUR FUR IS SO BEAUTIFUL!
Brock
THIS IS SPECIAL POKÉMON FOOD...
ZUBAAA!
HE USED TO BE A PEWTER CITY GYM LEADER, BUT NOW HE WANTS TO BE THE WORLD'S GREATEST POKÉMON BREEDER.
NIXX!
EAT UP, EVERY-ONE!
GEEEOO!

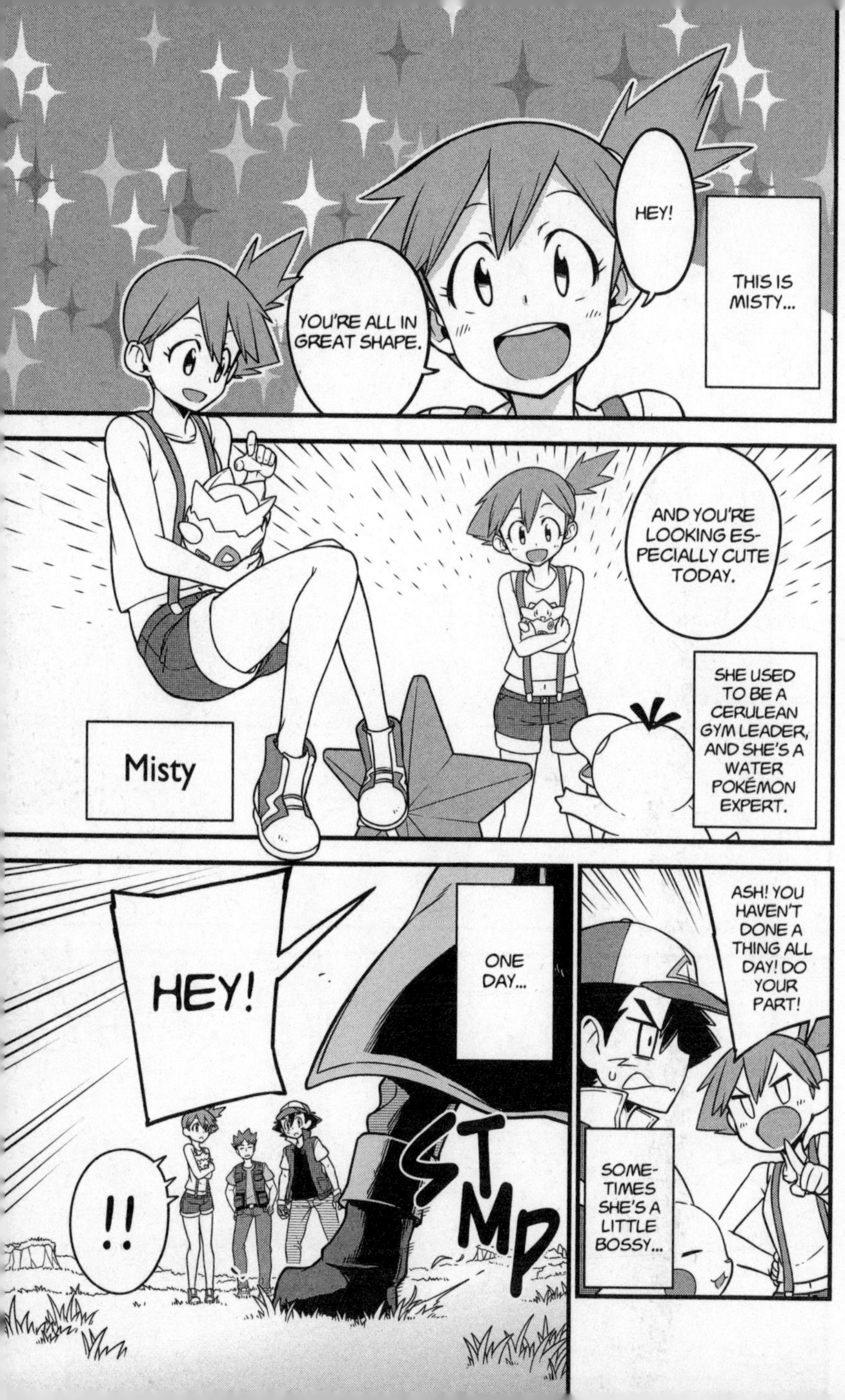
THIS IS MISTY...
HEY!
YOU'RE ALL IN GREAT SHAPE.
AND YOU'RE LOOKING ES-PECIALLY CUTE TODAY.
SHE USED TO BE A CERULEAN GYM LEADER, AND SHE'S A WATER POKÉMON EXPERT.
Misty
ASH! YOU HAVEN'T DONE A THING ALL DAY! DO YOUR PART!
SOME-TIMES SHE'S A LITTLE BOSSY...
ONE DAY...
HEY!
STMP
!!

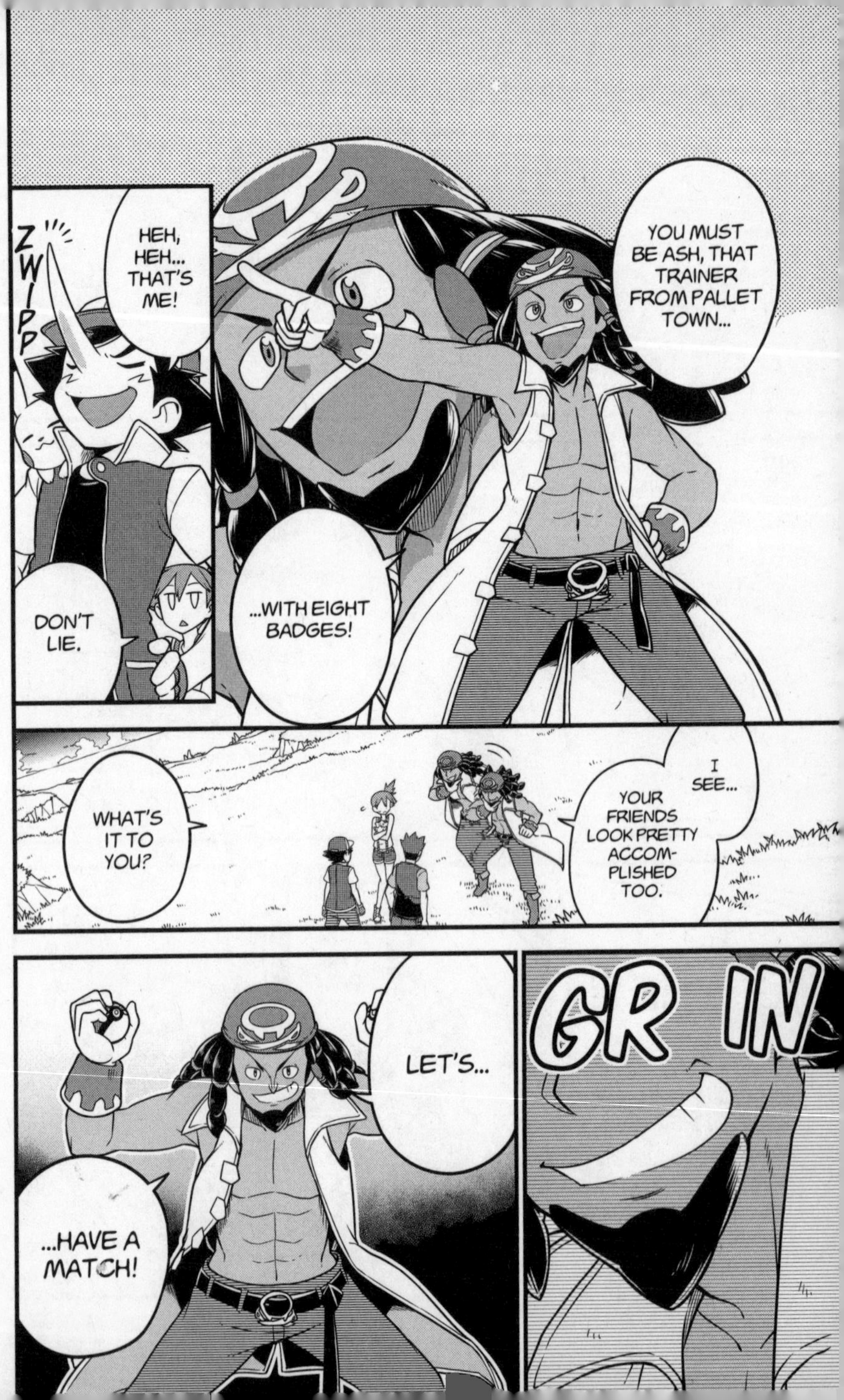
YOU MUST BE ASH, THAT TRAINER FROM PALLET TOWN...
...WITH EIGHT BADGES!
ZWIPP
HEH, HEH... THAT'S ME!
DON'T LIE.
I SEE... YOUR FRIENDS LOOK PRETTY ACCOM-PLISHED TOO.
WHAT'S IT TO YOU?
GR IN
LET'S...
...HAVE A MATCH!

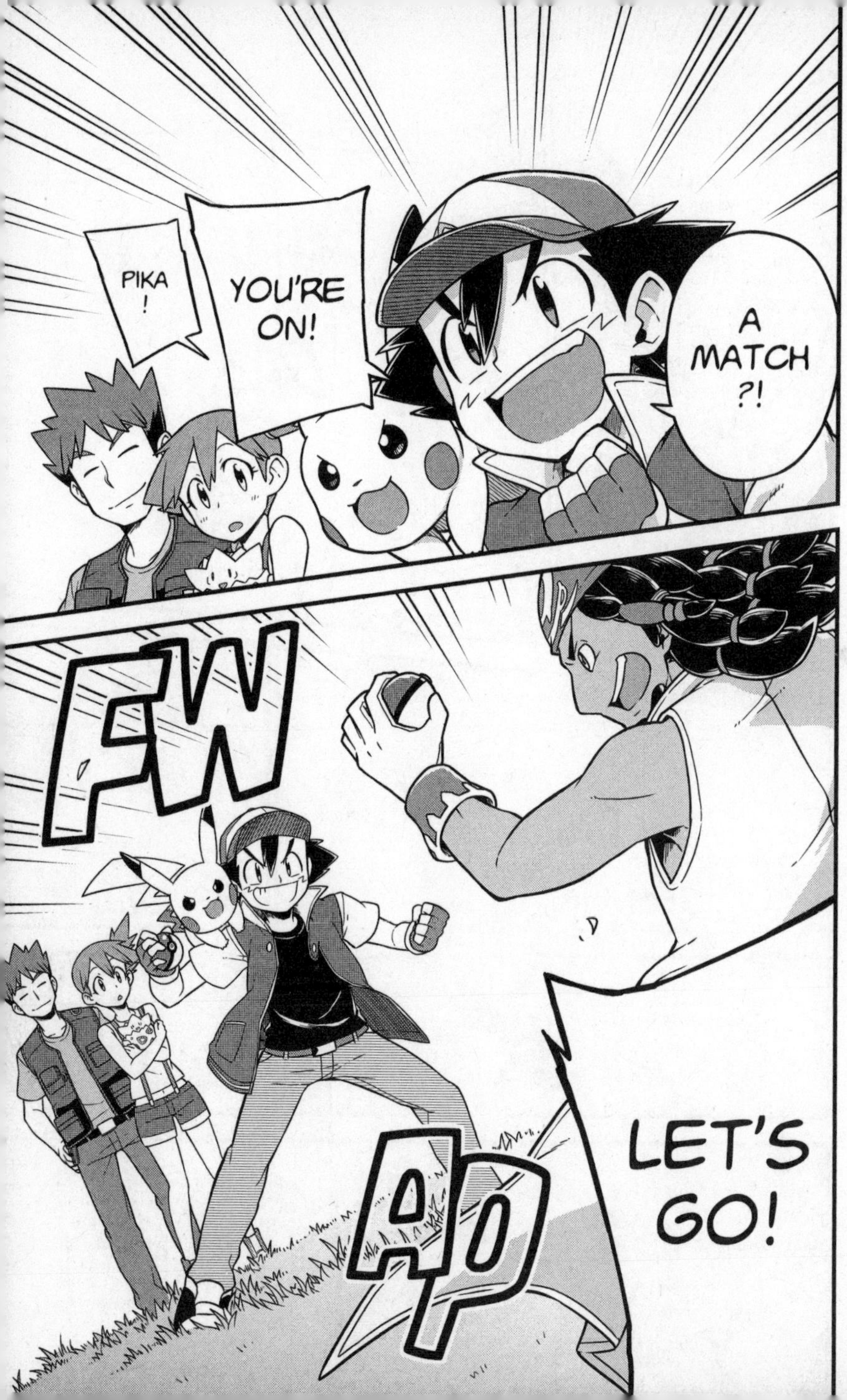
A MATCH ?!
YOU'RE ON!
PIKA !
FW
LET'S GO!
AP

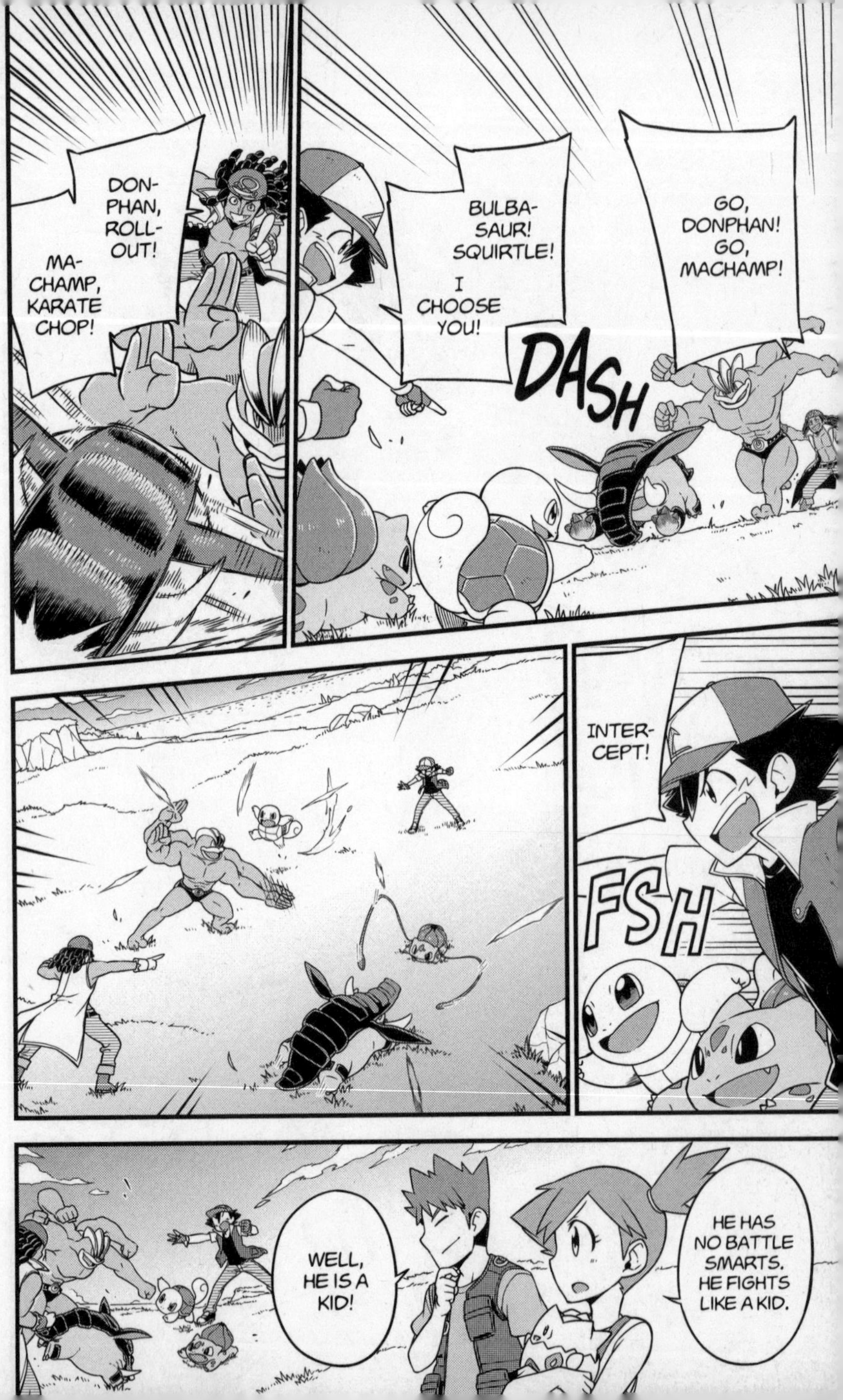
GO, DONPHAN! GO, MACHAMP!
DASH
BULBA-SAUR! SQUIRTLE!
I CHOOSE YOU!
DON-PHAN, ROLL-OUT!
MA-CHAMP, KARATE CHOP!
INTER-CEPT!
FSH
HE HAS NO BATTLE SMARTS. HE FIGHTS LIKE A KID.
WELL, HE IS A KID!

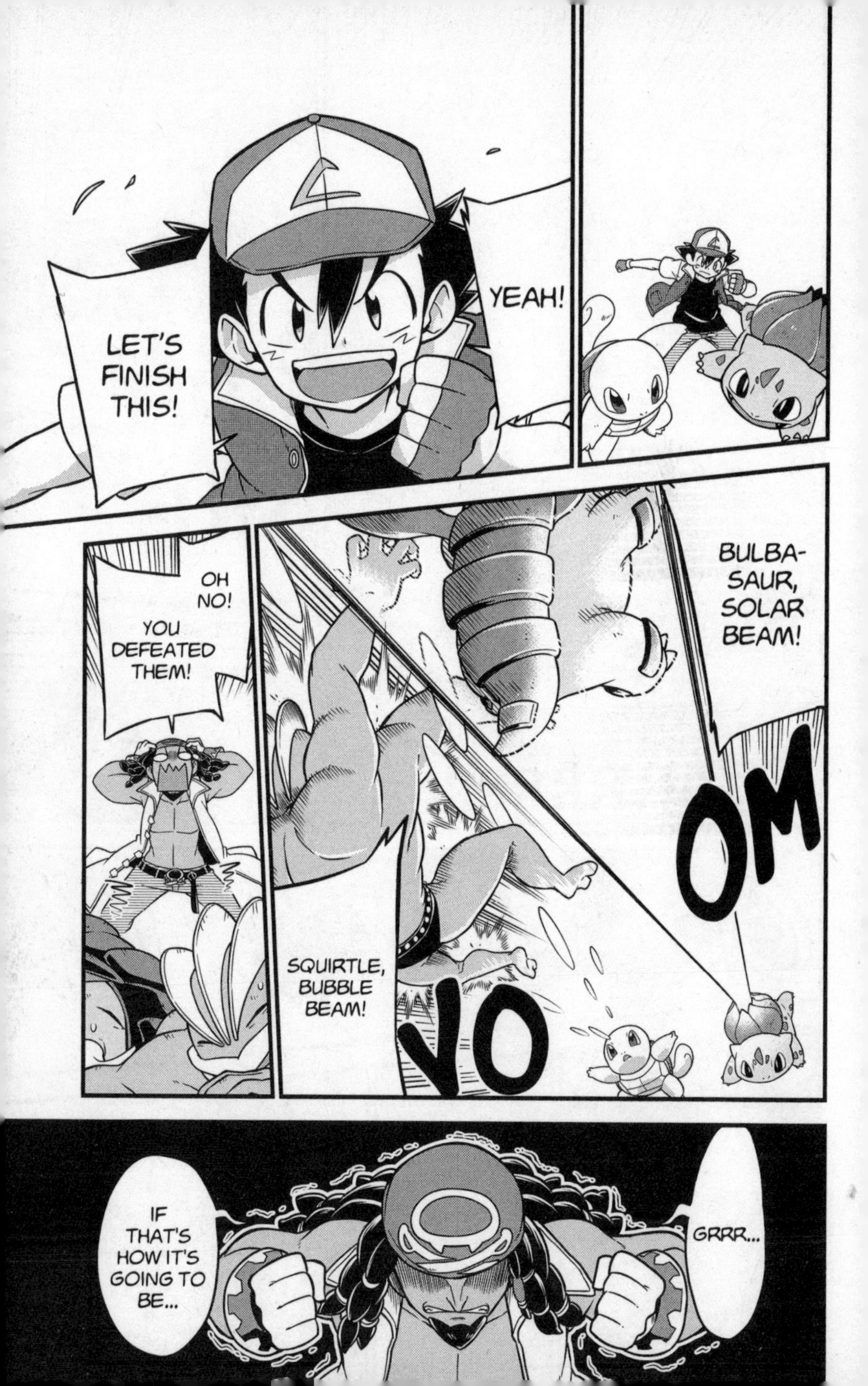
LET'S FINISH THIS!
YEAH!
BULBA-SAUR, SOLAR BEAM!
OM
SQUIRTLE, BUBBLE BEAM!
VO
OH NO!
YOU DEFEATED THEM!
GRRR...
IF THAT'S HOW IT'S GOING TO BE...

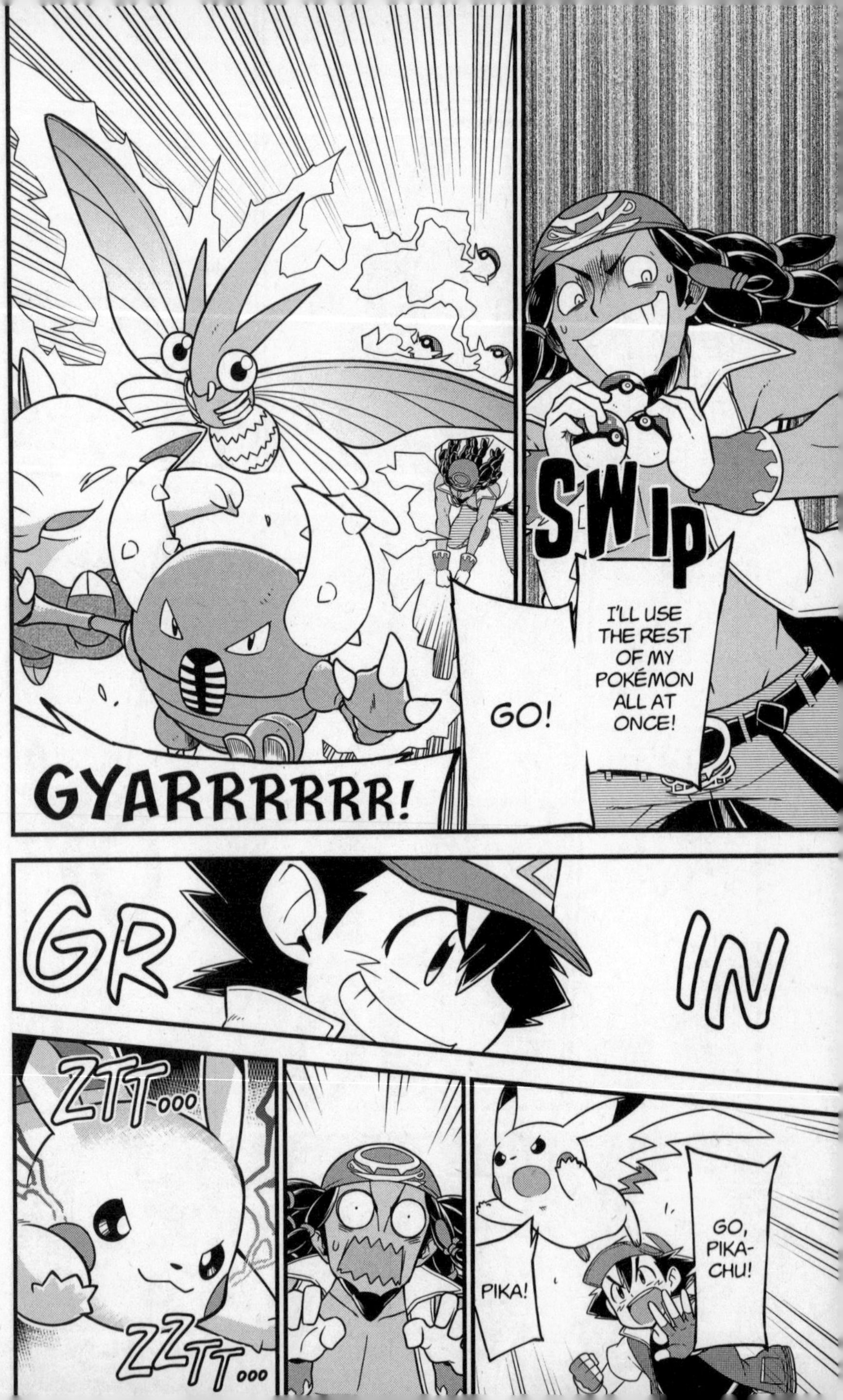
SWIP
I'LL USE THE REST OF MY POKÉMON ALL AT ONCE!
GO!
GYARRRRRRR!
GR IN
GO, PIKA-CHU!
PIKA!
ZTT...
ZZTT...

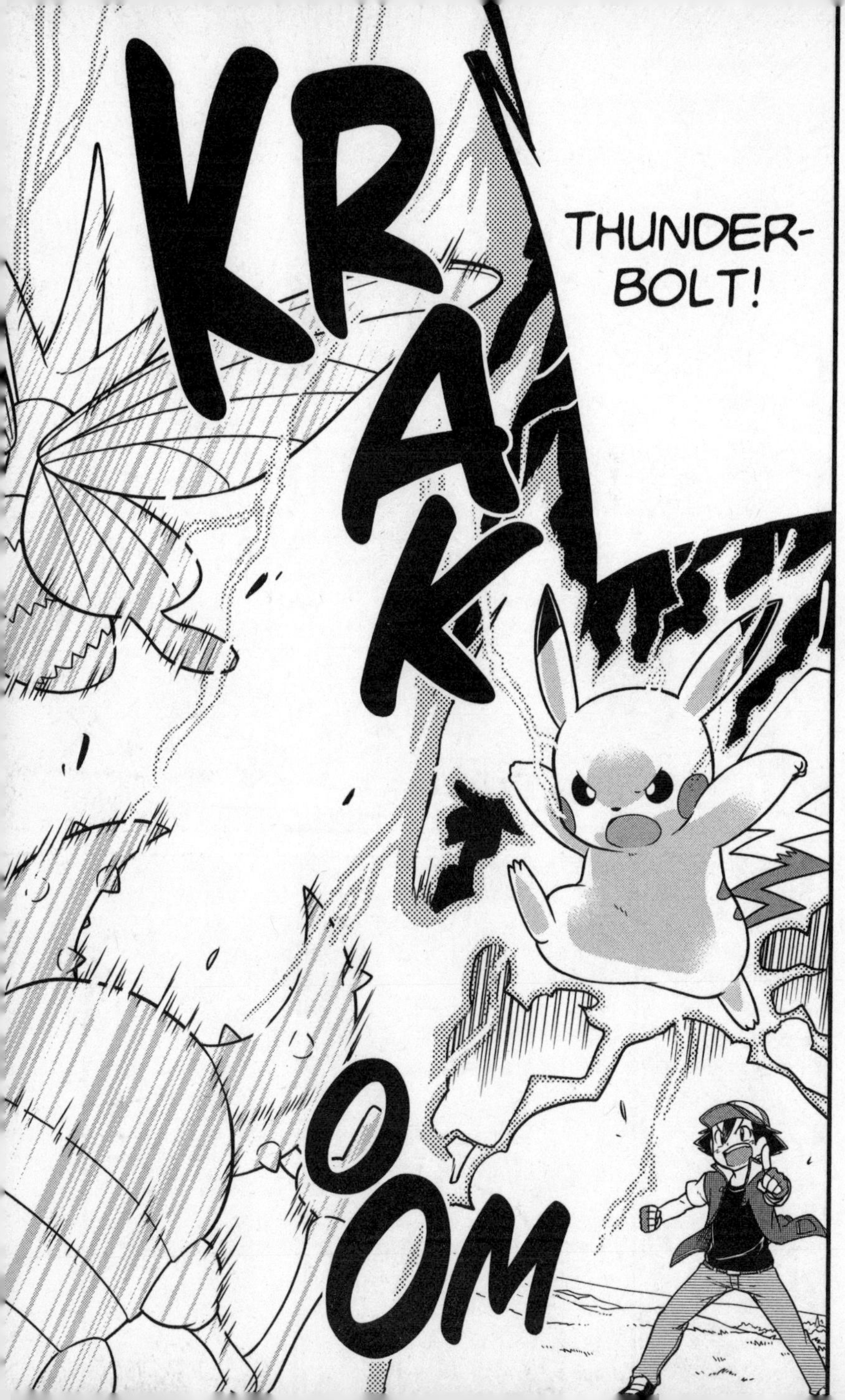
THUNDER-BOLT!
KRAKA
OOOM

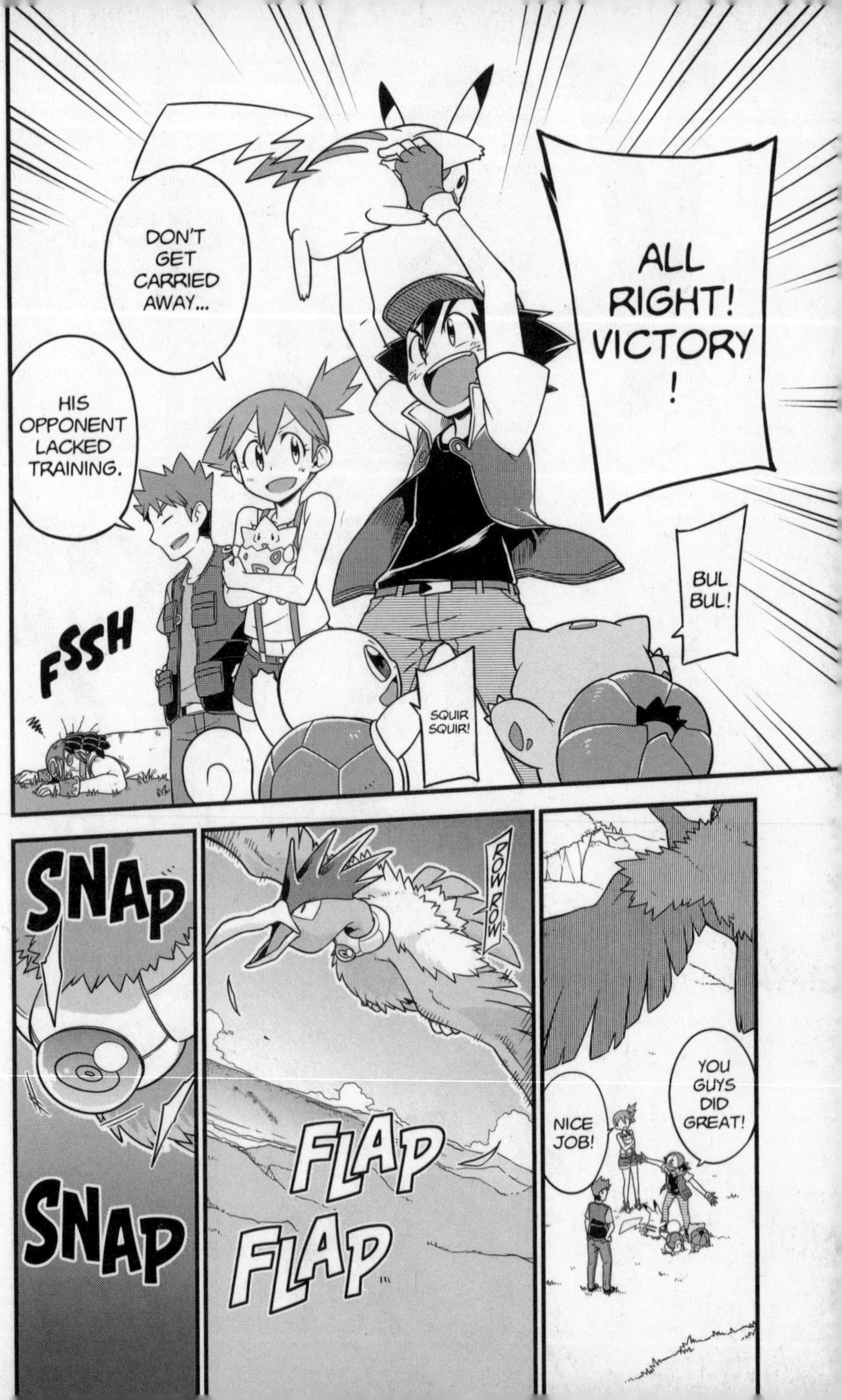
ALL RIGHT! VICTORY!
DON'T GET CARRIED AWAY...
BUL BUL!
HIS OPPONENT LACKED TRAINING.
SQUIR SQUIR!
FSSH
YOU GUYS DID GREAT!
NICE JOB!
ROW ROW
FLAP
FLAP
SNAP
SNAP

MASTER...

S
N
A
P

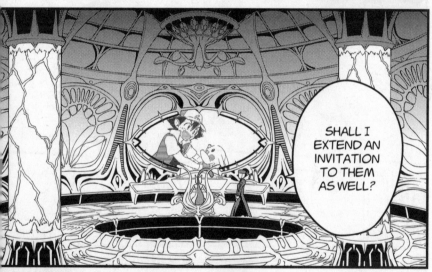

SHALL I
EXTEND AN
INVITATION
TO THEM
AS WELL?

I'LL
INVITE
THEM
TO...

AS
YOU
WISH.

SWF

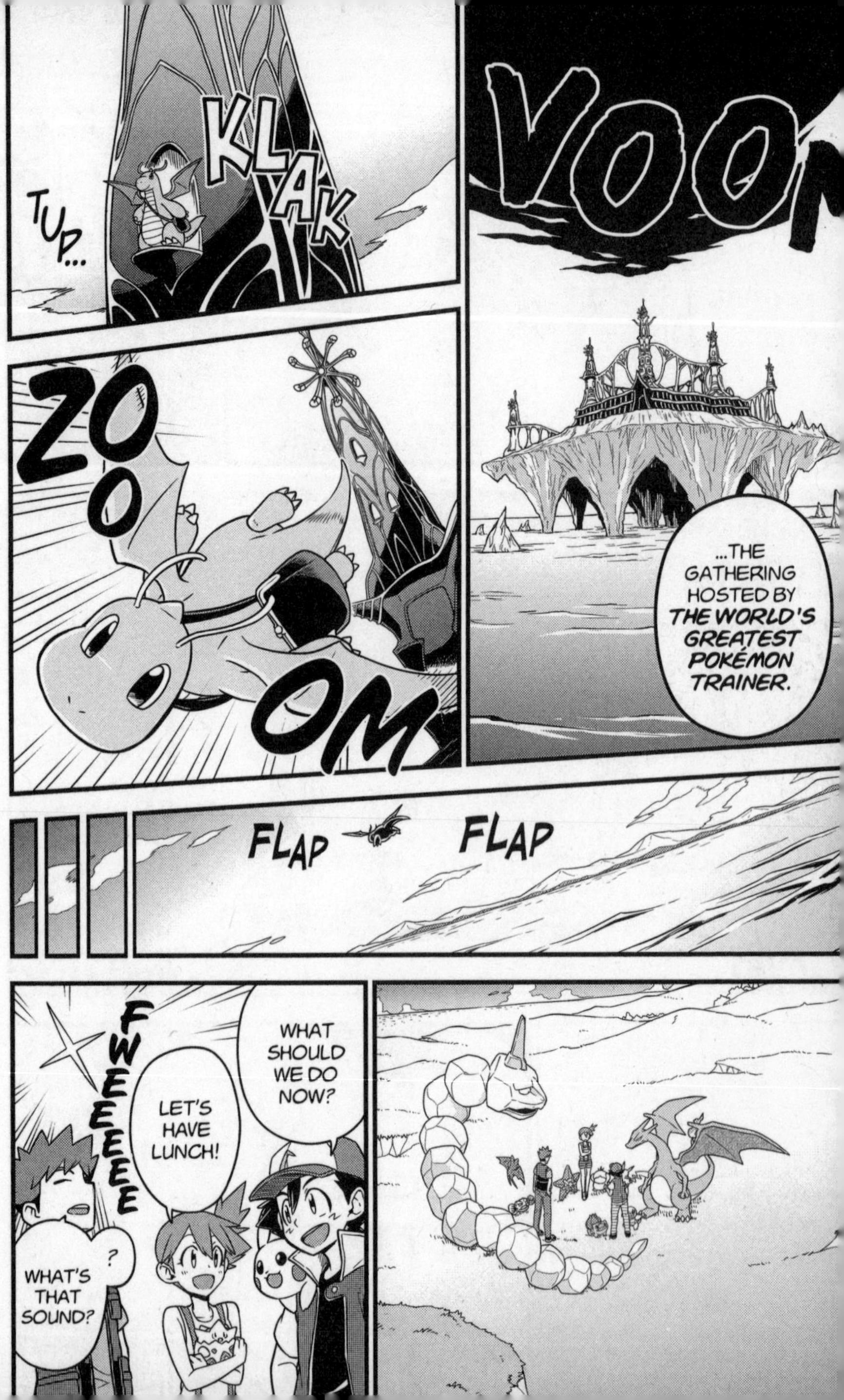
VOO
KLAK
TUP...
...THE GATHERING HOSTED BY THE WORLD'S GREATEST POKÉMON TRAINER.
ZOOOM
FLAP
FLAP
WHAT SHOULD WE DO NOW?
LET'S HAVE LUNCH!
FWEEEEEE
?
WHAT'S THAT SOUND?

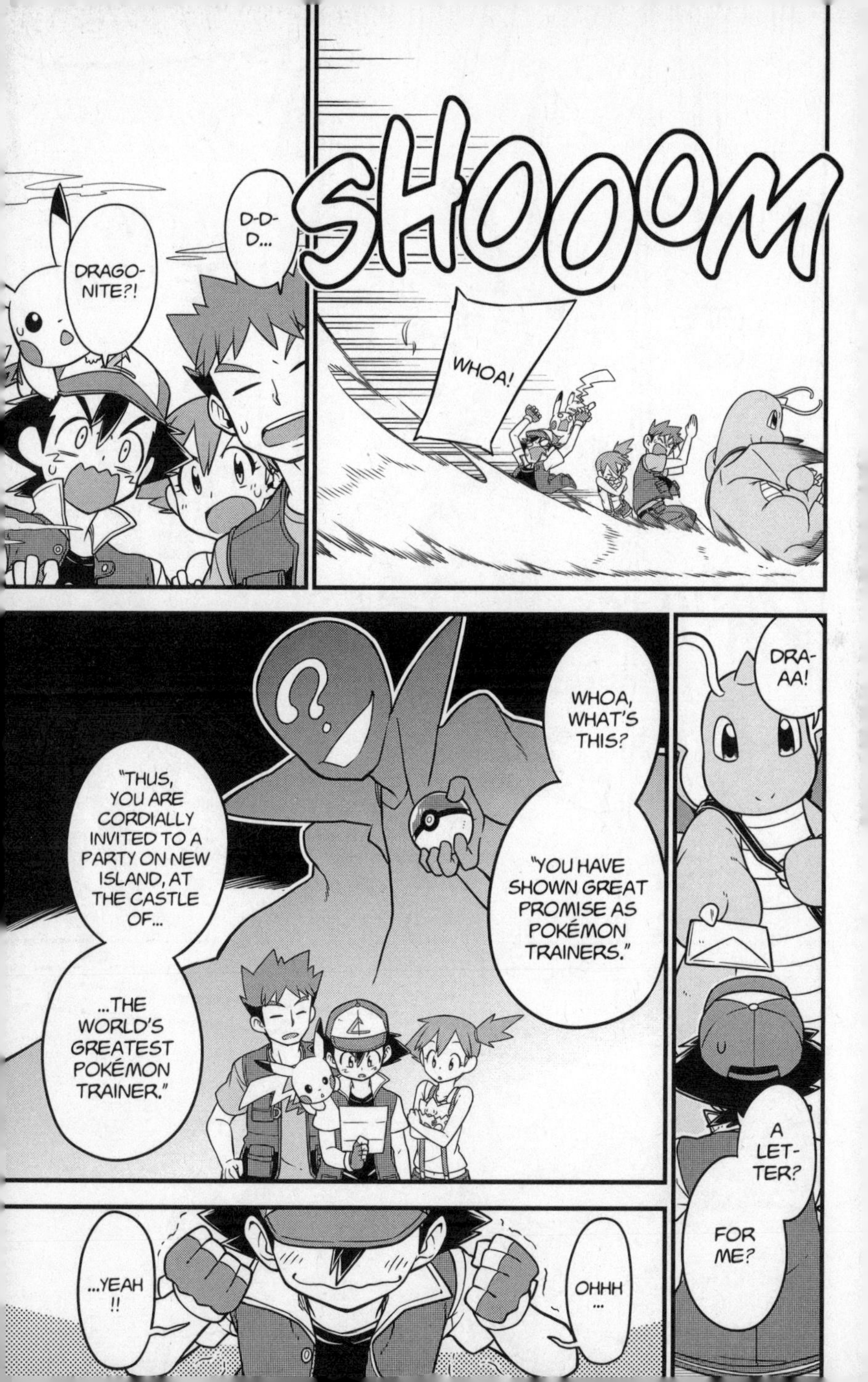
SHOOOM
WHOA!
D-D-D...
DRAGO-NITE?!
DRA-AA!
A LET-TER?
FOR ME?
WHOA, WHAT'S THIS?
"YOU HAVE SHOWN GREAT PROMISE AS POKÉMON TRAINERS."
"THUS, YOU ARE CORDIALLY INVITED TO A PARTY ON NEW ISLAND, AT THE CASTLE OF...
...THE WORLD'S GREATEST POKÉMON TRAINER."
OHHH...
...YEAH!!

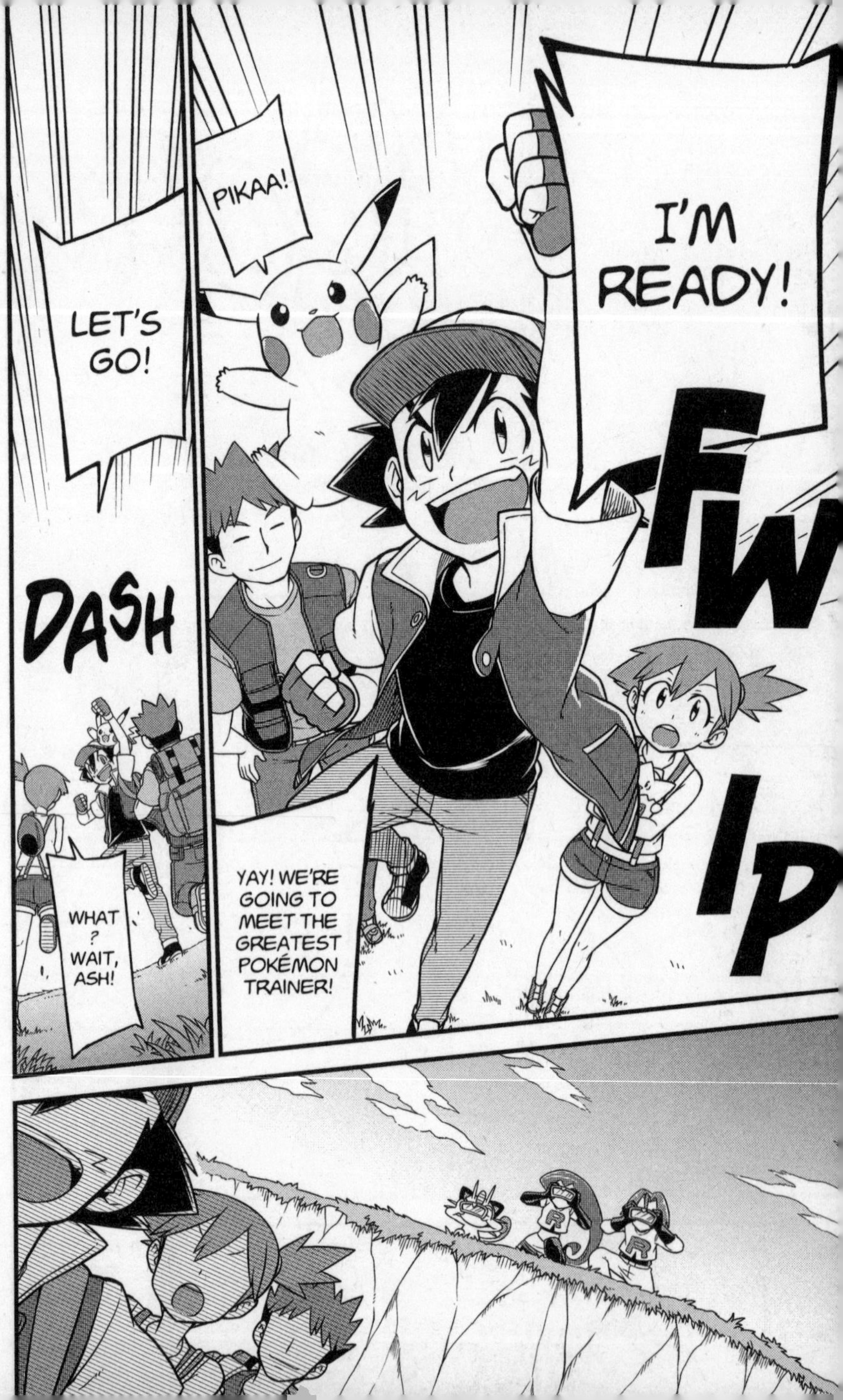
I'M READY!
PIKAA!
FWIP
YAY! WE'RE GOING TO MEET THE GREATEST POKÉMON TRAINER!
LET'S GO!
DASH
WHAT? WAIT, ASH!

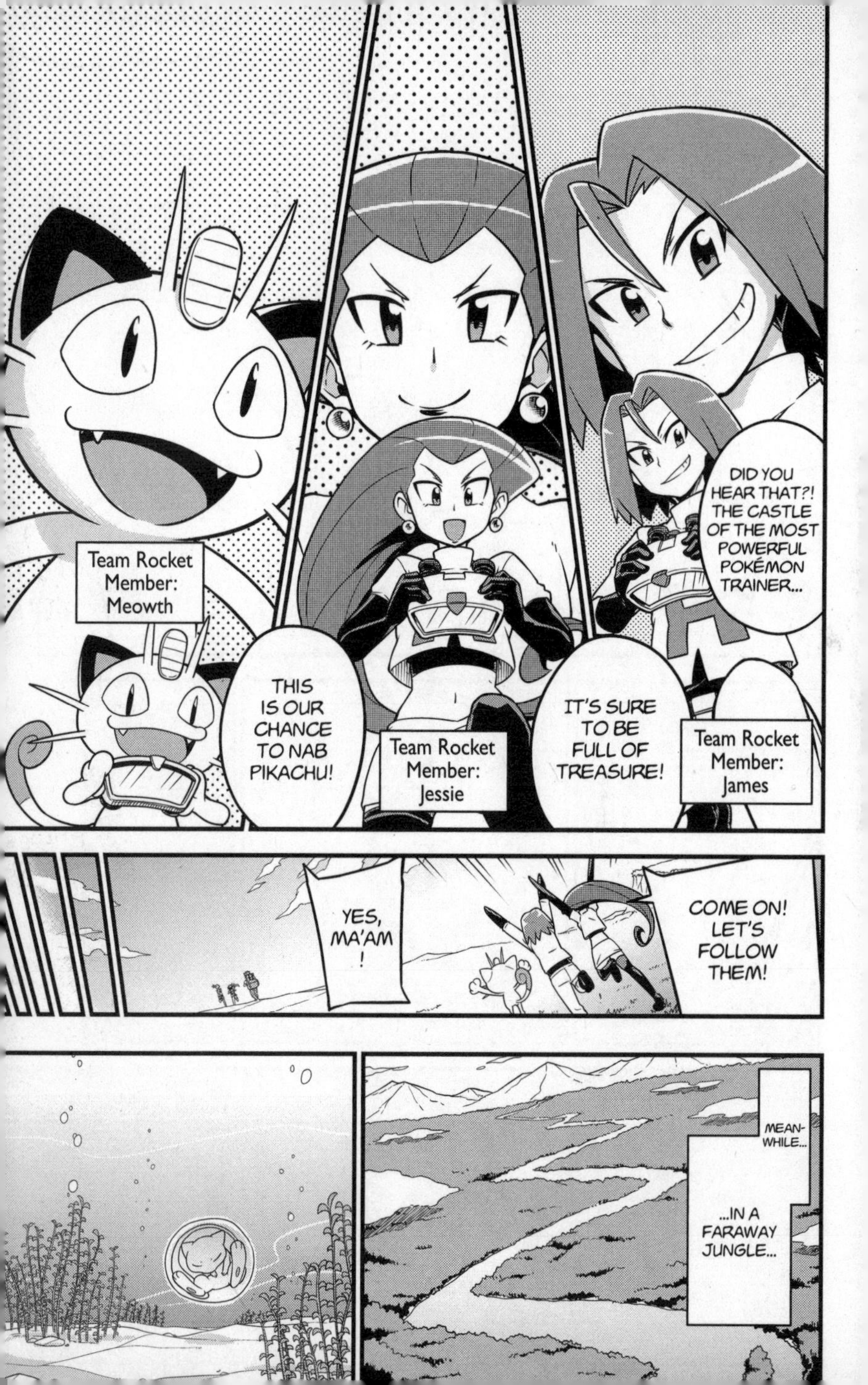
DID YOU HEAR THAT?! THE CASTLE OF THE MOST POWERFUL POKÉMON TRAINER...
Team Rocket Member: James
IT'S SURE TO BE FULL OF TREASURE!
Team Rocket Member: Jessie
THIS IS OUR CHANCE TO NAB PIKACHU!
Team Rocket Member: Meowth
COME ON! LET'S FOLLOW THEM!
YES, MA'AM!
MEAN-WHILE...
...IN A FARAWAY JUNGLE...

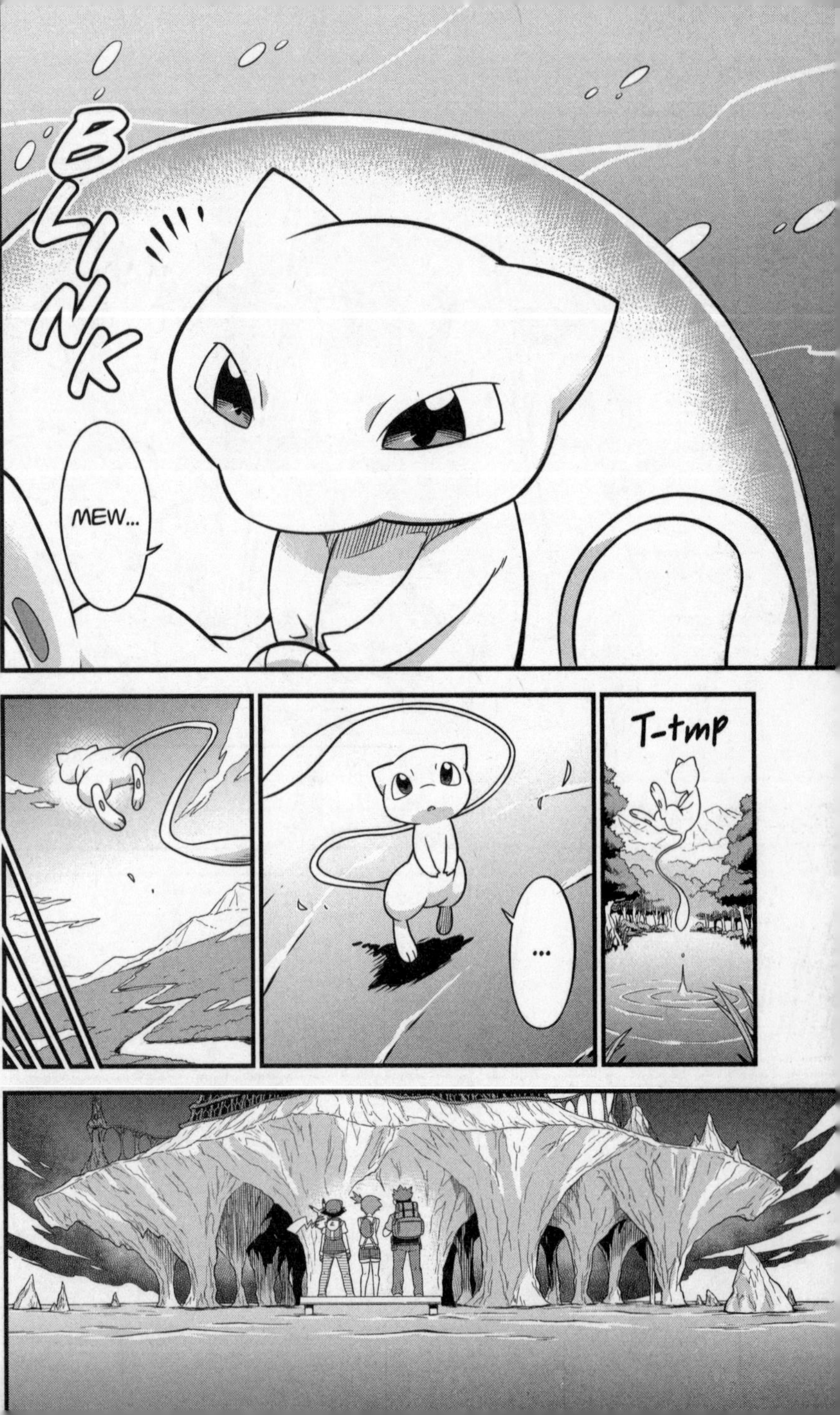
BLINK
MEW...
T-tmp
...

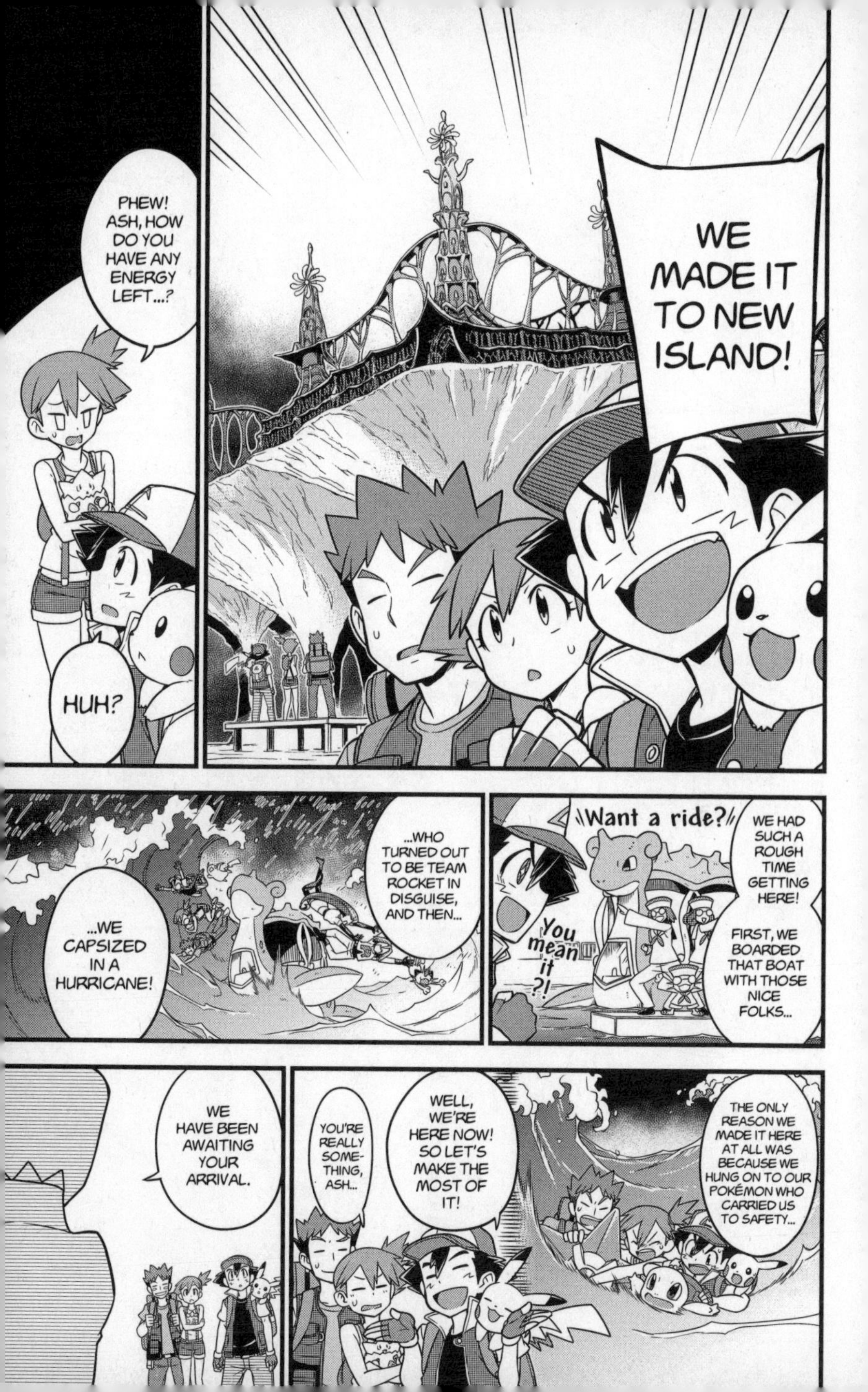
WE MADE IT TO NEW ISLAND!
PHEW! ASH, HOW DO YOU HAVE ANY ENERGY LEFT...?
HUH?
WE HAD SUCH A ROUGH TIME GETTING HERE!
Want a ride?
FIRST, WE BOARDED THAT BOAT WITH THOSE NICE FOLKS...
You mean it?!
...WHO TURNED OUT TO BE TEAM ROCKET IN DISGUISE, AND THEN...
...WE CAPSIZED IN A HURRICANE!
THE ONLY REASON WE MADE IT HERE AT ALL WAS BECAUSE WE HUNG ON TO OUR POKÉMON WHO CARRIED US TO SAFETY...
WELL, WE'RE HERE NOW! SO LET'S MAKE THE MOST OF IT!
YOU'RE REALLY SOME-THING, ASH...
WE HAVE BEEN AWAITING YOUR ARRIVAL.

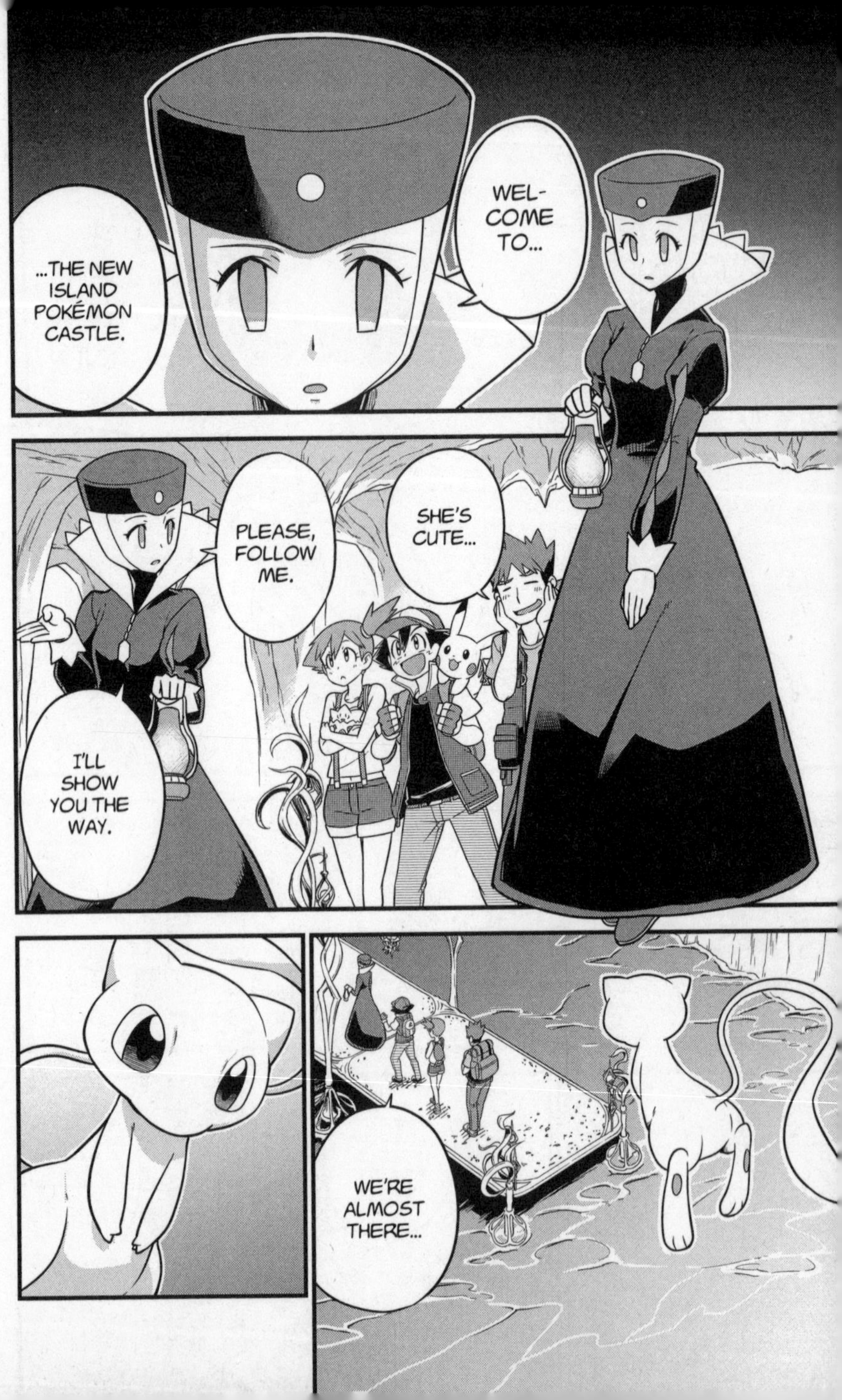
WEL-COME TO...
...THE NEW ISLAND POKÉMON CASTLE.
SHE'S CUTE...
PLEASE, FOLLOW ME.
I'LL SHOW YOU THE WAY.
WE'RE ALMOST THERE...

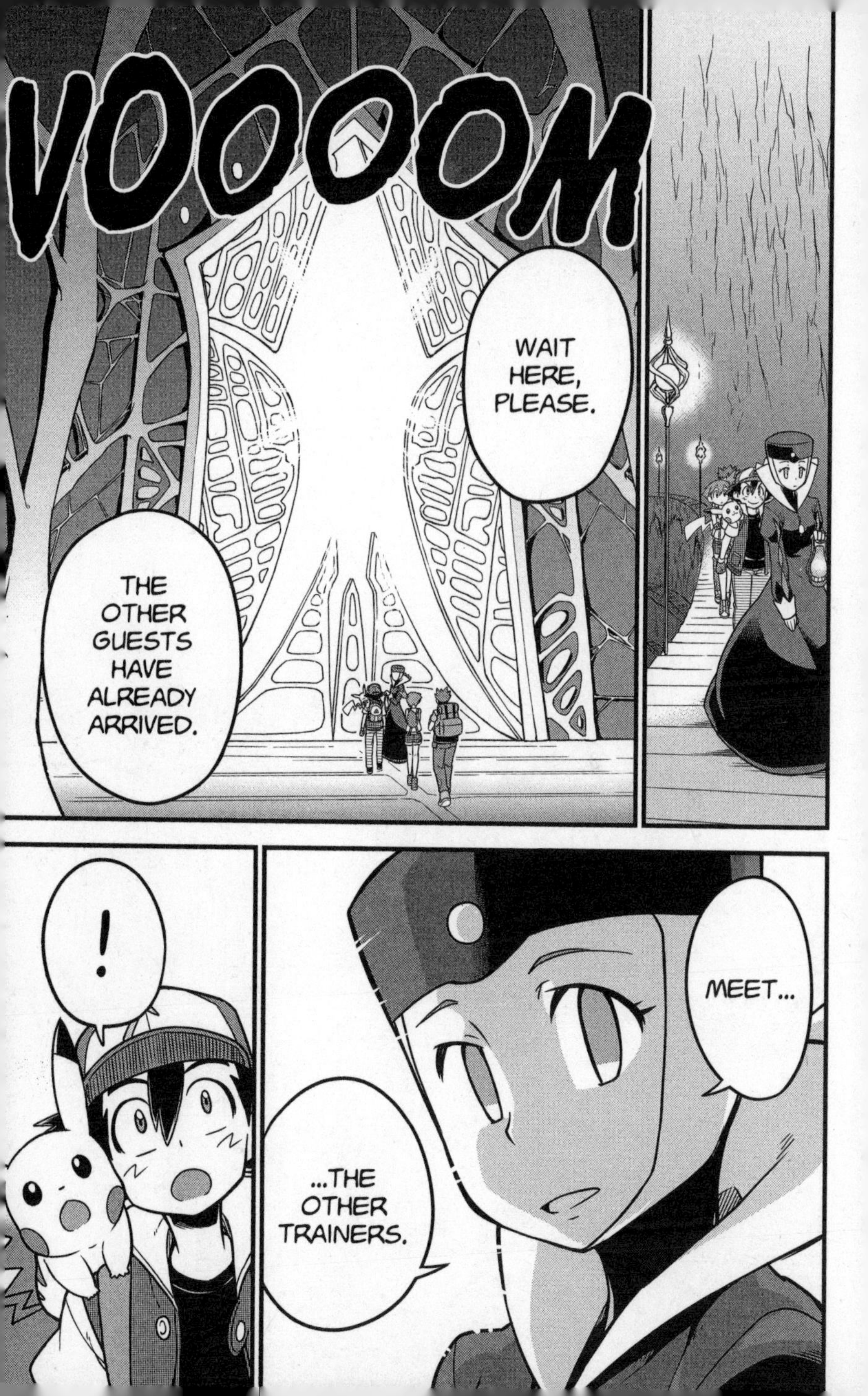
VOOOOM
WAIT HERE, PLEASE.
THE OTHER GUESTS HAVE ALREADY ARRIVED.
MEET...
...THE OTHER TRAINERS.
!

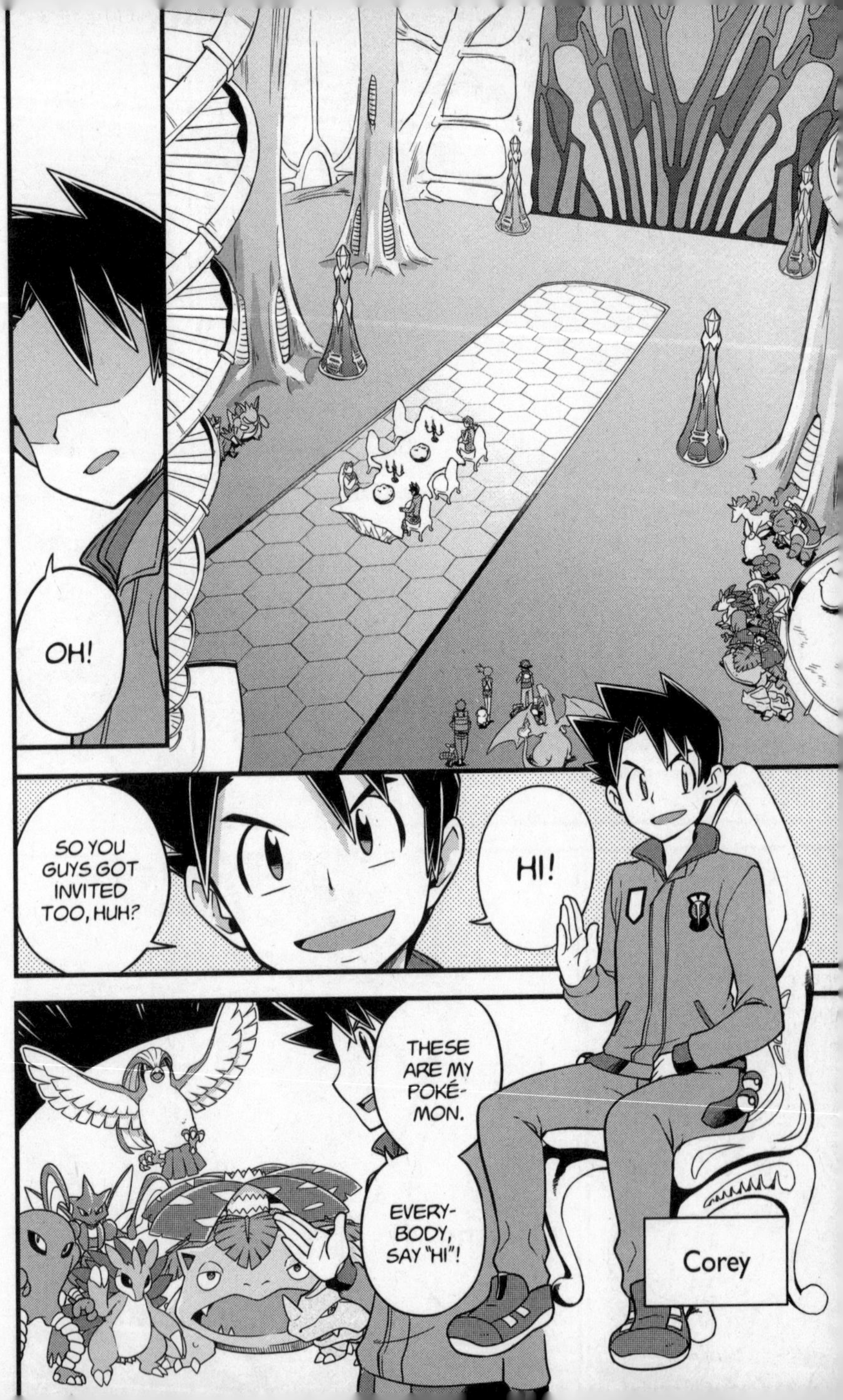
OH!
HI!
SO YOU GUYS GOT INVITED TOO, HUH?
THESE ARE MY POKÉ-MON.
EVERY-BODY, SAY "HI"!
Corey

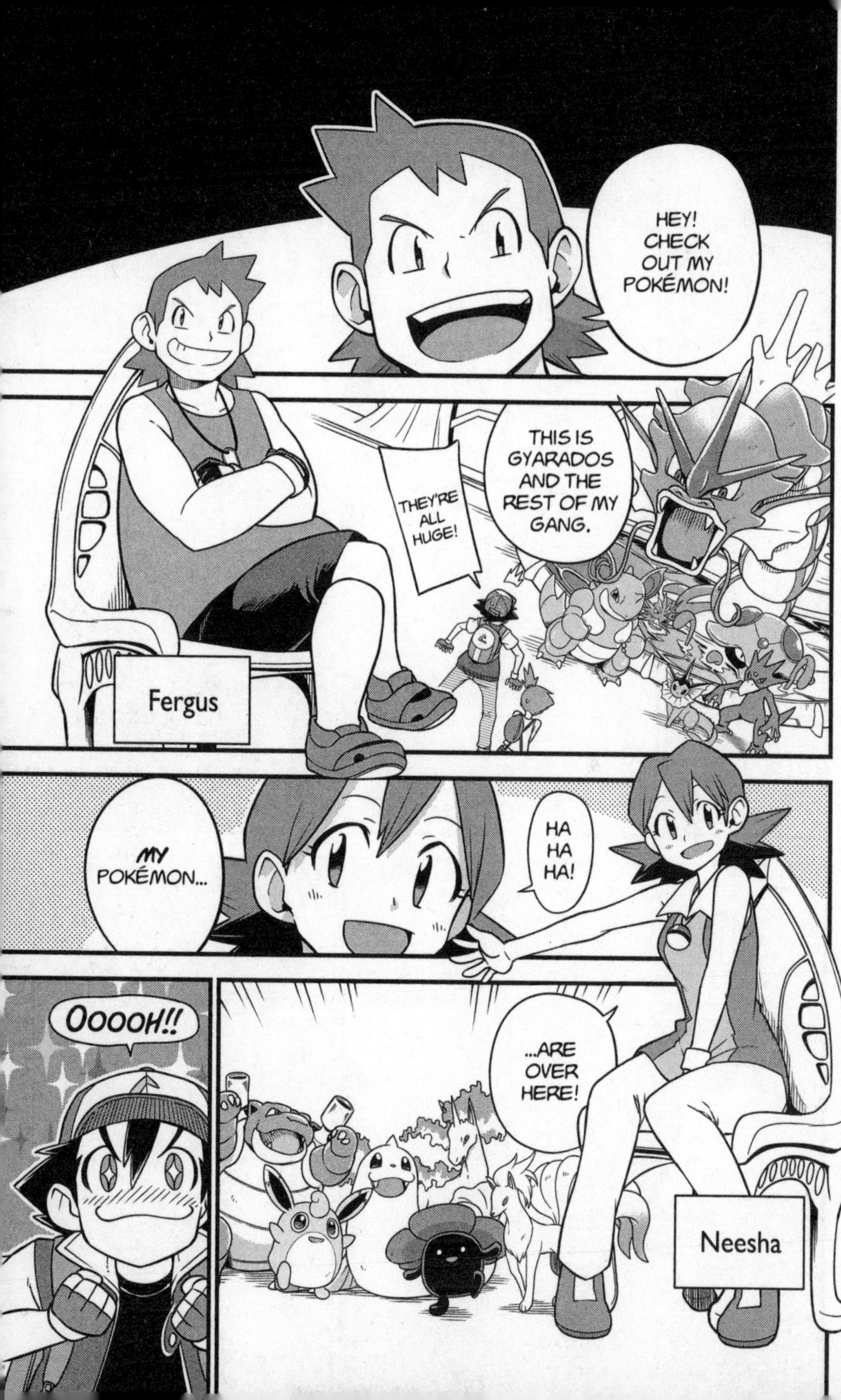
HEY! CHECK OUT MY POKÉMON!
THIS IS GYARADOS AND THE REST OF MY GANG.
THEY'RE ALL HUGE!
Fergus
HA HA HA!
MY POKÉMON...
...ARE OVER HERE!
Neesha
OOOOH!!

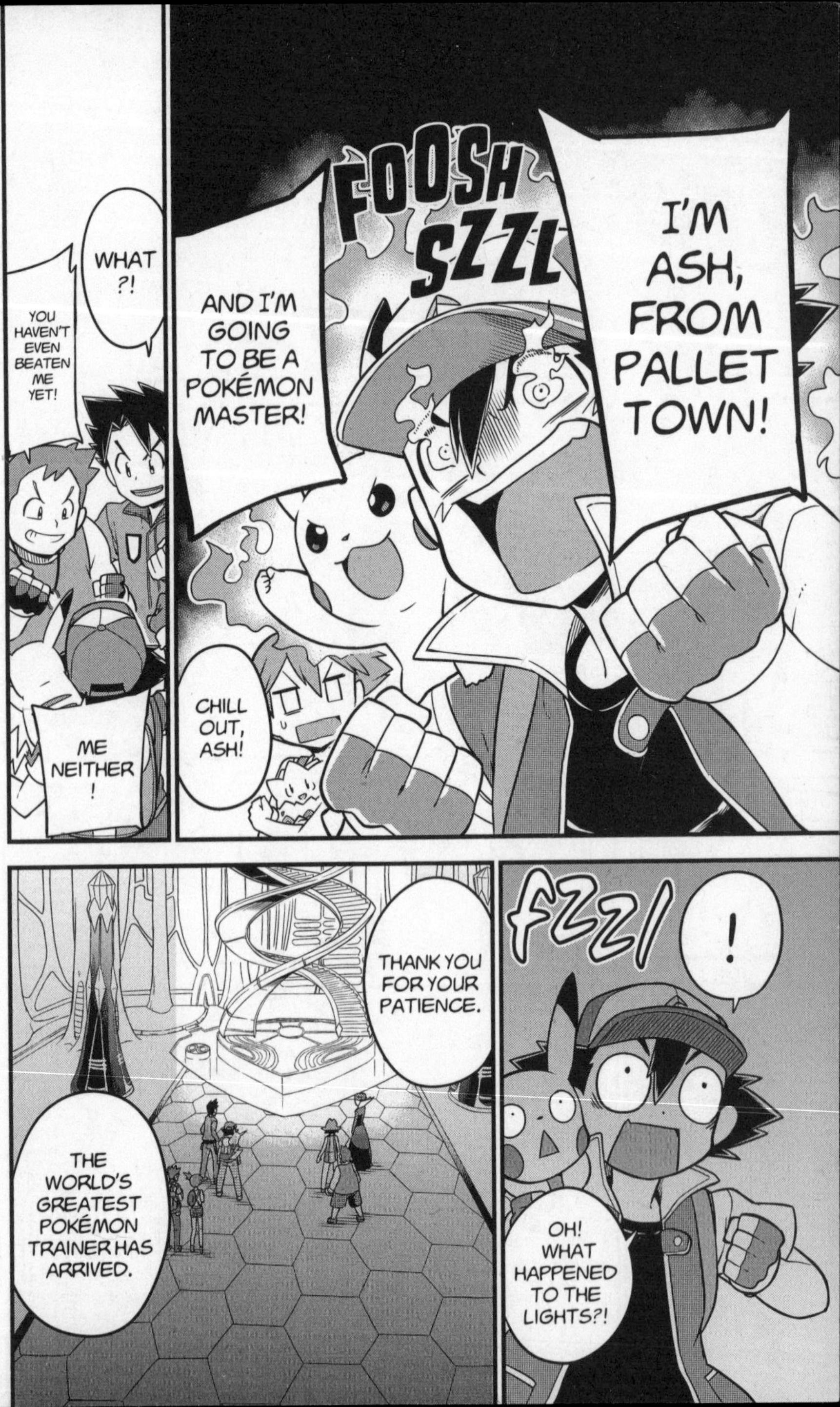
FOOSH
SZZL
I'M ASH, FROM PALLET TOWN!
AND I'M GOING TO BE A POKÉMON MASTER!
CHILL OUT, ASH!
WHAT?!
YOU HAVEN'T EVEN BEATEN ME YET!
ME NEITHER!
FZZL
!
OH! WHAT HAPPENED TO THE LIGHTS?!
THANK YOU FOR YOUR PATIENCE.
THE WORLD'S GREATEST POKÉMON TRAINER HAS ARRIVED.

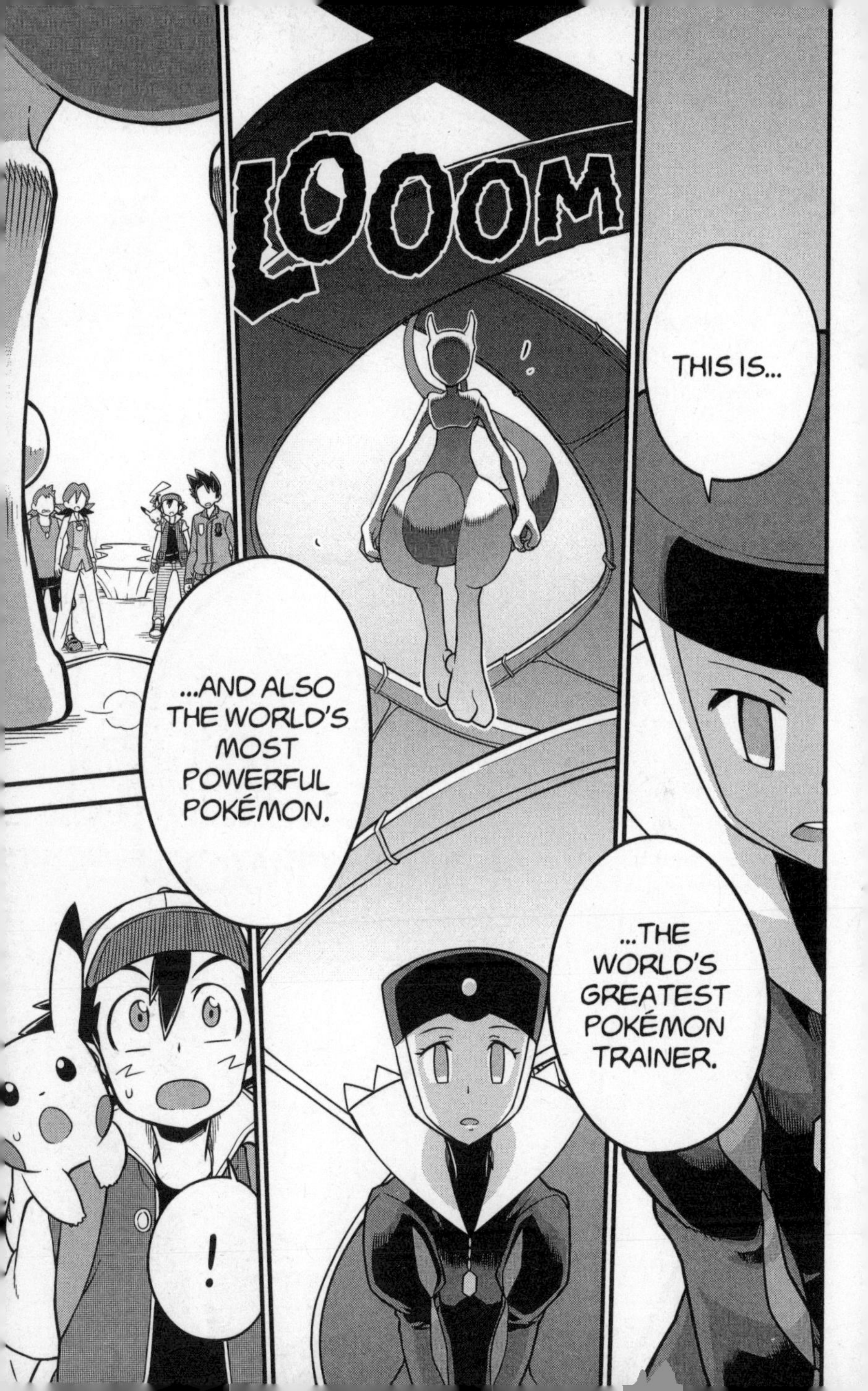
THIS IS...
...THE WORLD'S GREATEST POKÉMON TRAINER.
LOOOM
...AND ALSO THE WORLD'S MOST POWERFUL POKÉMON.
!

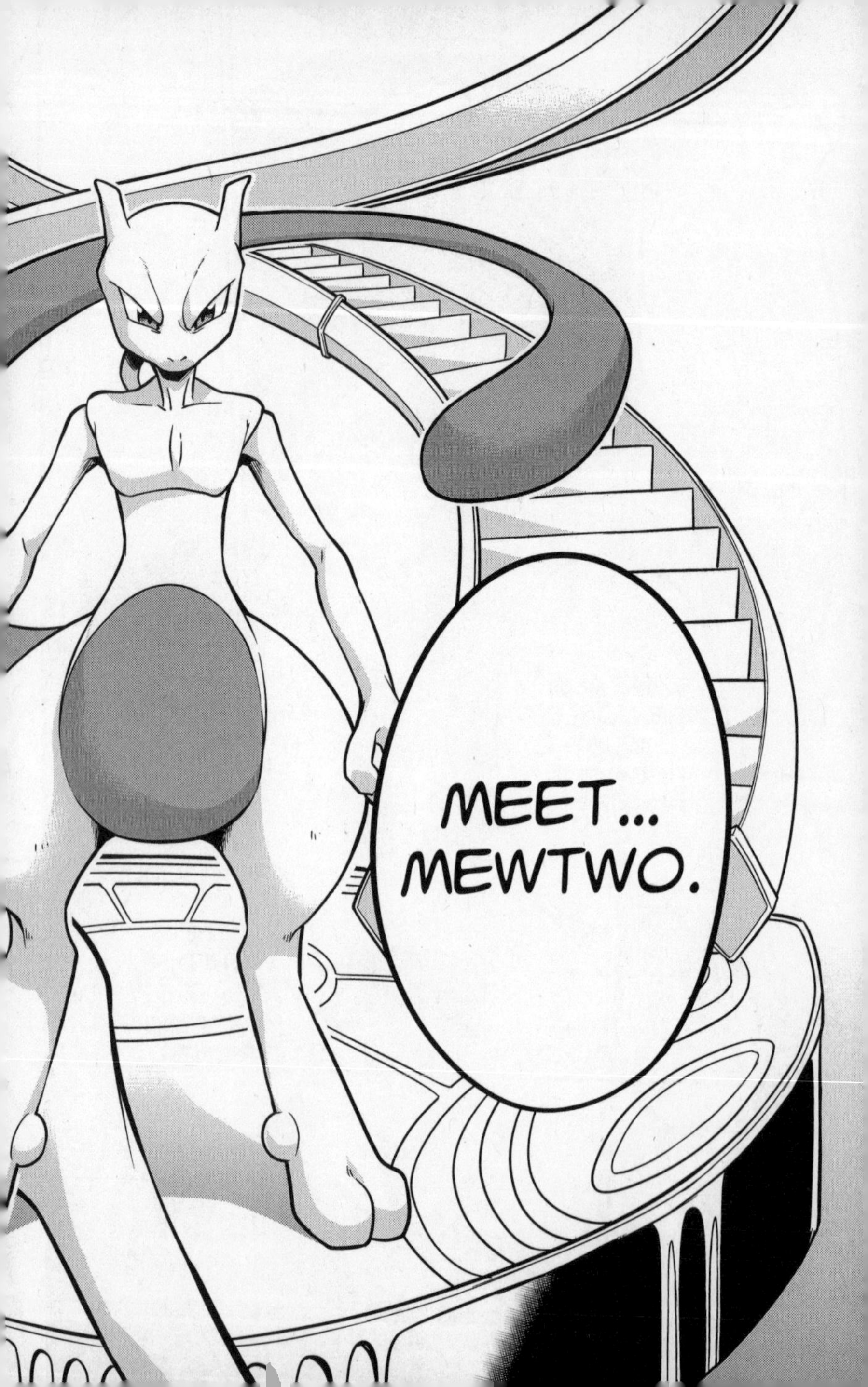
MEET... MEWTWO.

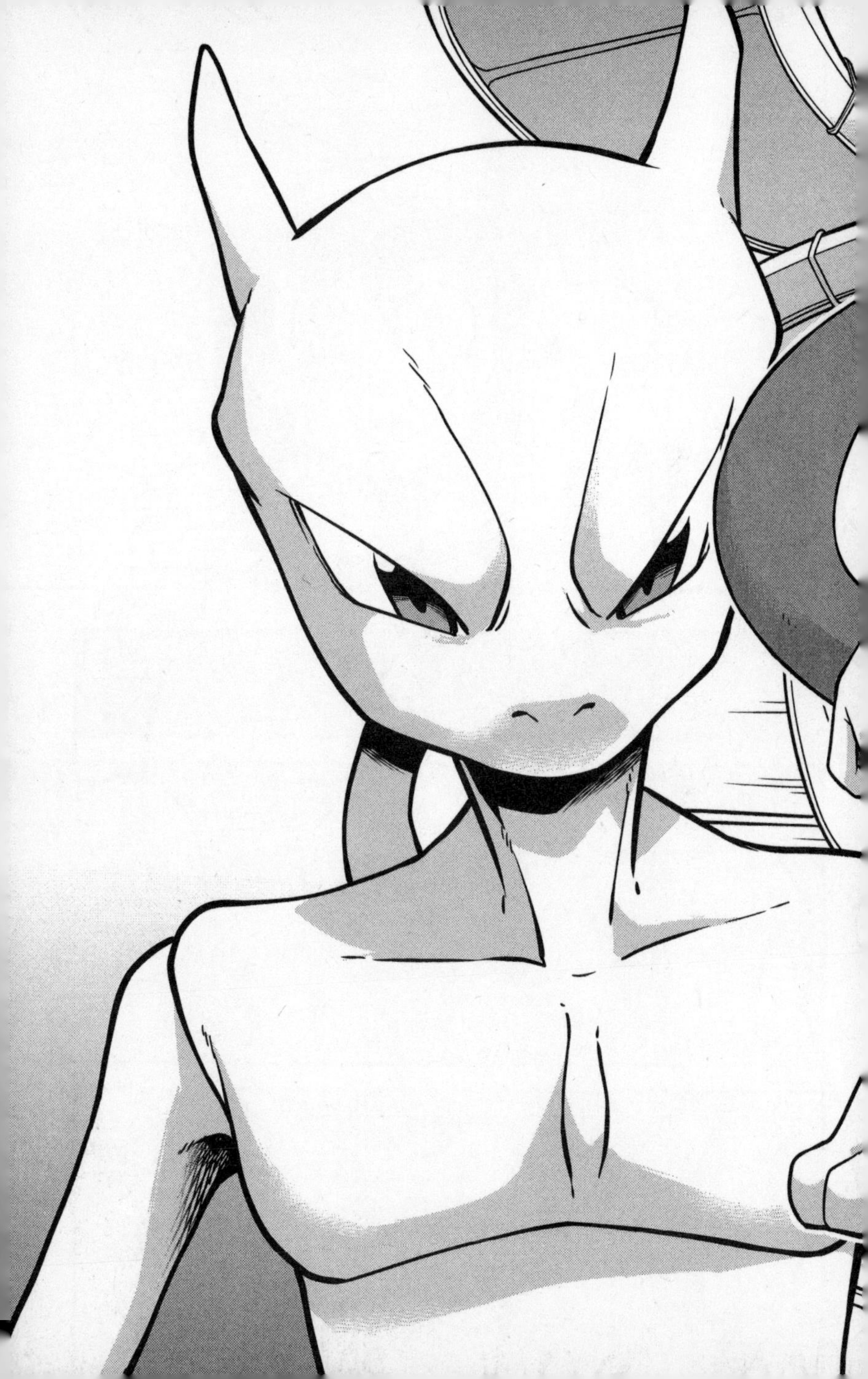

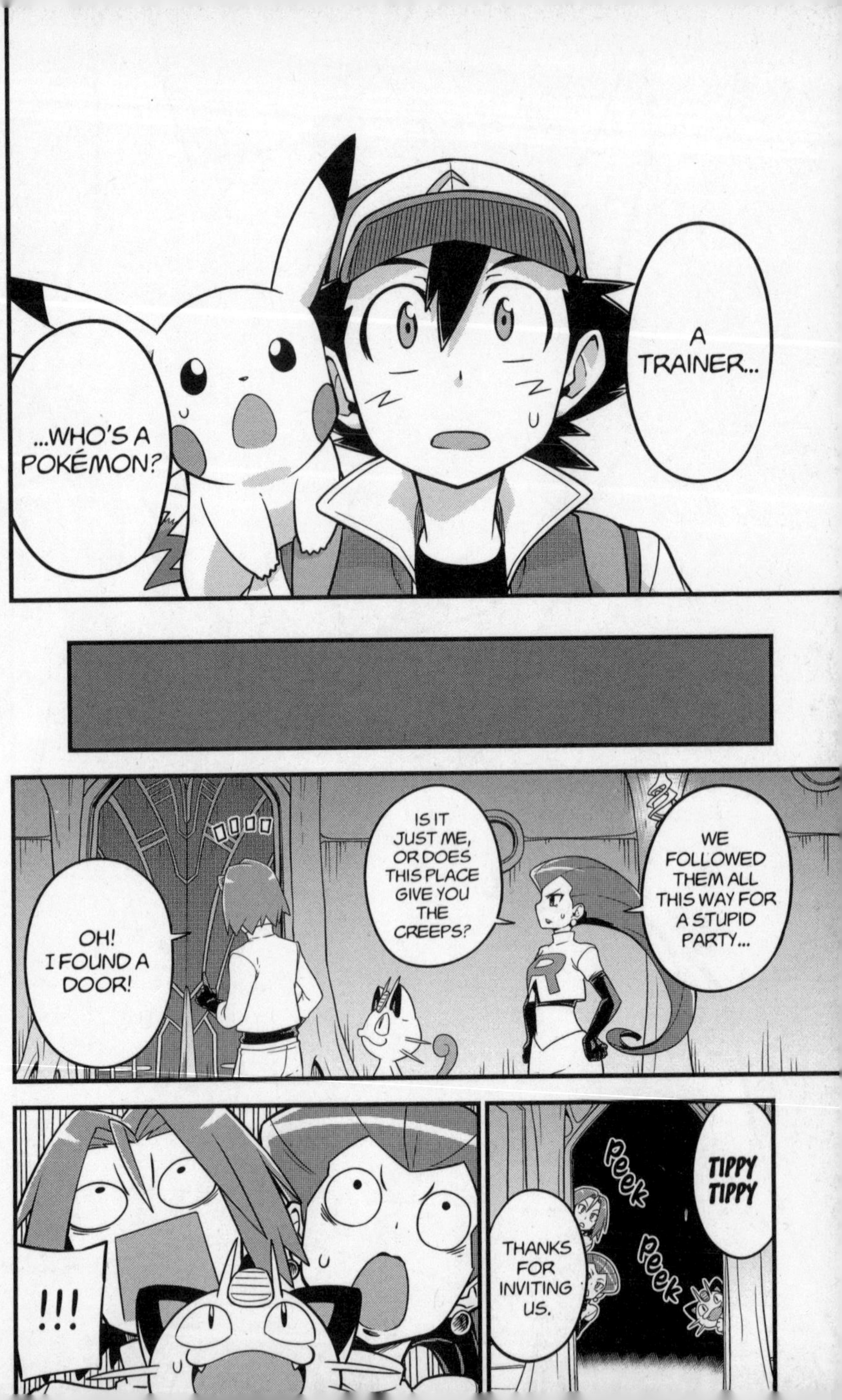
A TRAINER...
...WHO'S A POKÉMON?
WE FOLLOWED THEM ALL THIS WAY FOR A STUPID PARTY...
IS IT JUST ME, OR DOES THIS PLACE GIVE YOU THE CREEPS?
OH! I FOUND A DOOR!
TIPPY TIPPY
Peek peek
THANKS FOR INVITING US.
!!!

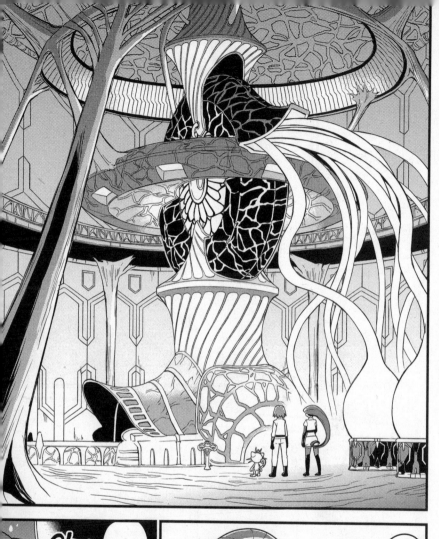

GLUB !

WHAT IS THIS ROOM?

THAT THING IS HUGE!

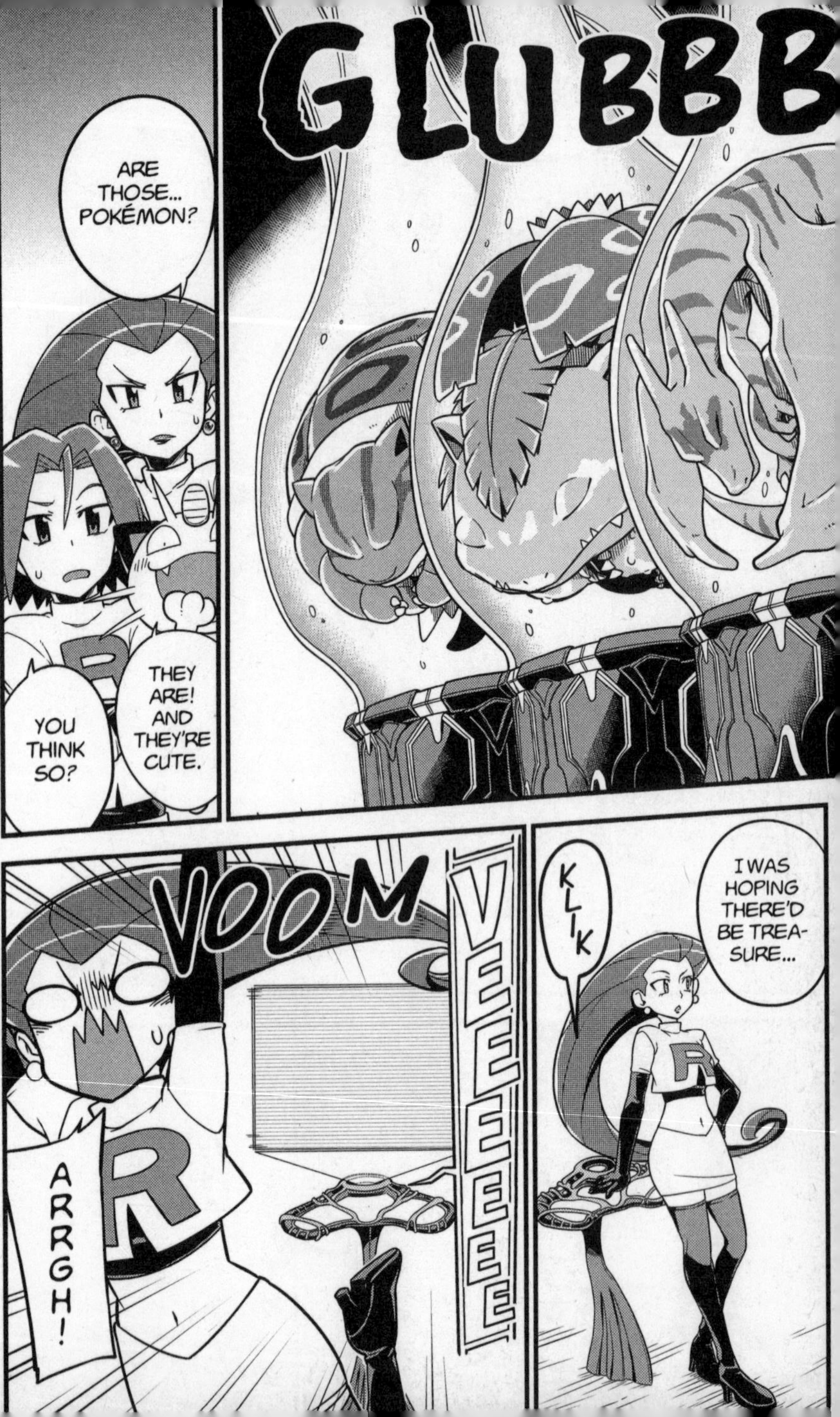
GLUBBB
ARE THOSE... POKÉMON?
THEY ARE! AND THEY'RE CUTE.
YOU THINK SO?
I WAS HOPING THERE'D BE TREA-SURE...
KLIK
VEEEEEE
VOOM
ARRGH!

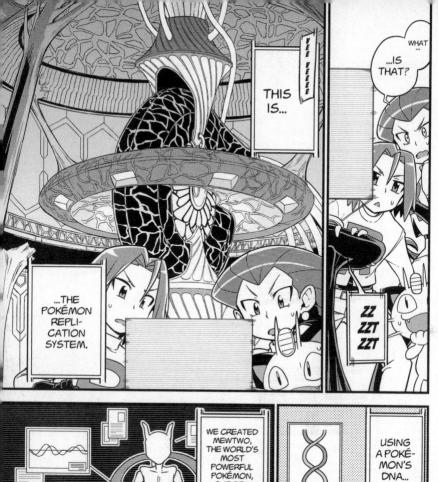

WHAT...
...IS THAT?
ZZ ZZT ZZT
VEE VEEEE
THIS IS...
...THE POKÉMON REPLI-CATION SYSTEM.
USING A POKÉ-MON'S DNA...
...WE CREATE A CLONE OF THE ORIGI-NAL.
WE CREATED MEWTWO, THE WORLD'S MOST POWERFUL POKÉMON, OUT OF A FOSSILIZED EYELASH FROM MEW.
BUT...

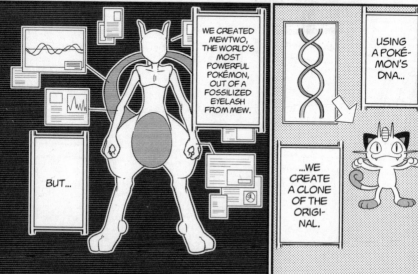

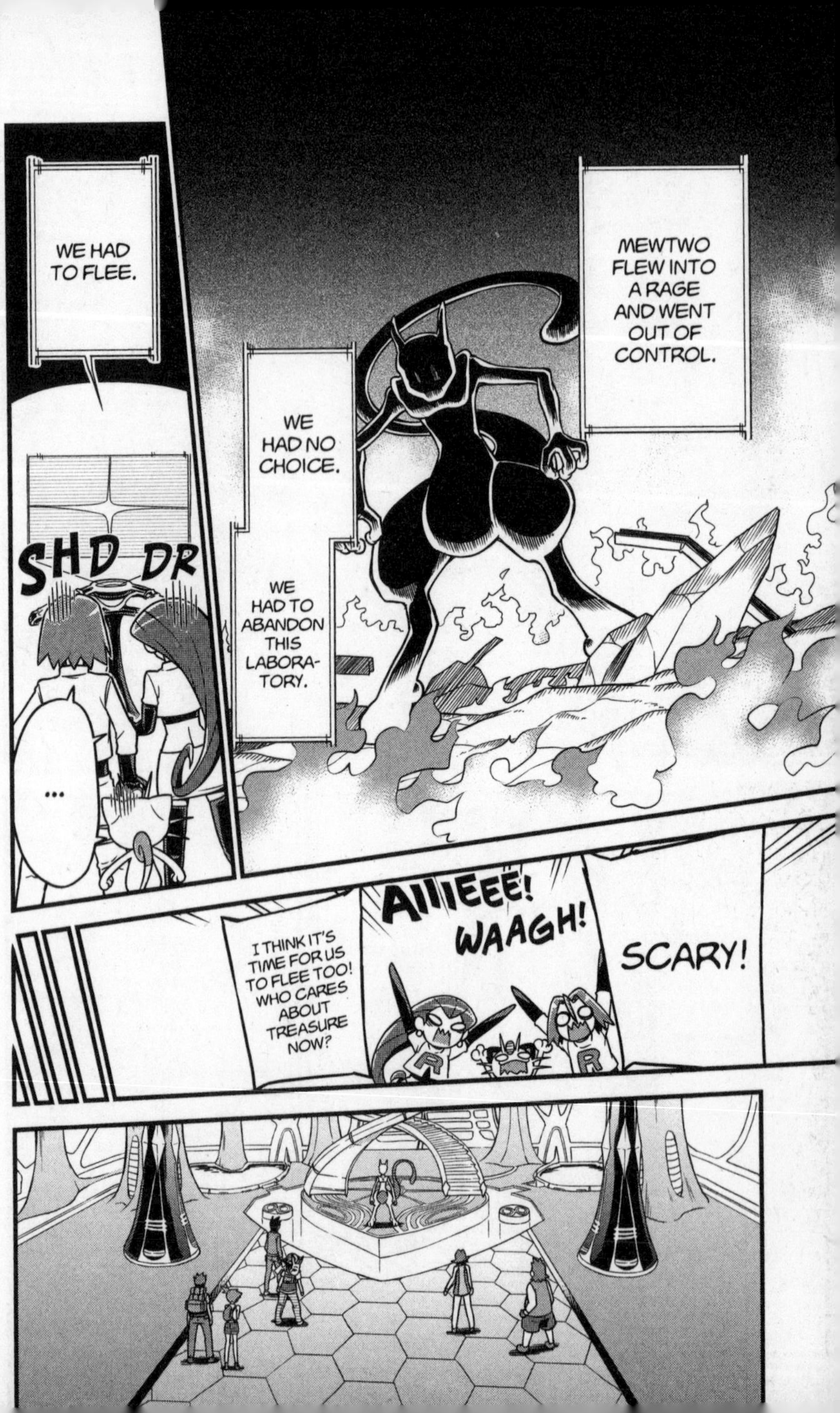
MEWTWO FLEW INTO A RAGE AND WENT OUT OF CONTROL.
WE HAD NO CHOICE.
WE HAD TO ABANDON THIS LABORATORY.
WE HAD TO FLEE.
SHD DR
...
SCARY!
AIIIEEE! WAAGH!
I THINK IT'S TIME FOR US TO FLEE TOO! WHO CARES ABOUT TREASURE NOW?

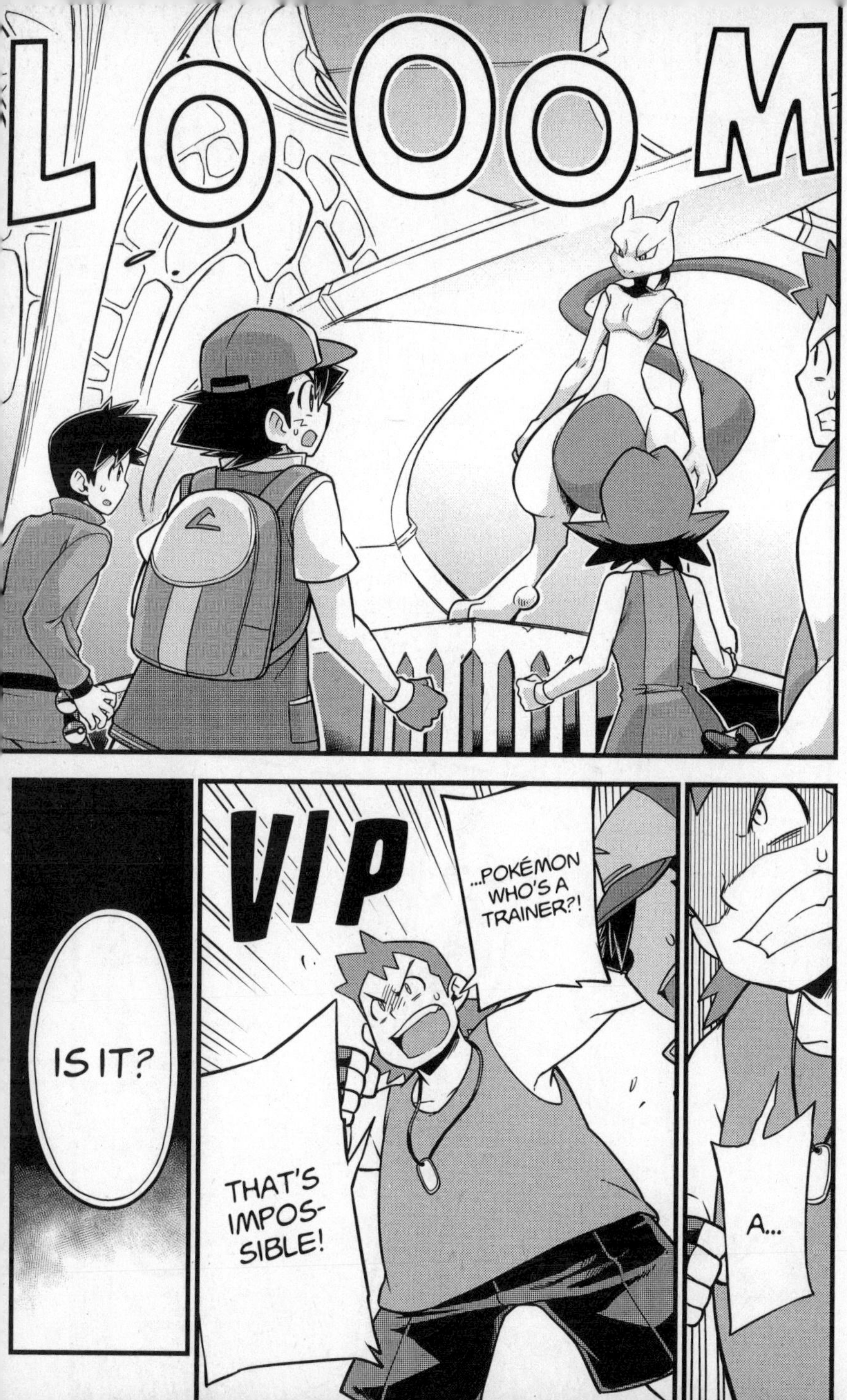
LOOOM
A...
...POKÉMON WHO'S A TRAINER?!
VIP
THAT'S IMPOSSIBLE!
IS IT?

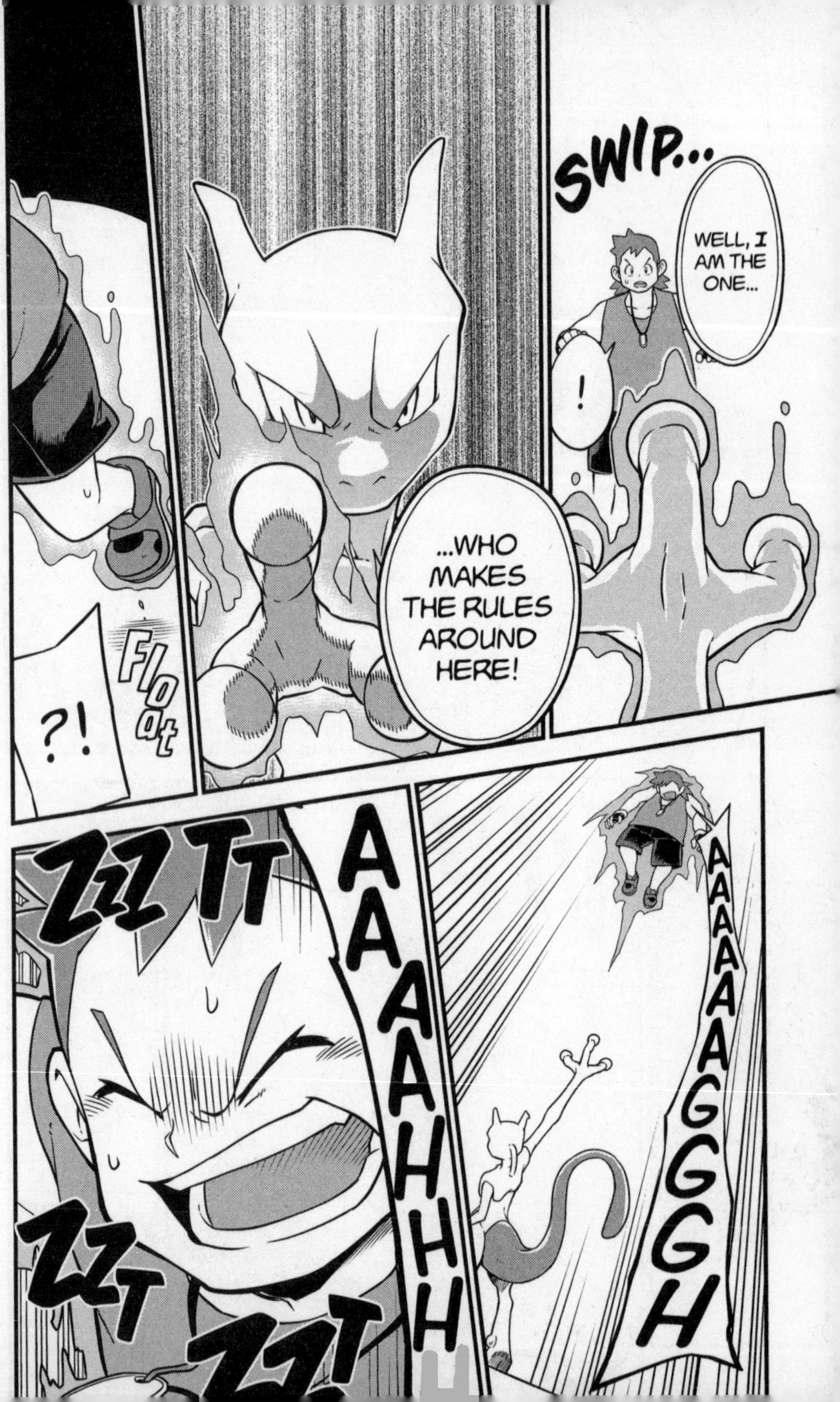
SWIP...
WELL, I AM THE ONE...
!
...WHO MAKES THE RULES AROUND HERE!
Float
?!
AAAAAAAGGGGH
ZZZTT
AAAHHHH
ZZZT
ZZZT

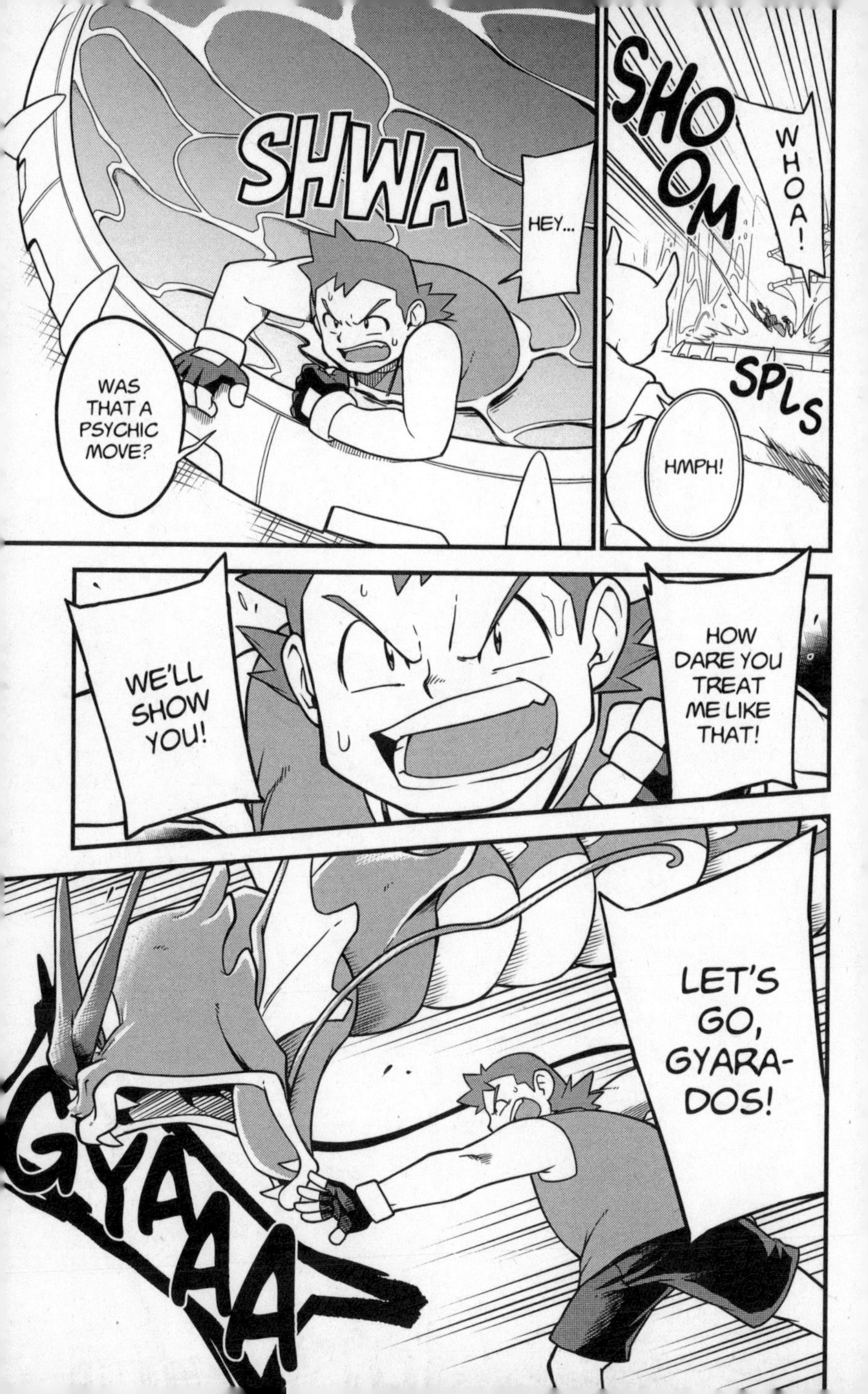
SHOOM
WHOA!
SPLS
HMPH!
SHWA
HEY...
WAS THAT A PSYCHIC MOVE?
HOW DARE YOU TREAT ME LIKE THAT!
WE'LL SHOW YOU!
LET'S GO, GYARA-DOS!
GYAAA

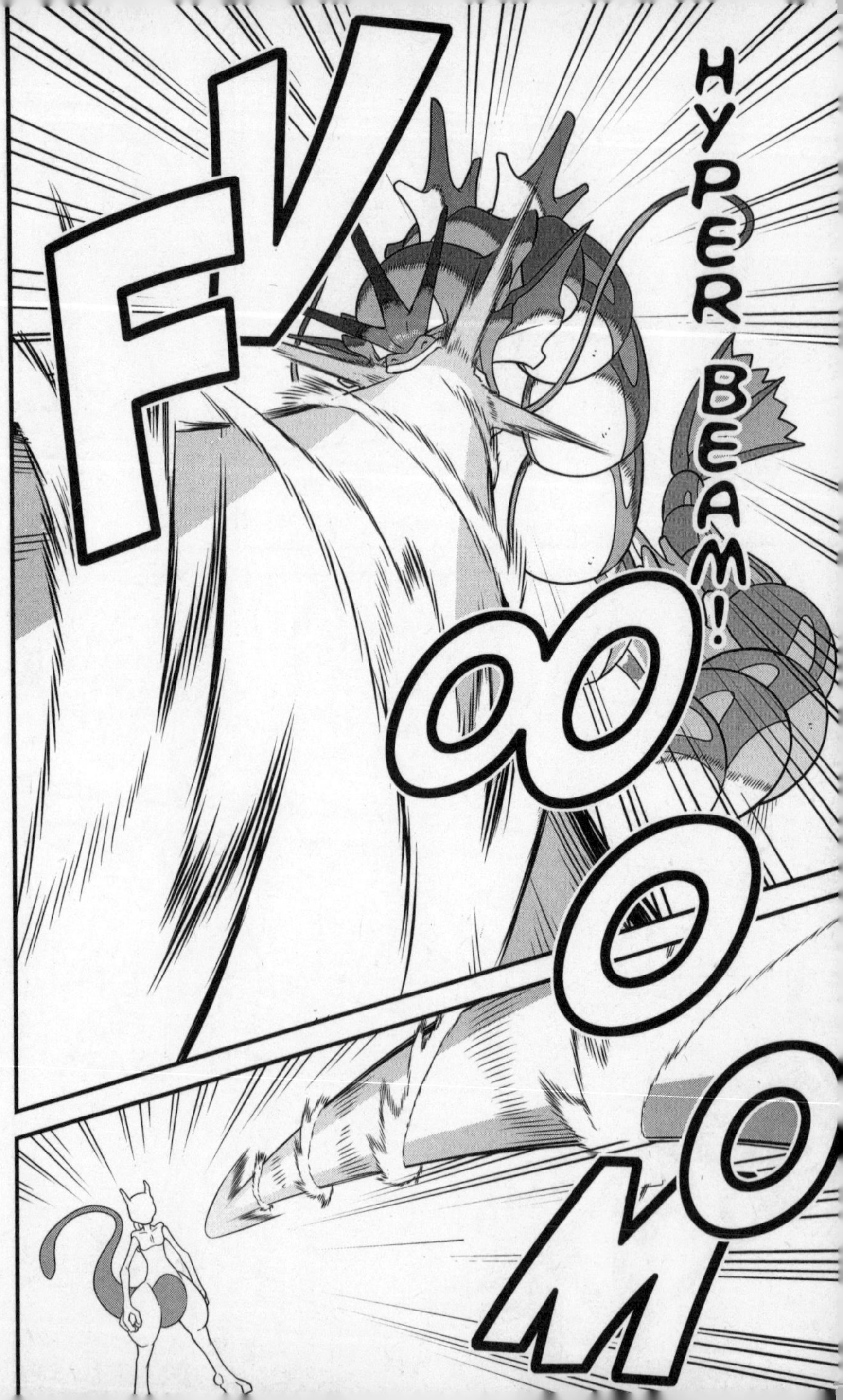
HYPER BEAM!
FWOOOM

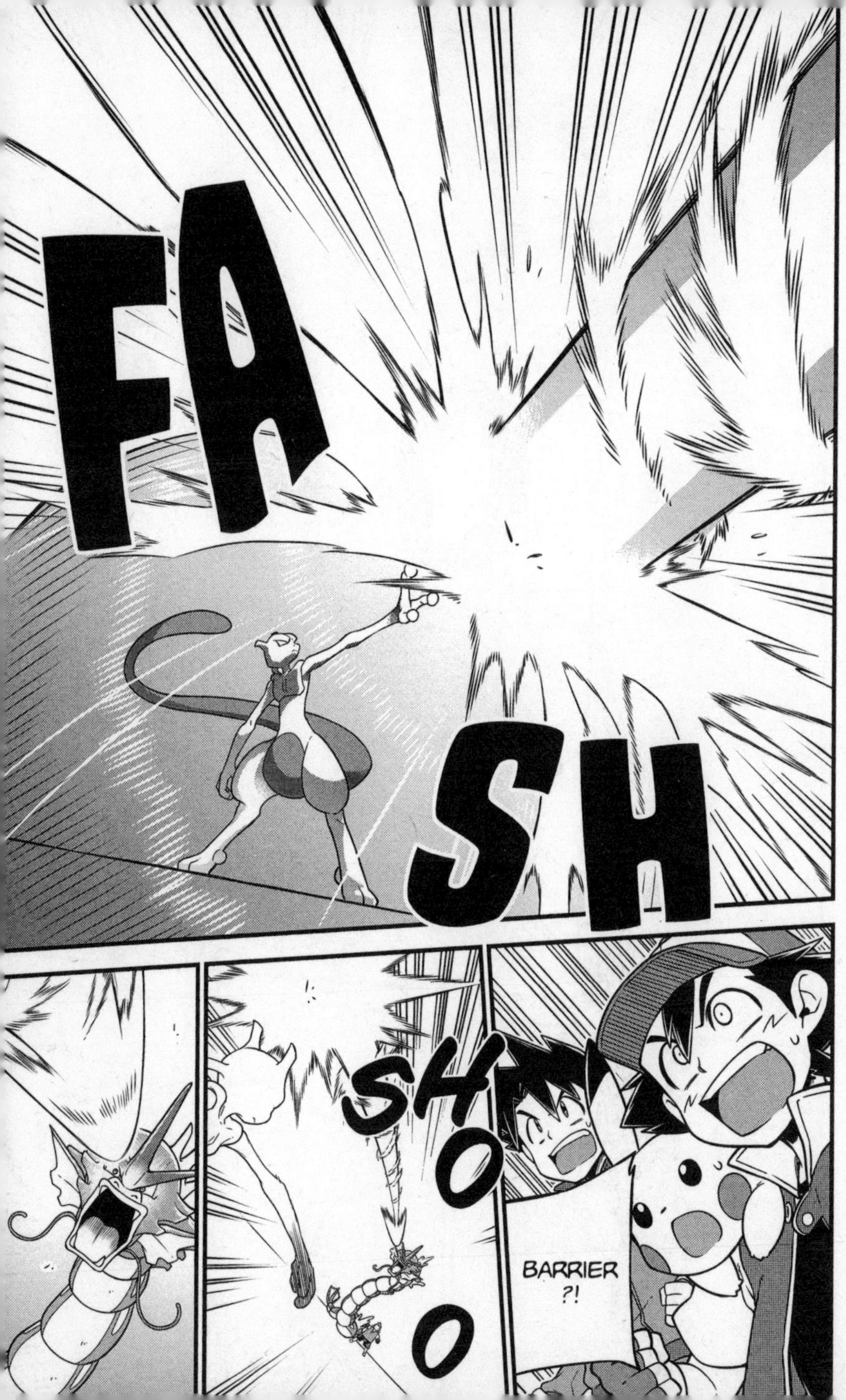
FA
SH
BARRIER ?!
SH
O
O

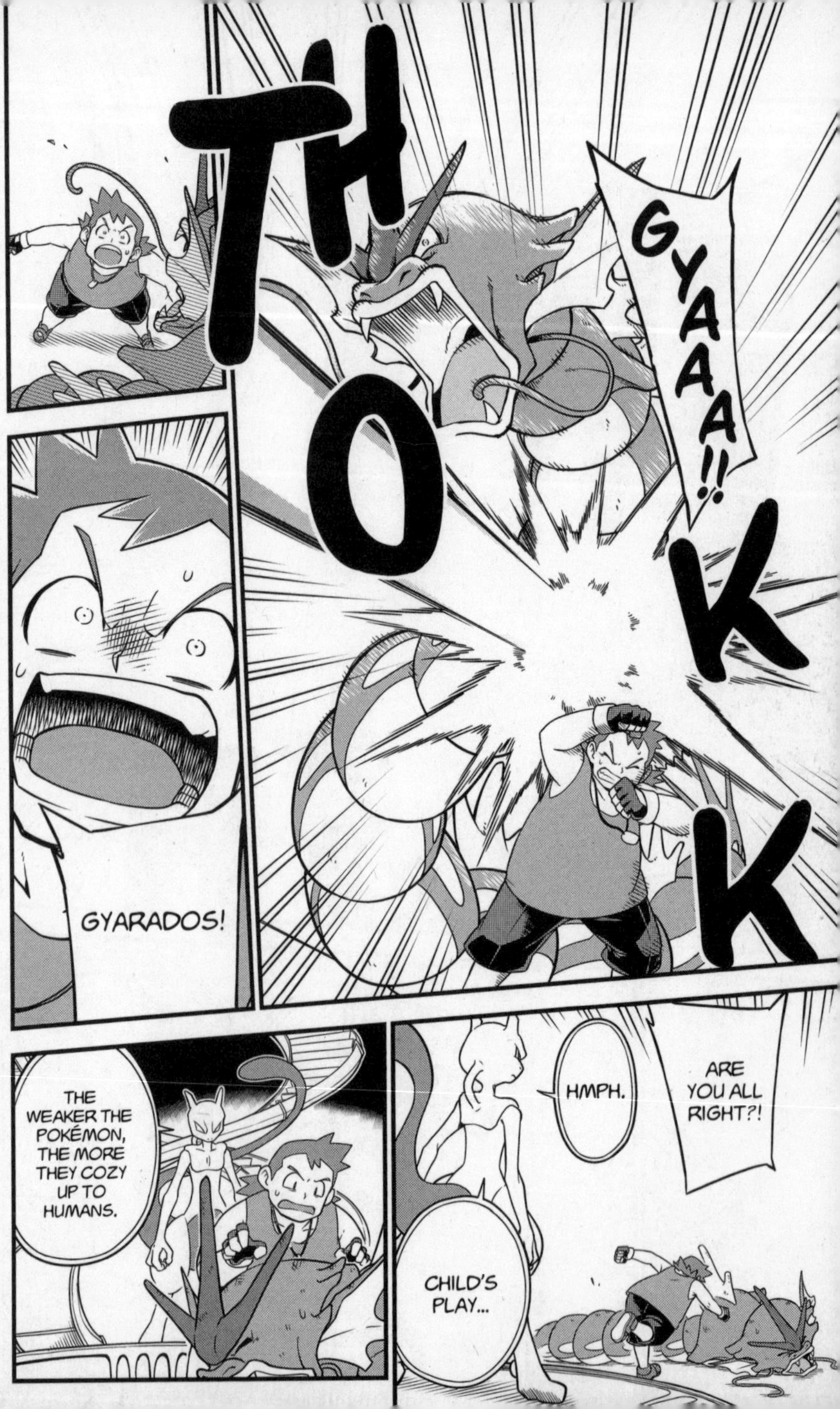
THOKK
GYAAA!!
GYARADOS!
ARE YOU ALL RIGHT?!
HMPH.
CHILD'S PLAY...
THE WEAKER THE POKÉMON, THE MORE THEY COZY UP TO HUMANS.

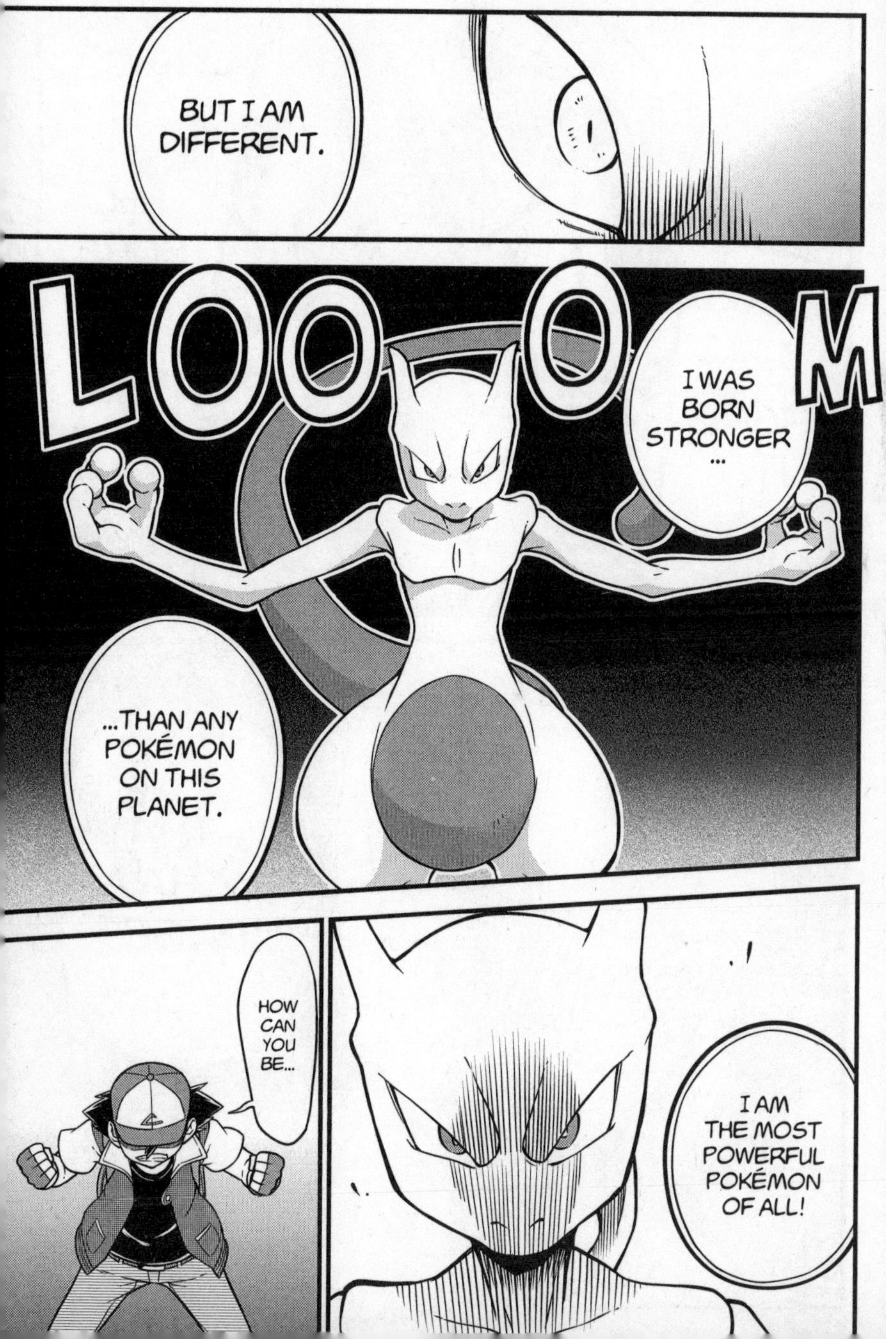
BUT I AM DIFFERENT.
LOOOM
I WAS BORN STRONGER ...
...THAN ANY POKÉMON ON THIS PLANET.
I AM THE MOST POWERFUL POKÉMON OF ALL!
HOW CAN YOU BE...

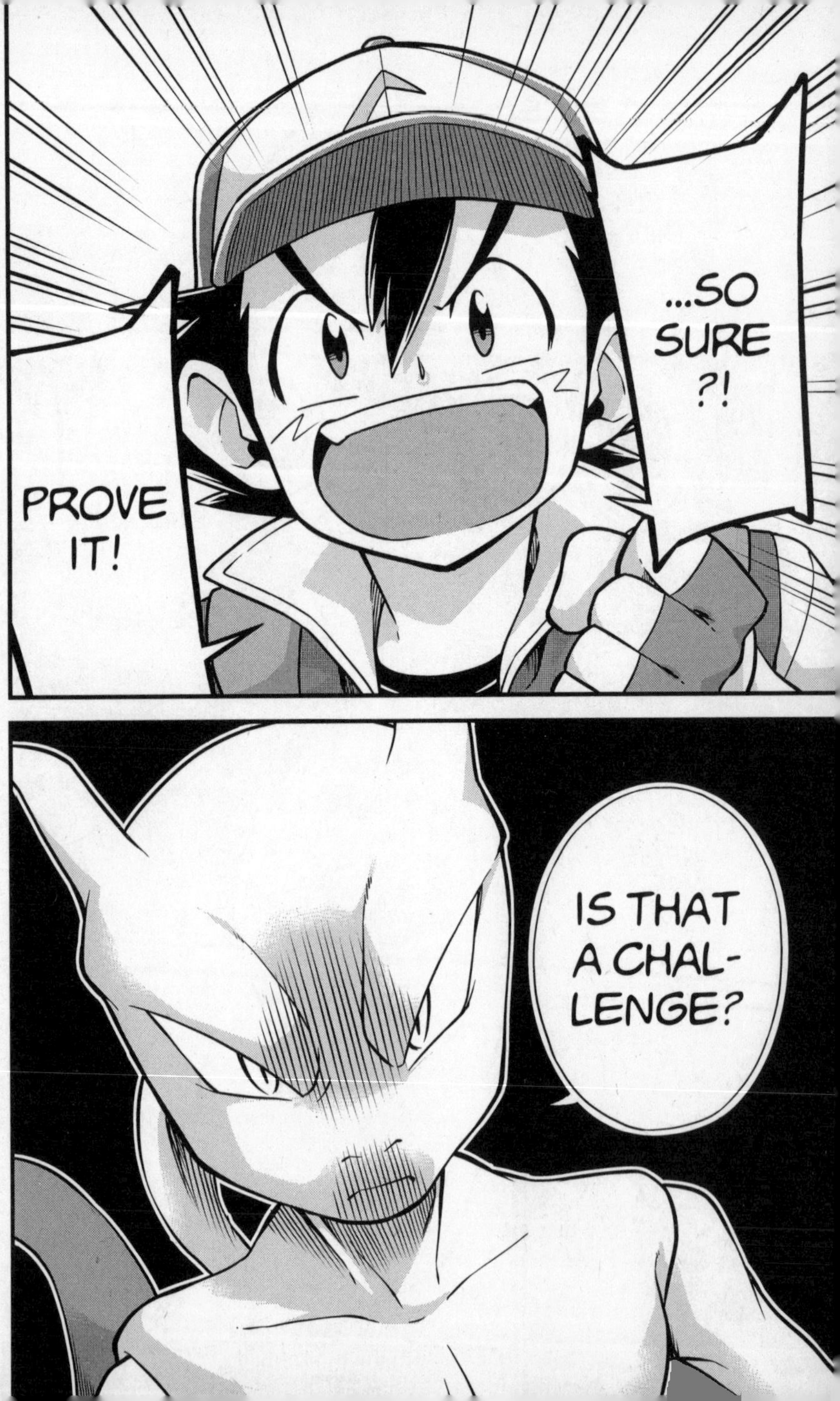
...SO SURE?!
PROVE IT!
IS THAT A CHALLENGE?

Pokémon™

MEWTWO STRIKES BACK

EVOLUTION

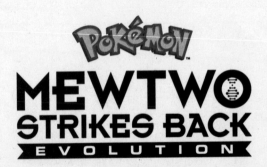

Part 2

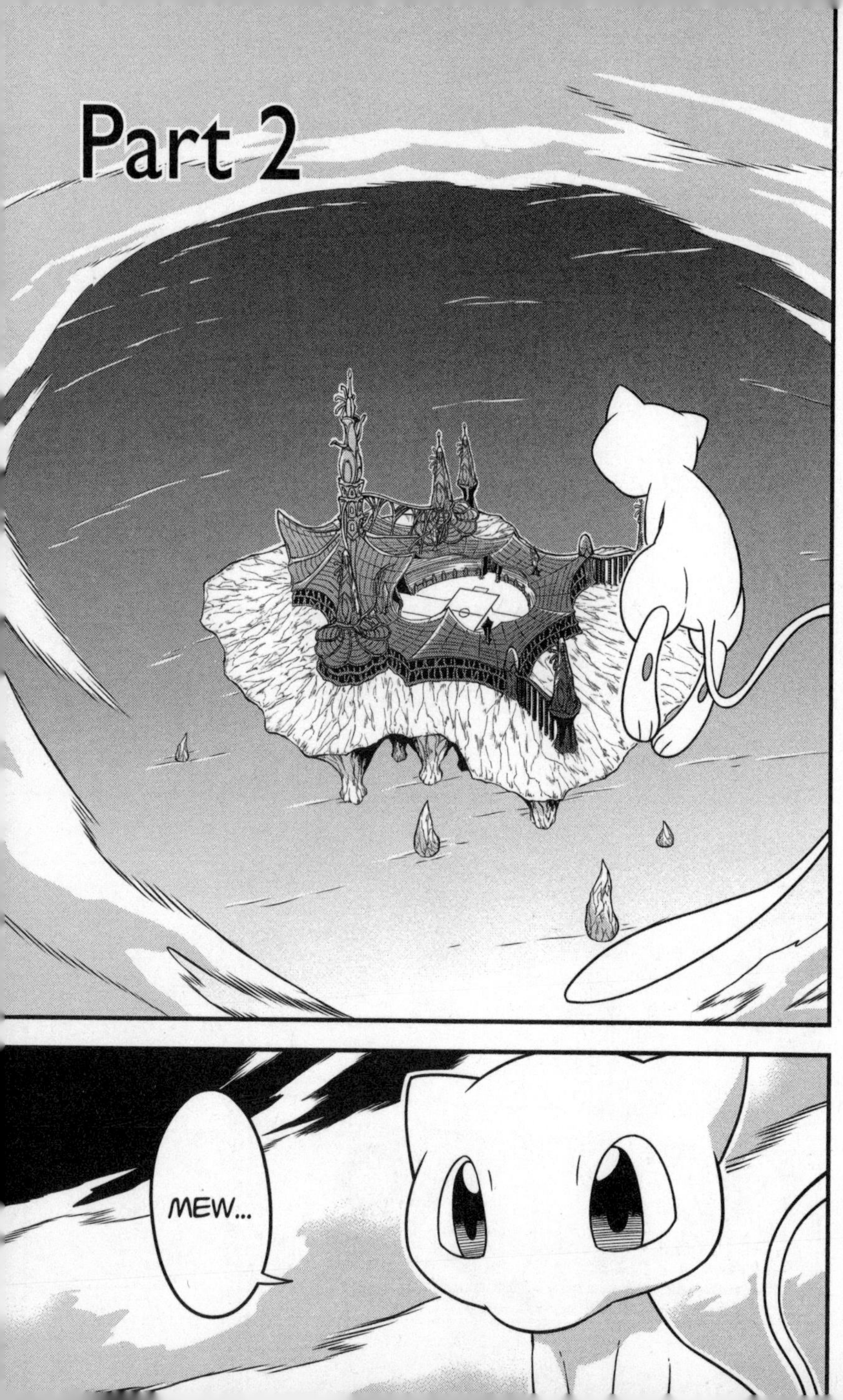
MEW...

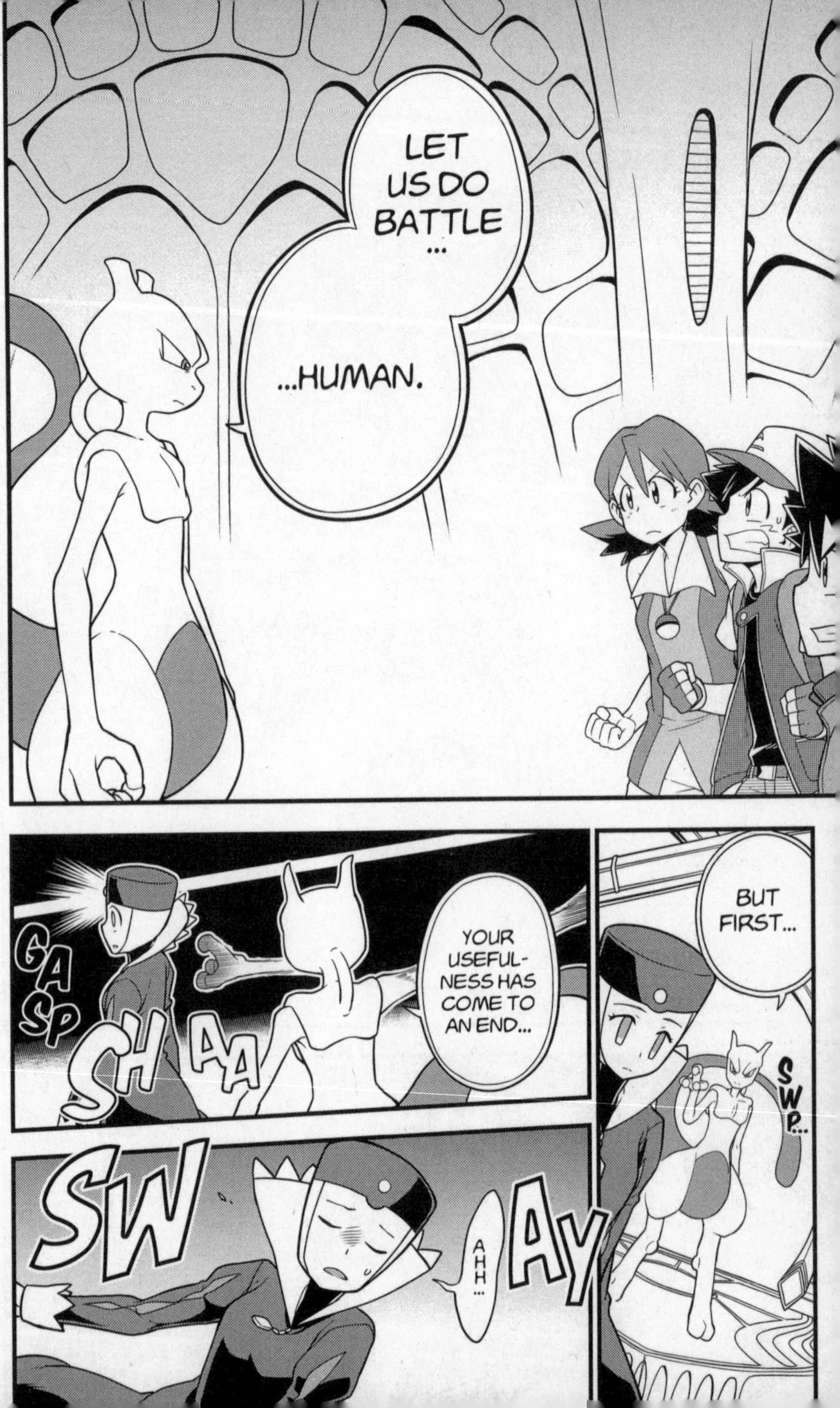
LET US DO BATTLE ...
...HUMAN.
BUT FIRST...
SWP...
YOUR USEFUL-NESS HAS COME TO AN END...
SHAA
GASP
SWAY
AHH...

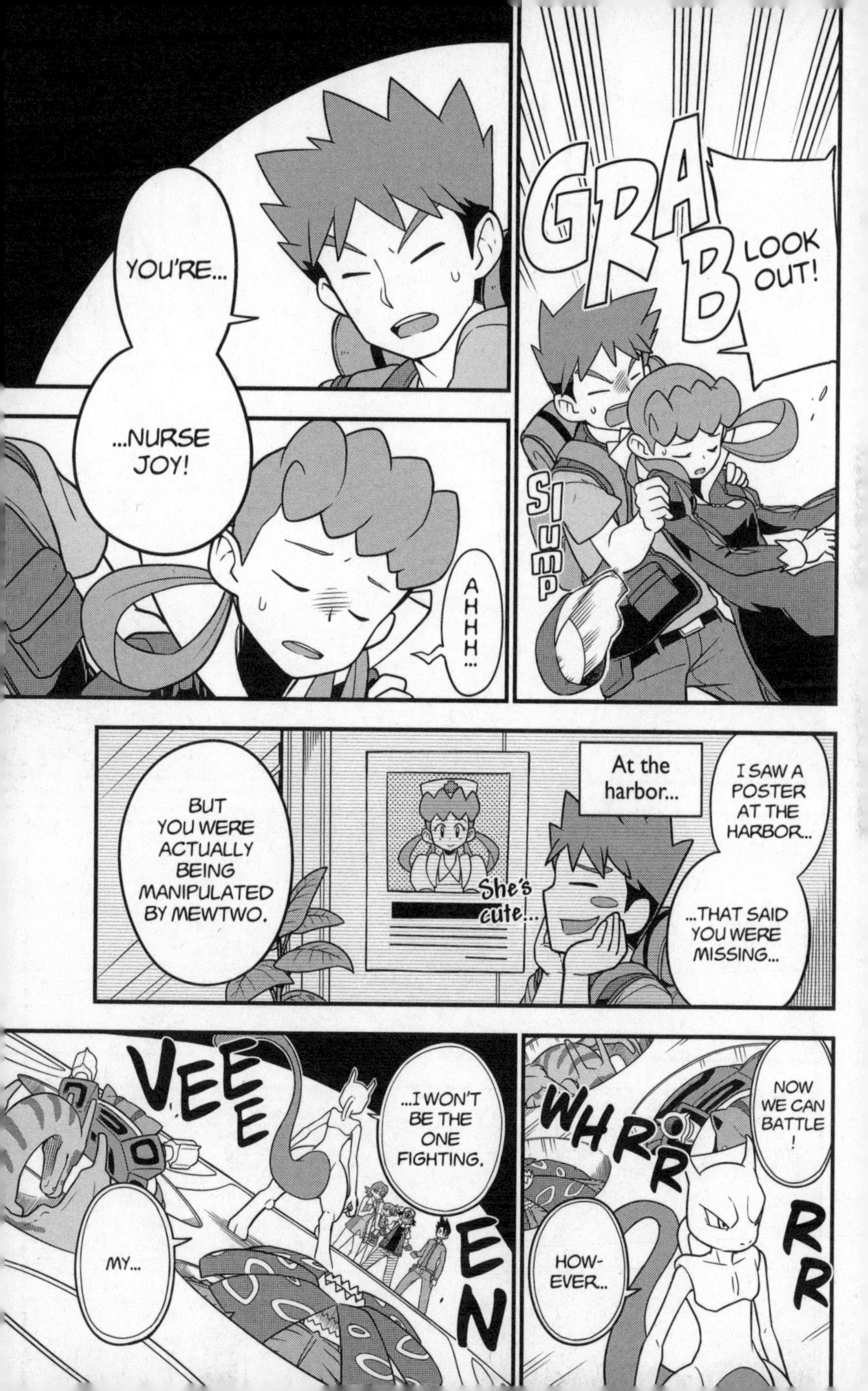
GRAB
LOOK OUT!
SLUMP
YOU'RE...
...NURSE JOY!
AHHH...
At the harbor...
I SAW A POSTER AT THE HARBOR...
...THAT SAID YOU WERE MISSING...
She's cute...
BUT YOU WERE ACTUALLY BEING MANIPULATED BY MEWTWO.
NOW WE CAN BATTLE!
WHRRRR
HOW-EVER...
...I WON'T BE THE ONE FIGHTING.
VEEEEN
MY...

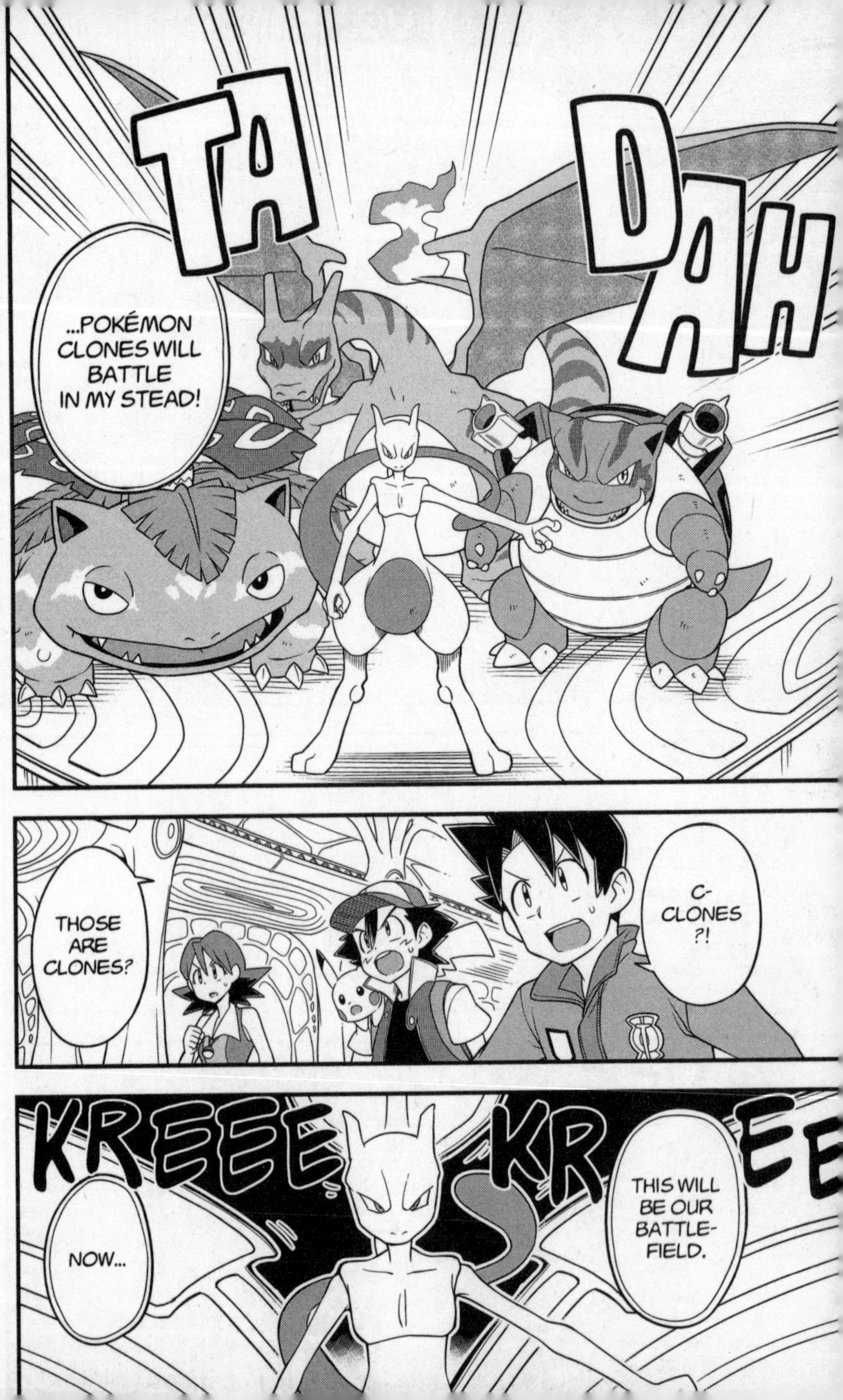
TA DAH
...POKÉMON CLONES WILL BATTLE IN MY STEAD!
C-CLONES?!
THOSE ARE CLONES?
KREEE KR EE
THIS WILL BE OUR BATTLE-FIELD.
NOW...

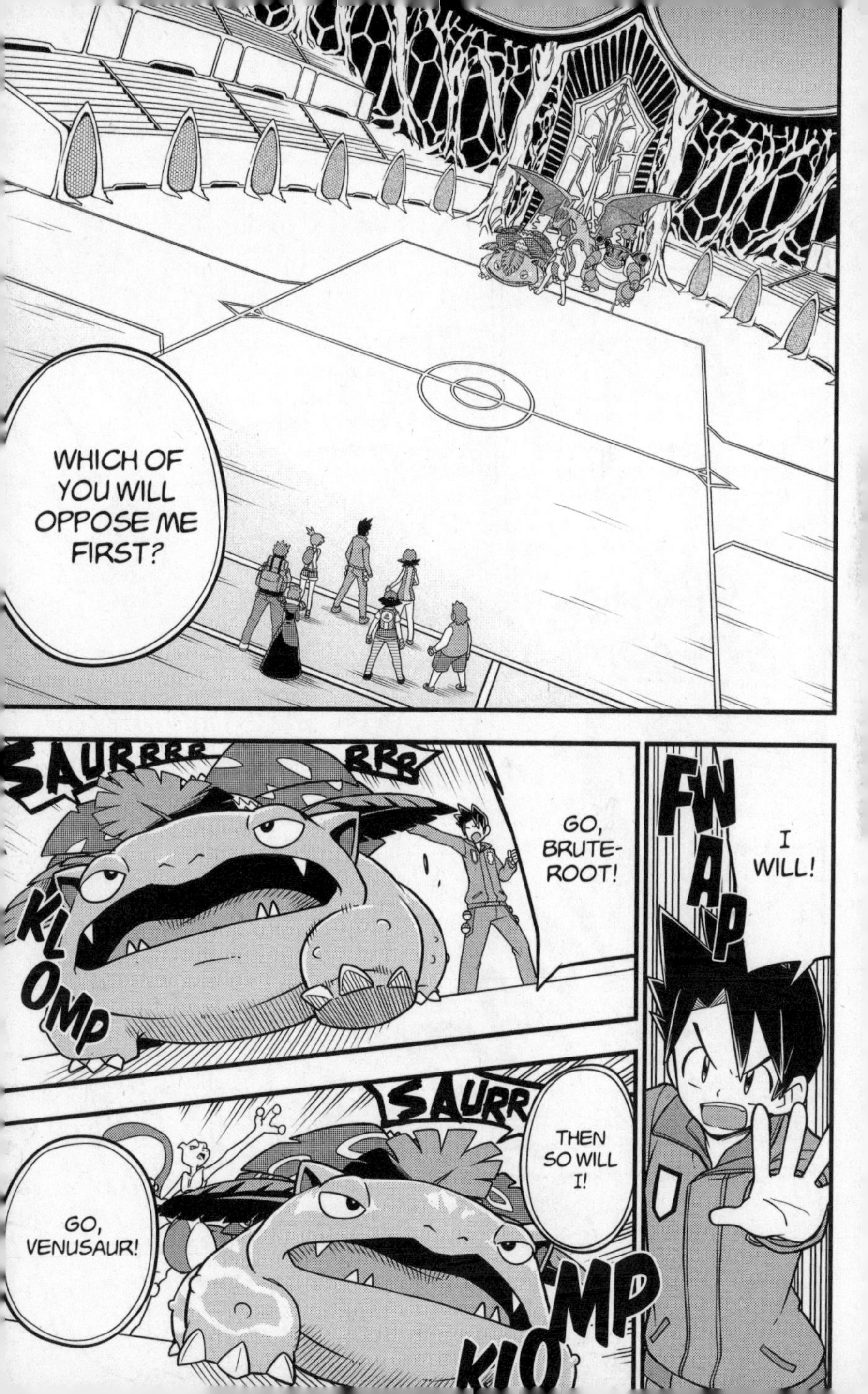
WHICH OF YOU WILL OPPOSE ME FIRST?
FWAP
I WILL!
SAURRRR RRR
GO, BRUTE-ROOT!
KLOMP
SAURR
THEN SO WILL I!
GO, VENUSAUR!
KLOMP

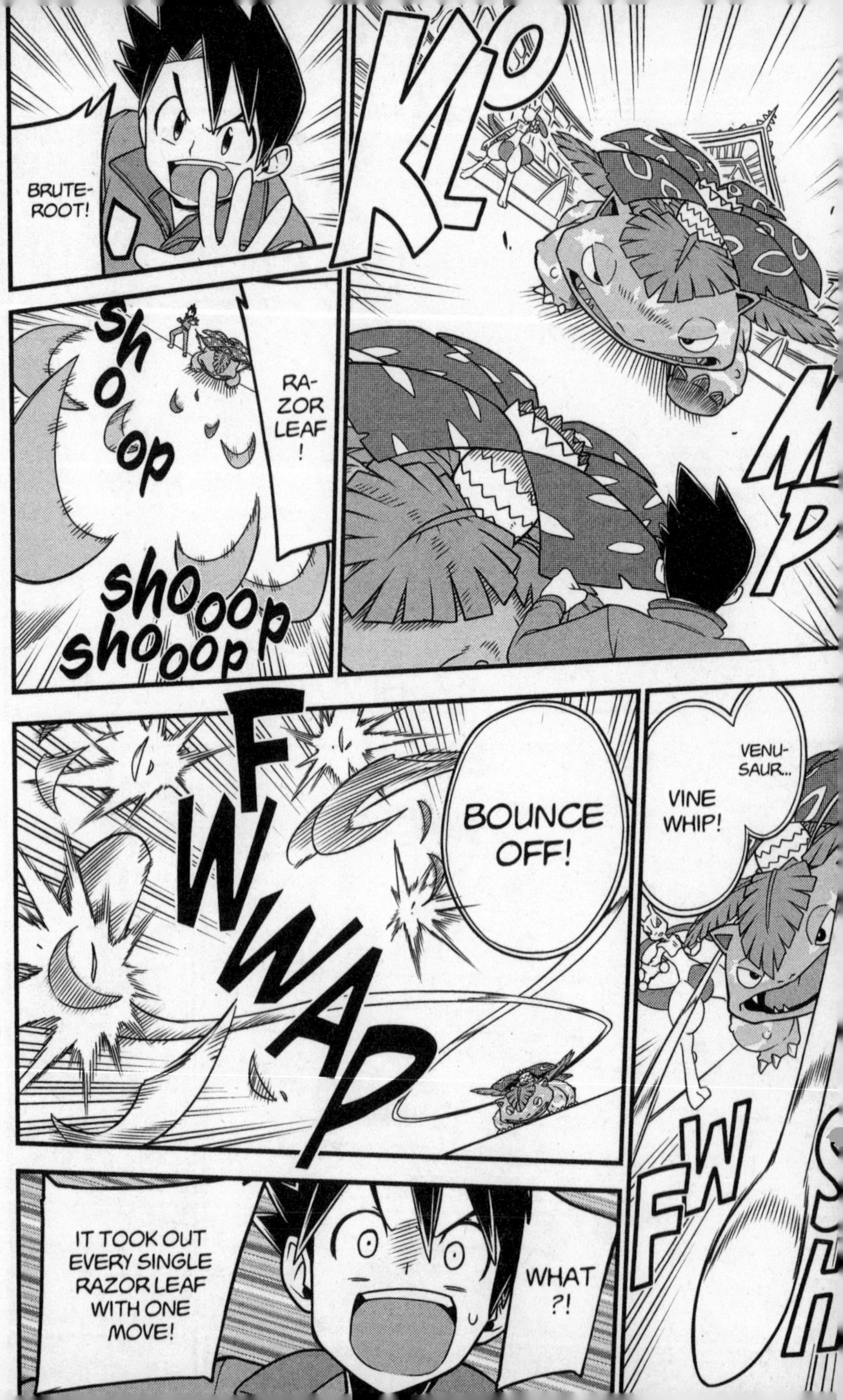
BRUTE-ROOT!
RA-ZOR LEAF!
shooop
shooop
shooop
VENU-SAUR...
VINE WHIP!
BOUNCE OFF!
FWWAP
WHAT?!
IT TOOK OUT EVERY SINGLE RAZOR LEAF WITH ONE MOVE!

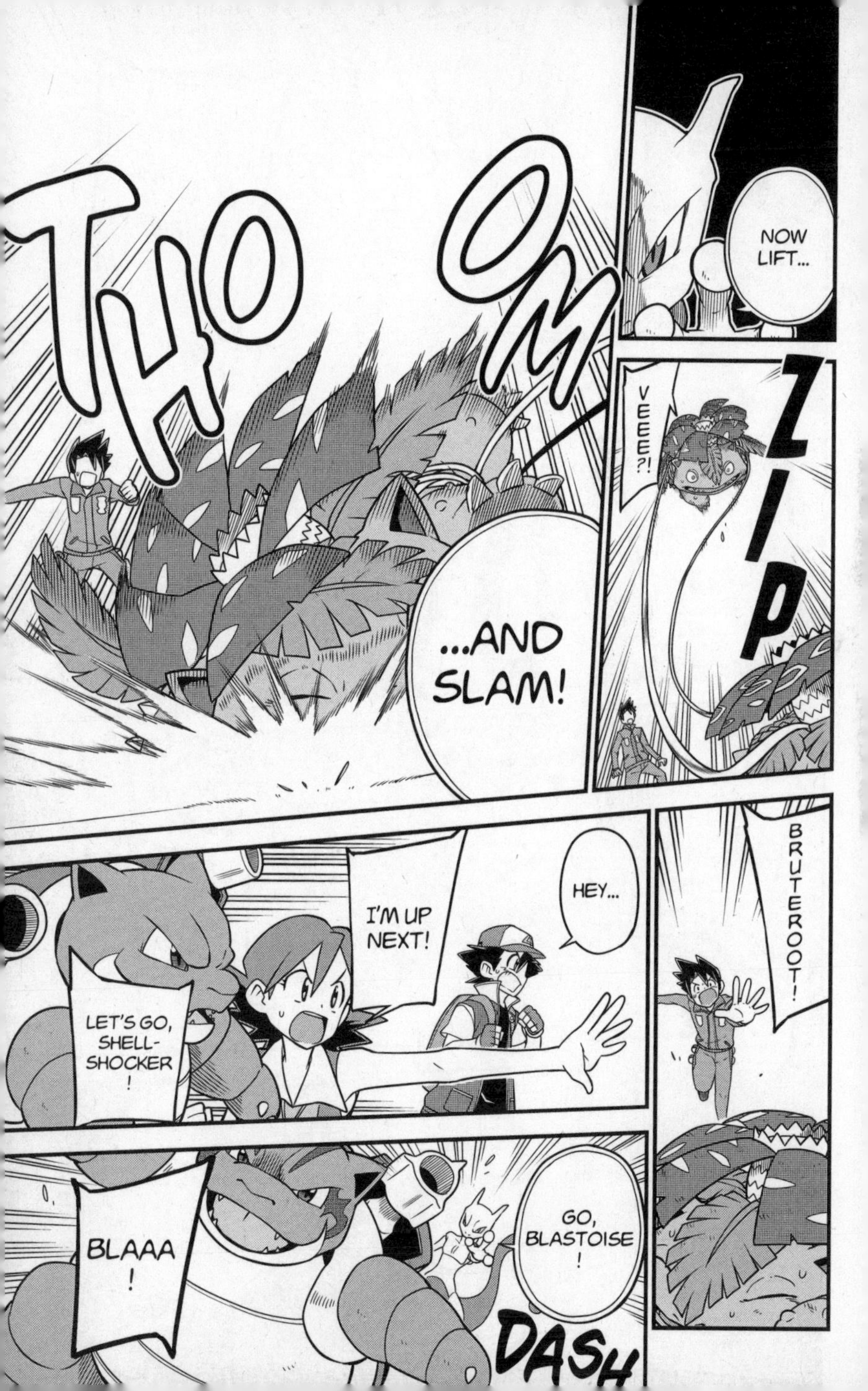
NOW LIFT...
VEEEE?!
ZIP
THOOM
...AND SLAM!
BRUTEROOT!
HEY...
I'M UP NEXT!
LET'S GO, SHELL-SHOCKER!
GO, BLASTOISE!
BLAAA!
DASH

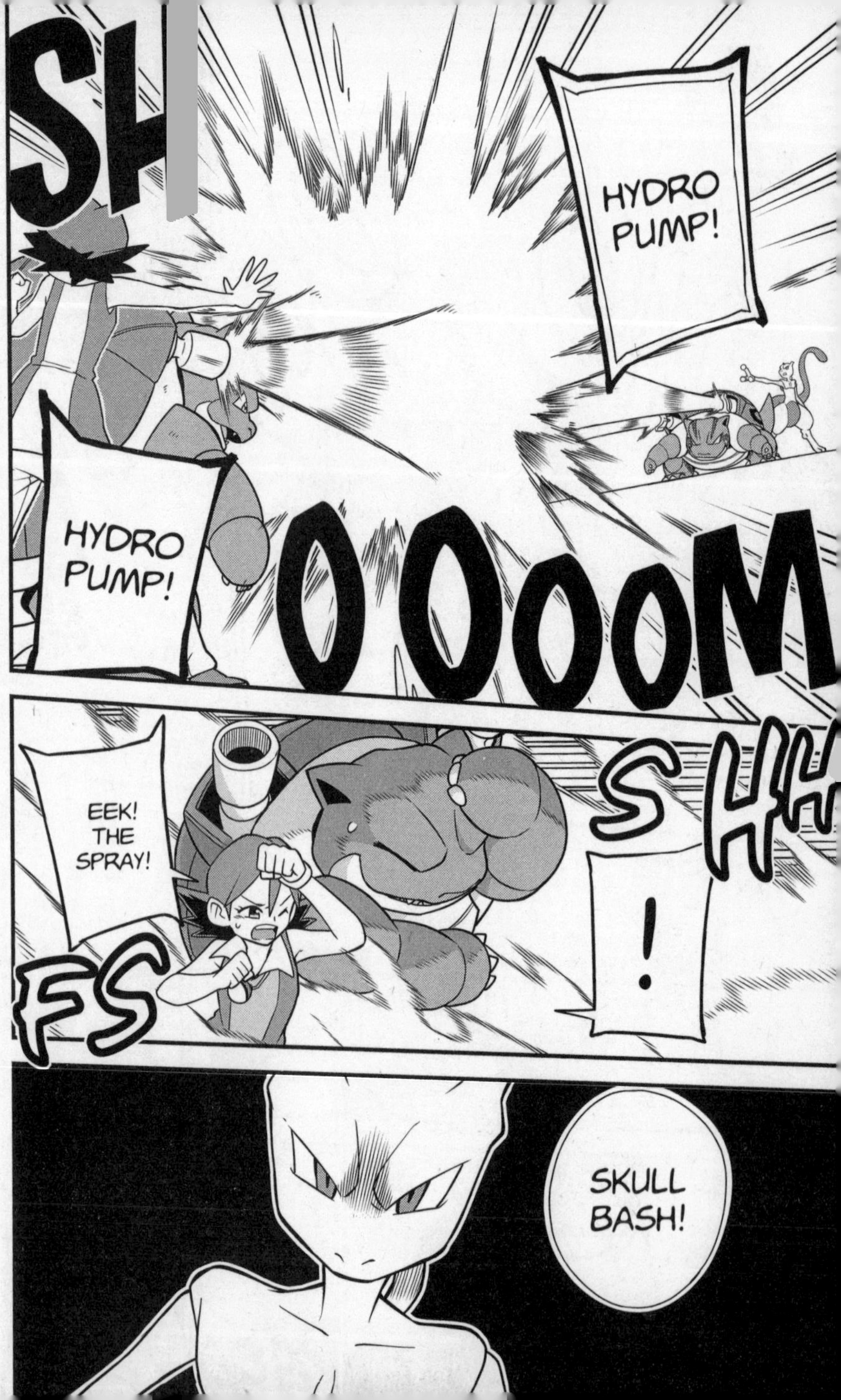
HYDRO PUMP!
SH
OOOOM
HYDRO PUMP!
SHH
!
EEK! THE SPRAY!
FS
SKULL BASH!

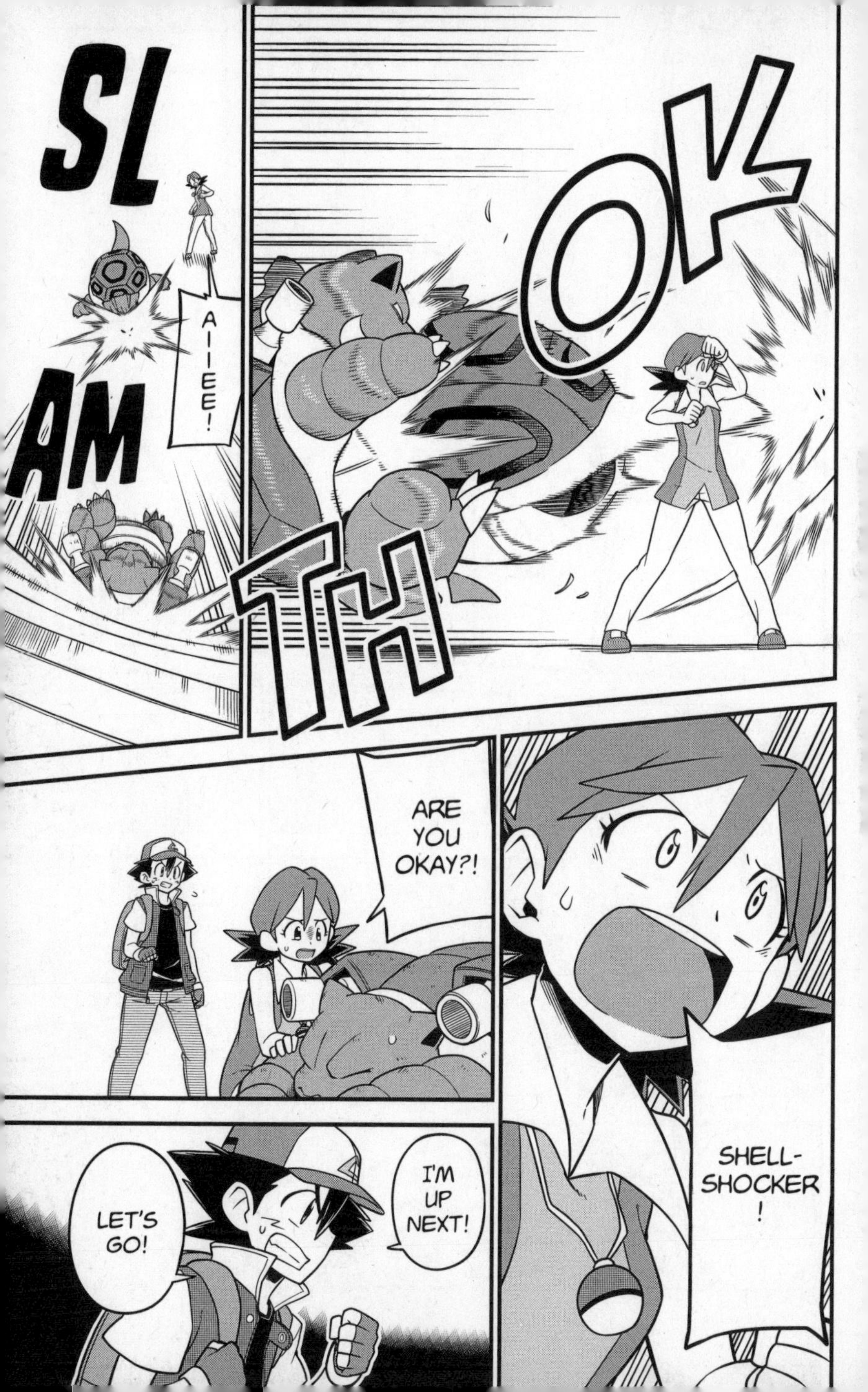
THOK
SLAM
AIIEE!
SHELL-SHOCKER!
ARE YOU OKAY?!
I'M UP NEXT!
LET'S GO!

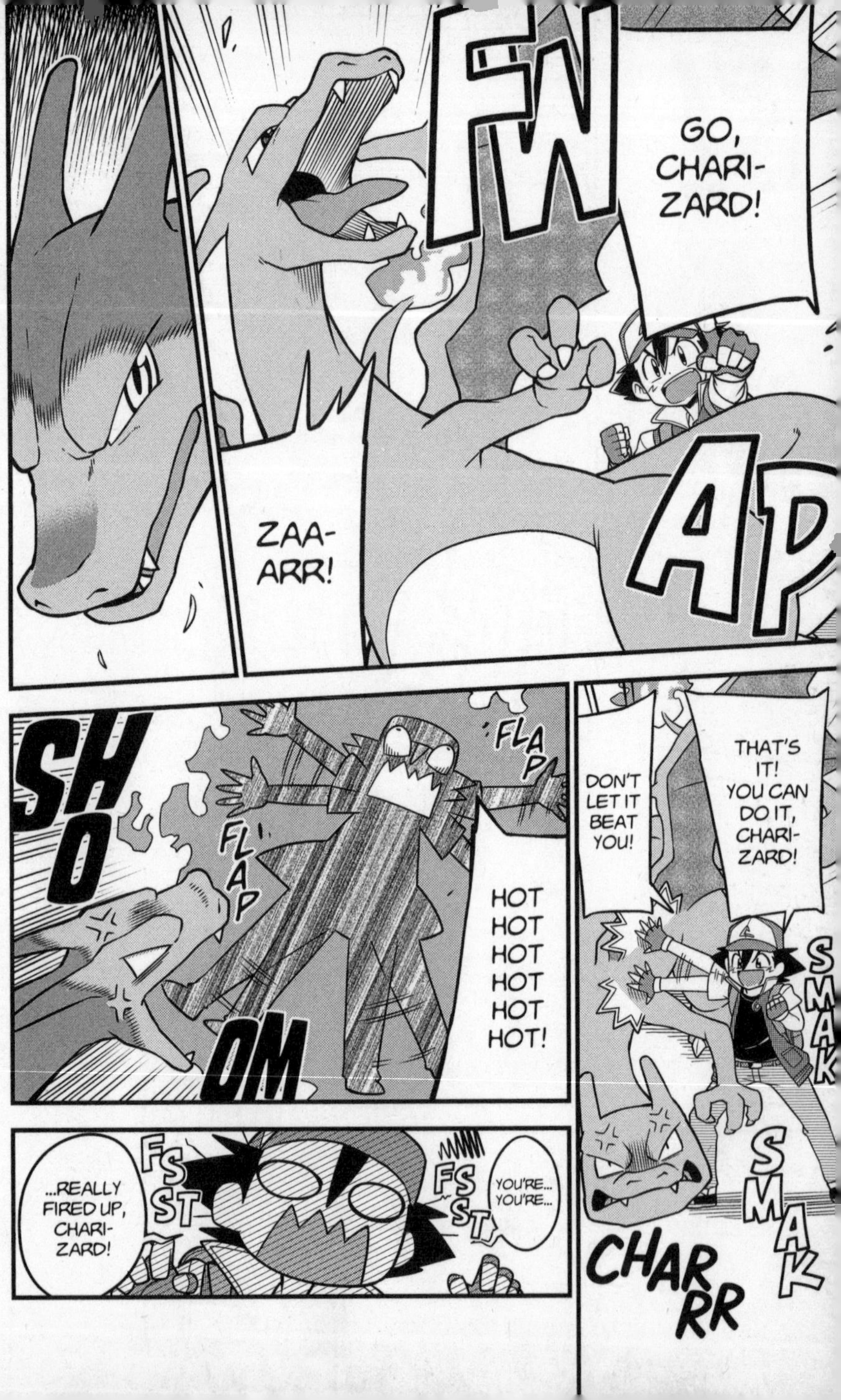

GO, CHARIZARD!
FW
AP
ZAA-ARR!
THAT'S IT! YOU CAN DO IT, CHARIZARD!
DON'T LET IT BEAT YOU!
SMAK
SMAK
CHARRR
FLAP
HOT HOT HOT HOT HOT HOT!
FLAP
SH
OOM
YOU'RE... YOU'RE...
FSST
FSST
...REALLY FIRED UP, CHARIZARD!

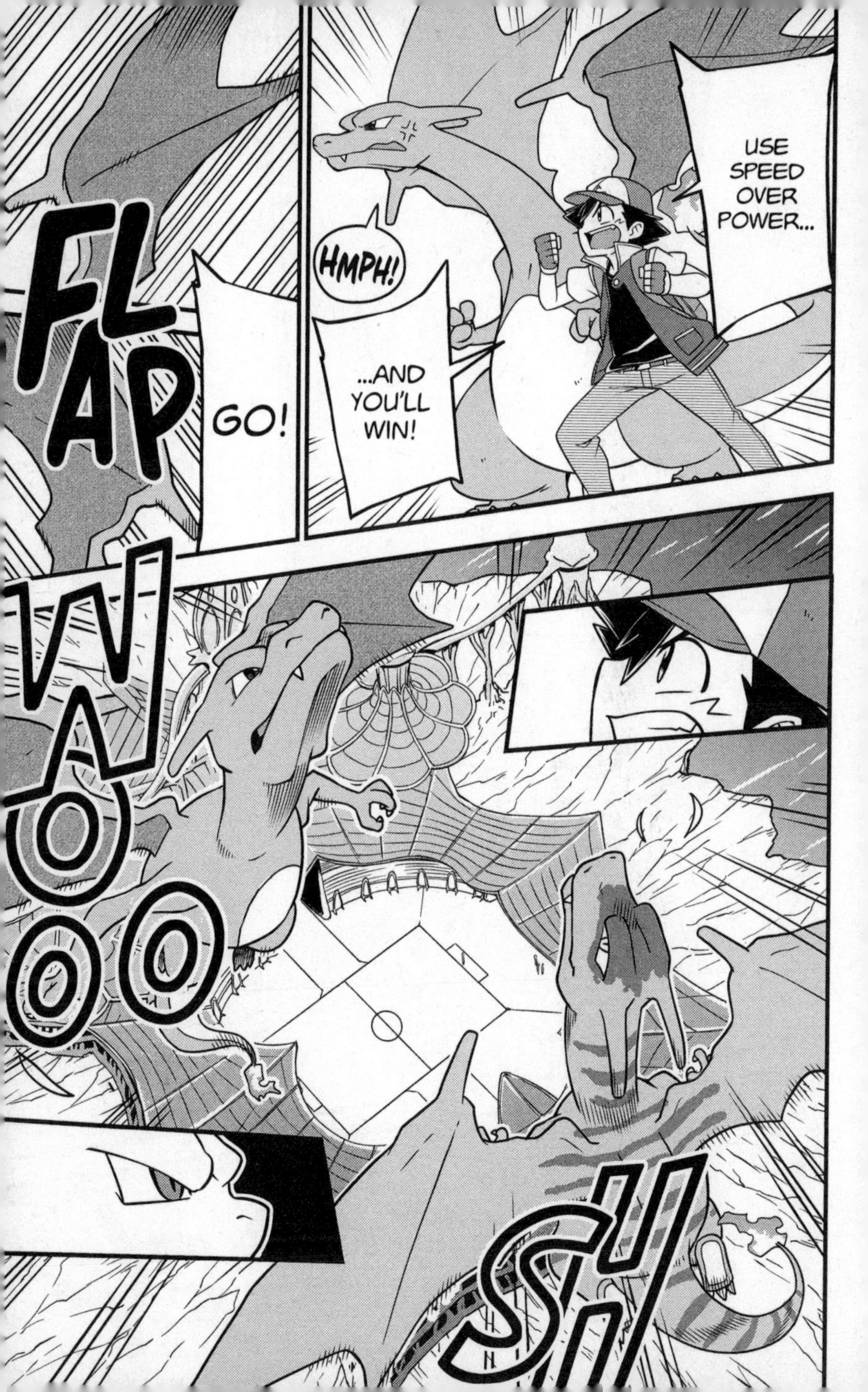

USE SPEED OVER POWER...
HMPH!
...AND YOU'LL WIN!
FLAP
GO!
WOOOO
SH

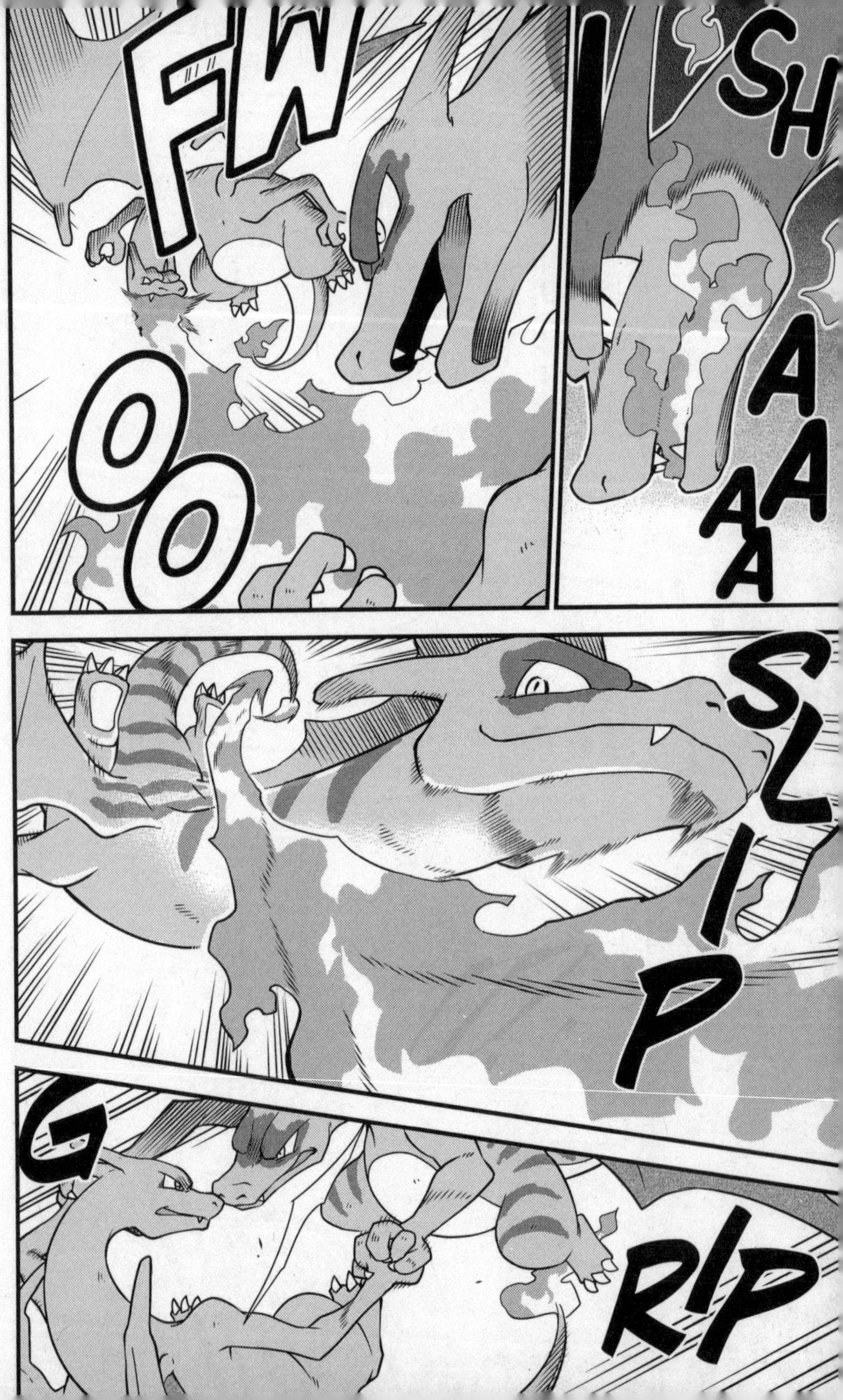
SHAAAA
FWOOO
SLIP
G
RIP

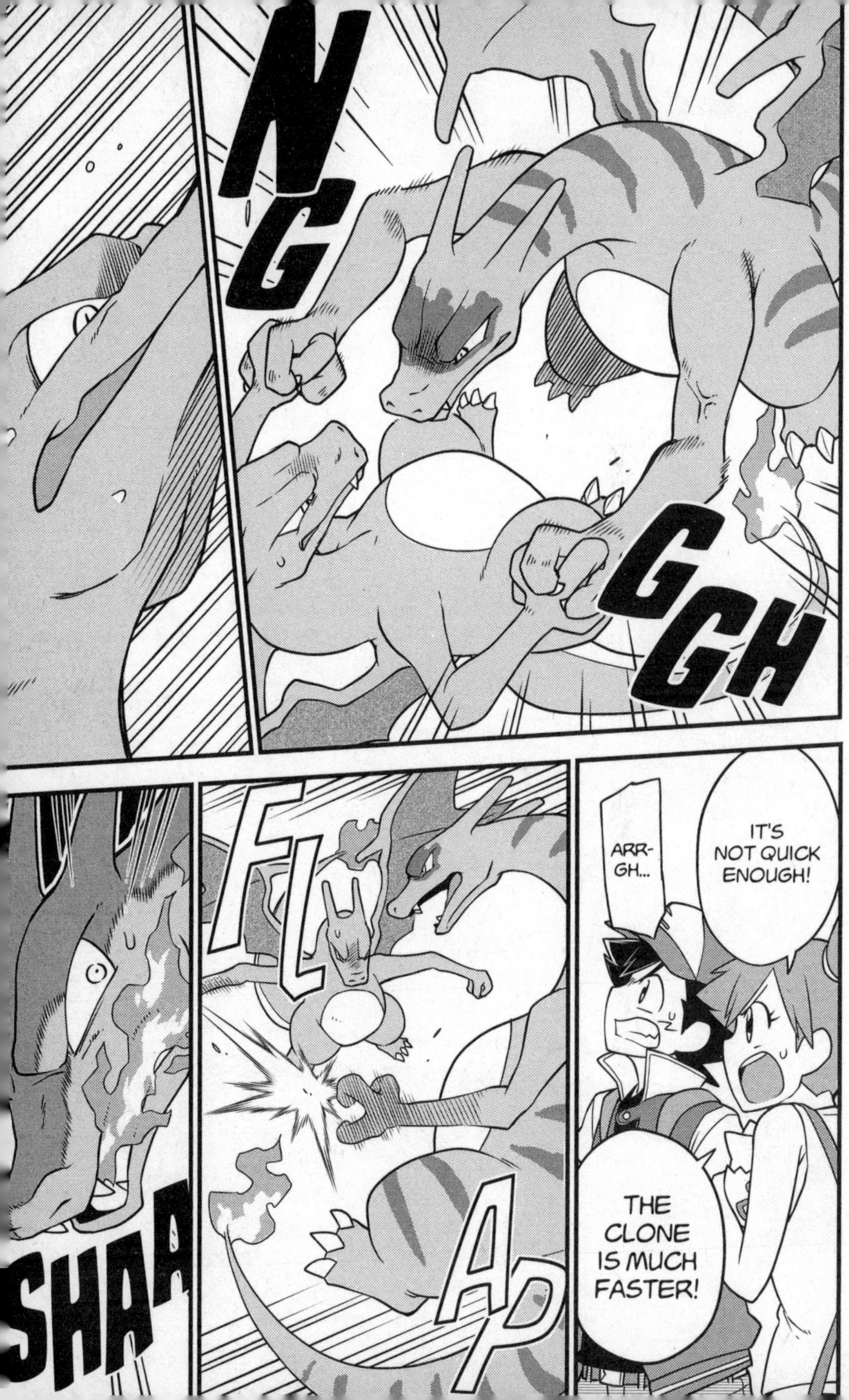
NG
GGH
IT'S NOT QUICK ENOUGH!
ARR-GH...
THE CLONE IS MUCH FASTER!
FL
AP
SHAA

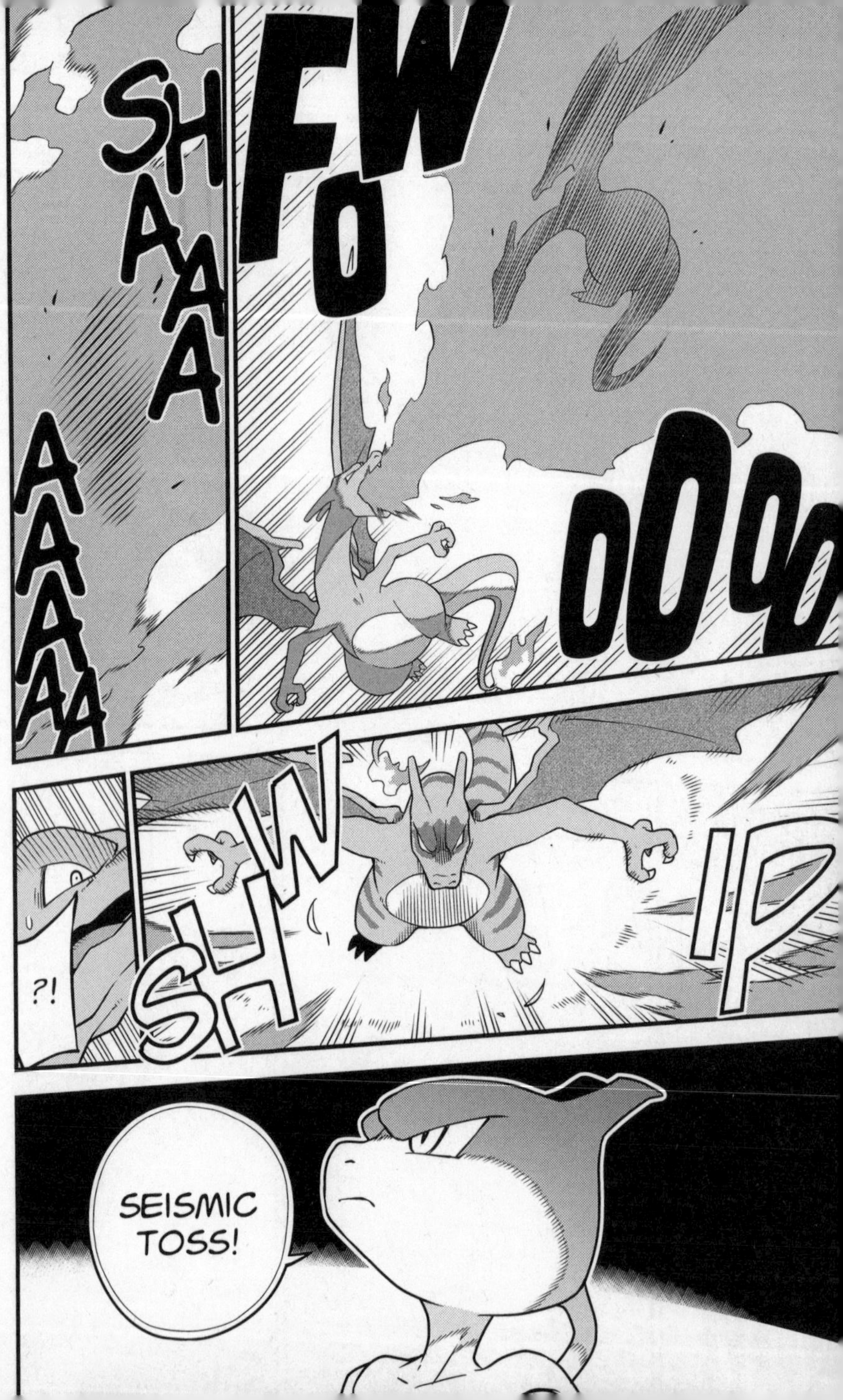
FWOOOO
SHAAAAAAAAA
SHWIP
?!
SEISMIC TOSS!

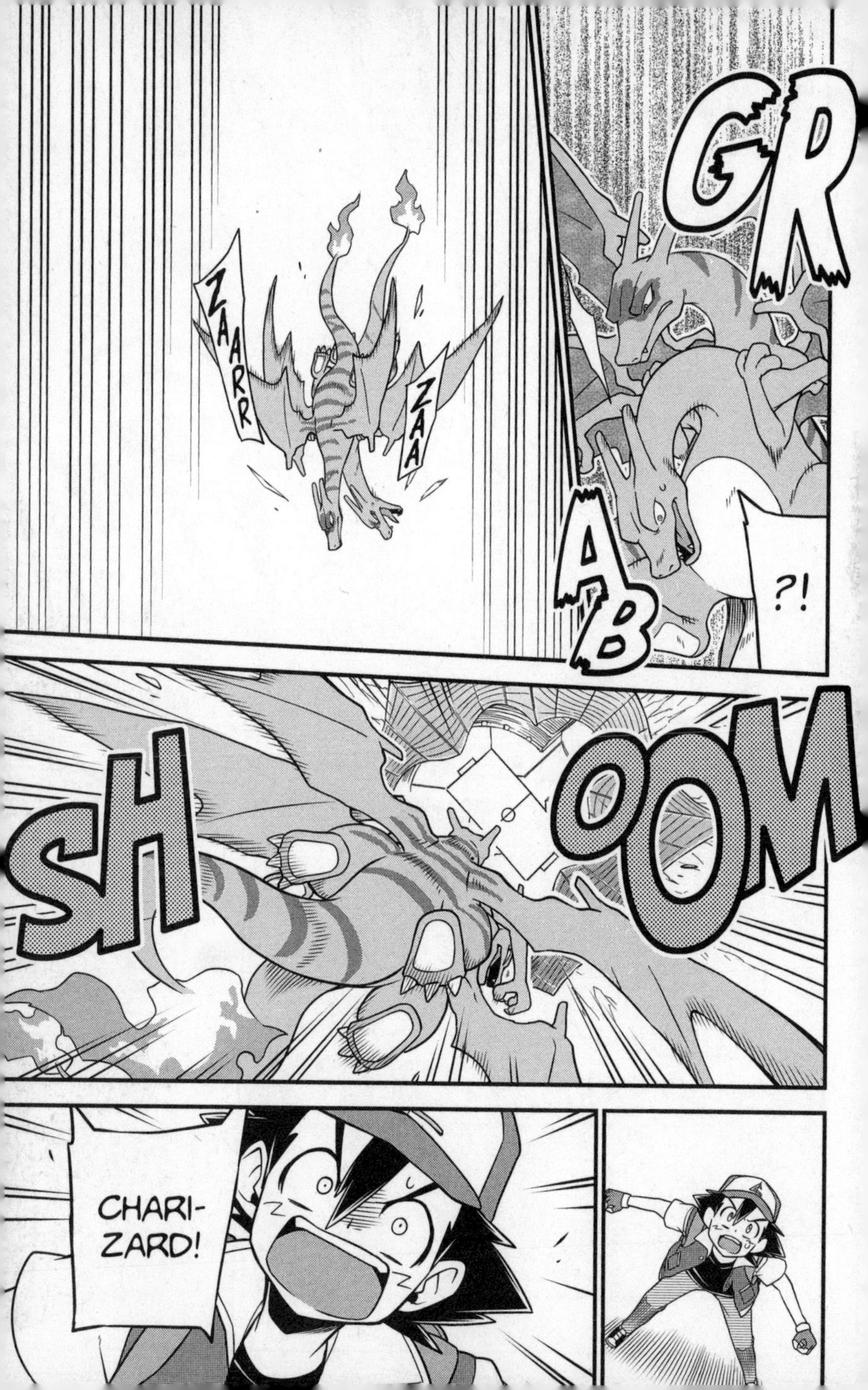
GR
AB
?!
ZAARR
ZAA
SHOOM
CHARI-
ZARD!

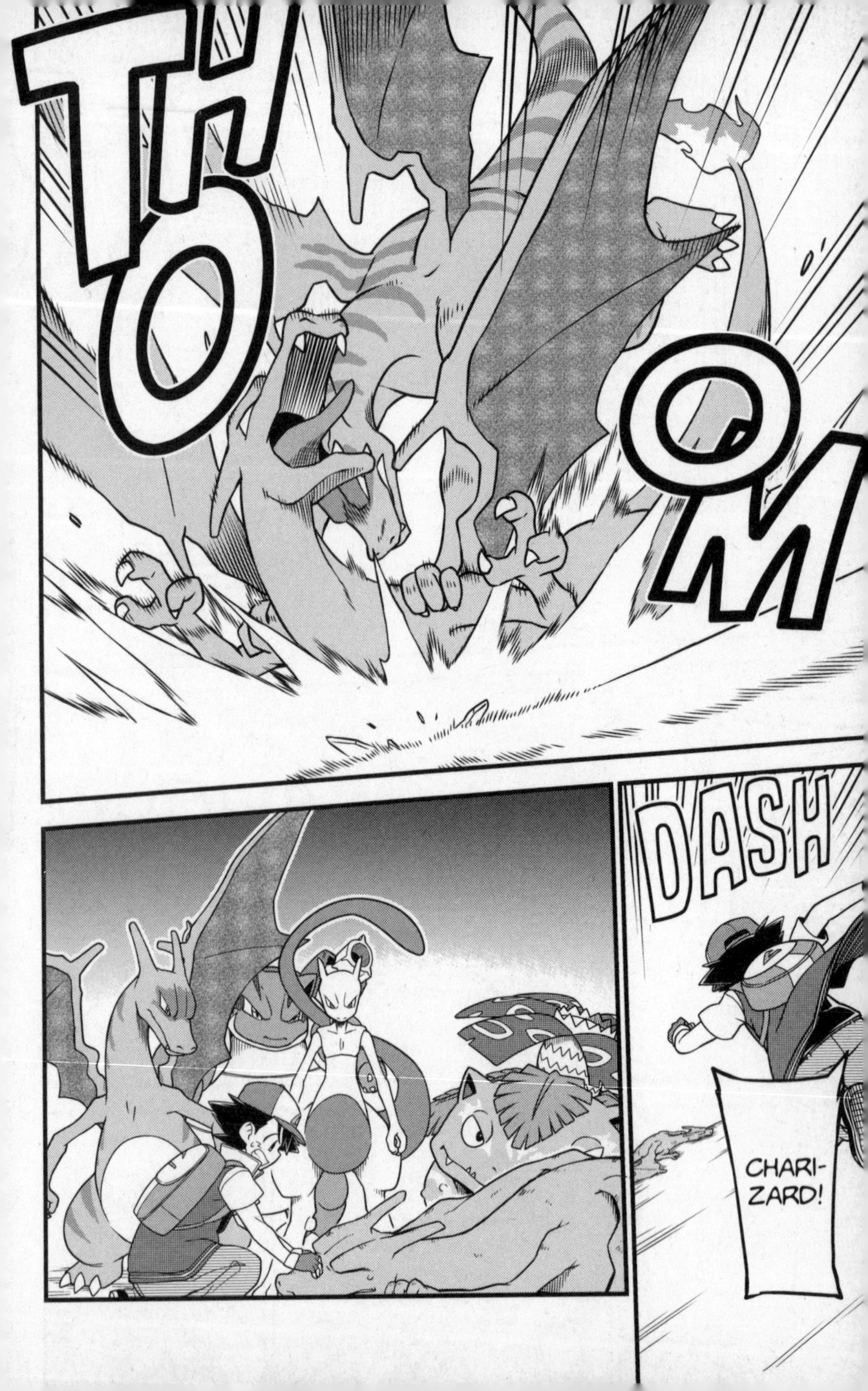
THOOM
DASH
CHARI-
ZARD!

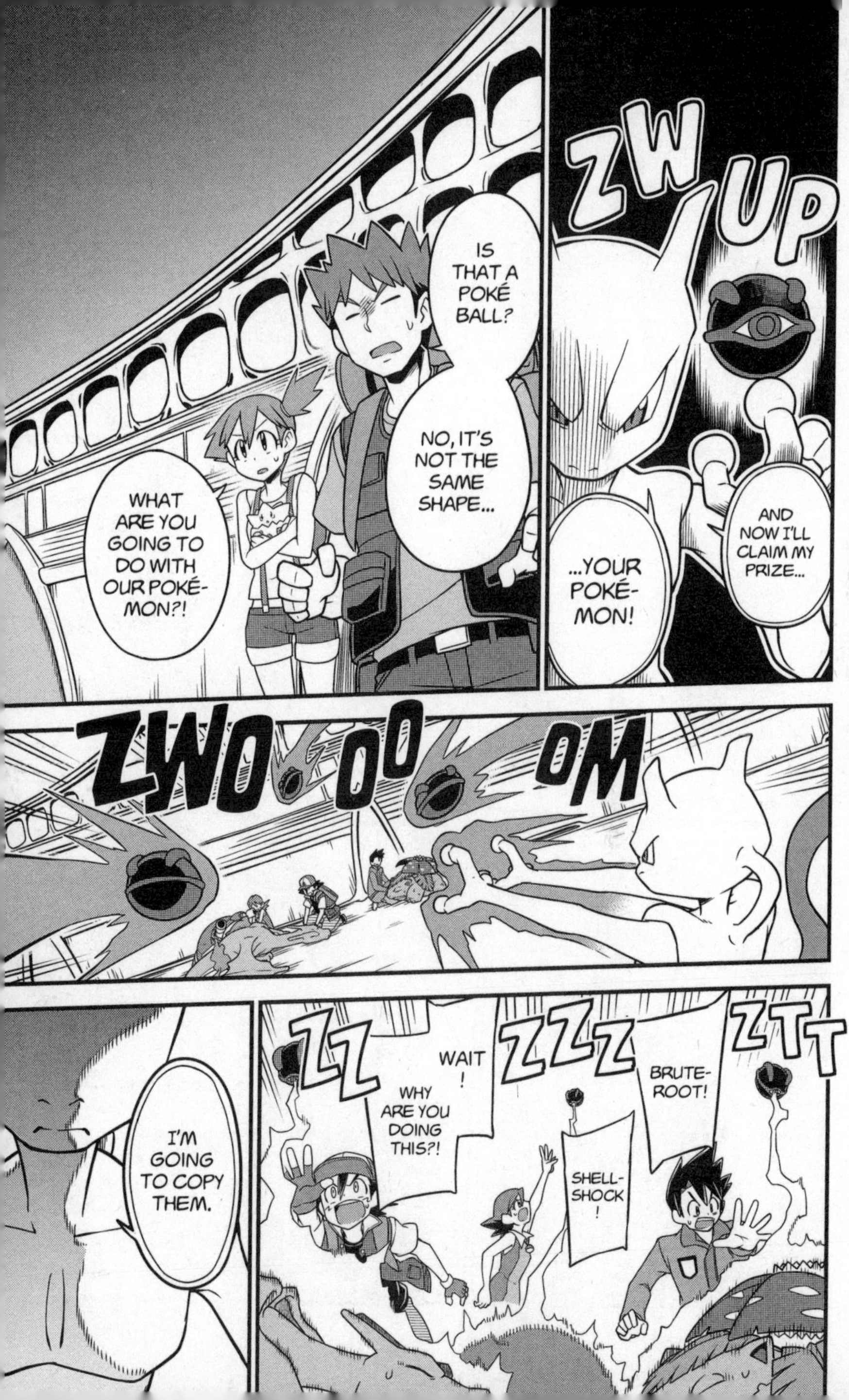
ZW UP
AND NOW I'LL CLAIM MY PRIZE...
...YOUR POKÉMON!
IS THAT A POKÉ BALL?
NO, IT'S NOT THE SAME SHAPE...
WHAT ARE YOU GOING TO DO WITH OUR POKÉMON?!
ZWOOOOM
ZTT
BRUTE-ROOT!
ZZZ
SHELL-SHOCK!
WAIT! WHY ARE YOU DOING THIS?!
ZZ
I'M GOING TO COPY THEM.

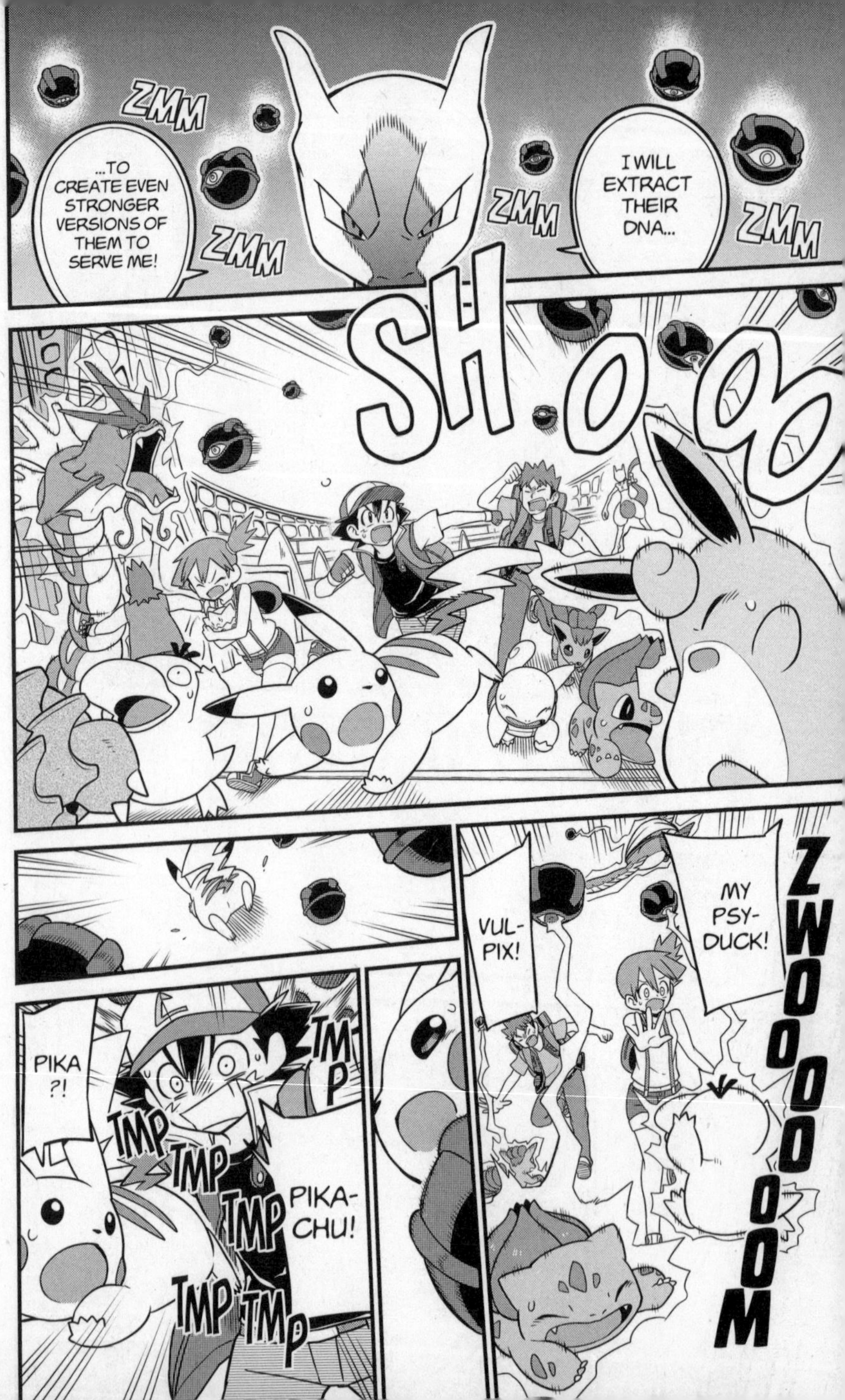
ZMM
I WILL EXTRACT THEIR DNA...
ZMM
ZMM
...TO CREATE EVEN STRONGER VERSIONS OF THEM TO SERVE ME!
ZMM
SHOOO
MY PSY-DUCK!
VUL-PIX!
ZWOOOOOOM
TMP
PIKA ?!
TMP TMP TMP
PIKA-CHU!
TMP TMP

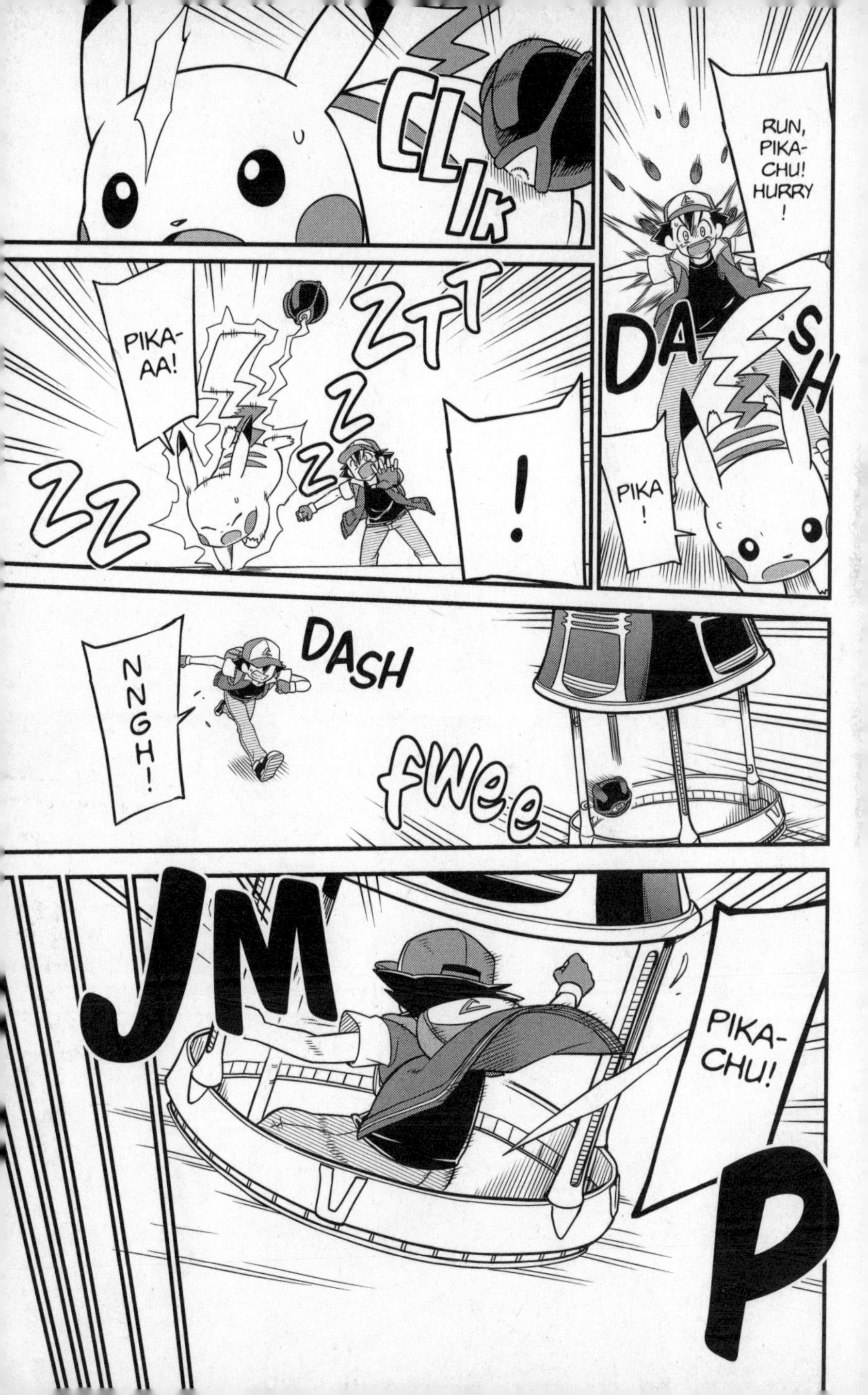
RUN, PIKA-CHU! HURRY!
DASH
PIKA!
CLIK
ZZTT
!
PIKA-AA!
ZZZZ
DASH
NNGH!
fwee
PIKA-CHU!
JMP

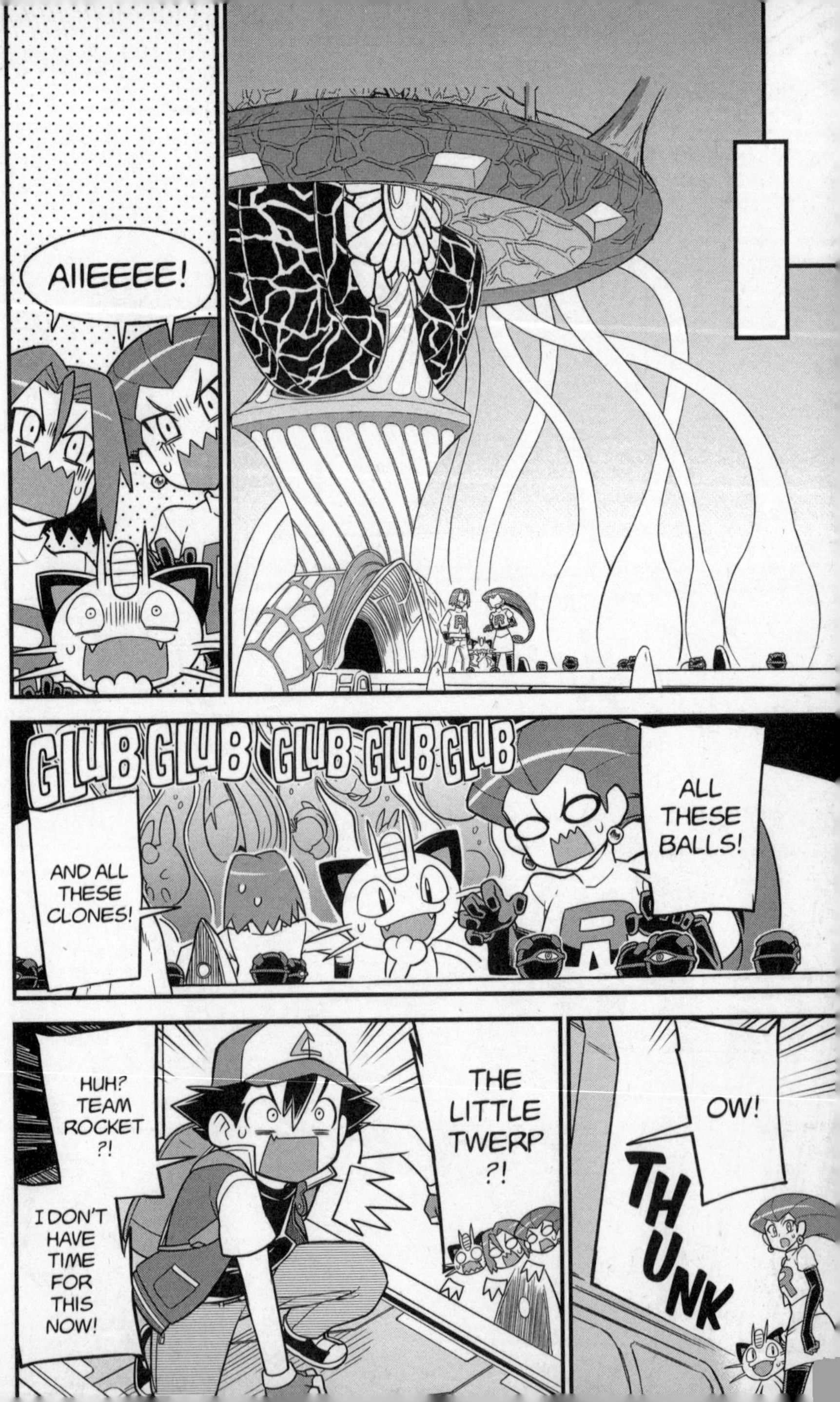
AIIEEEE!
GLUB GLUB GLUB GLUB GLUB
ALL THESE BALLS!
AND ALL THESE CLONES!
OW!
THUNK
THE LITTLE TWERP?!
HUH? TEAM ROCKET?!
I DON'T HAVE TIME FOR THIS NOW!

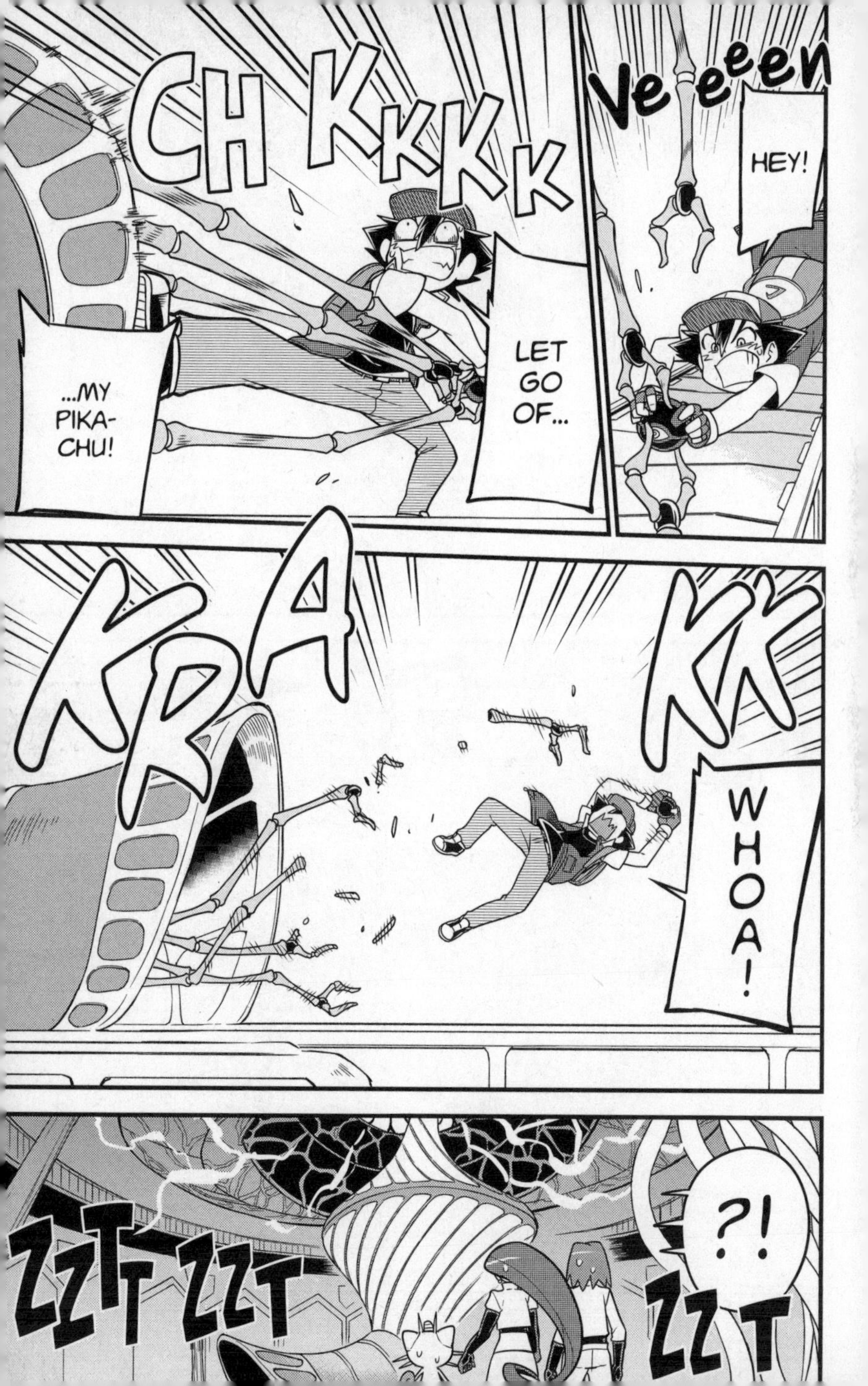
Veeeen
HEY!
CH KKKKK
LET GO OF...
...MY PIKA-CHU!
KRAKK
WHOA!
?!
ZZT
ZZTT ZZT

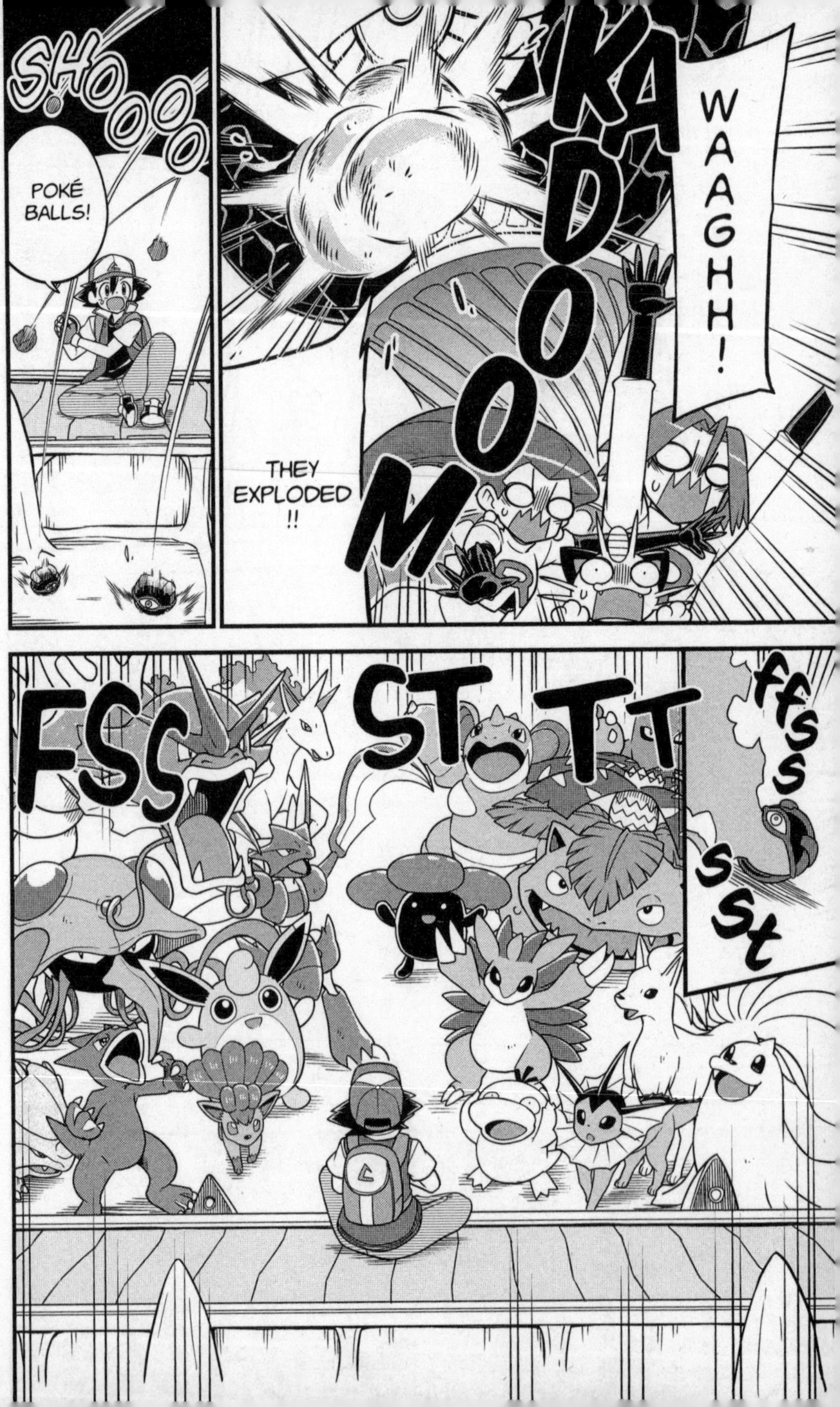
WAAAGH!
KADOOOM
THEY EXPLODED!!
SHOOOO
POKÉ BALLS!
ffss sst
FSSSTTT

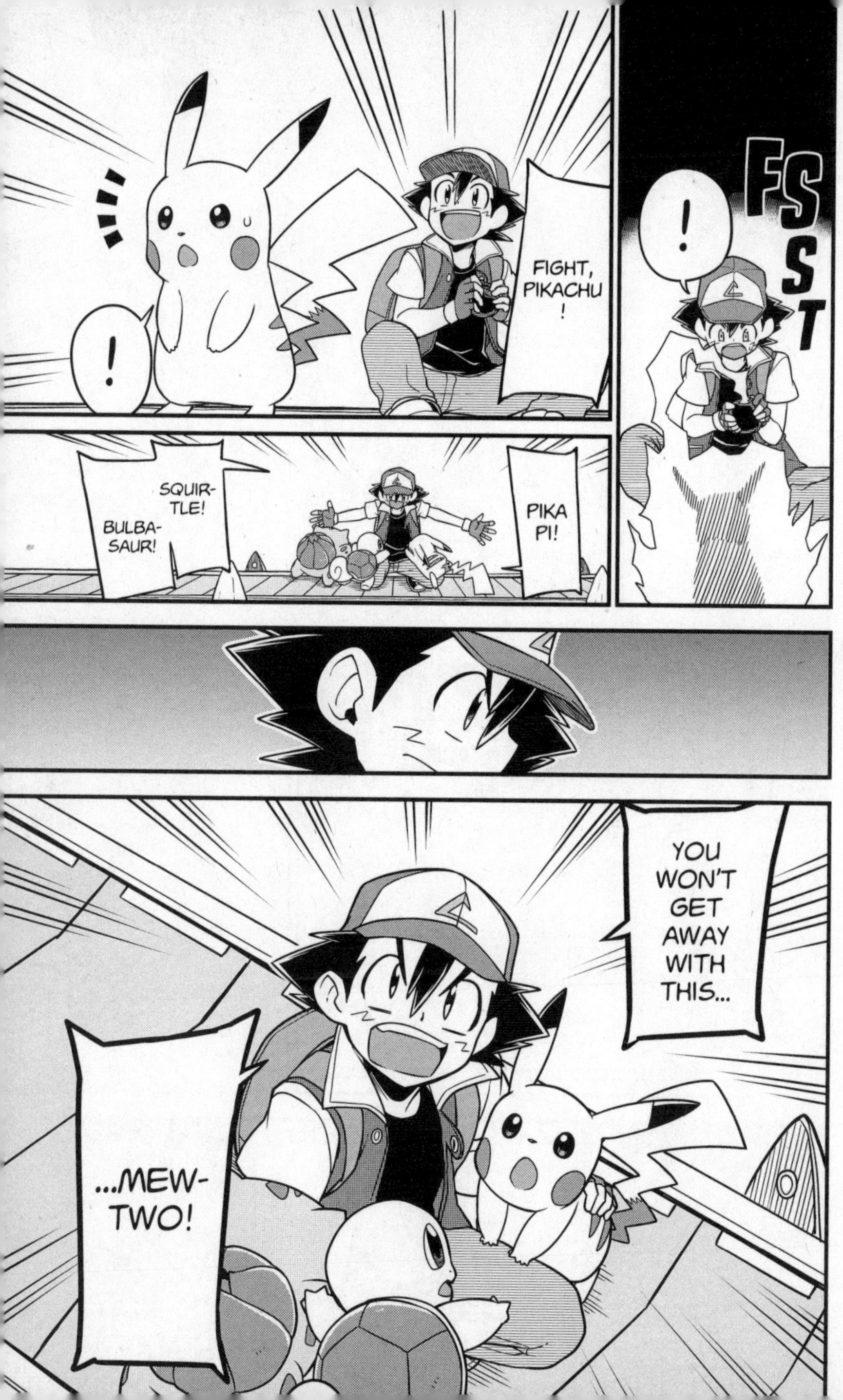
!
FSST
FIGHT, PIKACHU!
!
PIKA PI!
SQUIRTLE!
BULBASAUR!
YOU WON'T GET AWAY WITH THIS...
...MEWTWO!

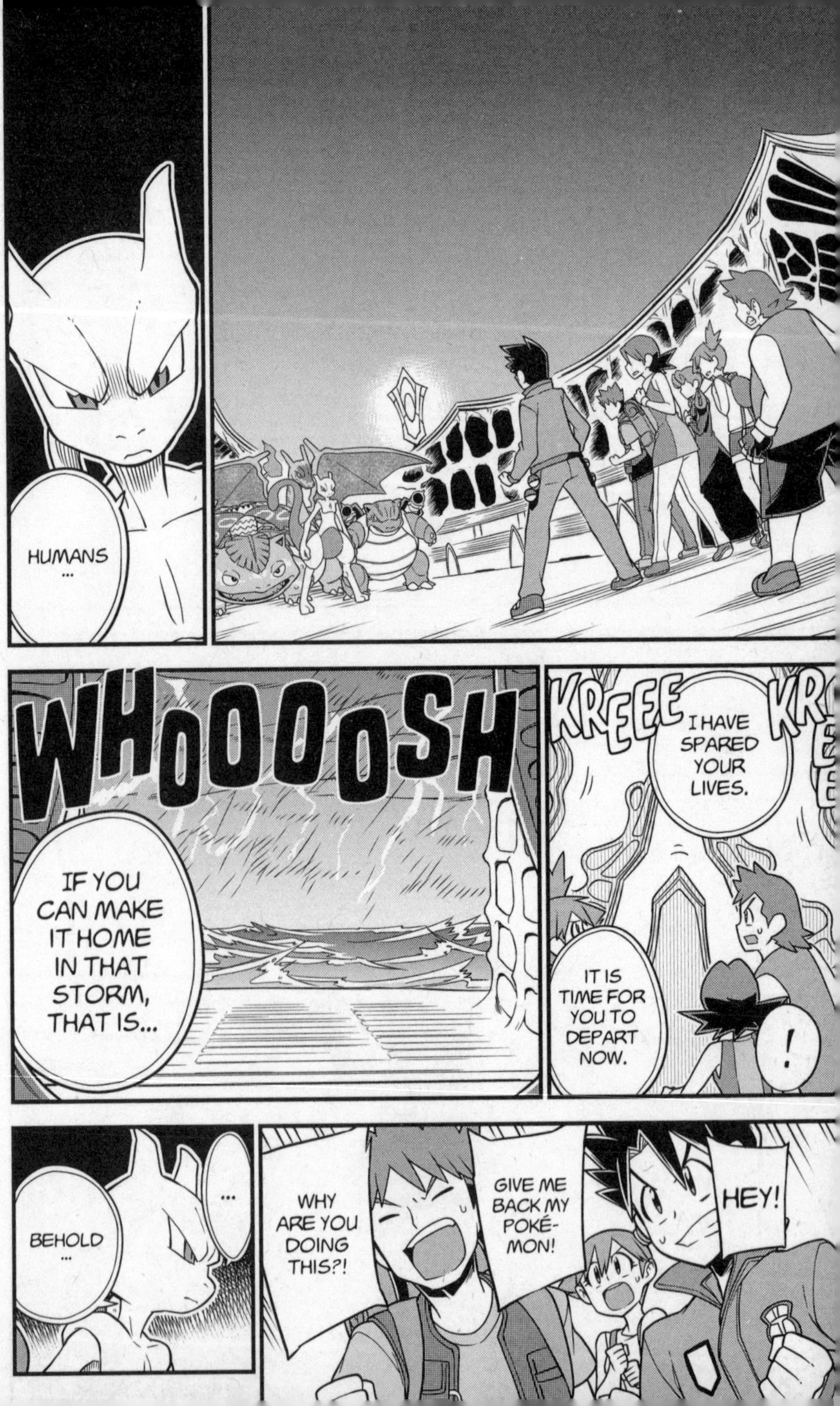
HUMANS ...
KREEE
I HAVE SPARED YOUR LIVES.
IT IS TIME FOR YOU TO DEPART NOW.
!
WHOOOOSH
IF YOU CAN MAKE IT HOME IN THAT STORM, THAT IS...
HEY!
GIVE ME BACK MY POKÉMON!
WHY ARE YOU DOING THIS?!
...
BEHOLD ...

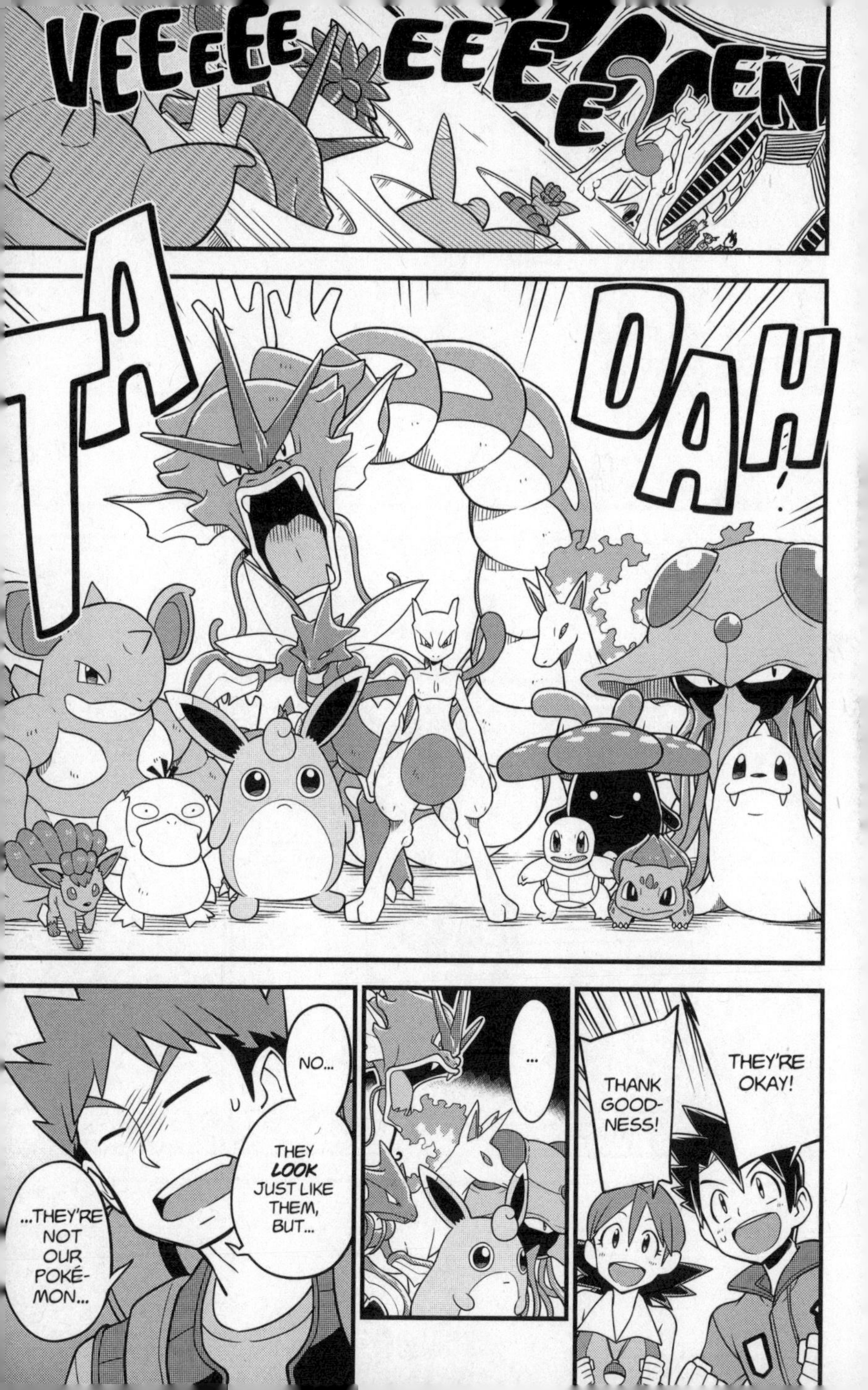
VEEEEE EEEEEEN
TA DAH
THEY'RE OKAY!
THANK GOOD-NESS!
...
NO...
THEY **LOOK** JUST LIKE THEM, BUT...
...THEY'RE NOT OUR POKÉ-MON...

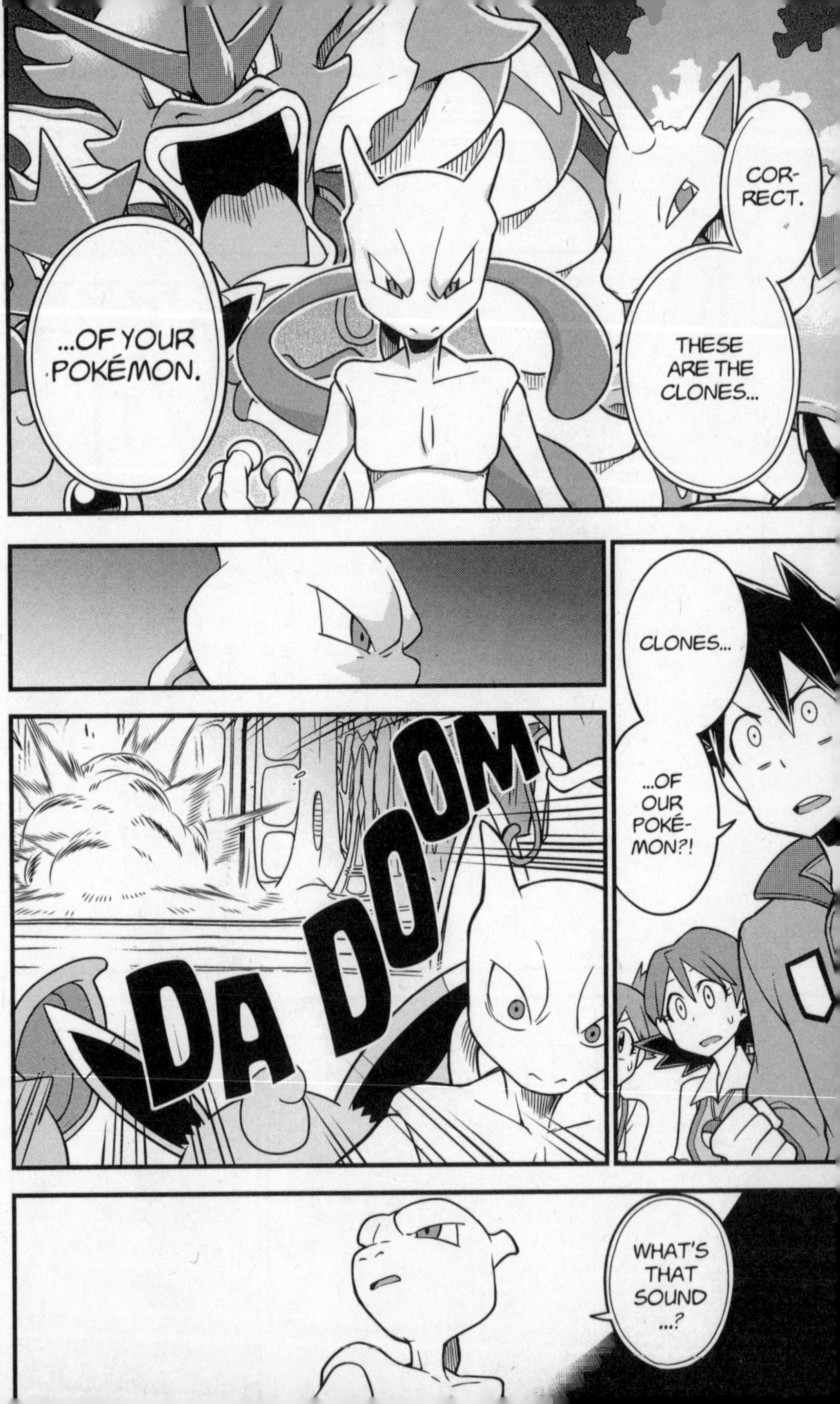
CORRECT.
THESE ARE THE CLONES...
...OF YOUR POKÉMON.
CLONES...
...OF OUR POKÉMON?!
DA DOOM
WHAT'S THAT SOUND ...?

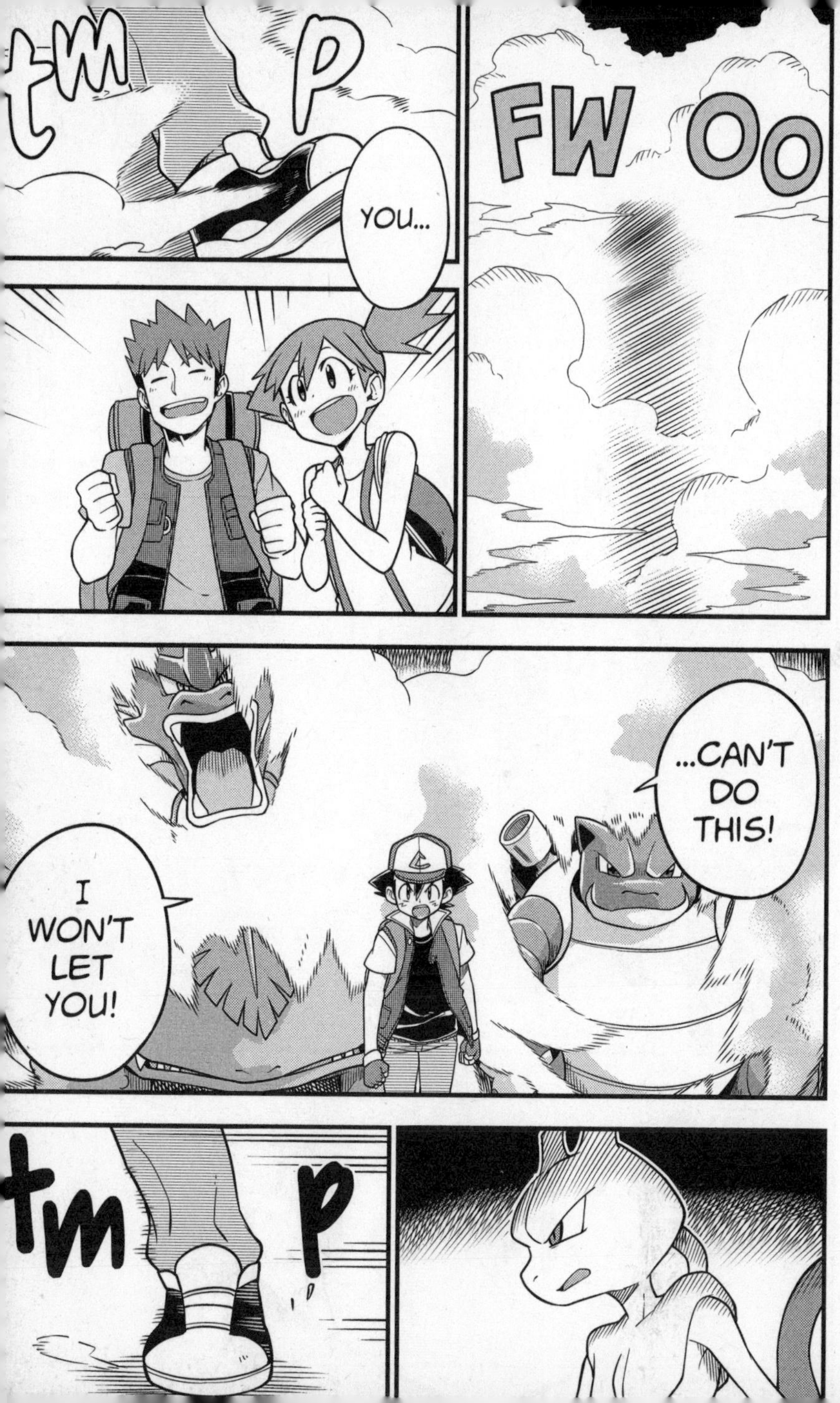
FW OO
tm p
YOU...
...CAN'T DO THIS!
I WON'T LET YOU!
tm p

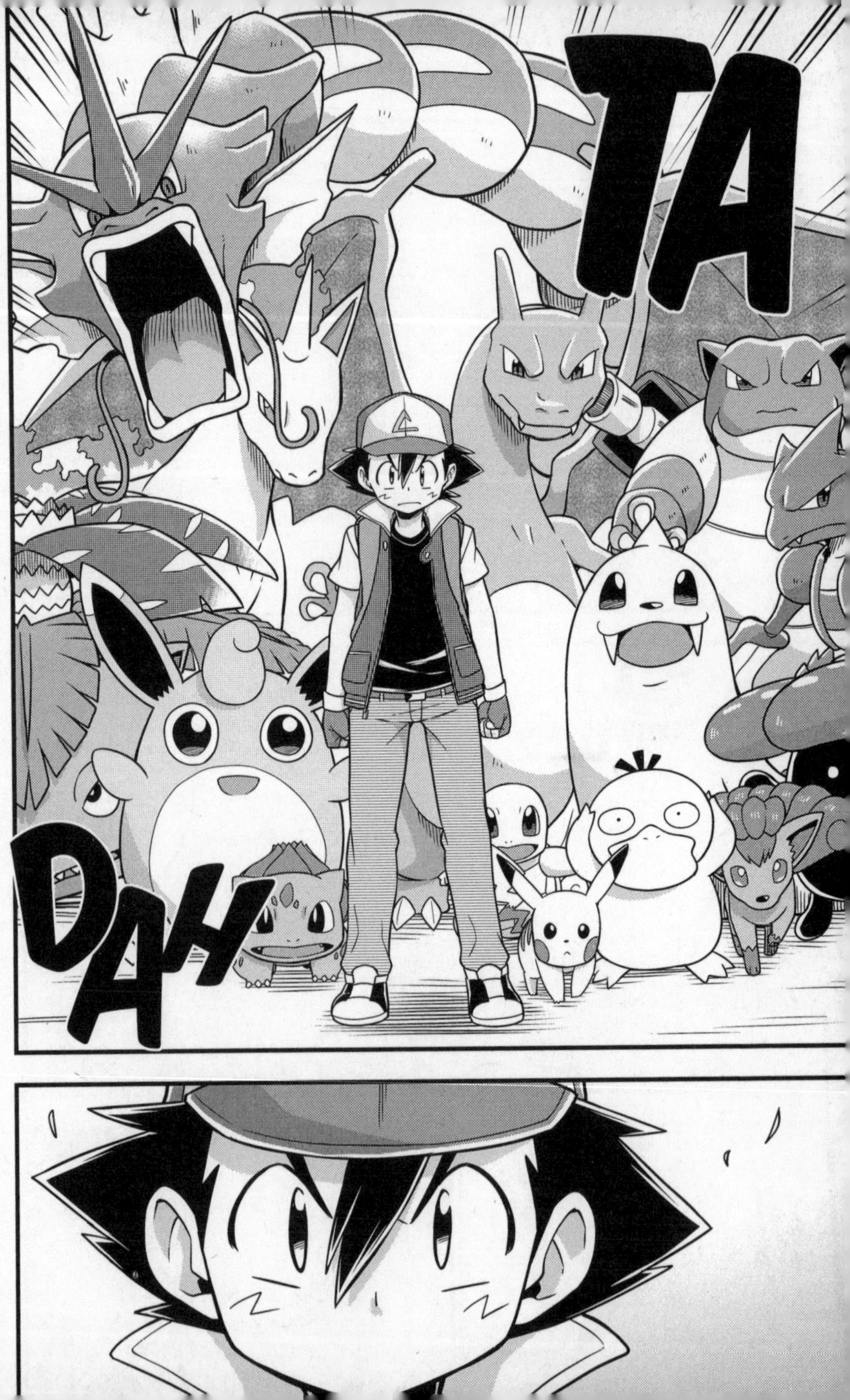
TA
DAH

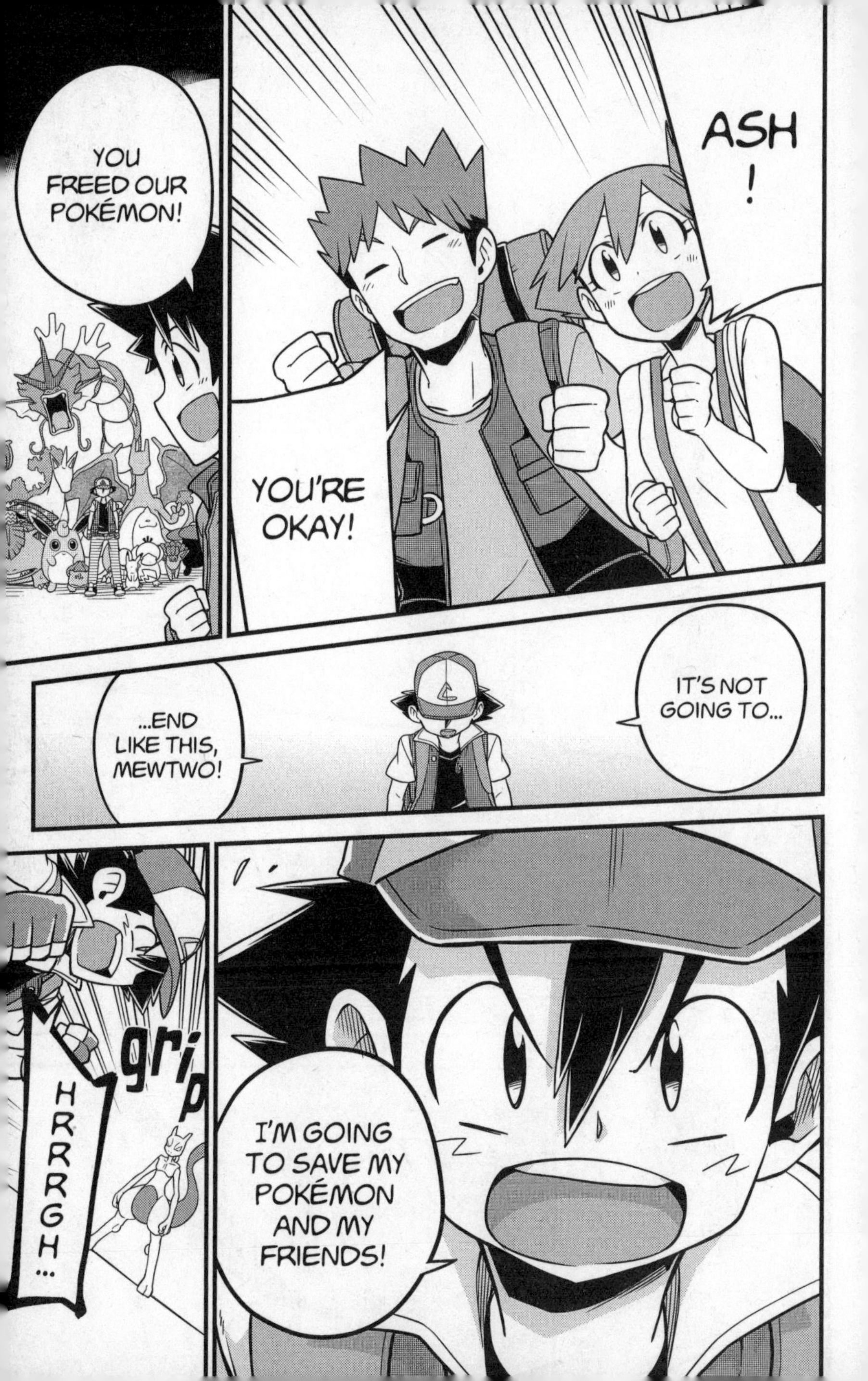
ASH!
YOU'RE OKAY!
YOU FREED OUR POKÉMON!
IT'S NOT GOING TO...
...END LIKE THIS, MEWTWO!
I'M GOING TO SAVE MY POKÉMON AND MY FRIENDS!
grip
HRRRGH...

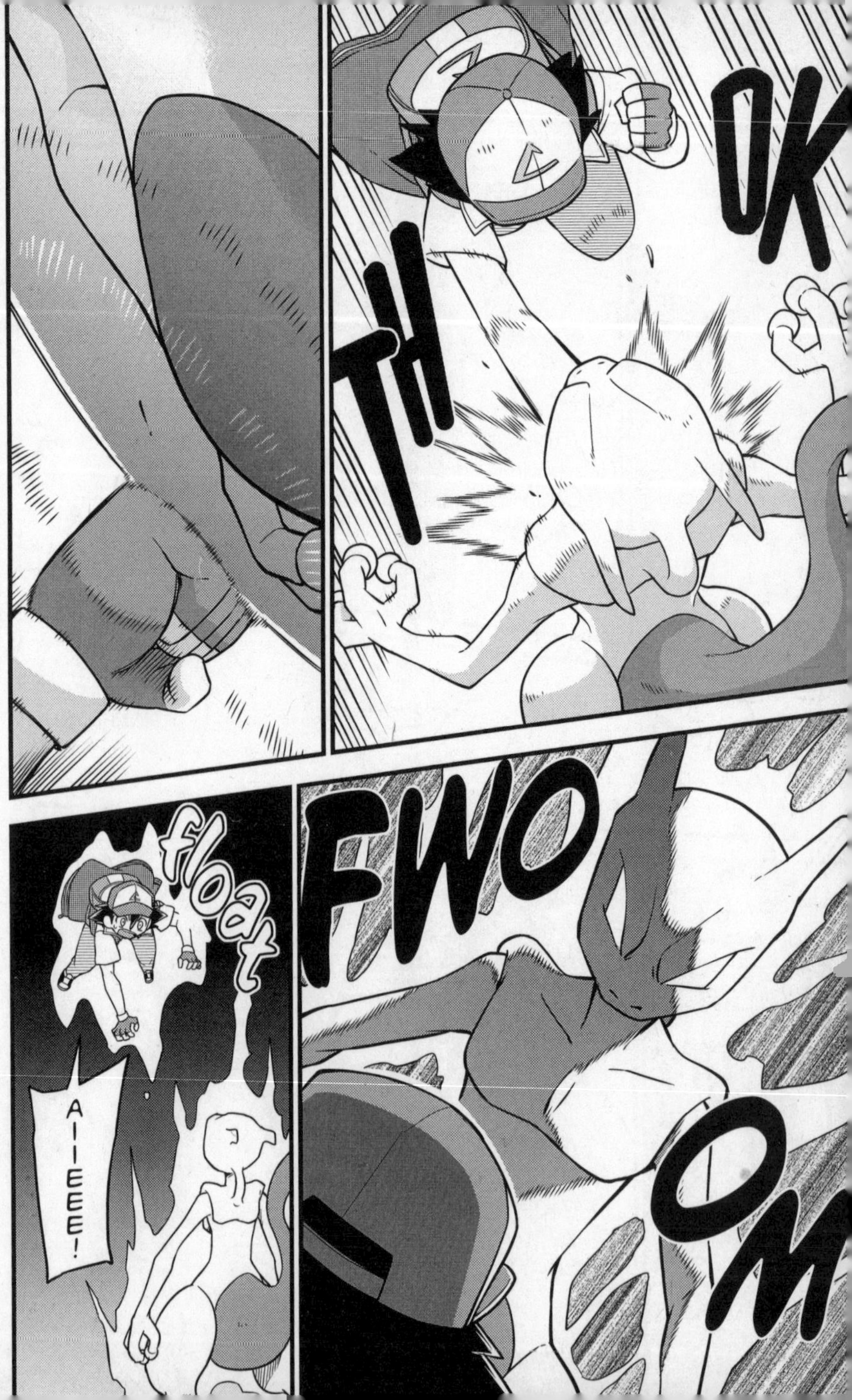
THOK
FWOOM
float
AIIEEE!

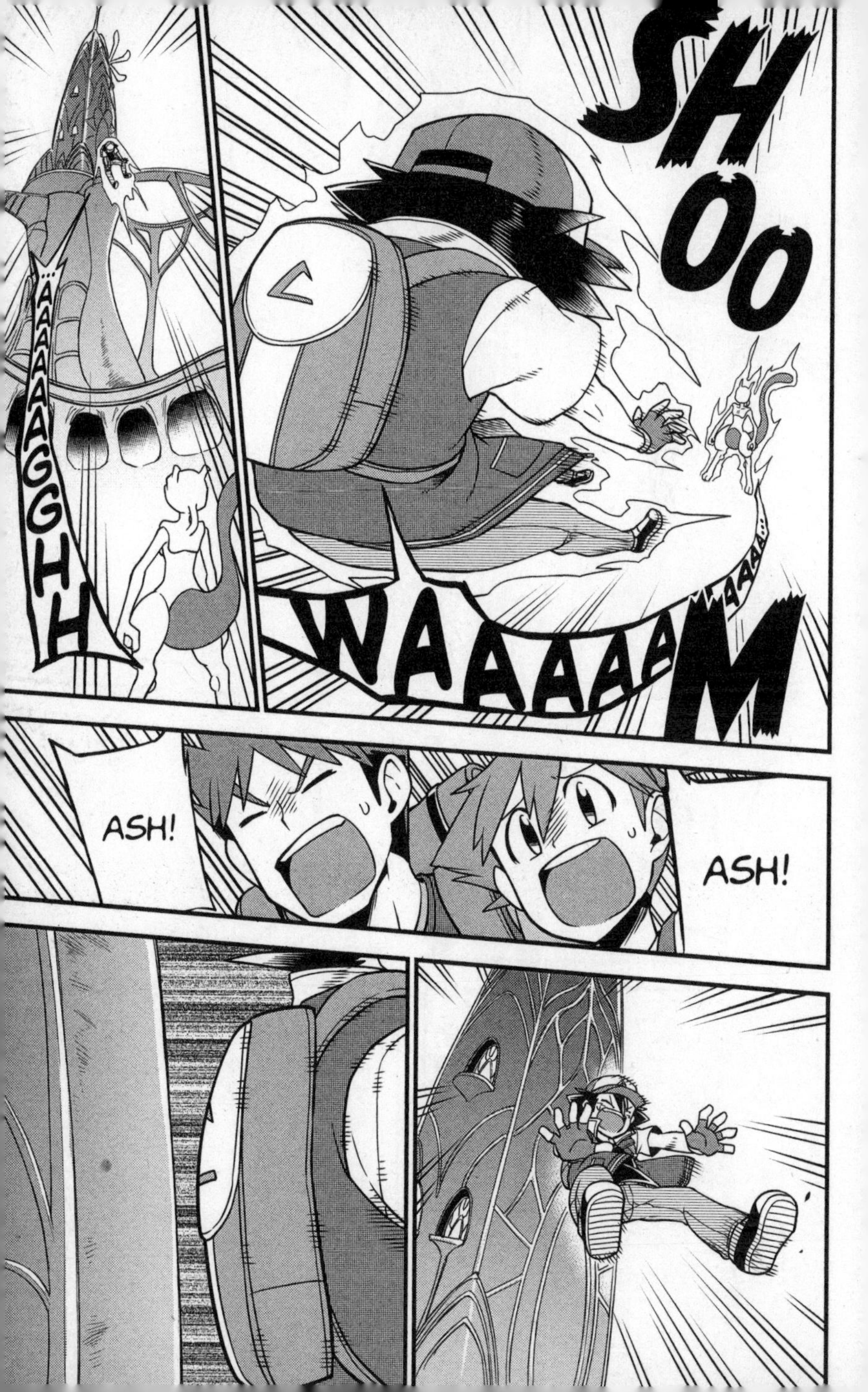
SHOO
...AAAA
WAAAAAM
...AAAAAAAGGHH
ASH!
ASH!

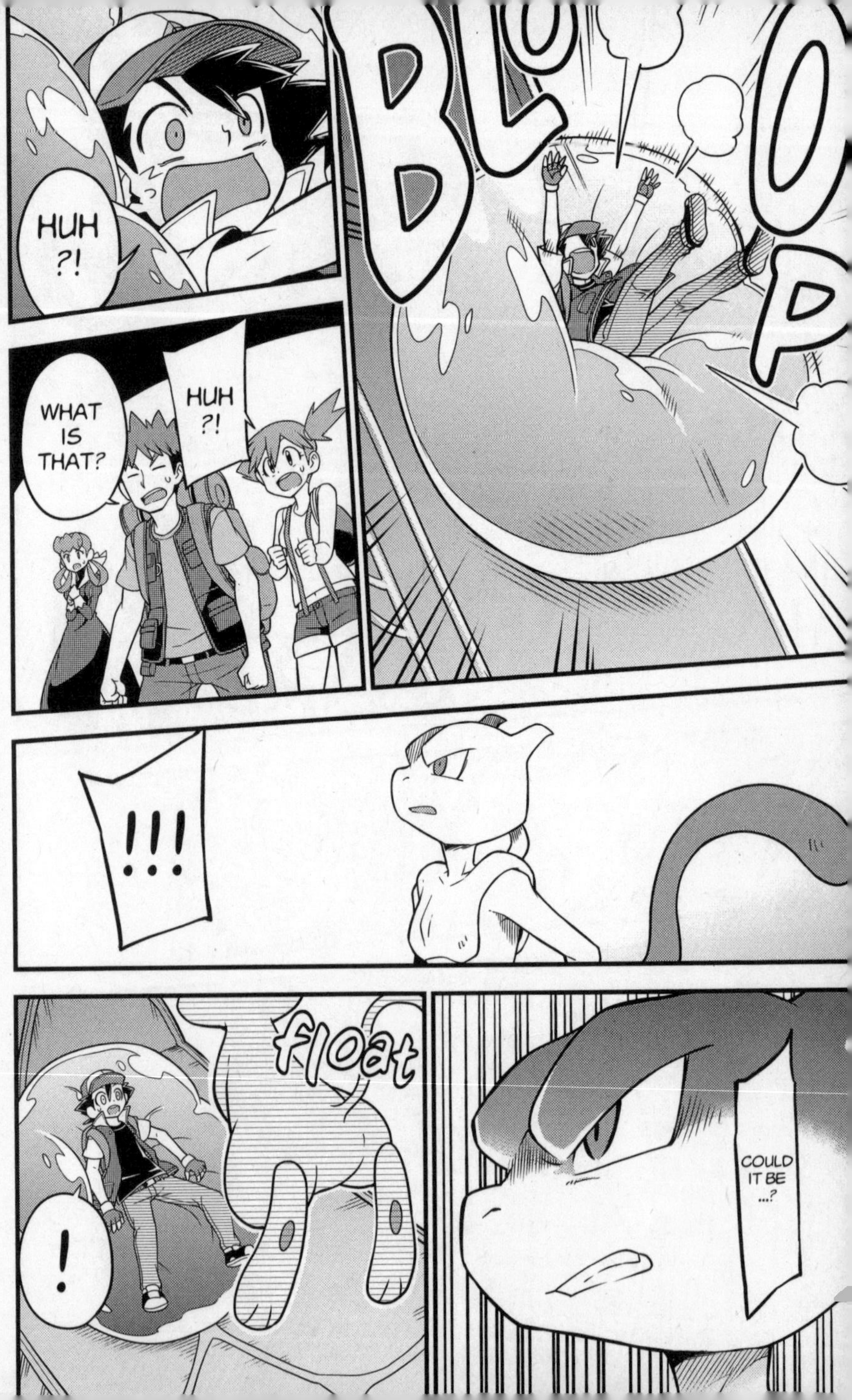

BLOOP
HUH ?!
HUH ?!
WHAT IS THAT?
!!!
COULD IT BE ...?
float
!

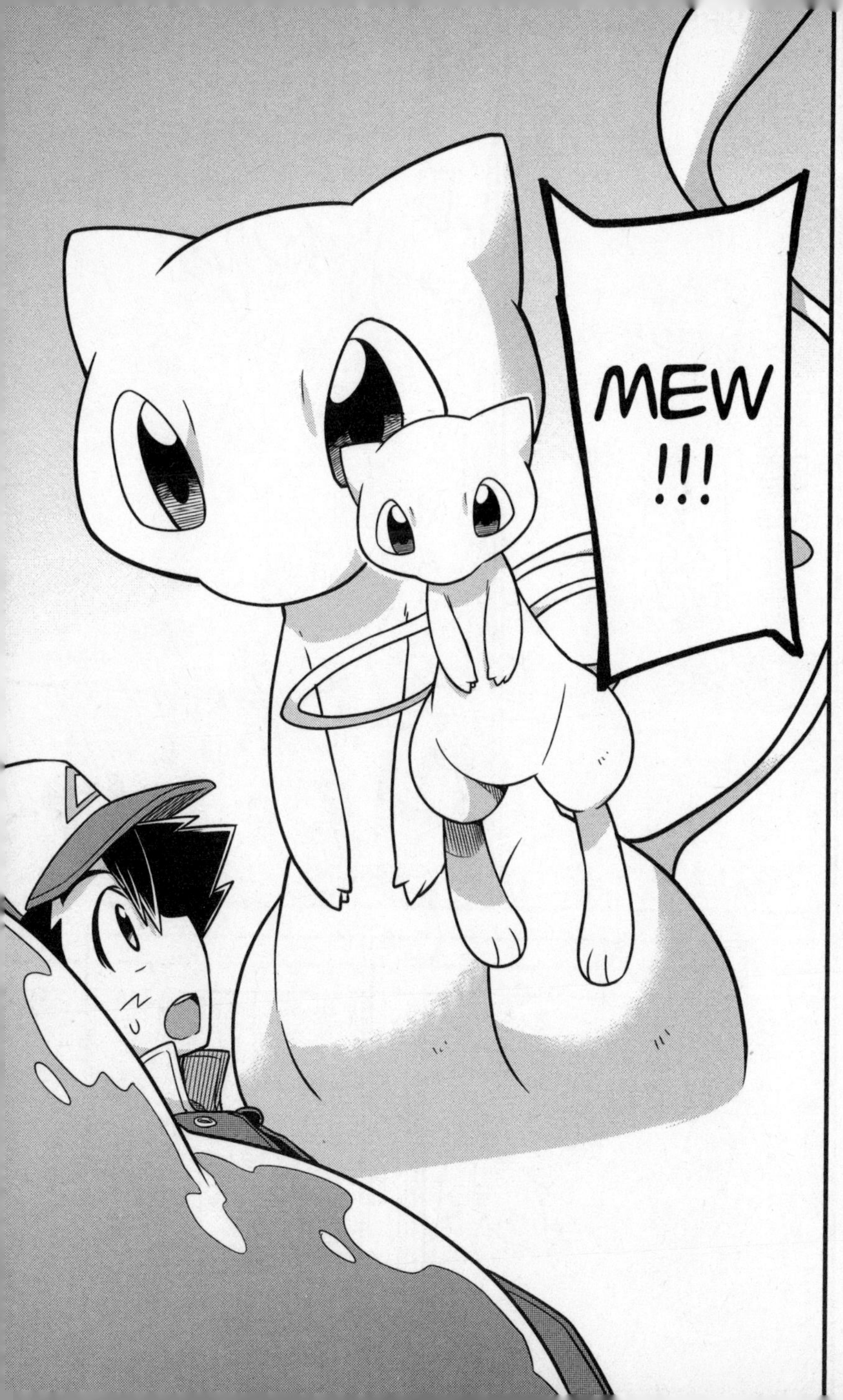
MEW !!!

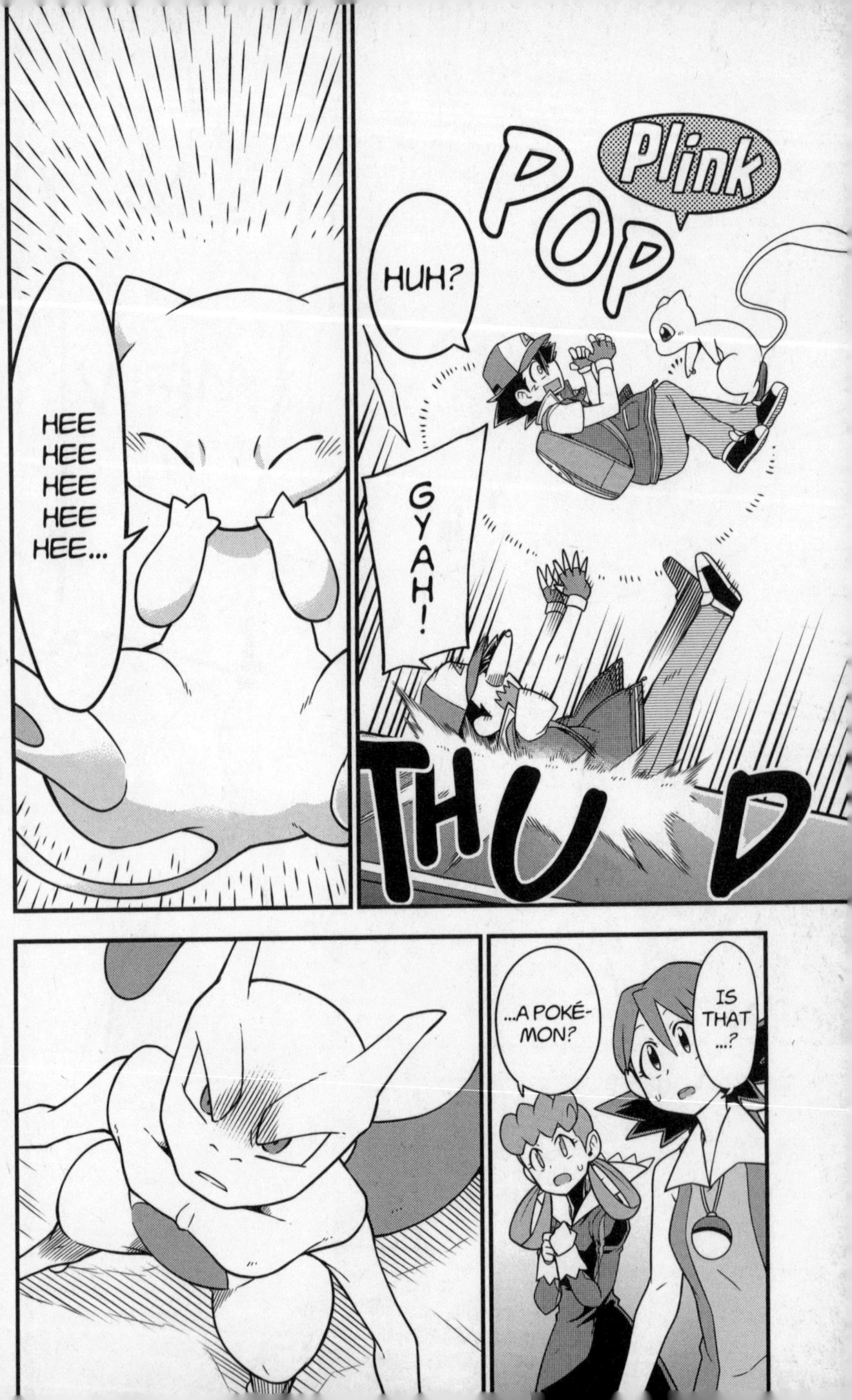
HUH?
POP
Plink
GYAH!
THUD
HEE HEE HEE HEE HEE...
IS THAT ...?
...A POKÉMON?

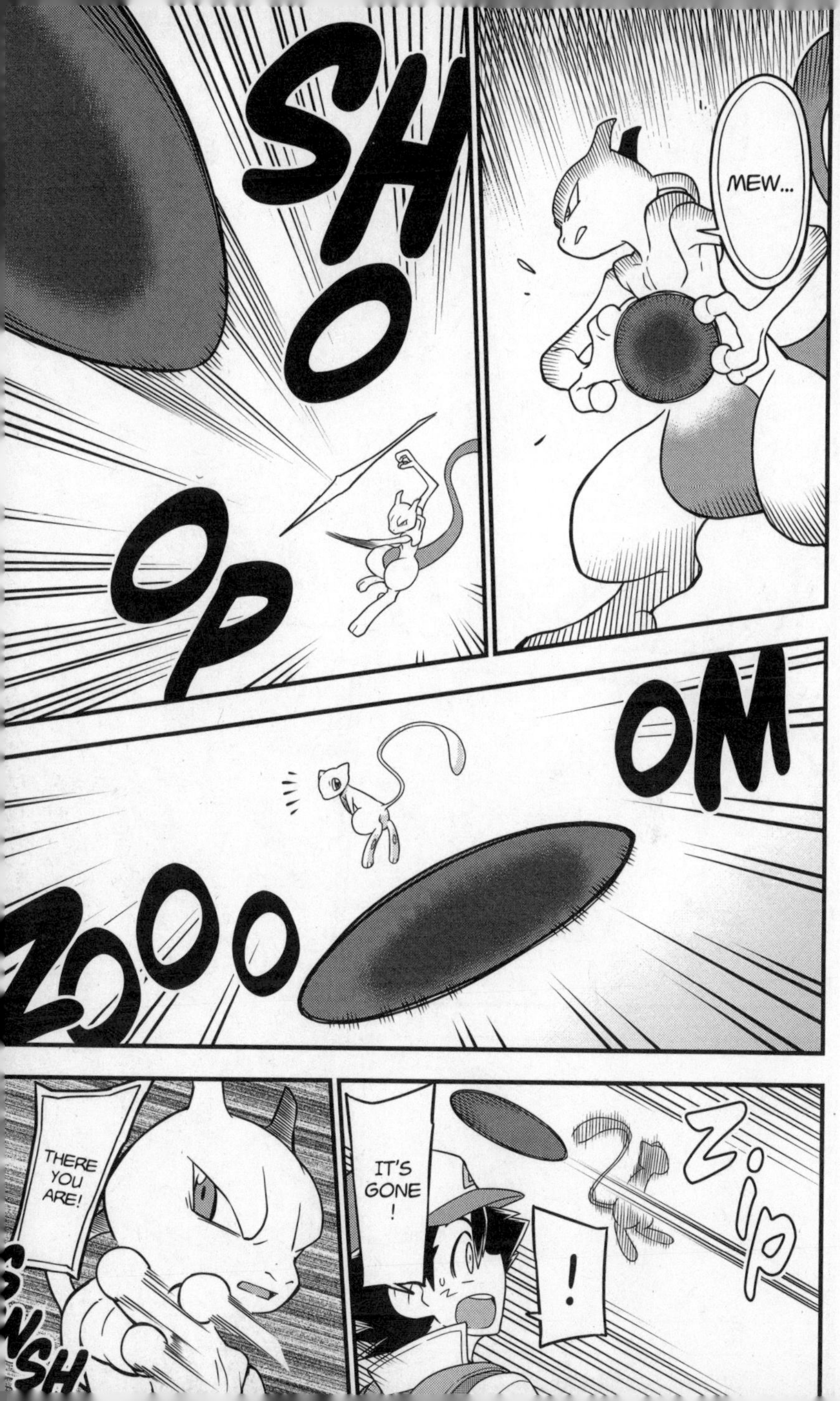
MEW...
SHOOP
ZOOOOM
ZIP
!
IT'S GONE!
THERE YOU ARE!

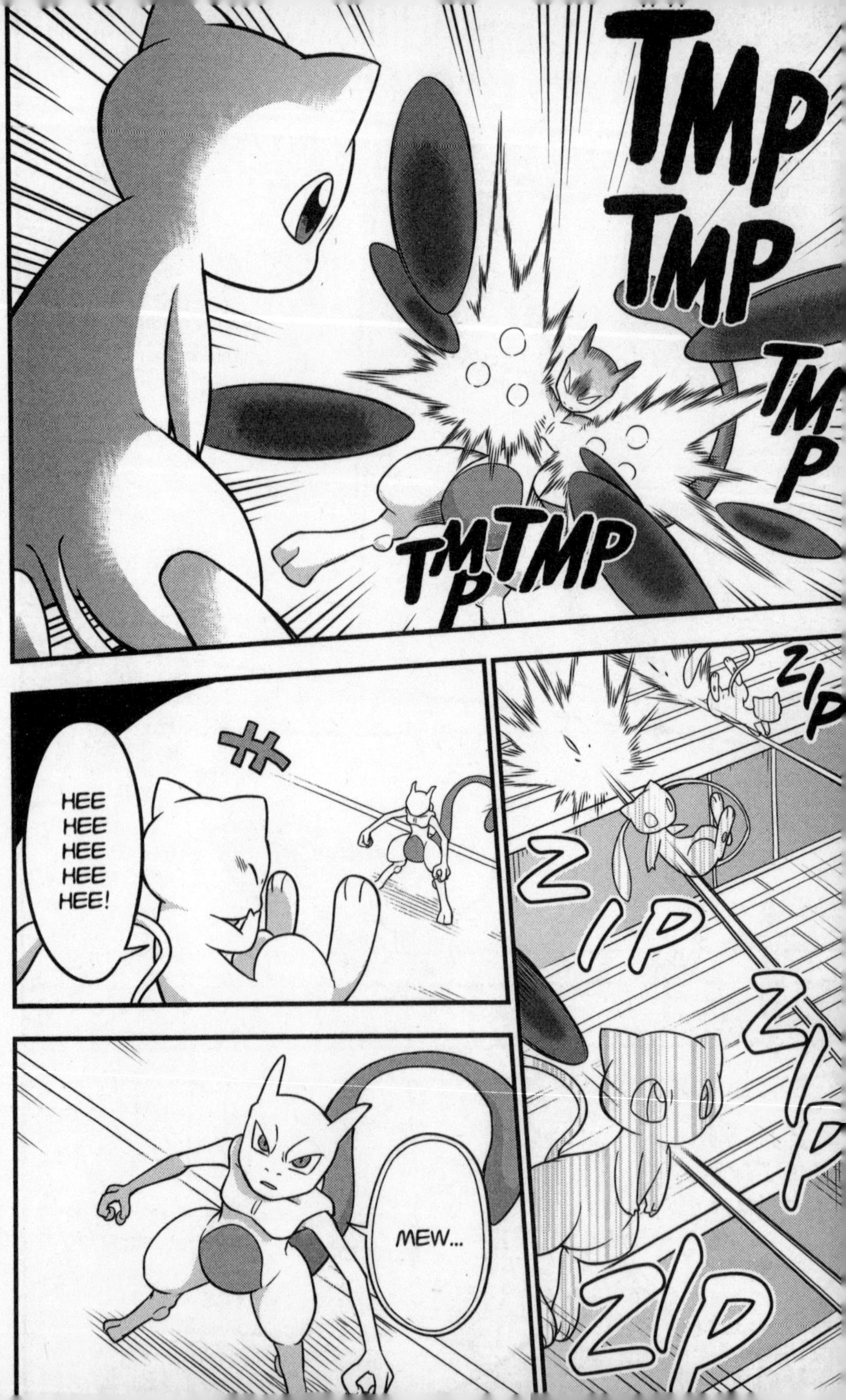
TMP
TMP
TMP
TMP TMP
ZIP
ZIP
ZIP
ZIP
HEE HEE HEE HEE HEE!
MEW...

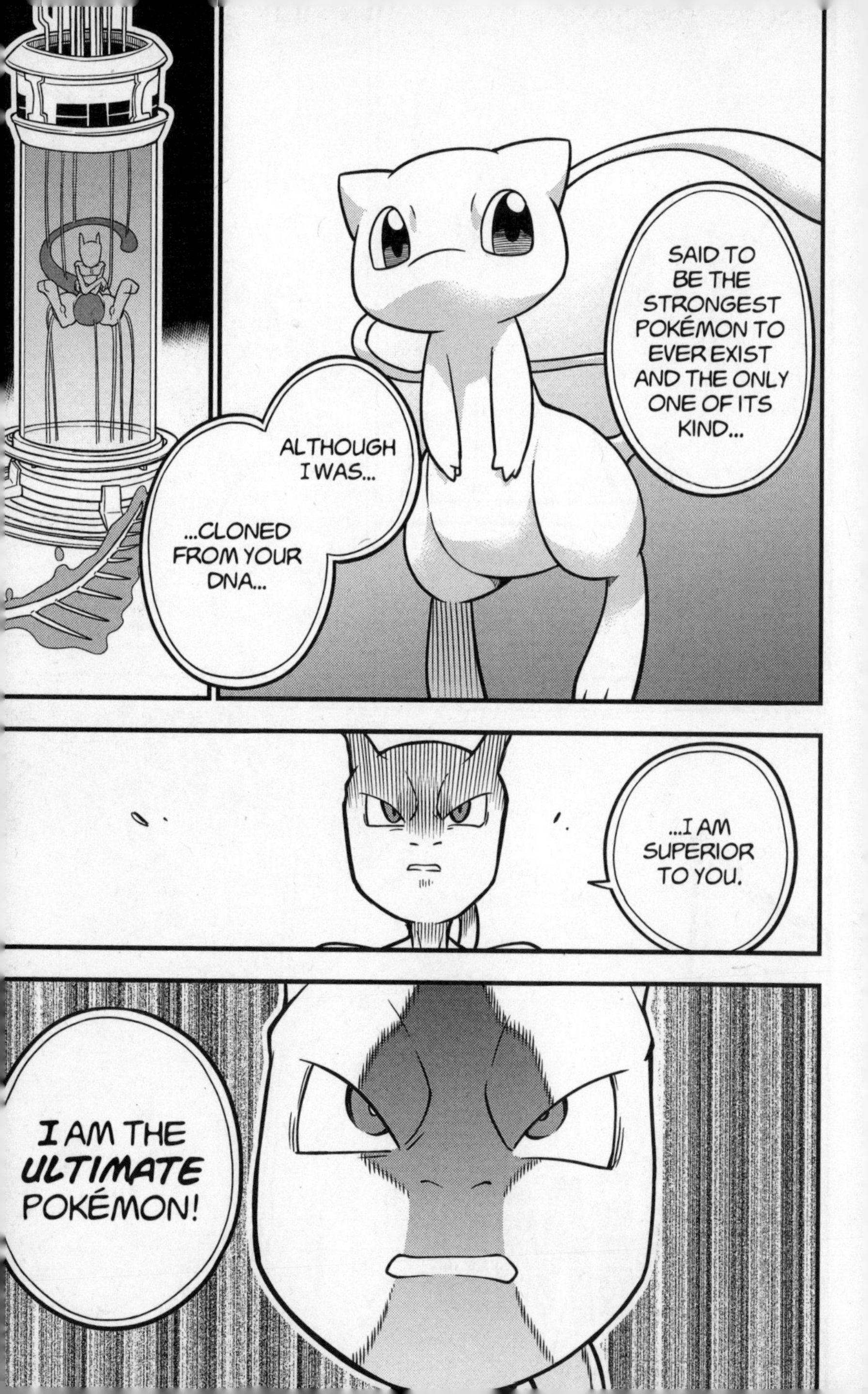
SAID TO BE THE STRONGEST POKÉMON TO EVER EXIST AND THE ONLY ONE OF ITS KIND...
ALTHOUGH I WAS...
...CLONED FROM YOUR DNA...
...I AM SUPERIOR TO YOU.
I AM THE *ULTIMATE* POKÉMON!

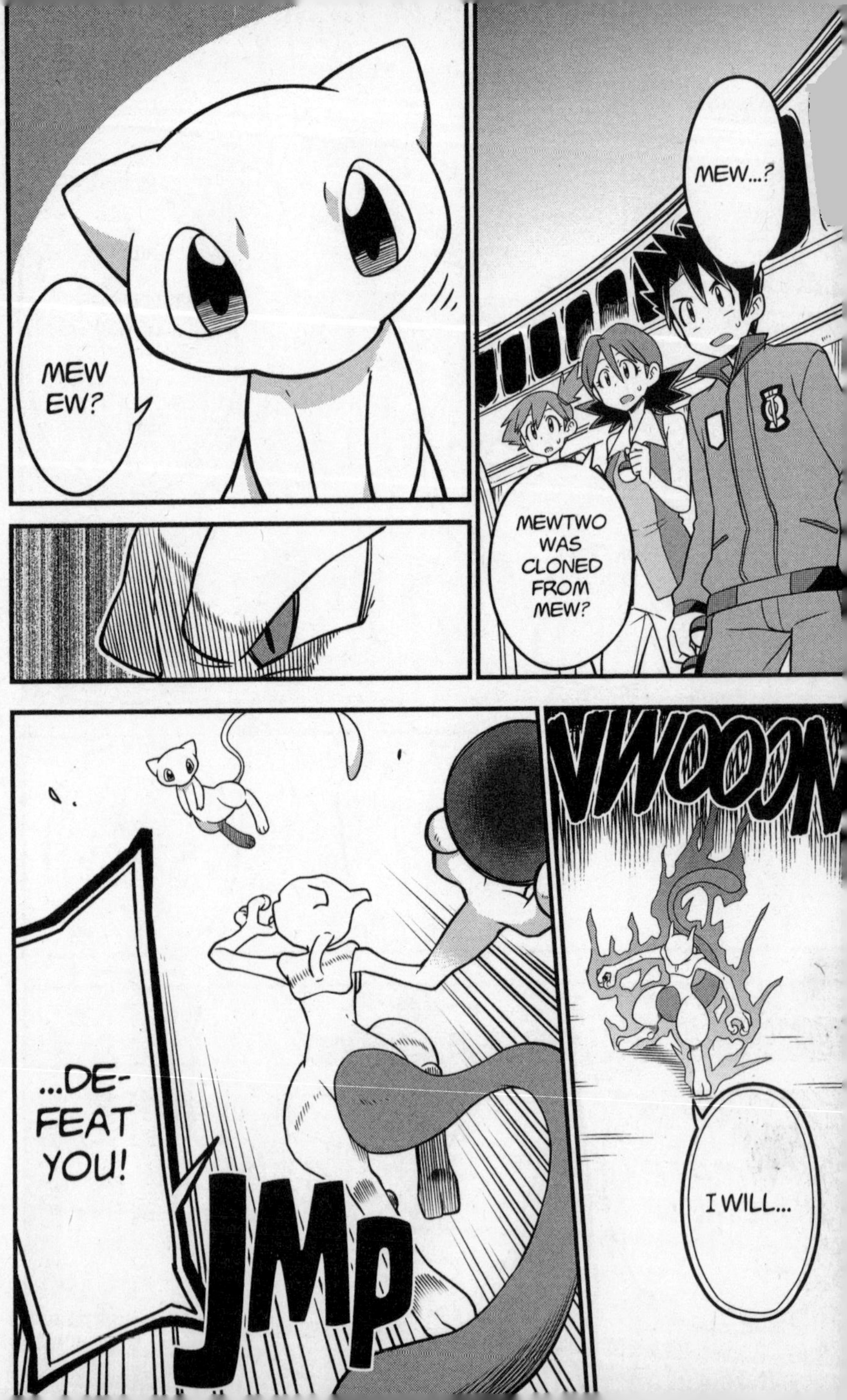
MEW...?
MEWTWO WAS CLONED FROM MEW?
MEW EW?
VWOOOM
I WILL...
...DE-FEAT YOU!
JMP

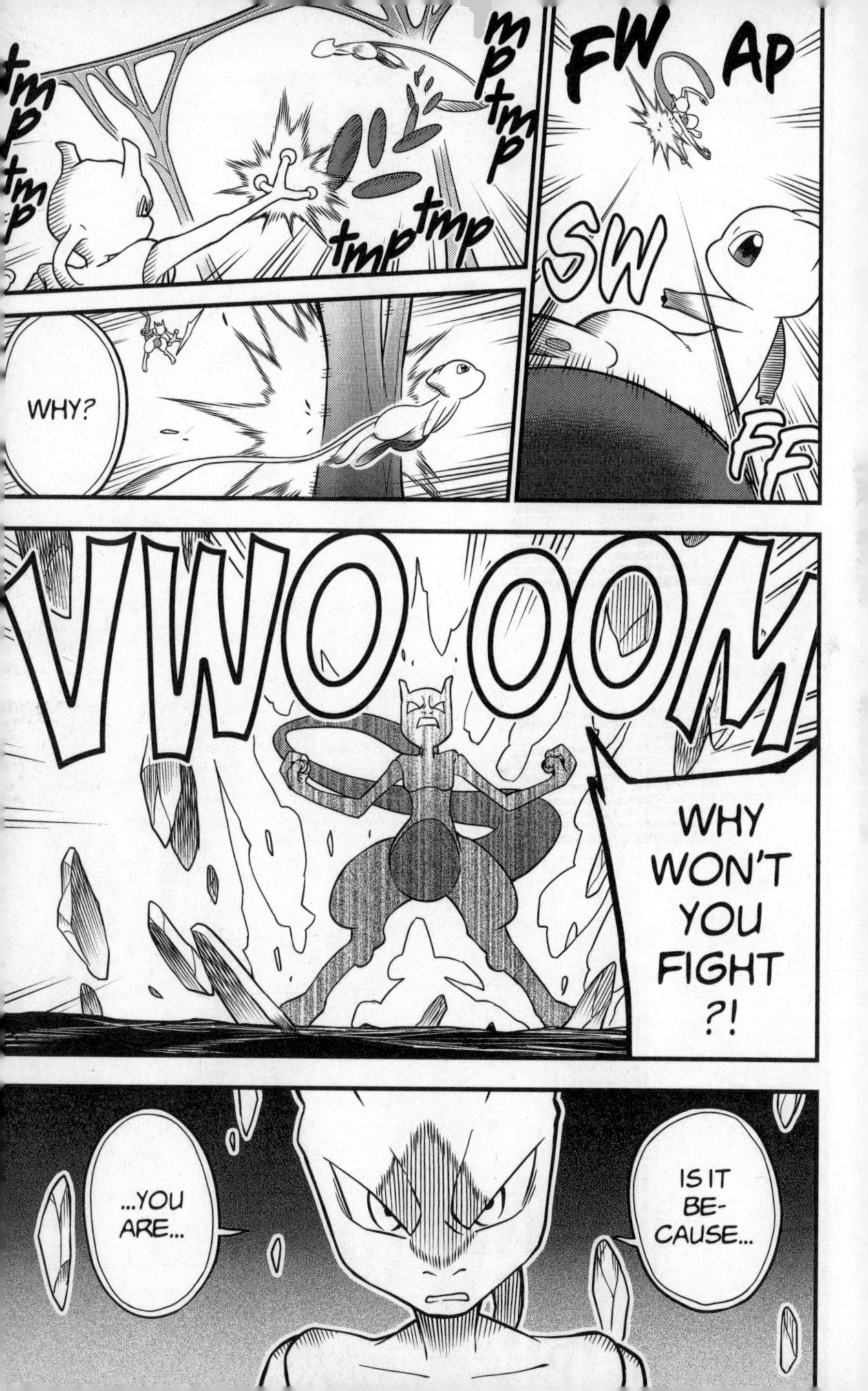
FWAP
SW
FF
mp tmp tmp
tmp tmp
tmp tmp
WHY?
VWOOOM
WHY WON'T YOU FIGHT ?!
IS IT BE-CAUSE...
...YOU ARE...

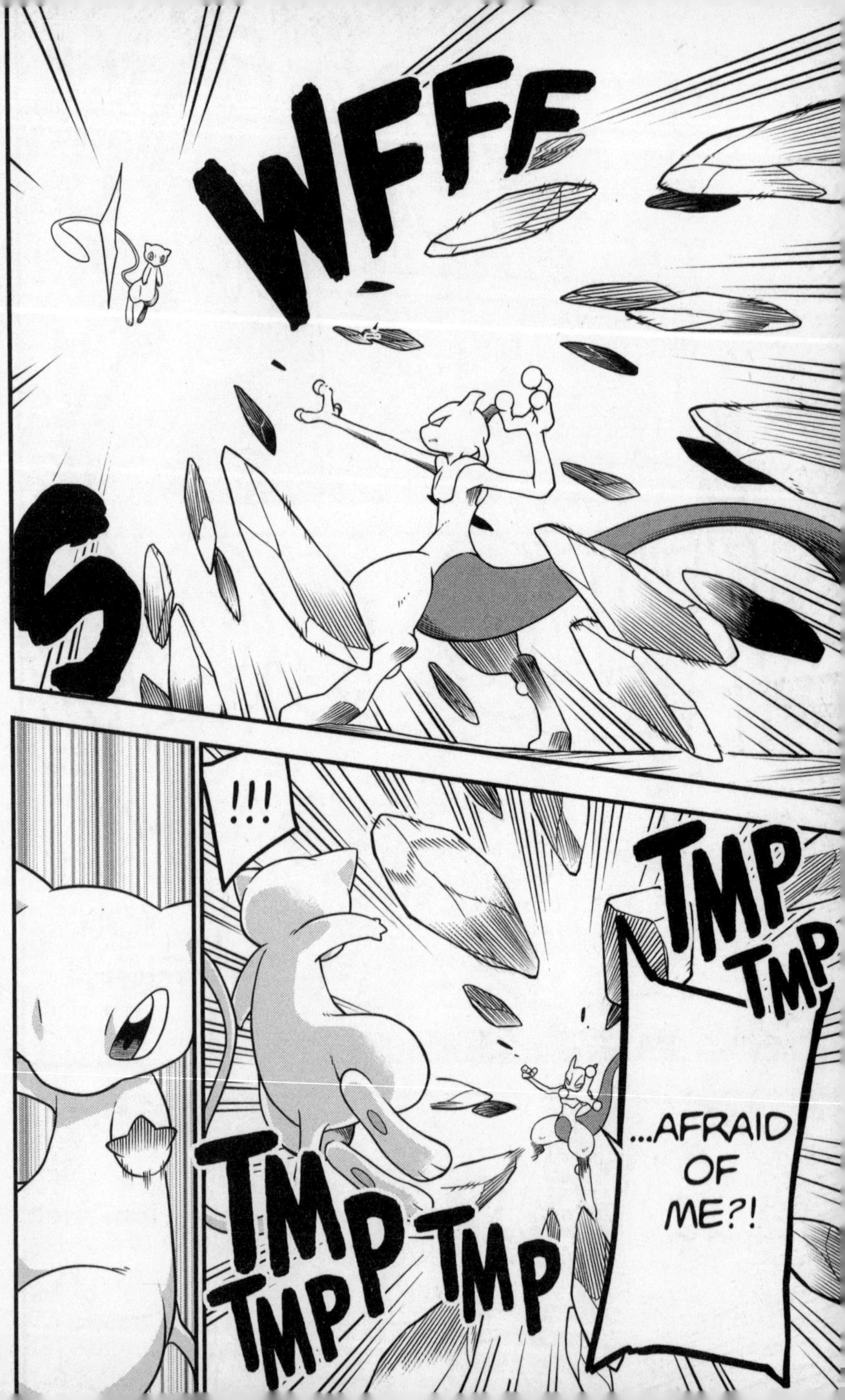
WFFF
S
TMP TMP
...AFRAID OF ME?!
!!!
TMP TMP TMP

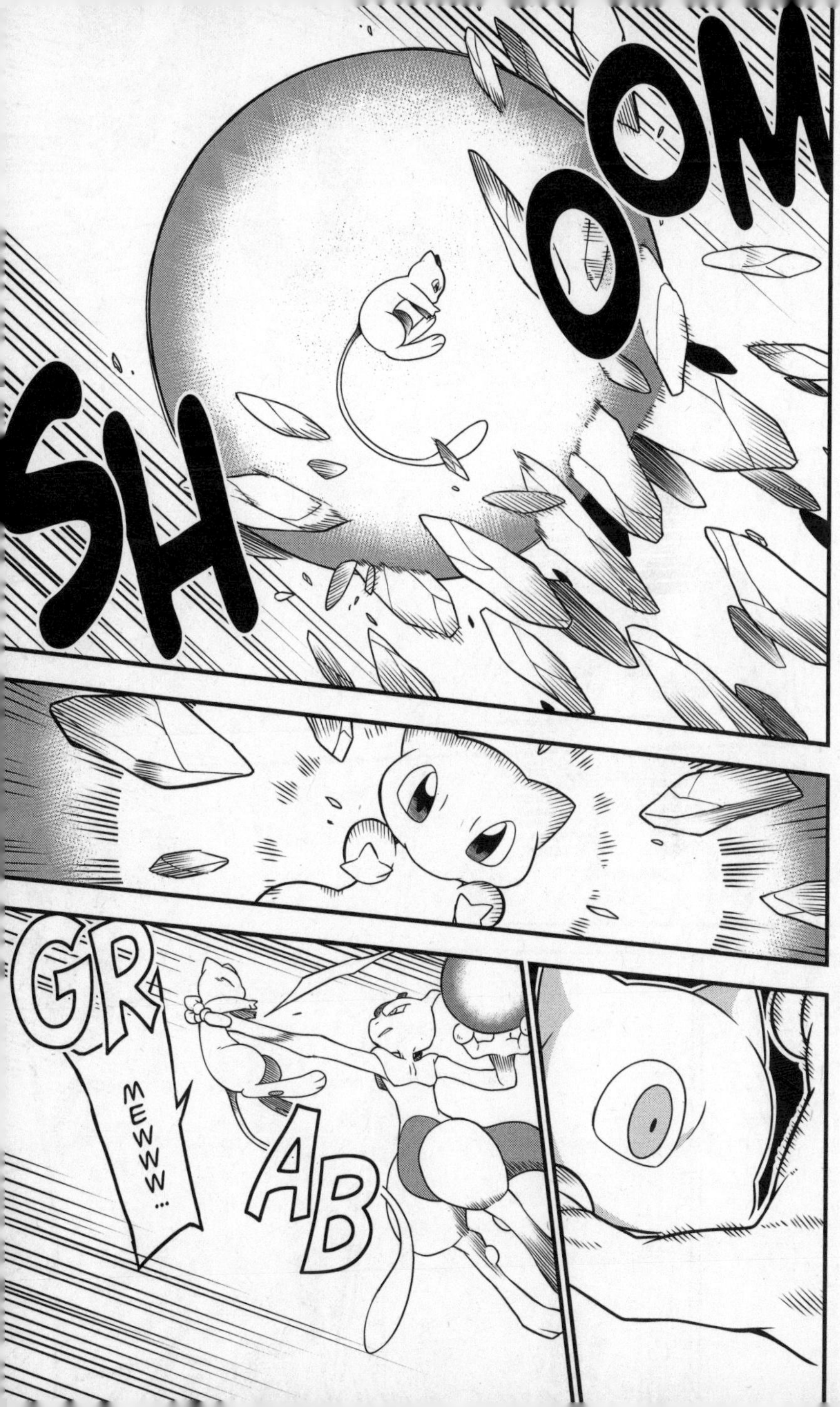
SHOOM
GRAB
MEWWW...

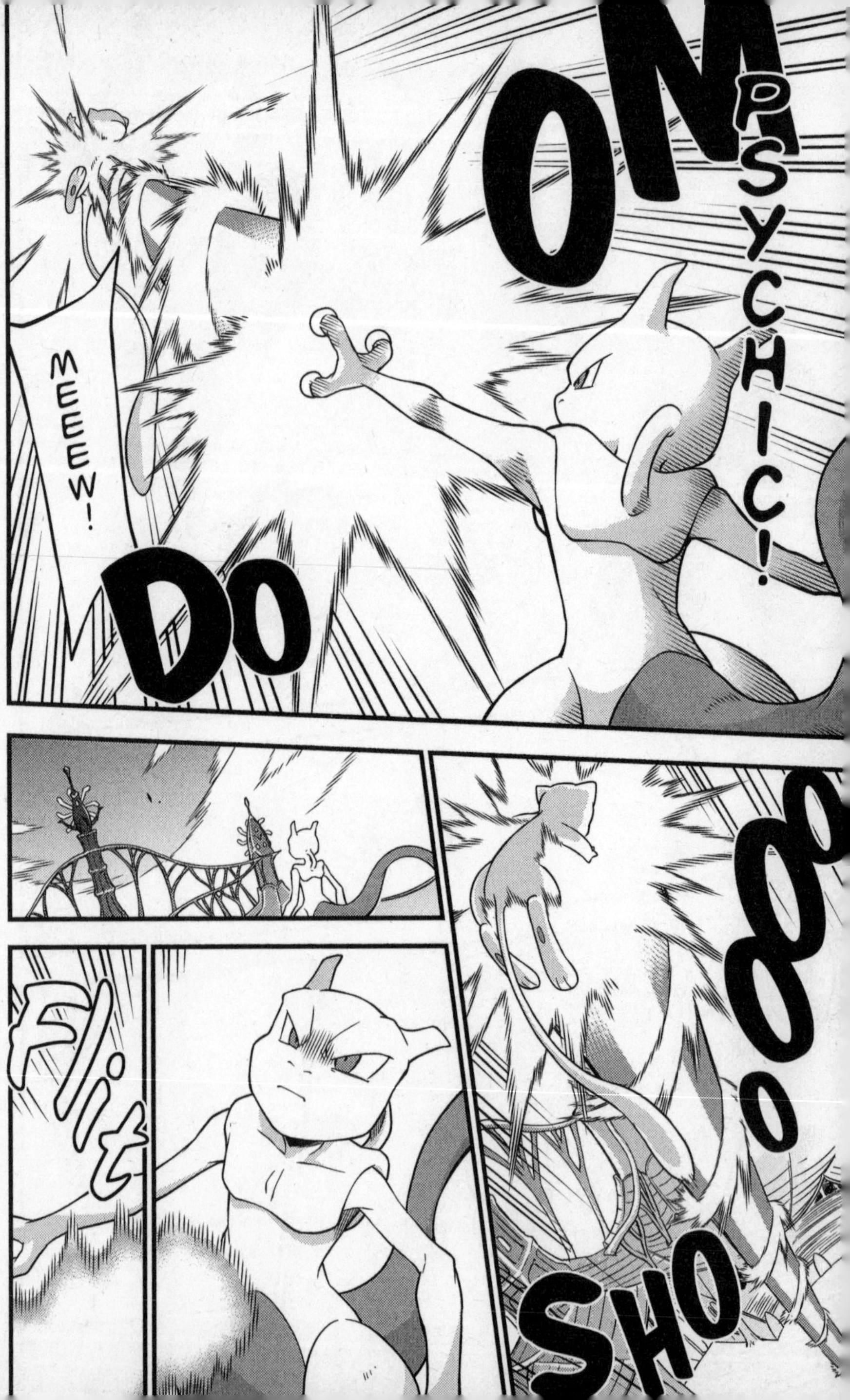
PSYCHIC!
DO OM
MEEEW!
SHOOOO
Flit

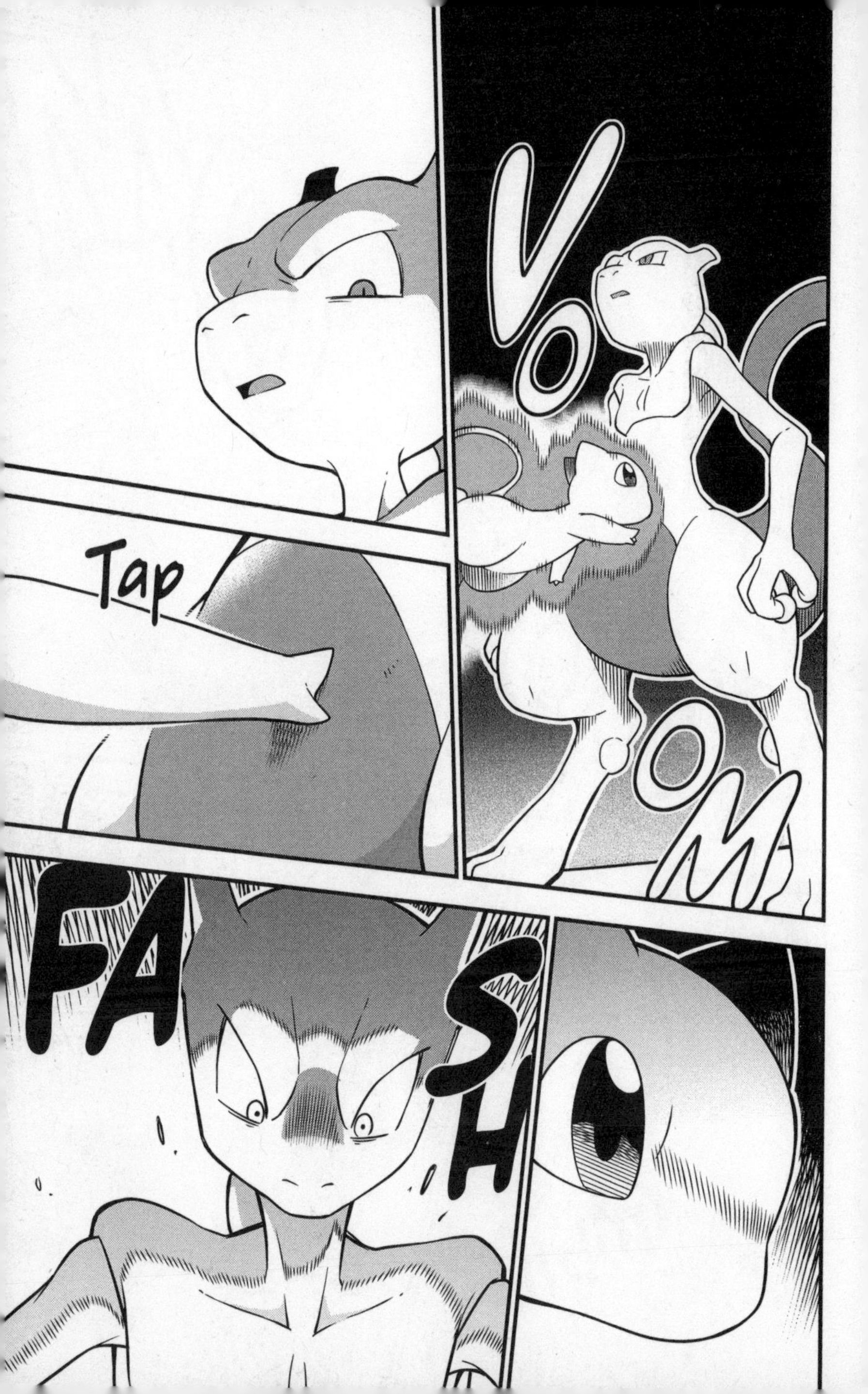
VOOM
Tap
FASH

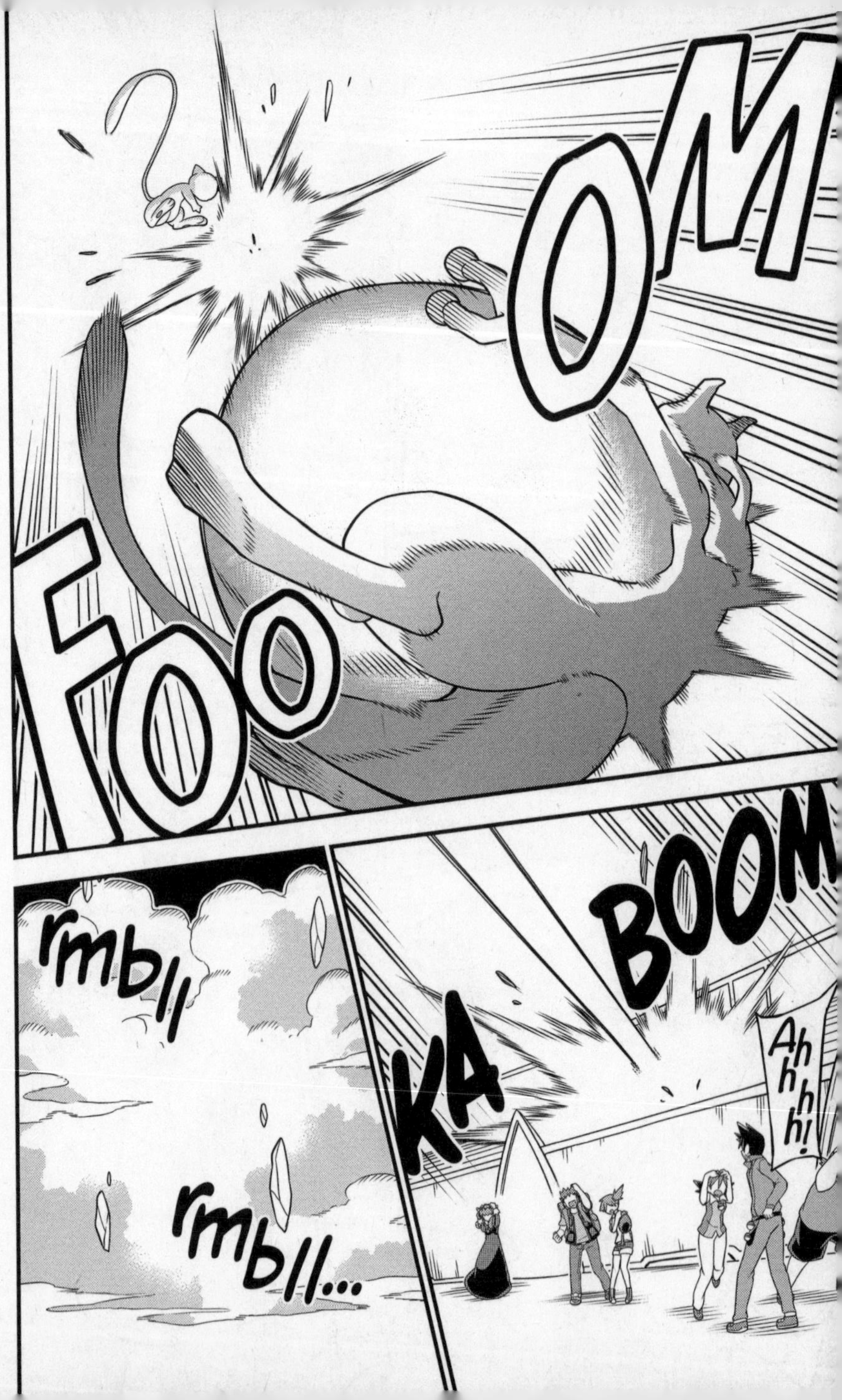
FOOOM
KA
BOOM
Ahhhh!
rmbll
rmbll...

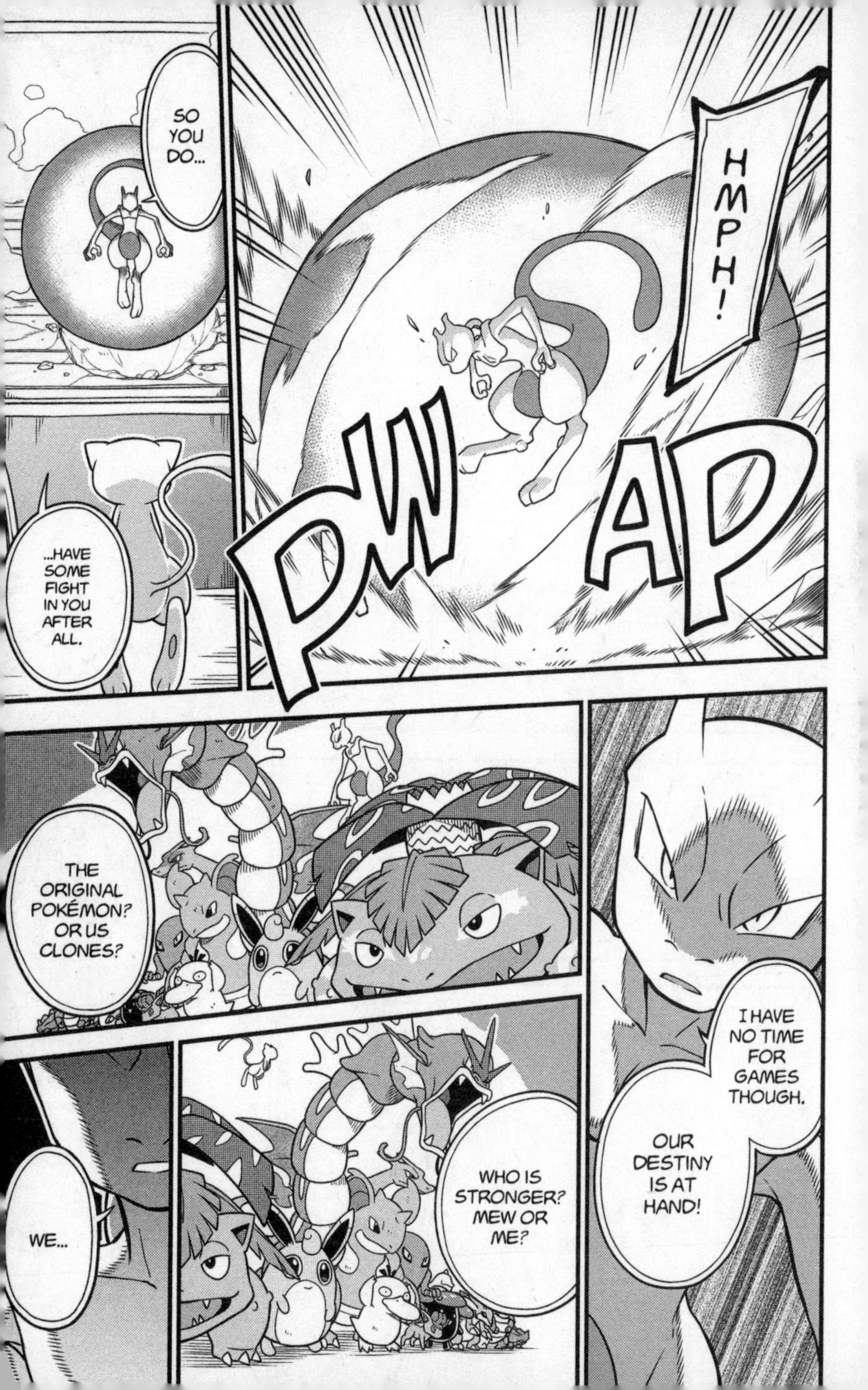
HMPH!
PWAP
SO YOU DO...
...HAVE SOME FIGHT IN YOU AFTER ALL.
I HAVE NO TIME FOR GAMES THOUGH.
OUR DESTINY IS AT HAND!
THE ORIGINAL POKÉMON? OR US CLONES?
WHO IS STRONGER? MEW OR ME?
WE...

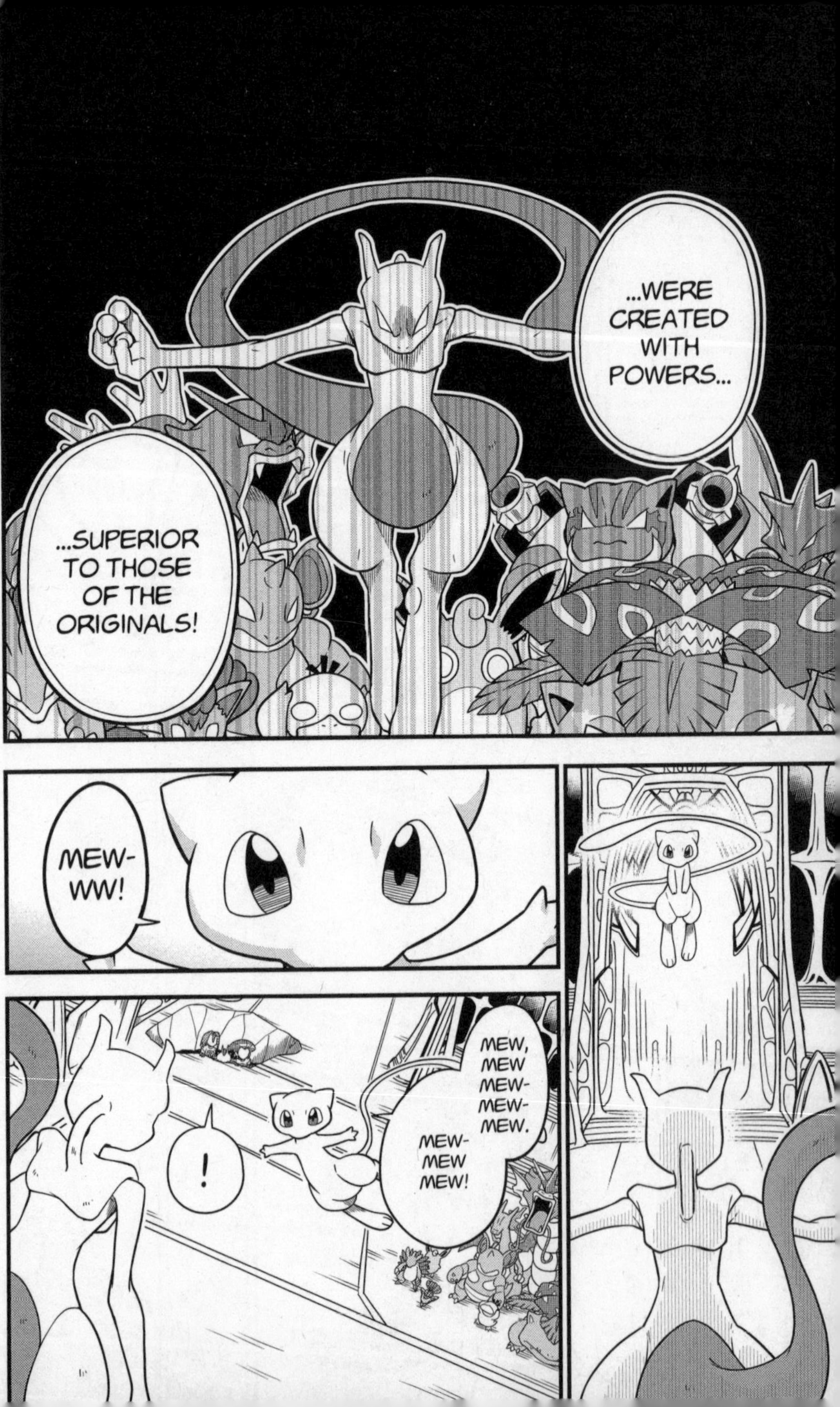
...WERE CREATED WITH POWERS...
...SUPERIOR TO THOSE OF THE ORIGINALS!
MEW-WW!
MEW, MEW MEW-MEW-MEW.
MEW-MEW MEW!
!

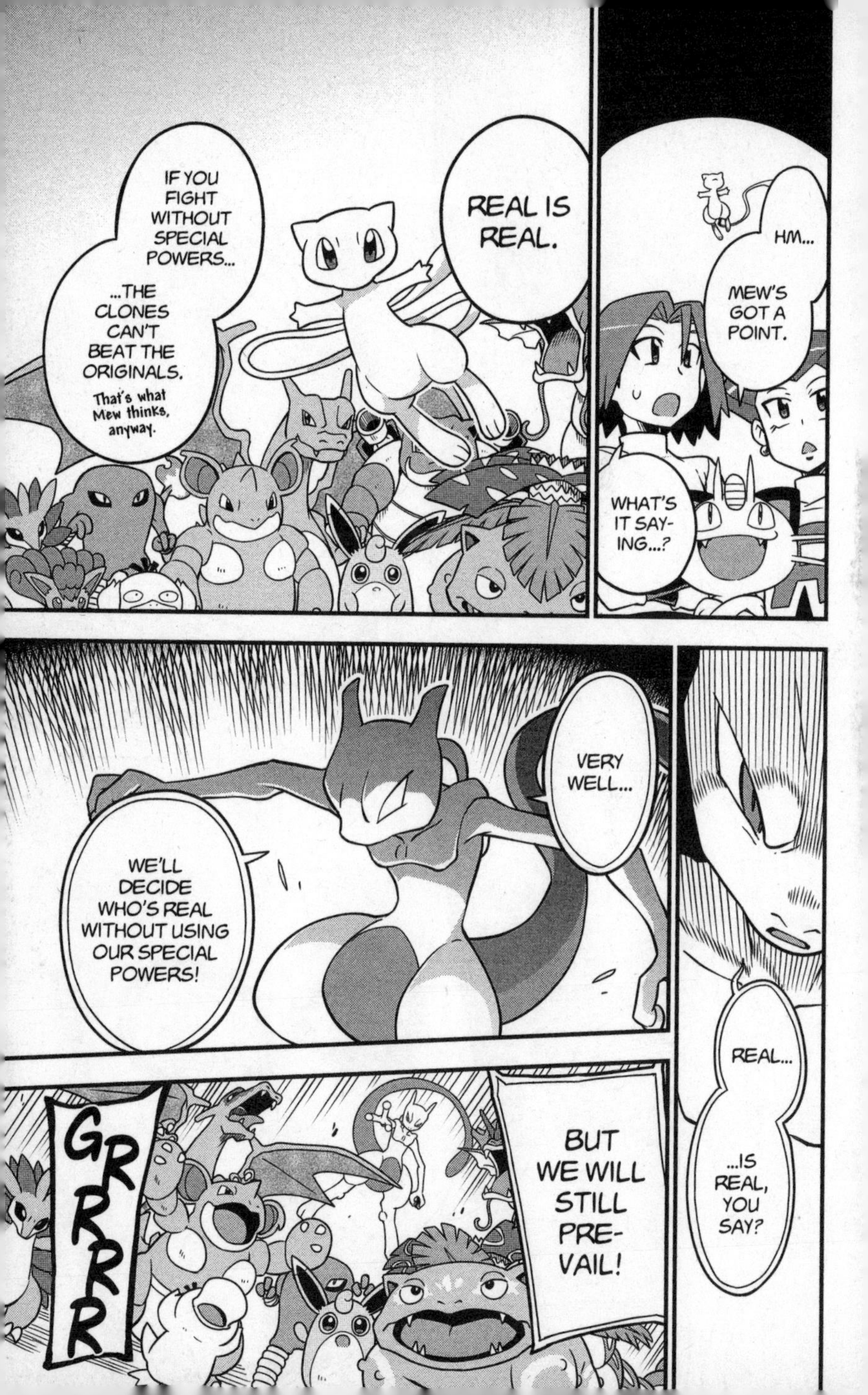
HM...
MEW'S GOT A POINT.
WHAT'S IT SAY-ING...?
REAL IS REAL.
IF YOU FIGHT WITHOUT SPECIAL POWERS...
...THE CLONES CAN'T BEAT THE ORIGINALS.
That's what Mew thinks, anyway.
REAL...
...IS REAL, YOU SAY?
VERY WELL...
WE'LL DECIDE WHO'S REAL WITHOUT USING OUR SPECIAL POWERS!
BUT WE WILL STILL PRE-VAIL!
GRRRR

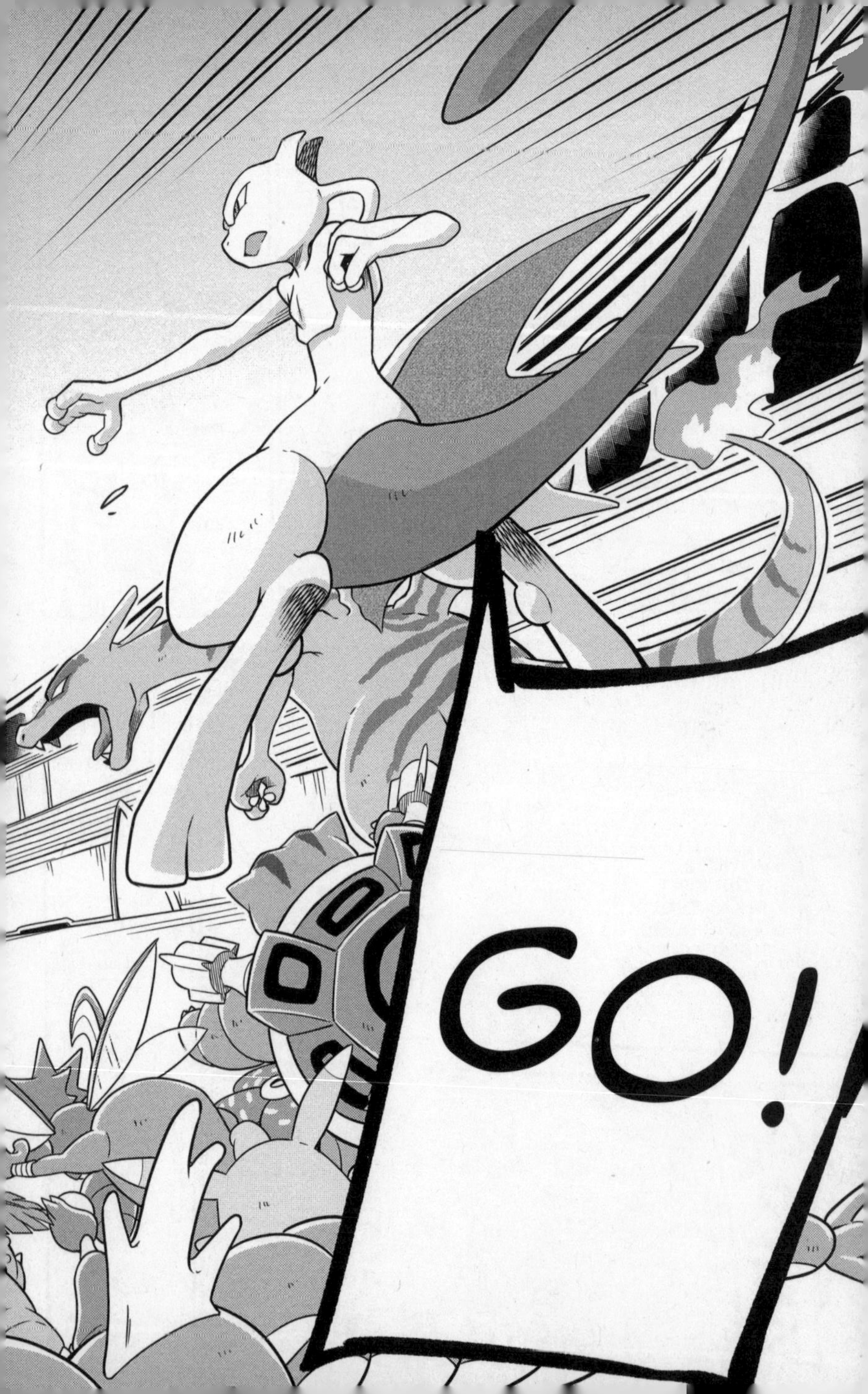
GO!

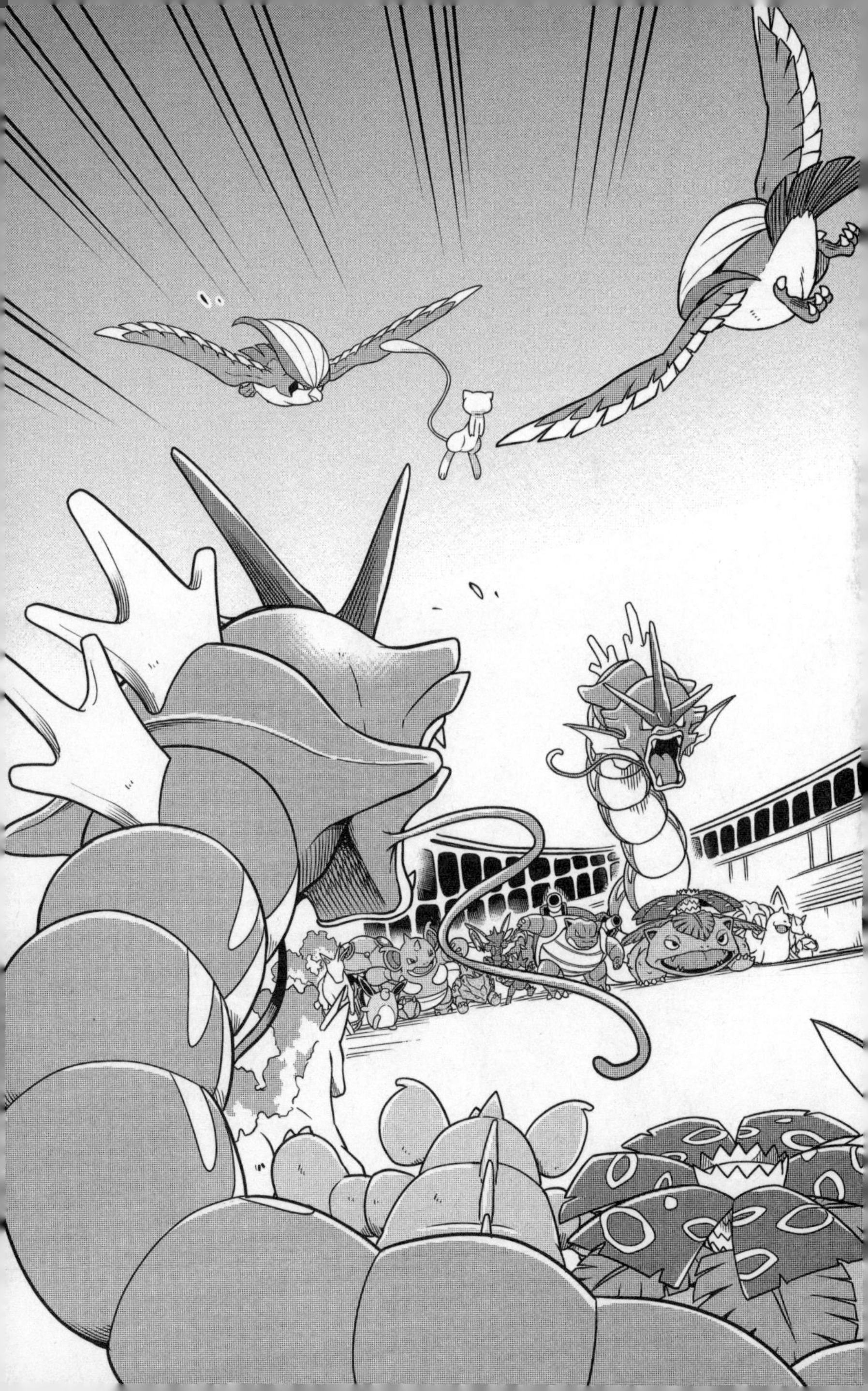

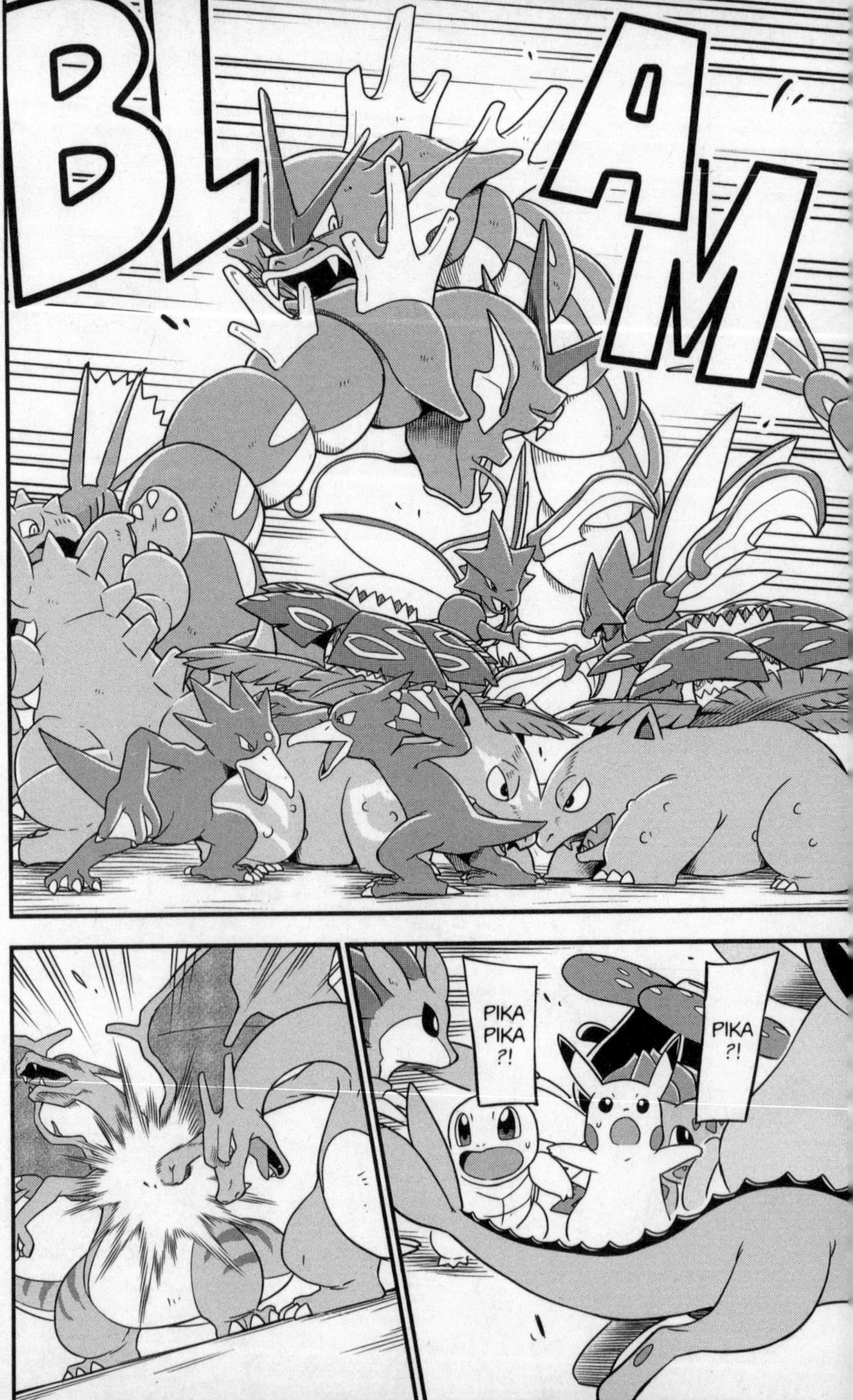
BLAM
PIKA ?!
PIKA PIKA ?!

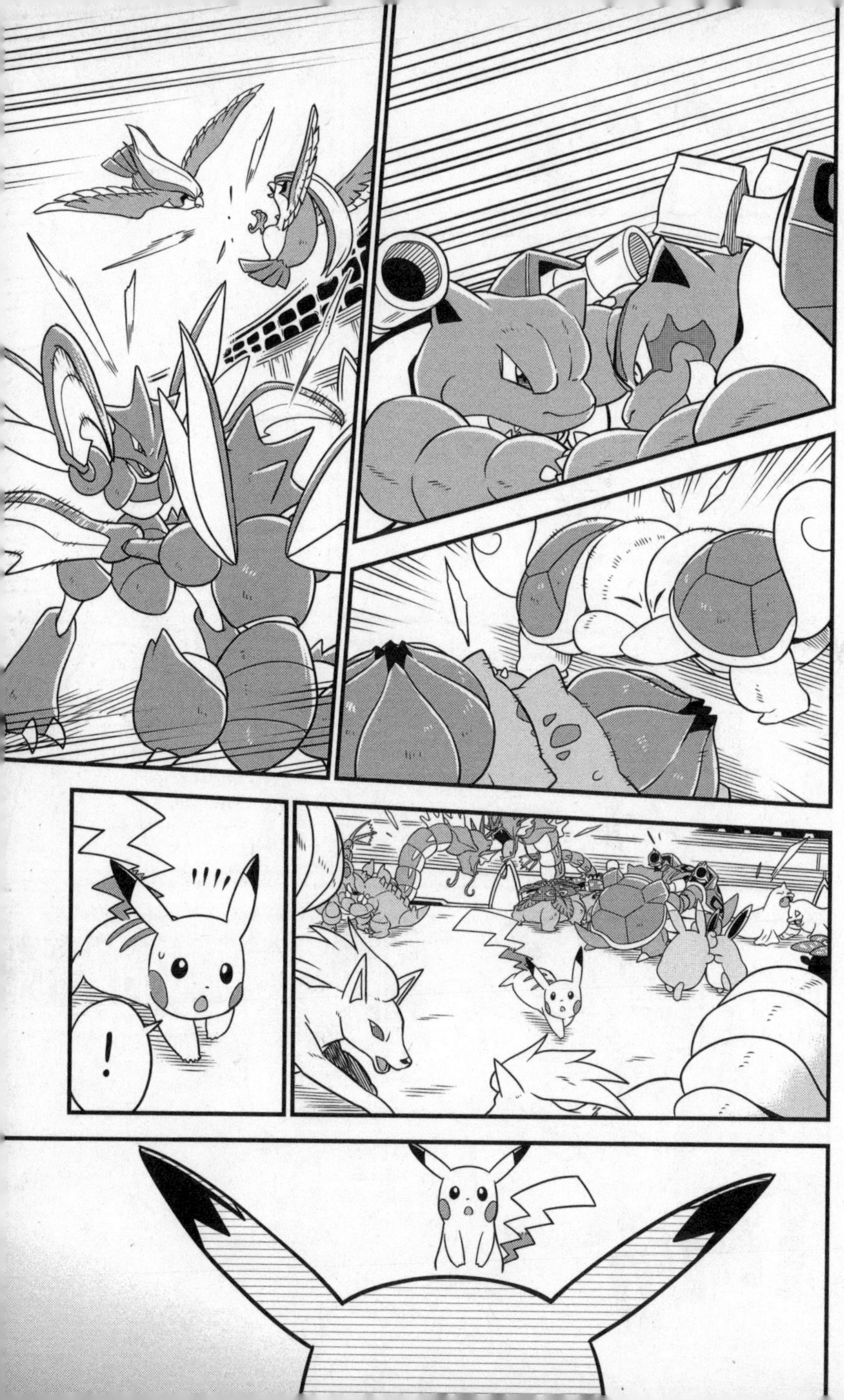
!

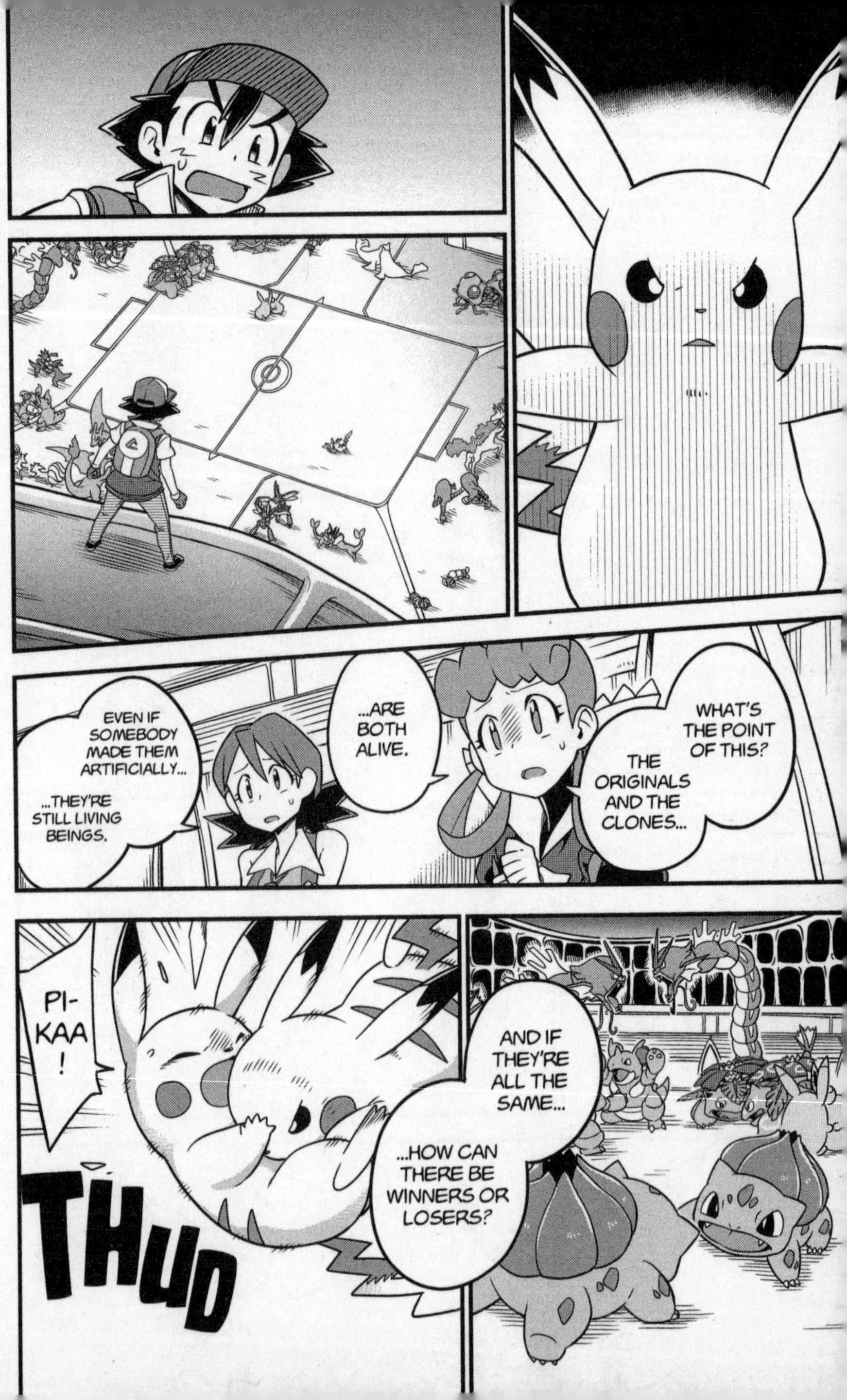
WHAT'S THE POINT OF THIS?
THE ORIGINALS AND THE CLONES...
...ARE BOTH ALIVE.
EVEN IF SOMEBODY MADE THEM ARTIFICIALLY...
...THEY'RE STILL LIVING BEINGS.
AND IF THEY'RE ALL THE SAME...
...HOW CAN THERE BE WINNERS OR LOSERS?
PI-KAA!
THUD

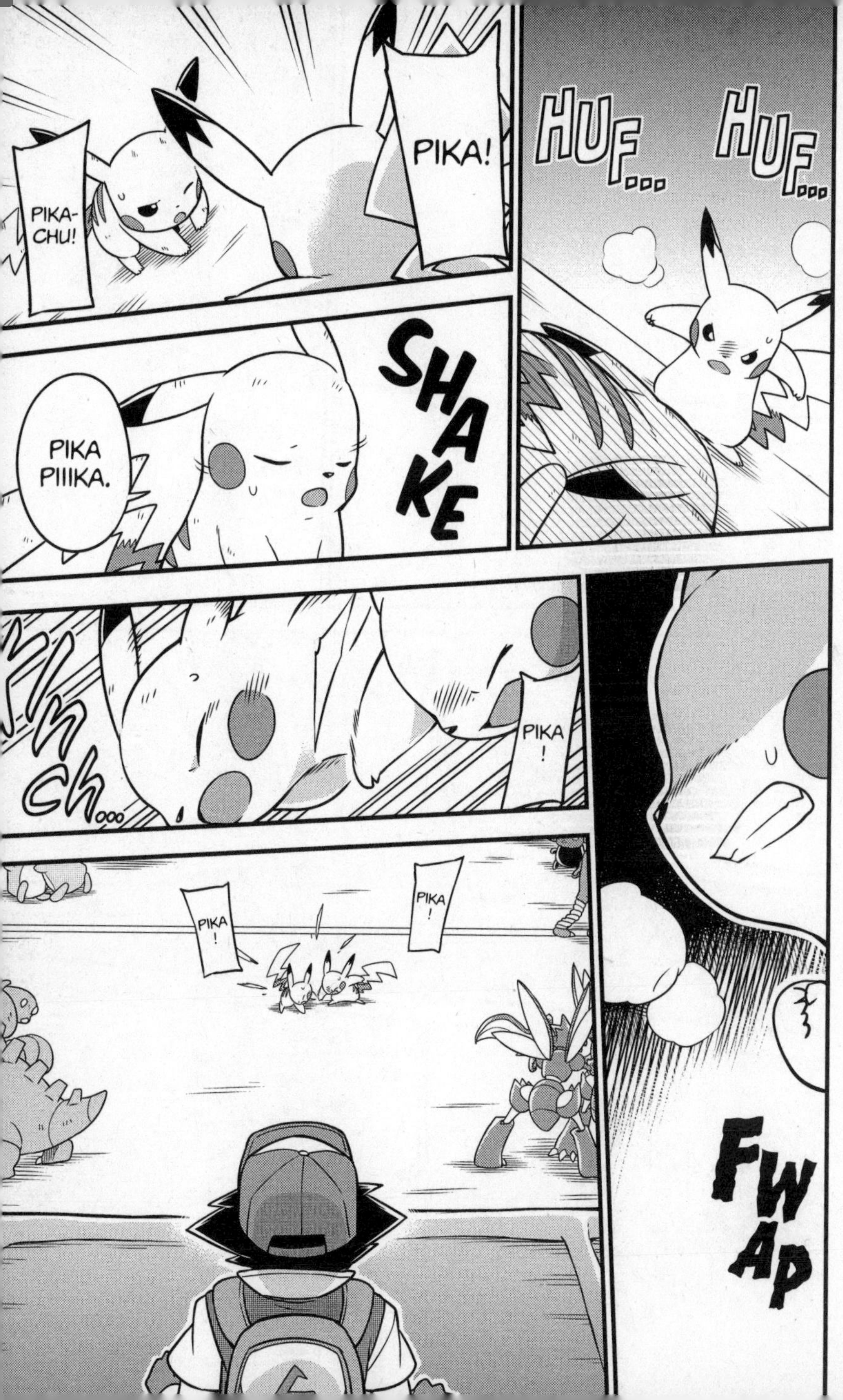
HUF... HUF...
PIKA!
PIKA-CHU!
SHAKE
PIKA PIIIKA.
FWAP
PIKA!
Mnch...
PIKA!
PIKA!

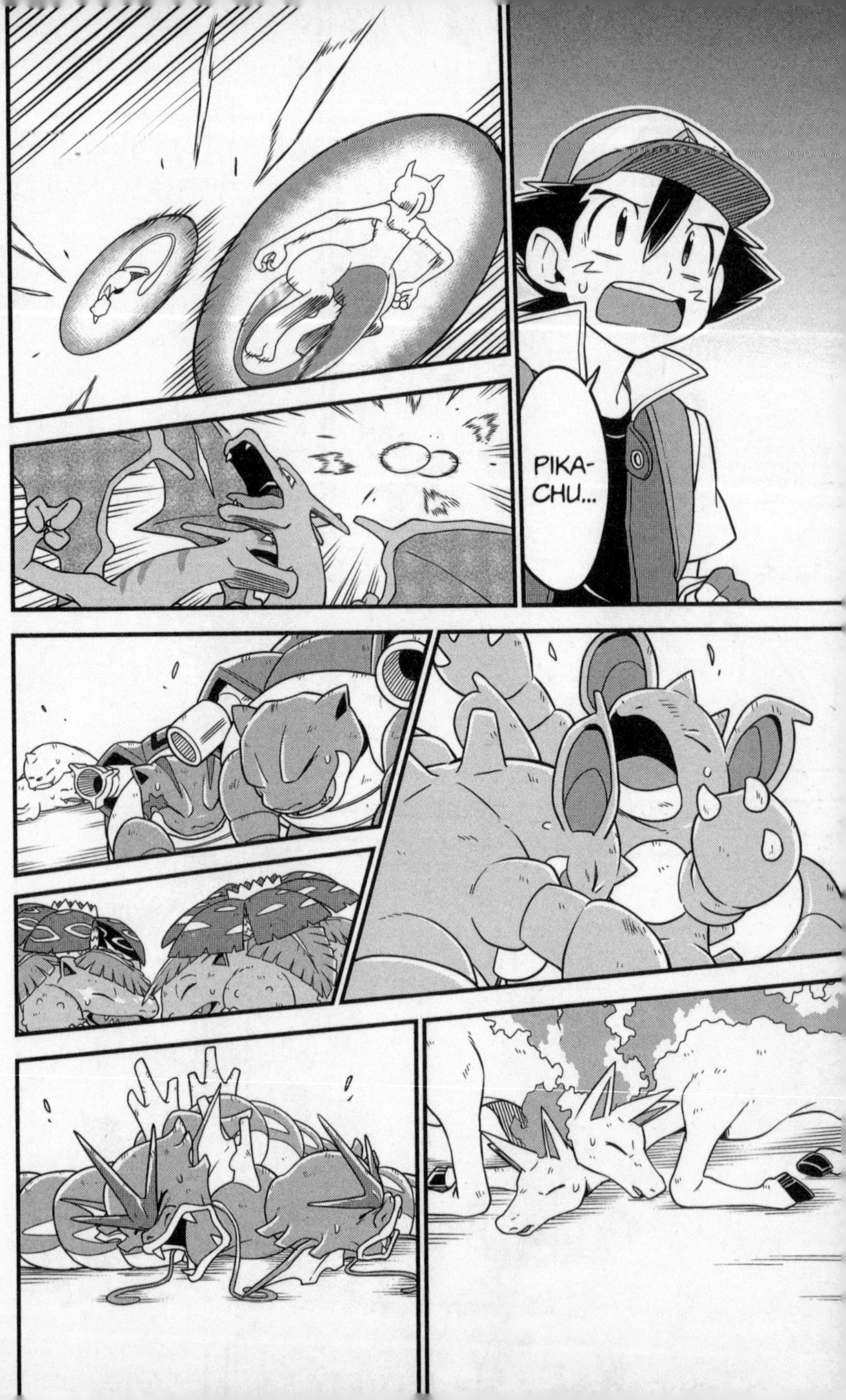
PIKA-
CHU...

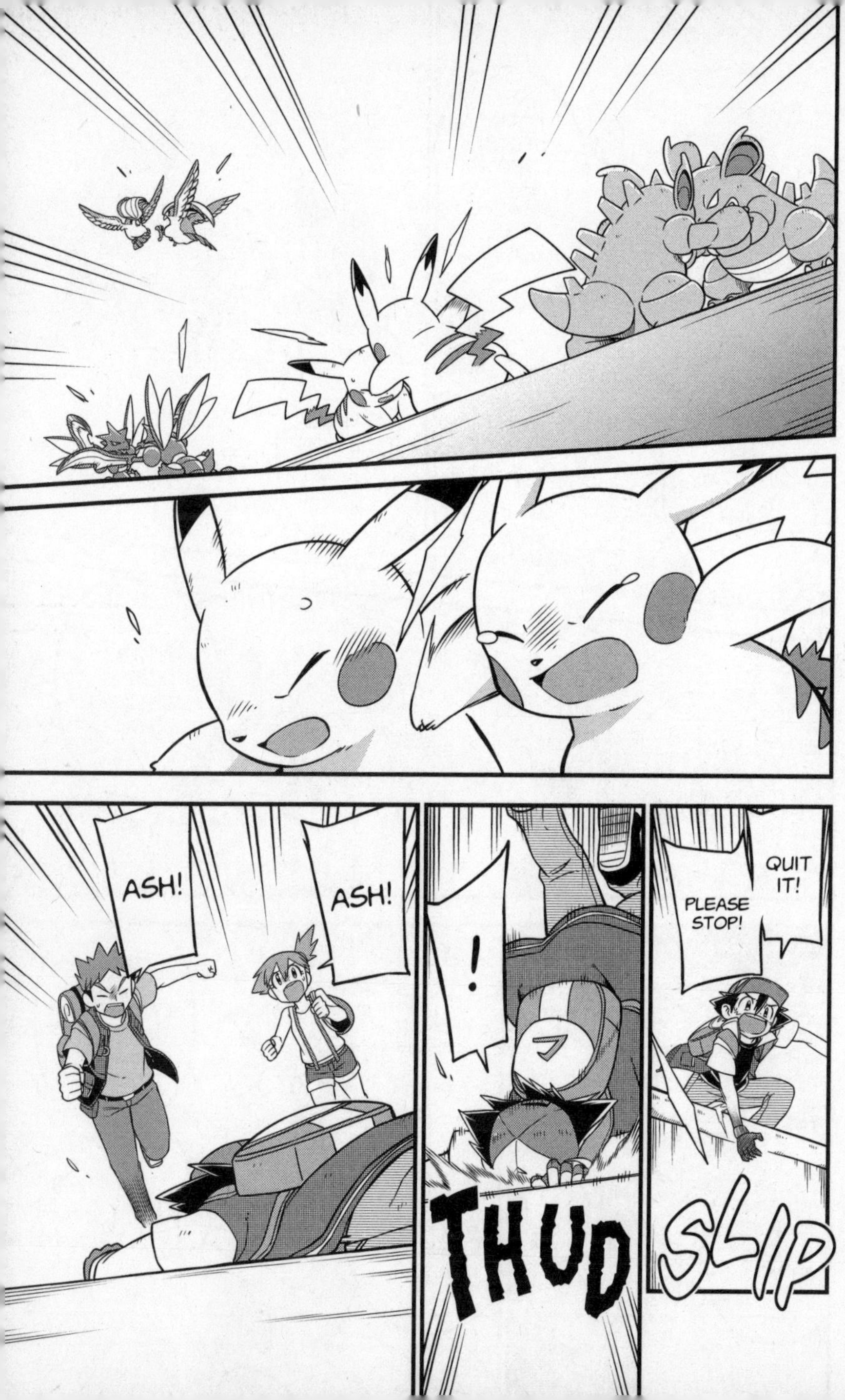
QUIT IT!
PLEASE STOP!
SLIP
!
THUD
ASH!
ASH!

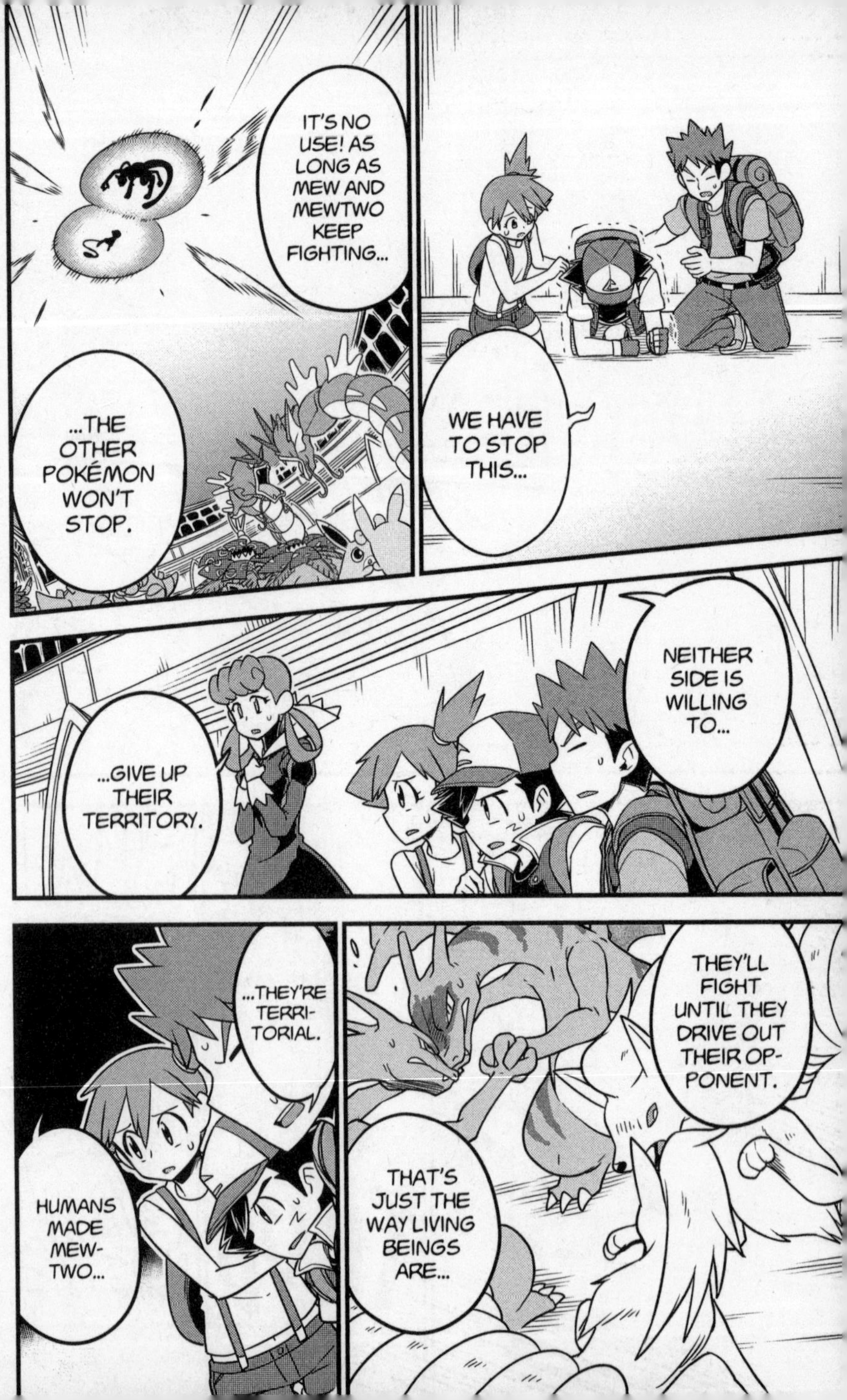
WE HAVE TO STOP THIS...
IT'S NO USE! AS LONG AS MEW AND MEWTWO KEEP FIGHTING...
...THE OTHER POKÉMON WON'T STOP.
NEITHER SIDE IS WILLING TO...
...GIVE UP THEIR TERRITORY.
THEY'LL FIGHT UNTIL THEY DRIVE OUT THEIR OPPONENT.
THAT'S JUST THE WAY LIVING BEINGS ARE...
...THEY'RE TERRITORIAL.
HUMANS MADE MEWTWO...

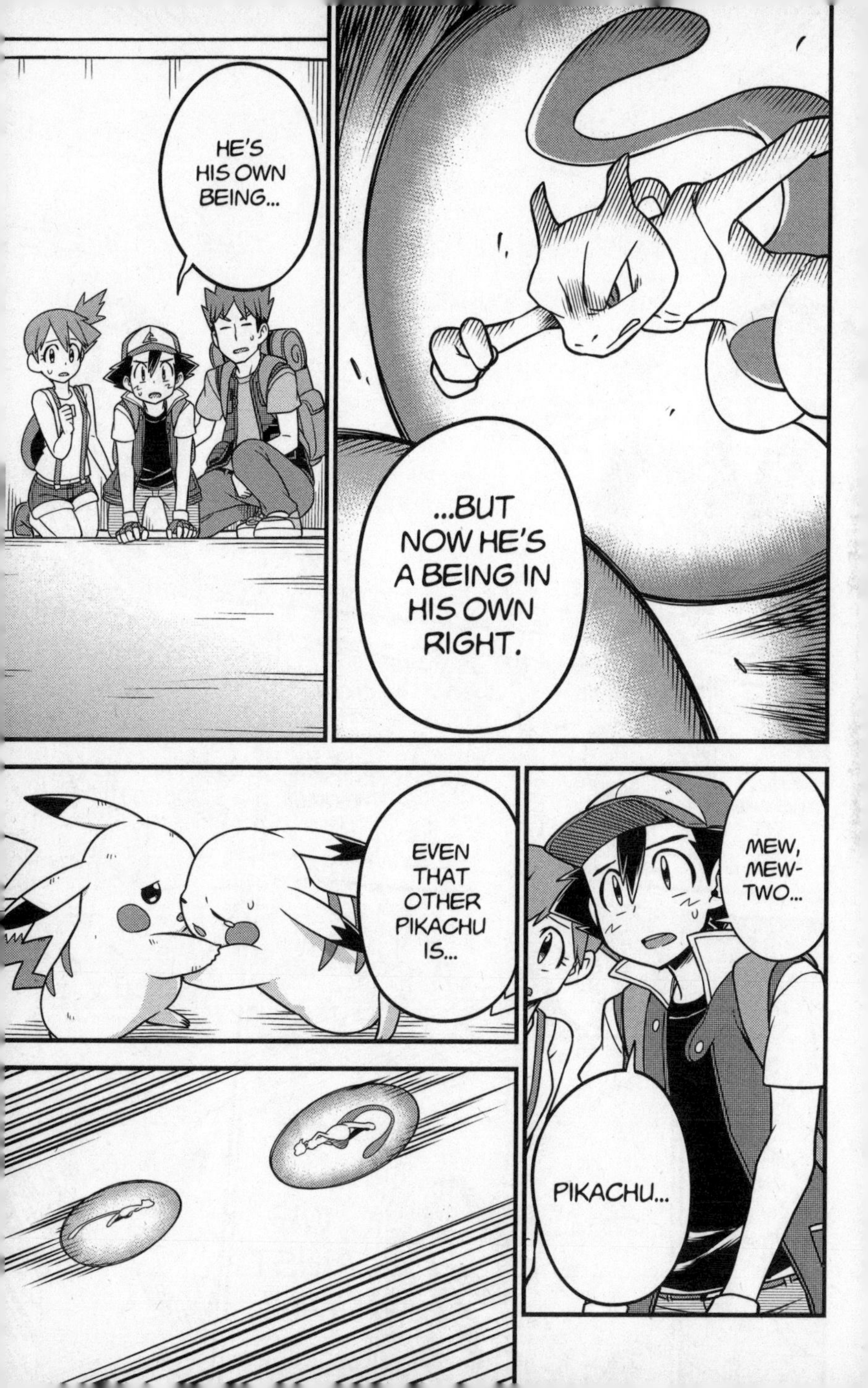
HE'S HIS OWN BEING...
...BUT NOW HE'S A BEING IN HIS OWN RIGHT.
EVEN THAT OTHER PIKACHU IS...
MEW, MEW-TWO...
PIKACHU...

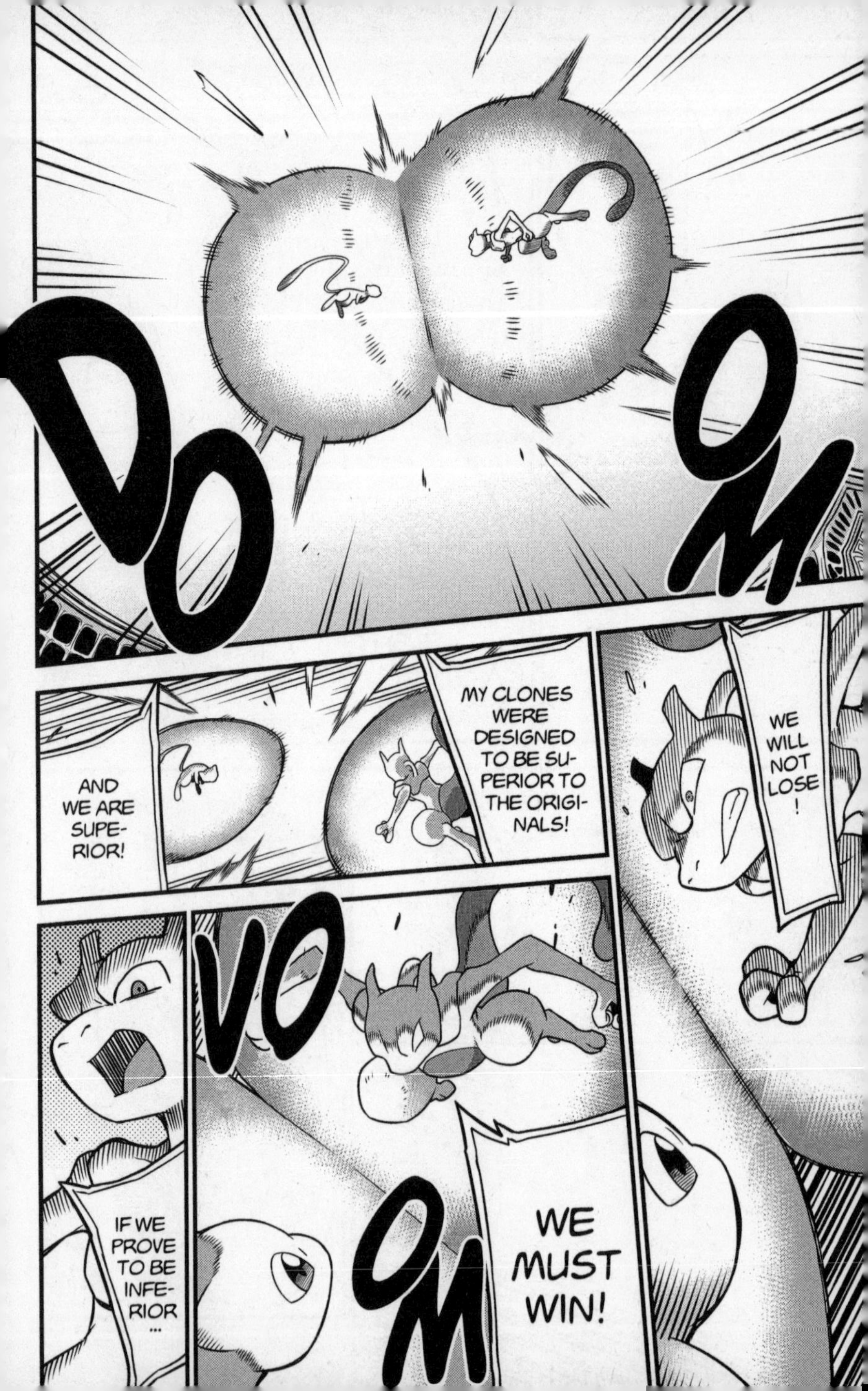
DOOM
WE WILL NOT LOSE!
MY CLONES WERE DESIGNED TO BE SU-PERIOR TO THE ORIGI-NALS!
AND WE ARE SUPE-RIOR!
VOOM
WE MUST WIN!
IF WE PROVE TO BE INFE-RIOR...

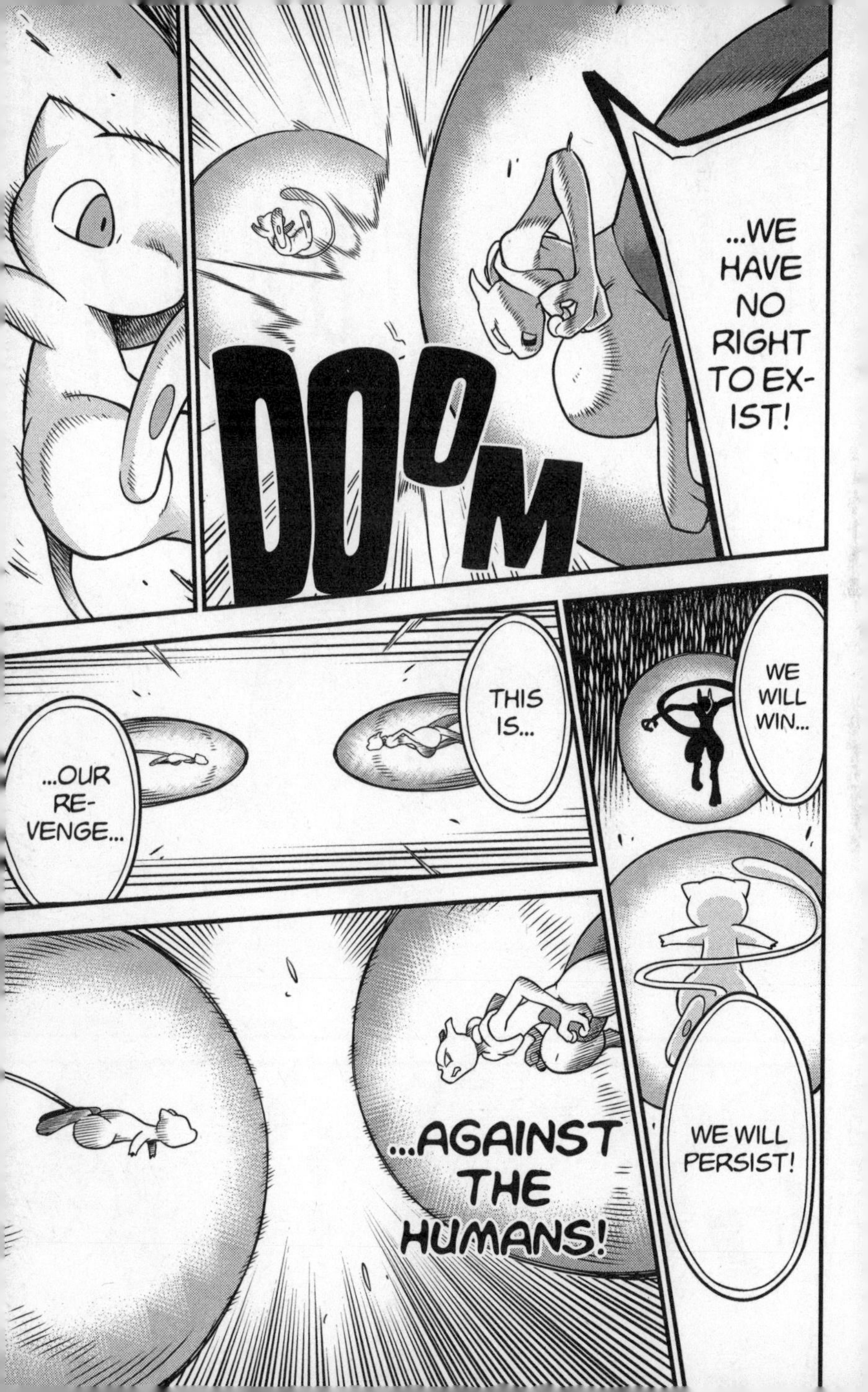
...WE HAVE NO RIGHT TO EXIST!
DOOOM
WE WILL WIN...
THIS IS...
...OUR REVENGE...
WE WILL PERSIST!
...AGAINST THE HUMANS!

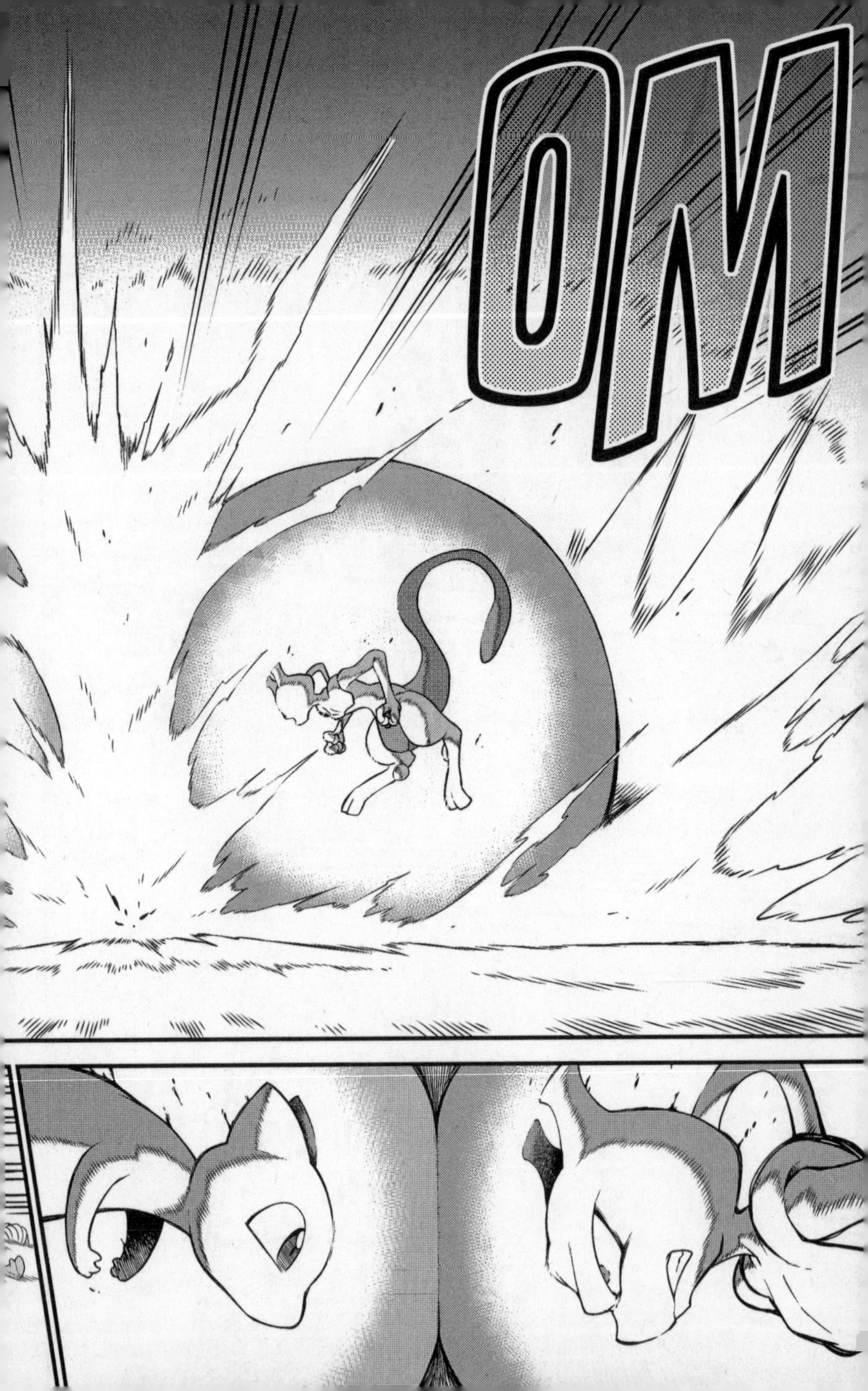
OM

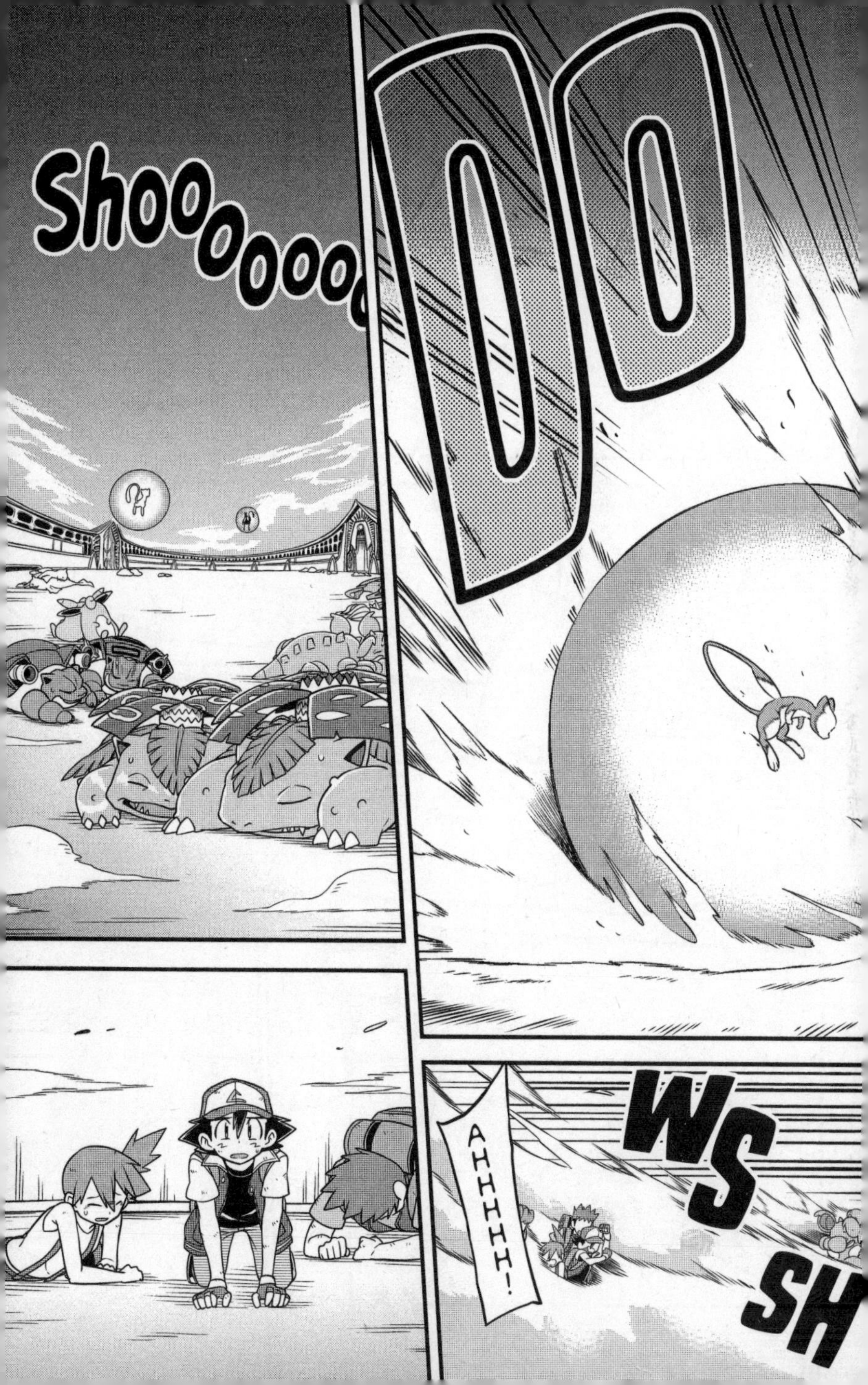
ShooooooOO
AHHHHH!
WSSH

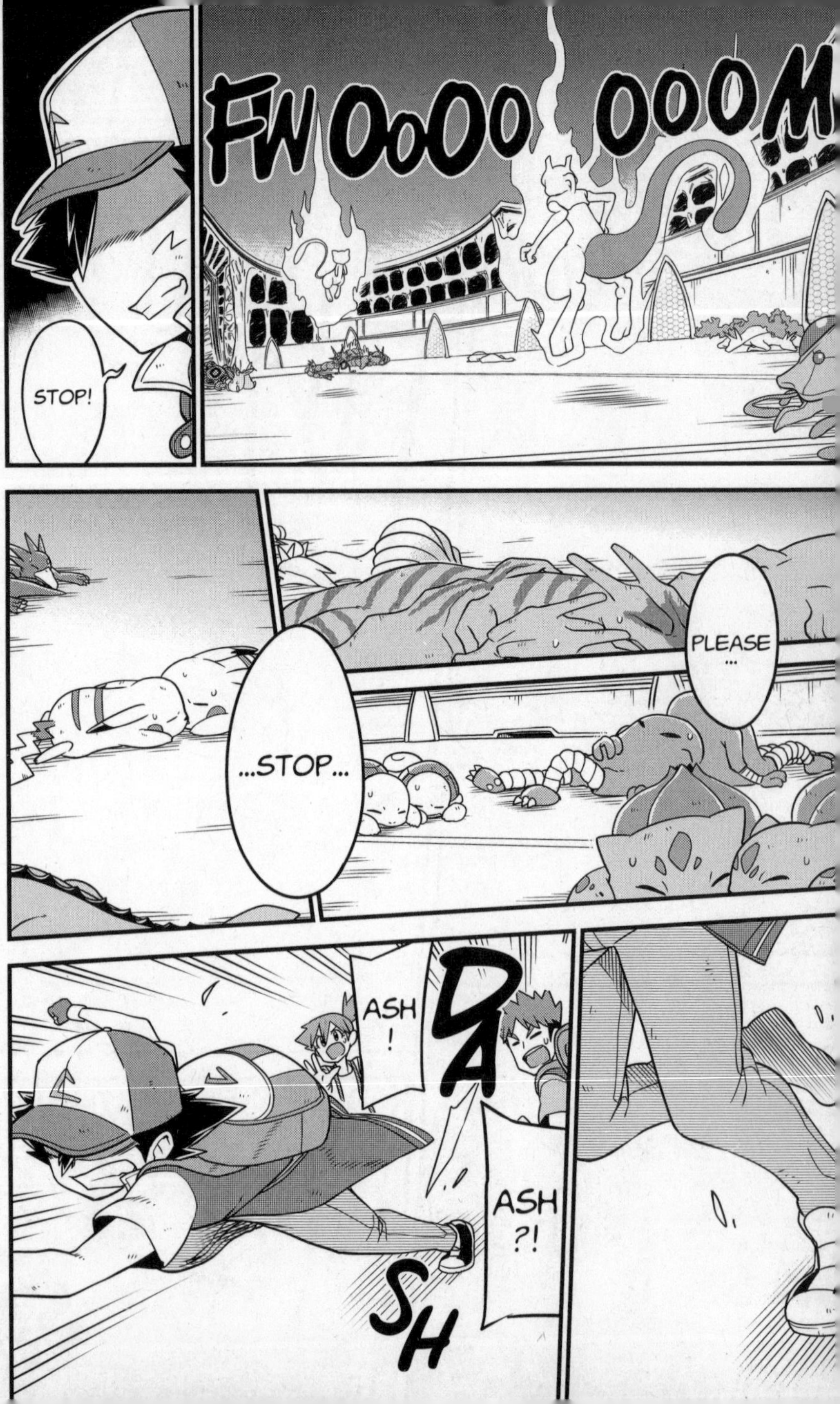
FWOOOO OOOM
STOP!
PLEASE ...
...STOP...
DA
ASH !
ASH ?!
SH

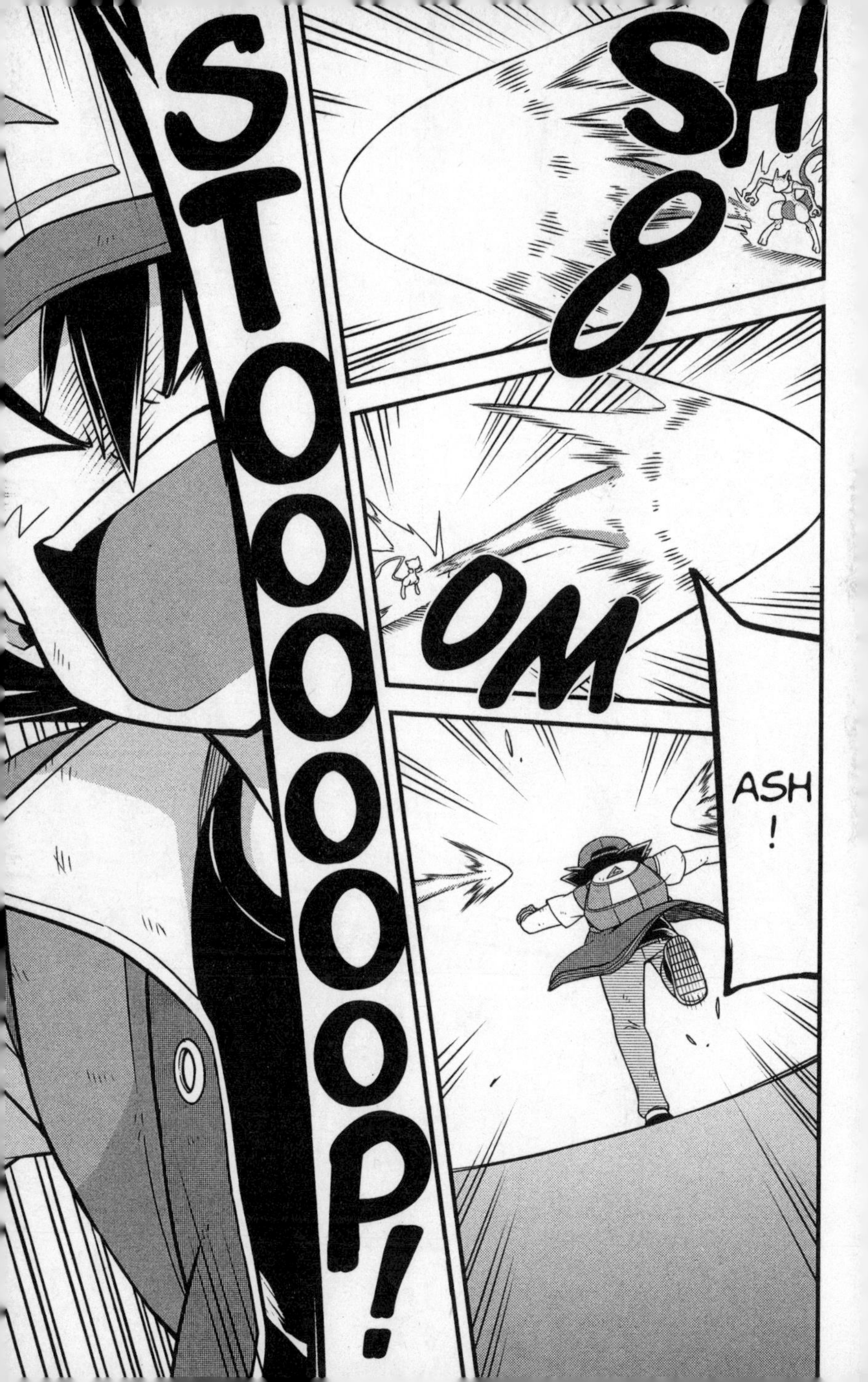
SHOOOM
ASH!
STOOOOOOOP!

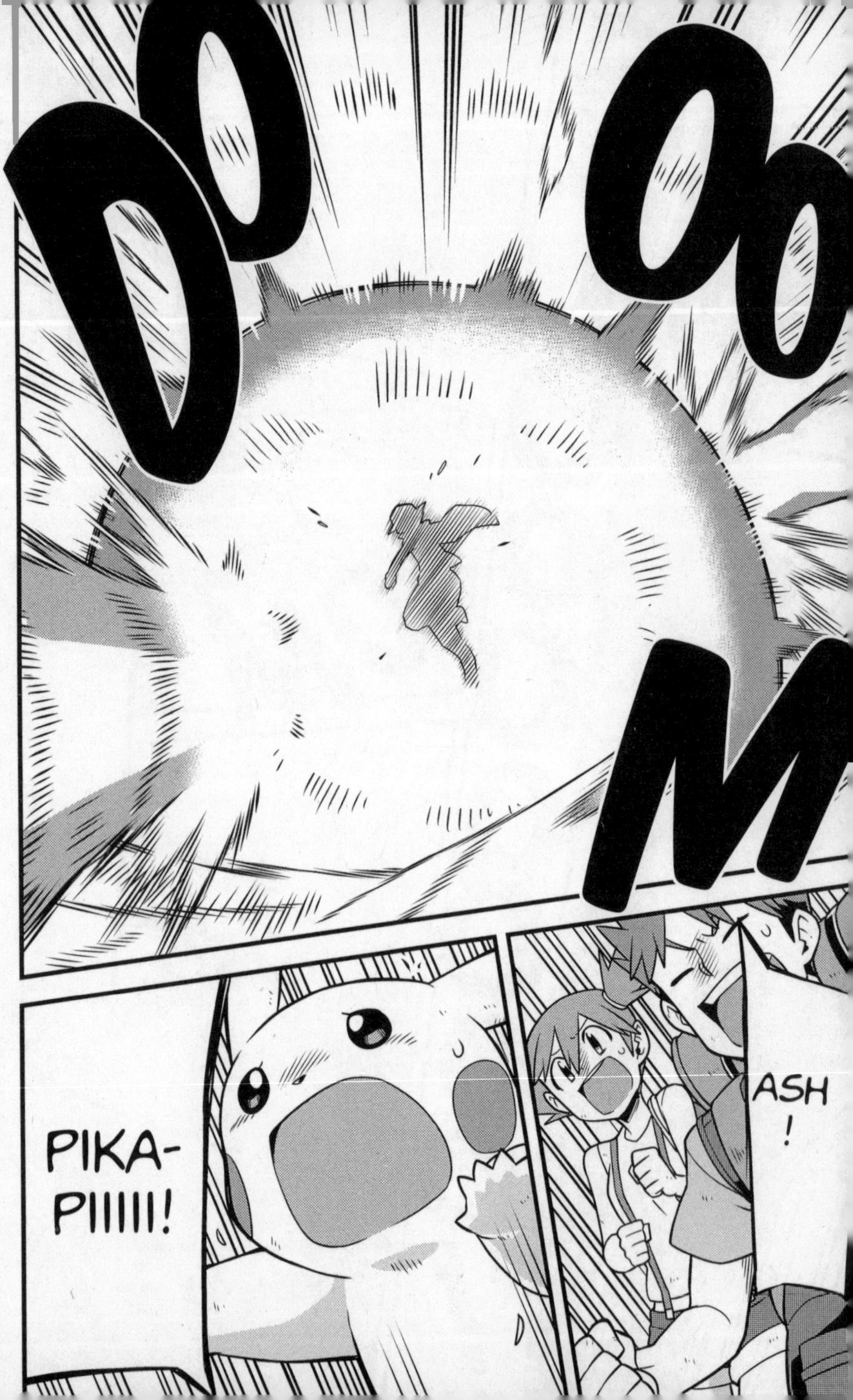
DOOOM
ASH!
PIKA-PIIIIII!

Pokémon™

MEWTWO STRIKES BACK

EVOLUTION

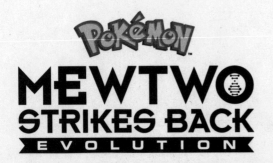

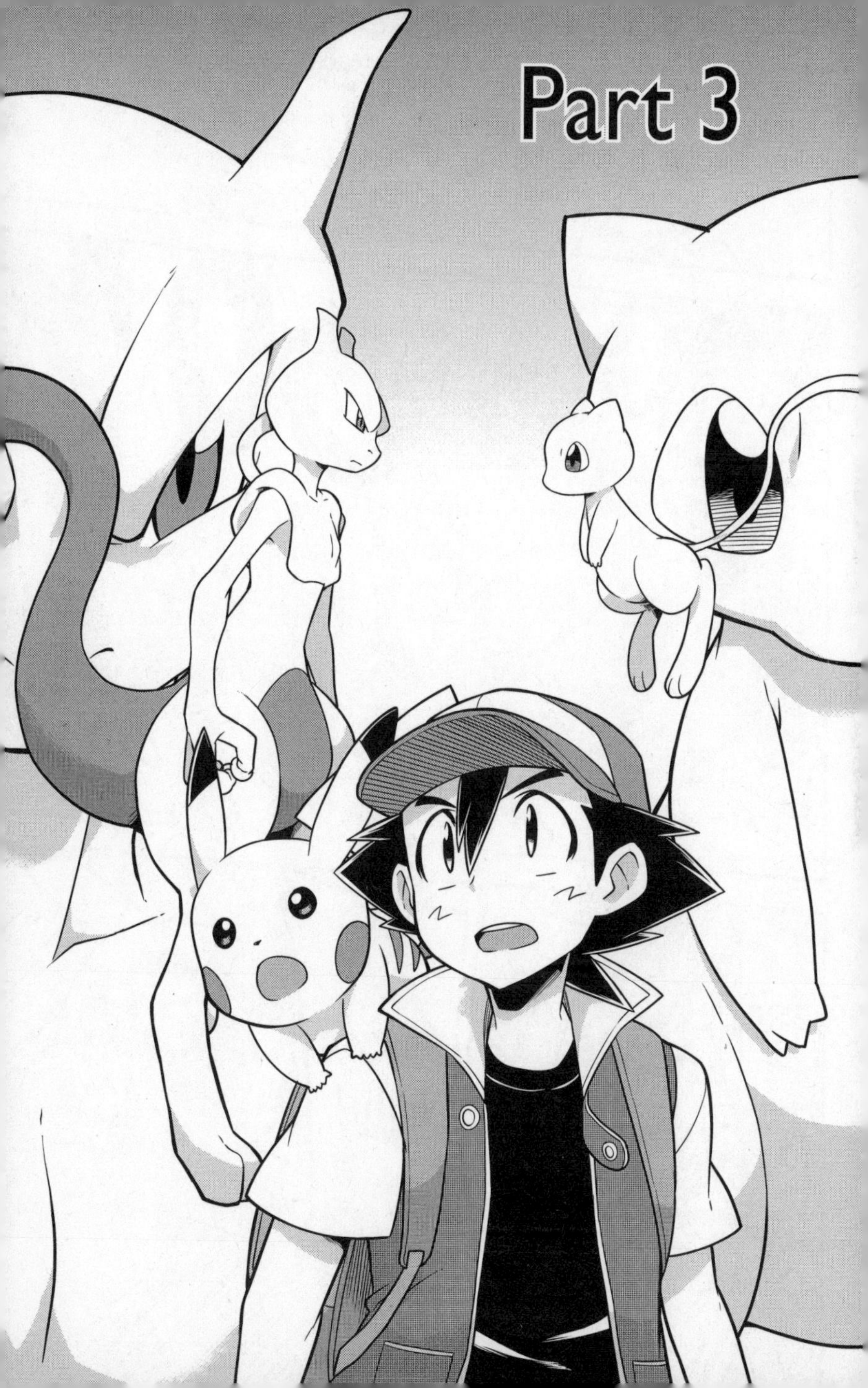
Part 3

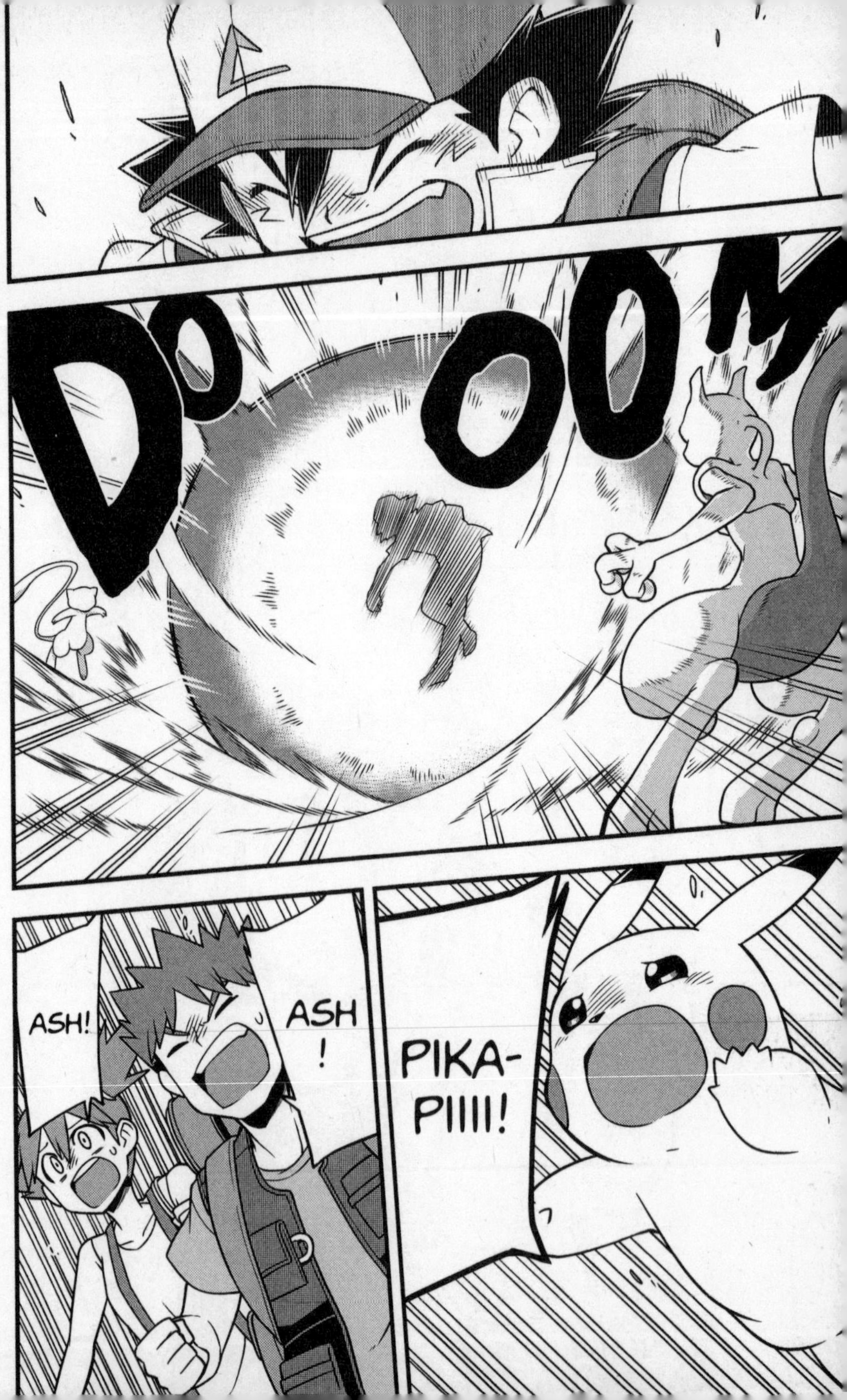
DOOOM
PIKA-PIIII!
ASH !
ASH!

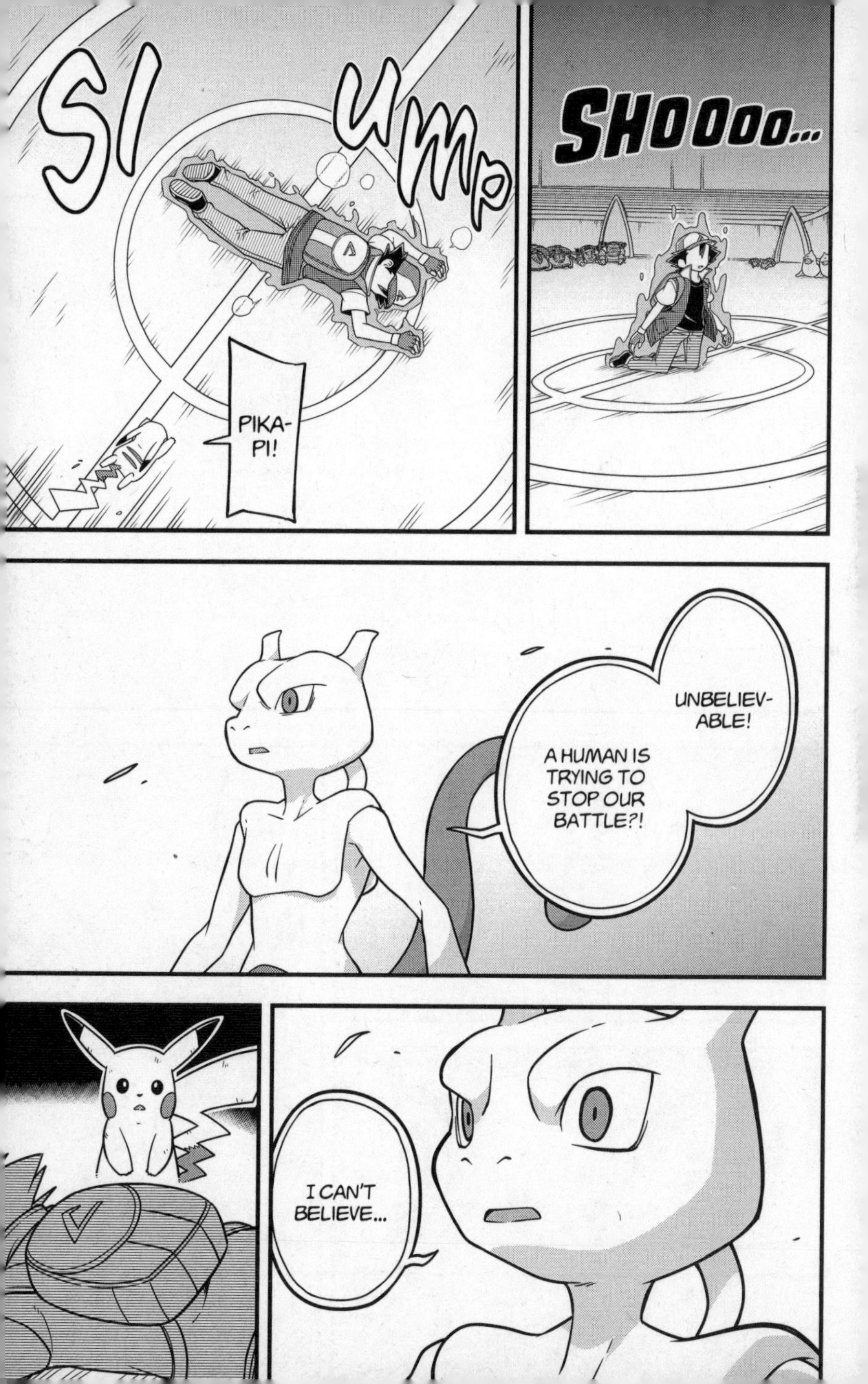
SHOOOO...
SLUMP
PIKA-PI!
UNBELIEVABLE!
A HUMAN IS TRYING TO STOP OUR BATTLE?!
I CAN'T BELIEVE...

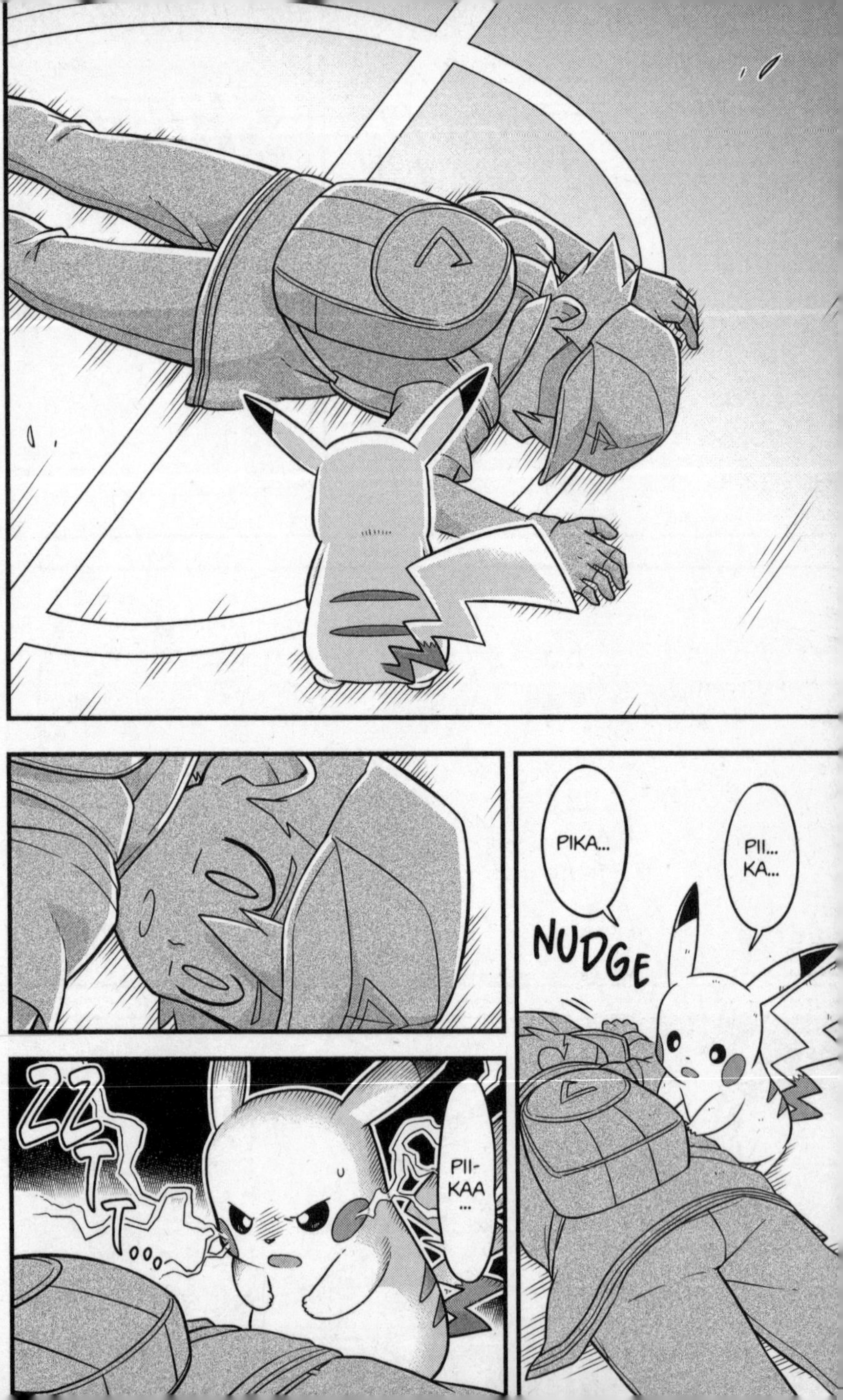
PII... KA...
PIKA...
NUDGE
PII-KAA...
ZZTT...

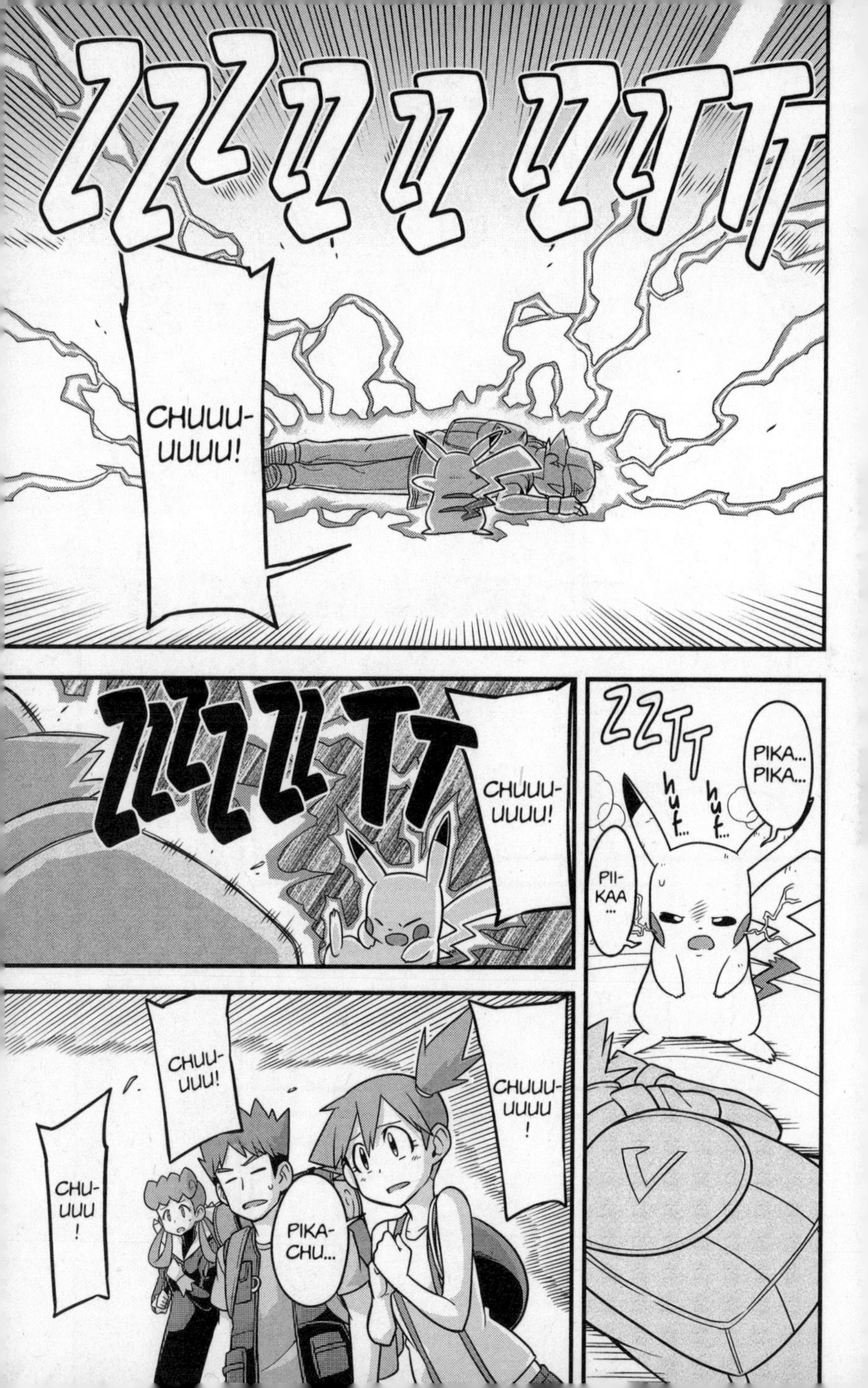
ZZZZZZZZZTTT
CHUUU-UUUU!
ZZTT
PIKA... PIKA...
huf... huf...
PII-KAA...
ZZZZZTT
CHUUU-UUUU!
CHUUU-UUUU!
CHUU-UUU!
PIKA-CHU...
CHU-UUU!

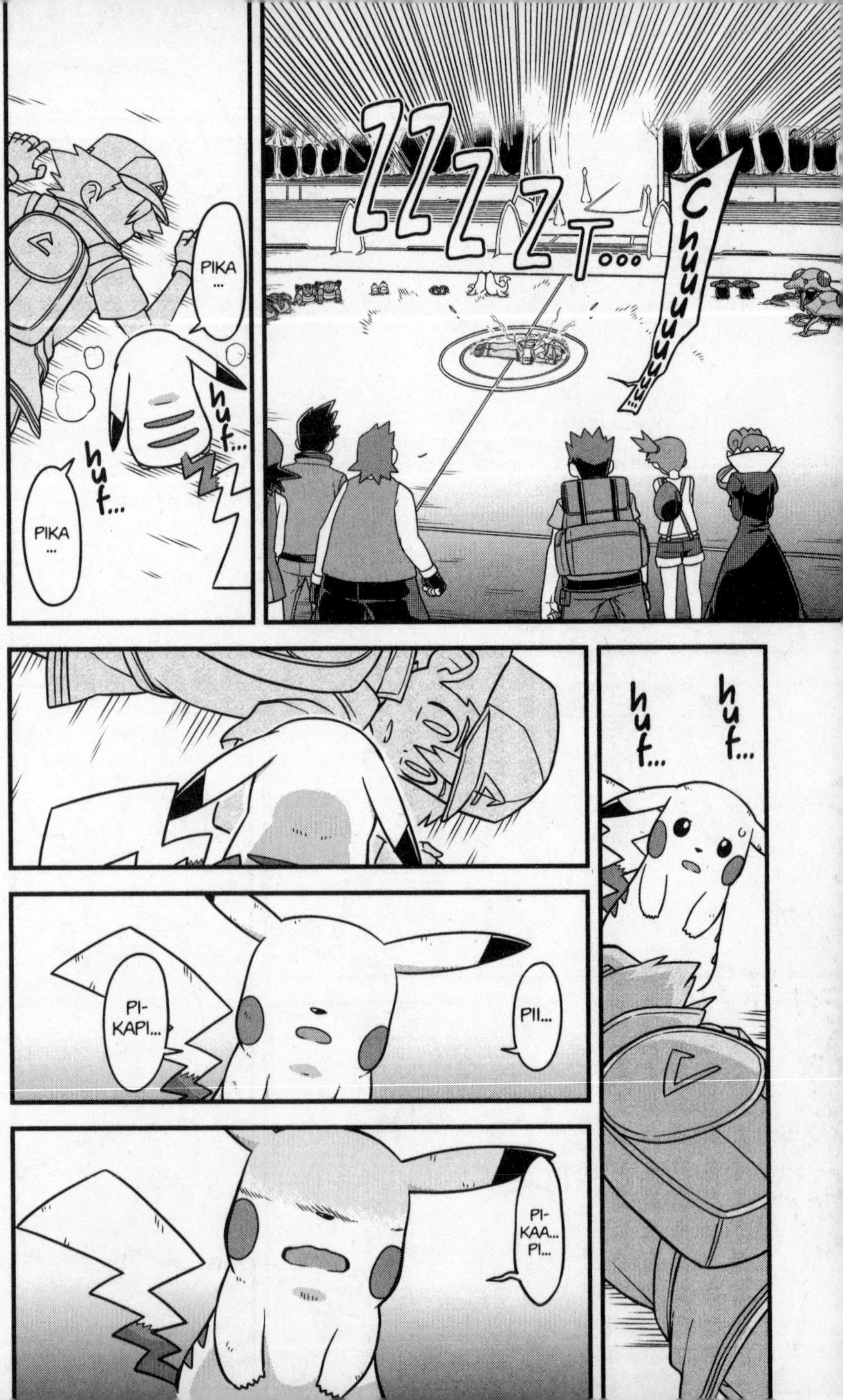
ZZZZZT...
Chuuuuuuuuu
PIKA...
huf...
huf...
PIKA...
huf...
huf...
PII...
PI-KAPI...
PI-KAAA... PI...

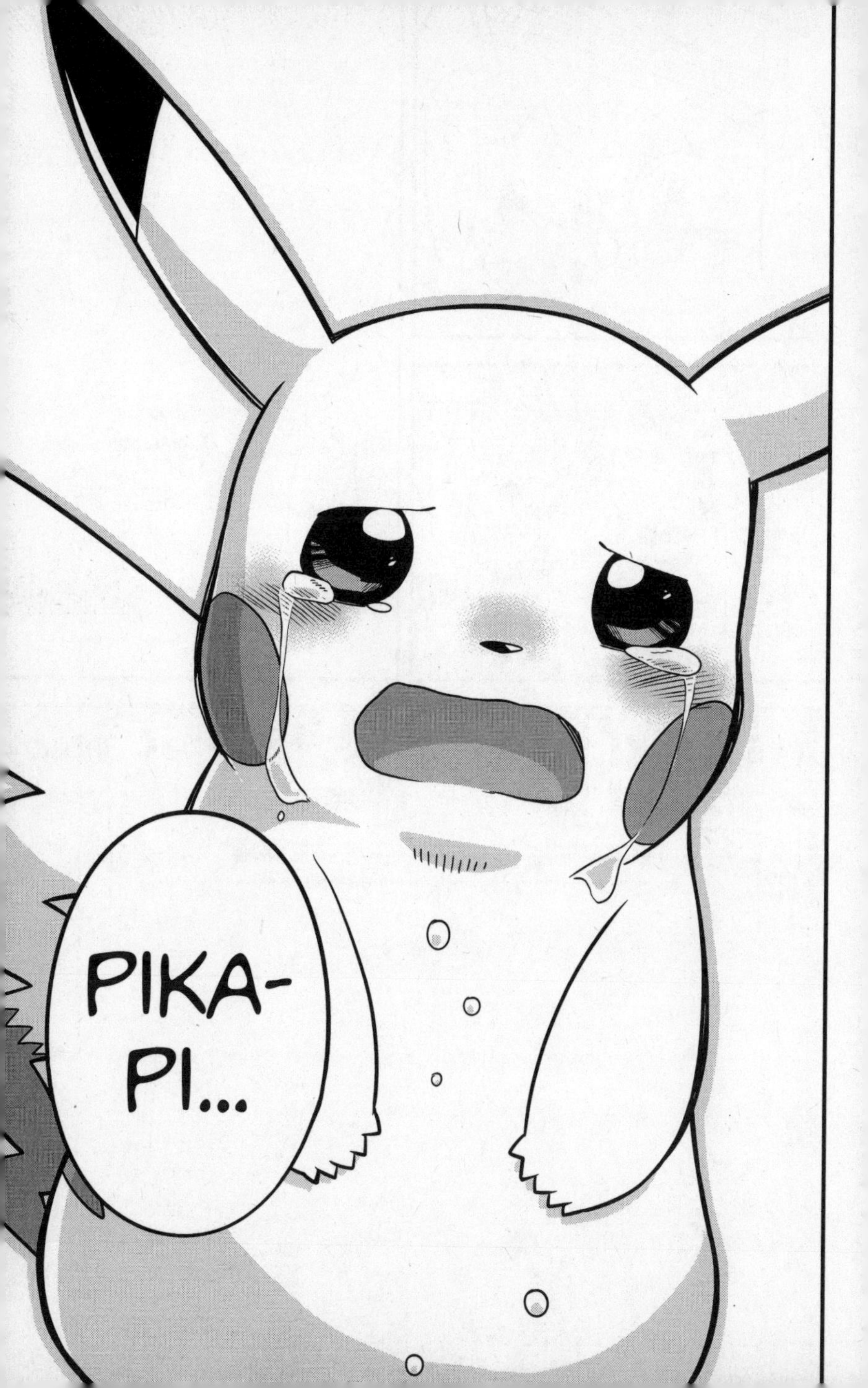
PIKA-PI...

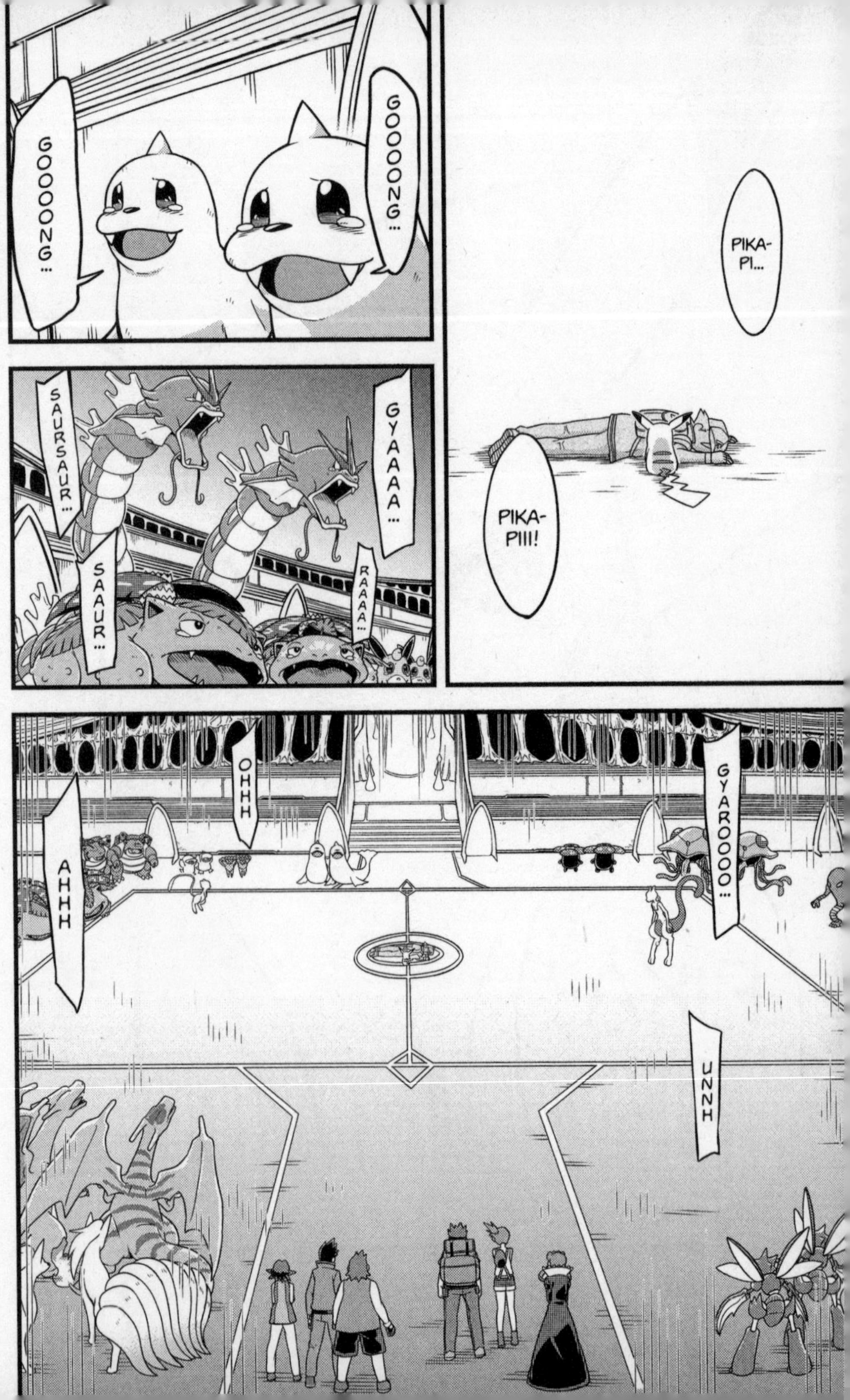
PIKA-PI...
PIKA-PIII!
GOOOOONG...
GOOOOONG...
GYAAAAA...
RAAAAA...
SAURSAUR...
SAAAUR...
GYAROOOO...
UNNH
OHHH
AHHH

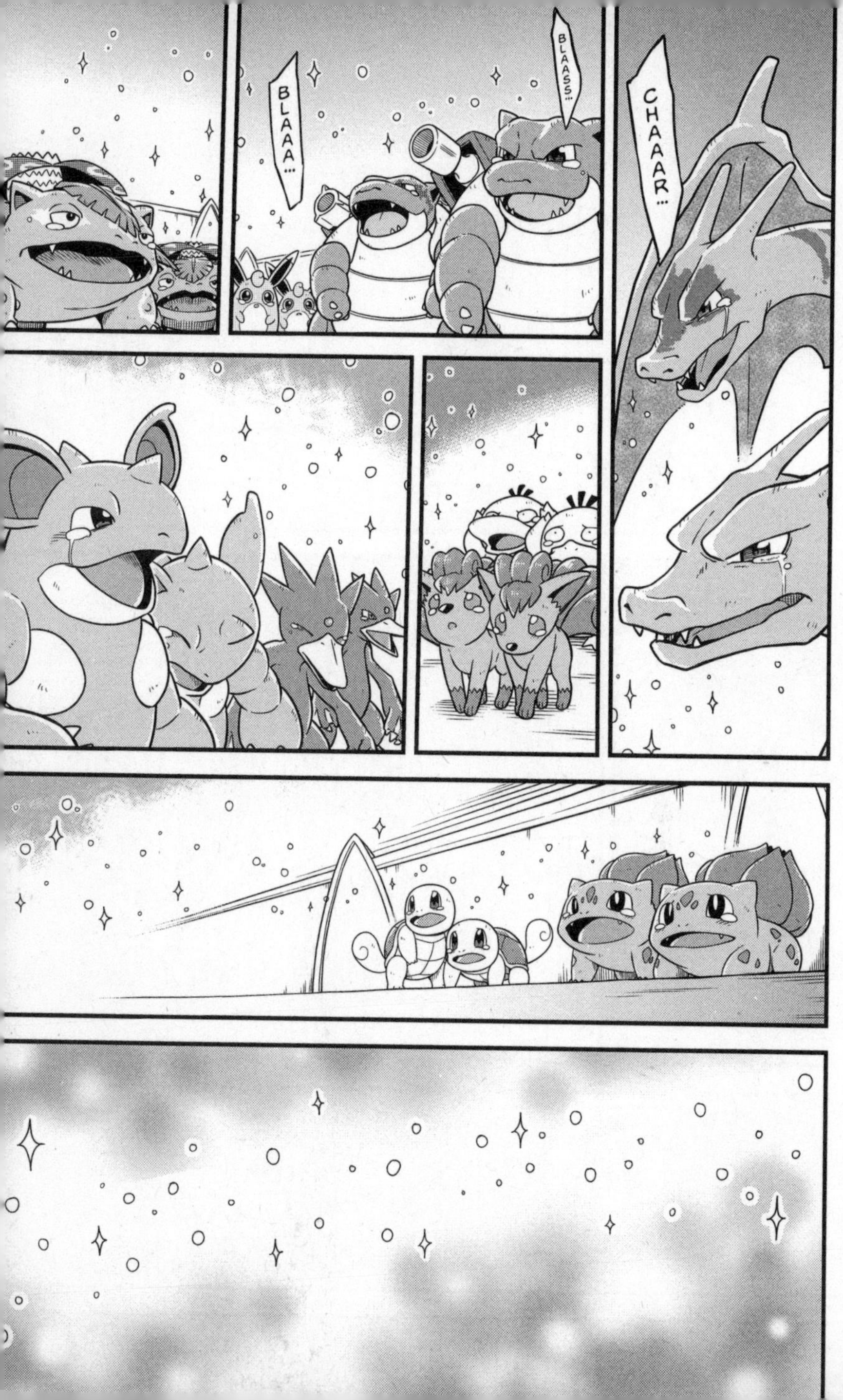
CHAAAR...
BLAAASS...
BLAAA...

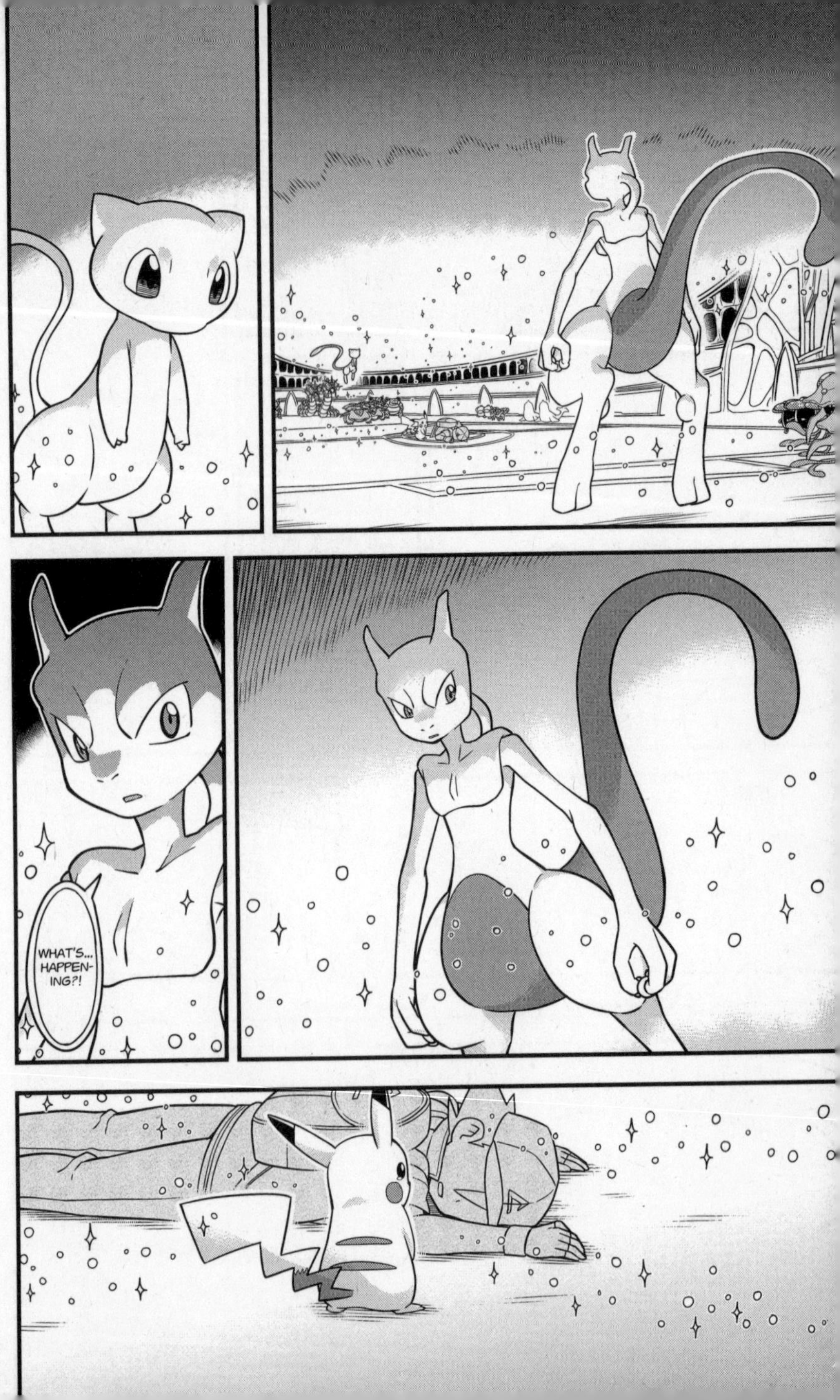
WHAT'S... HAPPENING?!

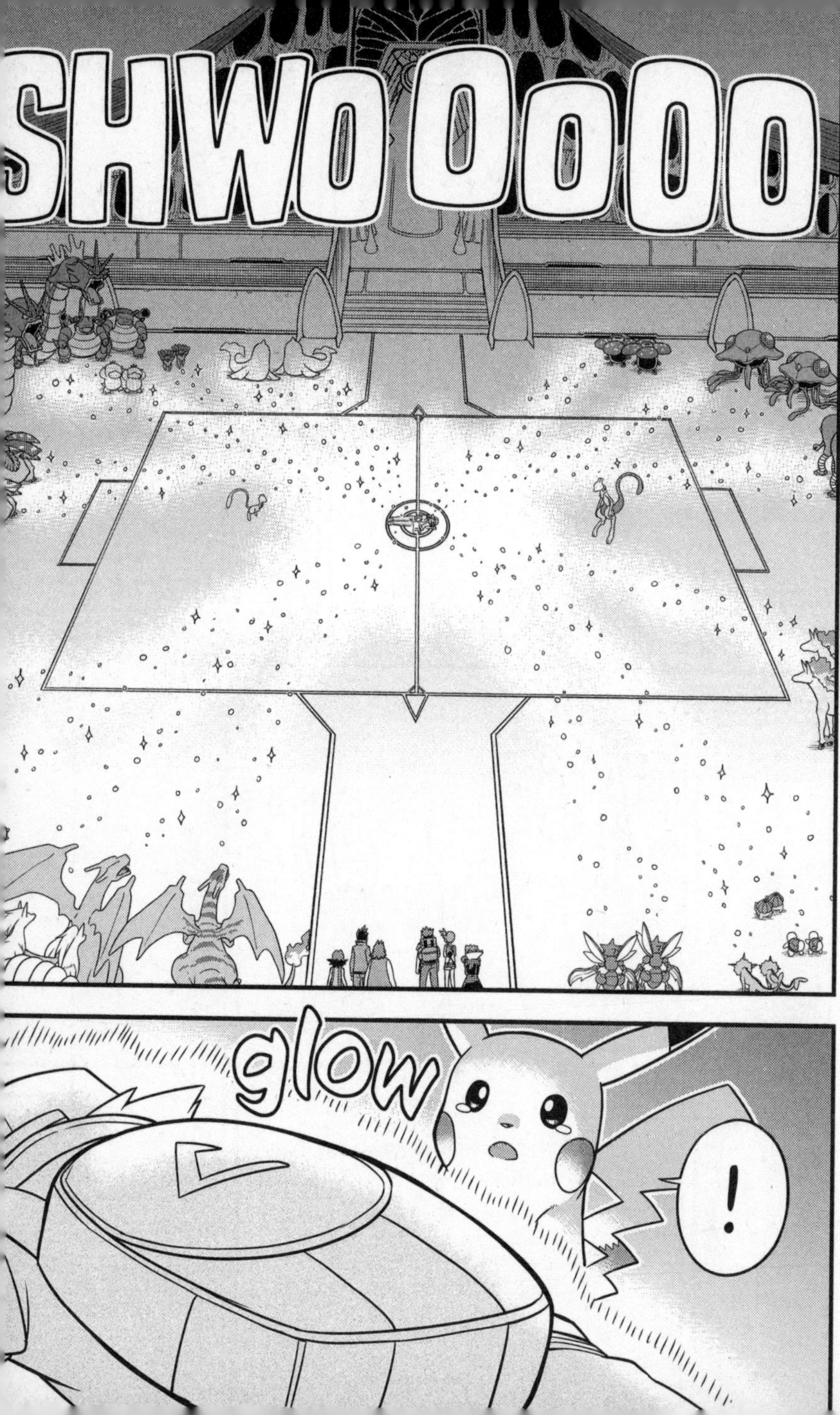
SHWOOOOO
glow
!

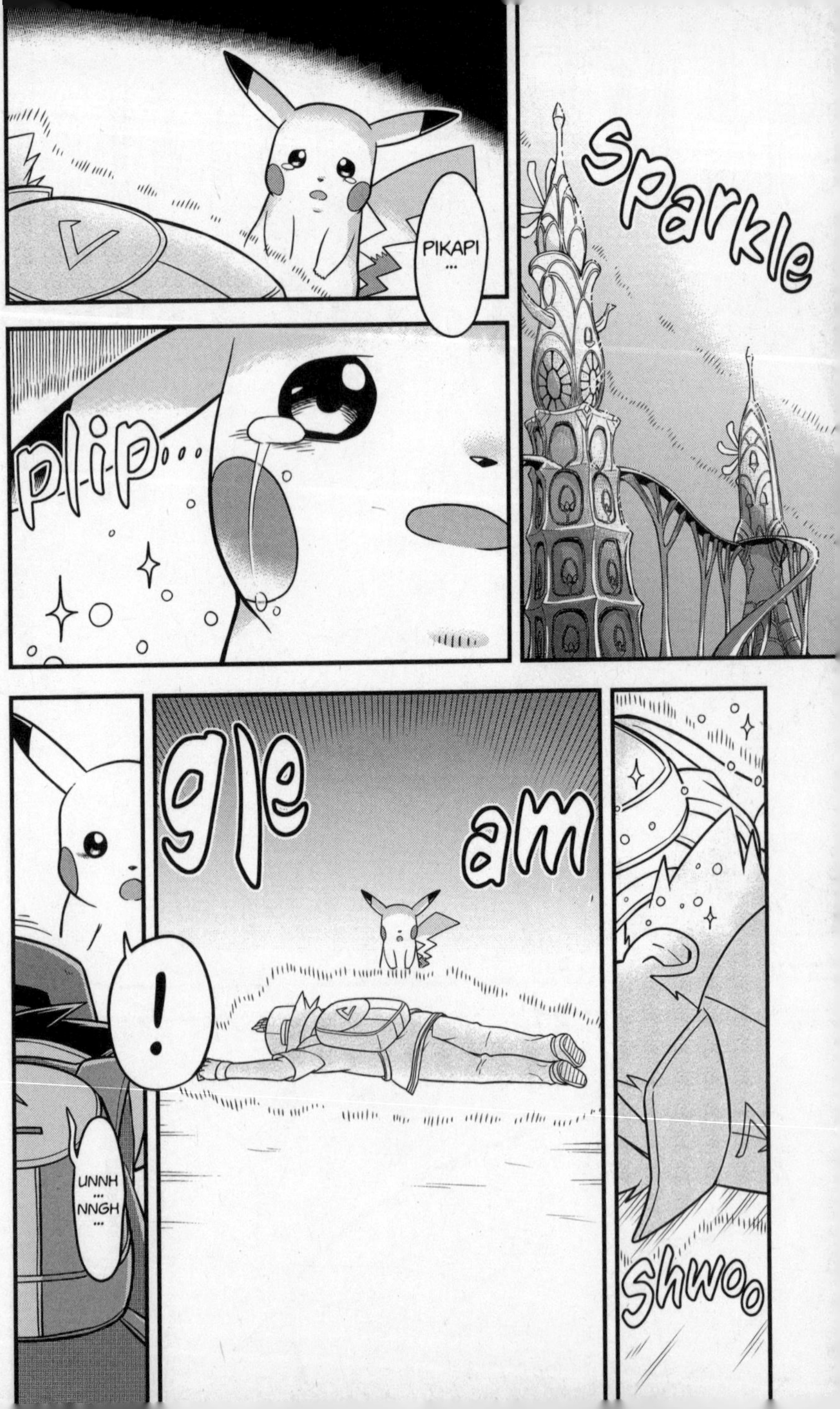
Sparkle
PIKAPI ...
plip...
Shwoo
gle
am
!
UNNH ... NNGH ...

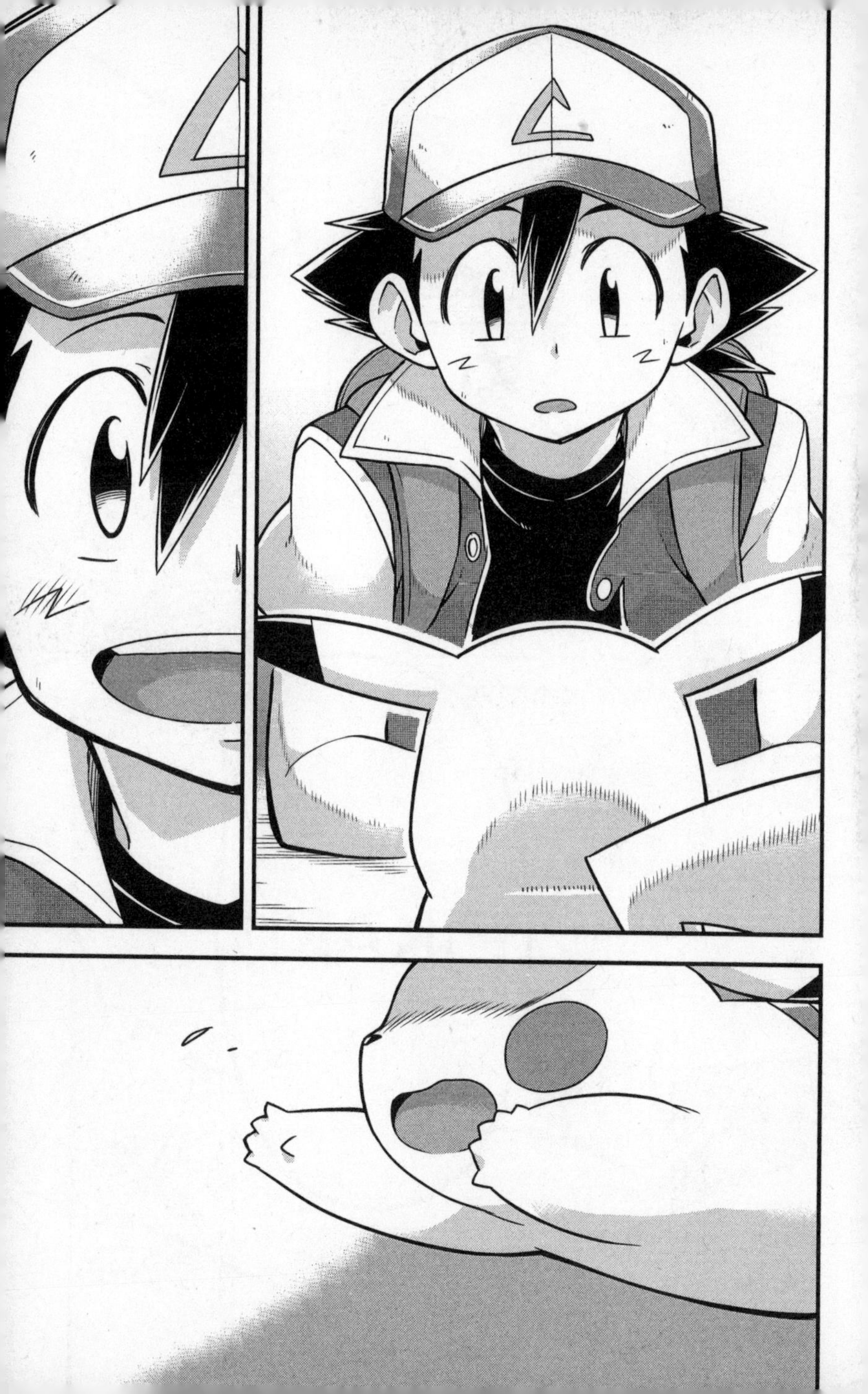

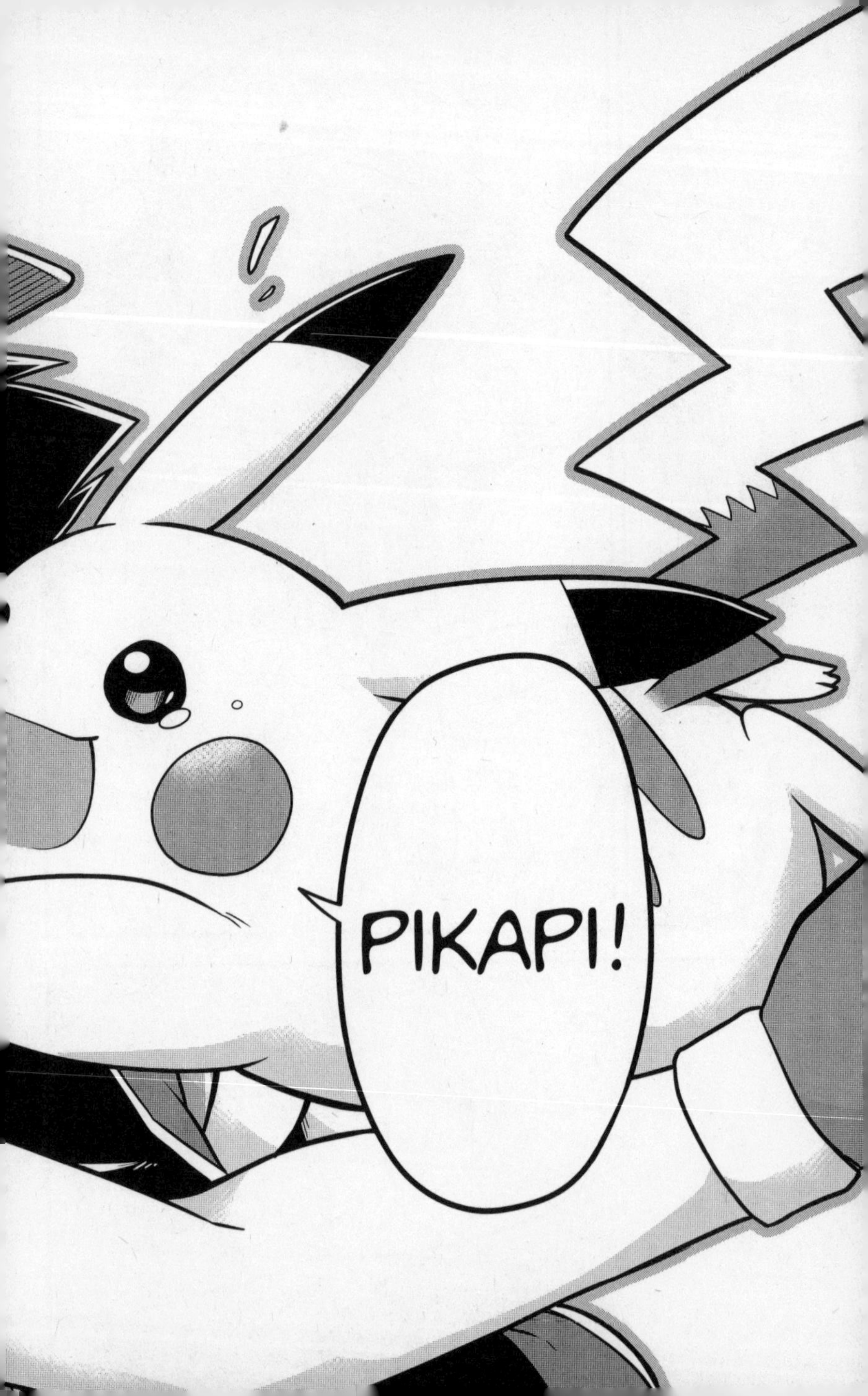
!
PIKAPI!

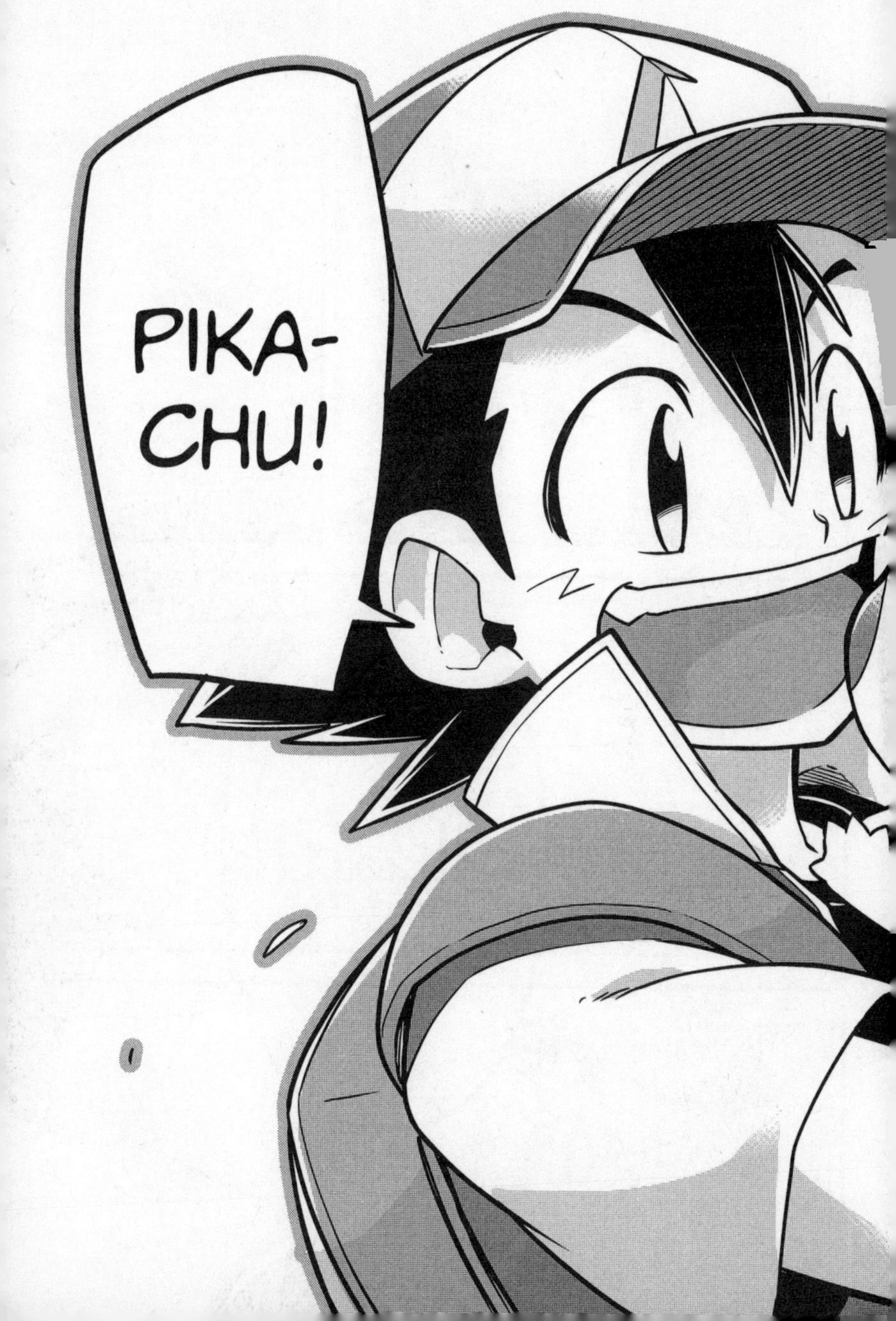
PIKA-CHU!

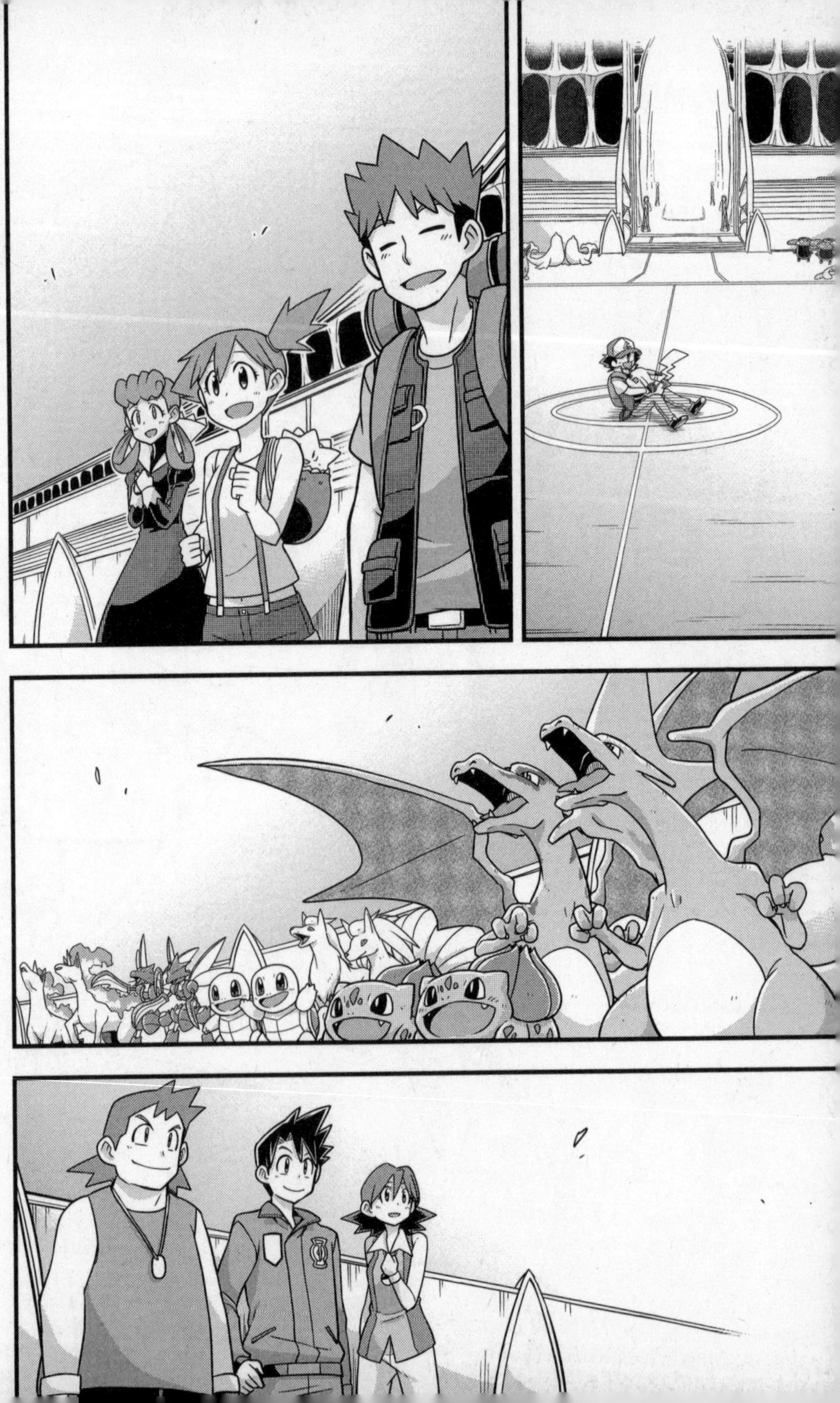

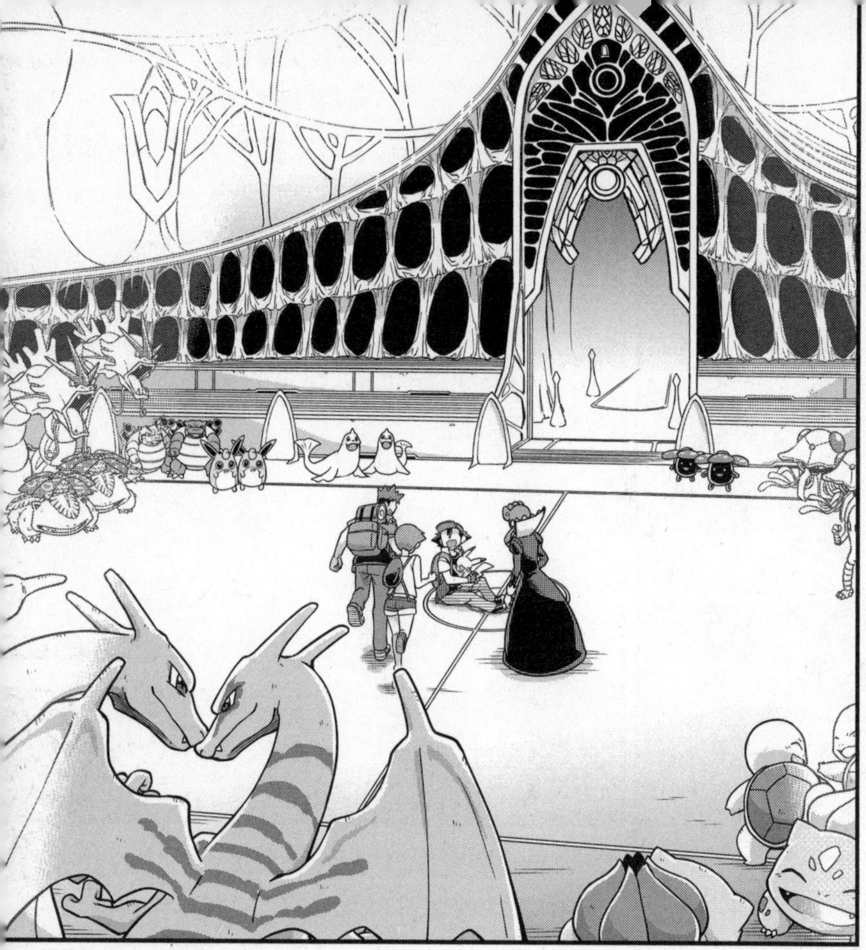
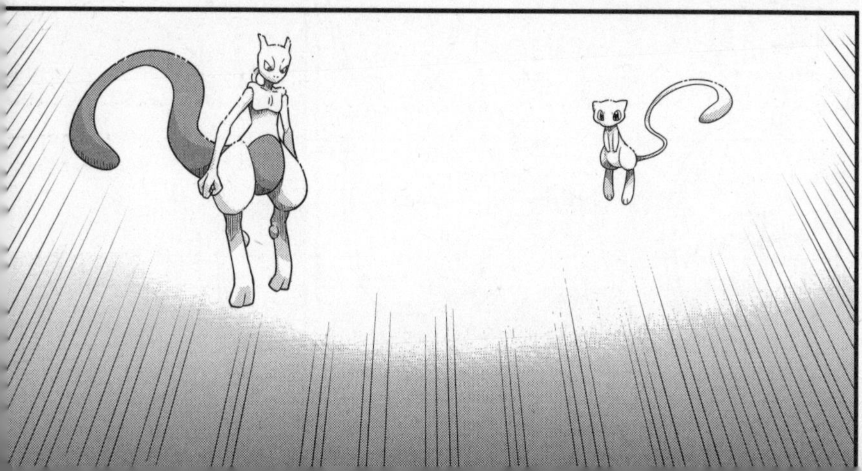

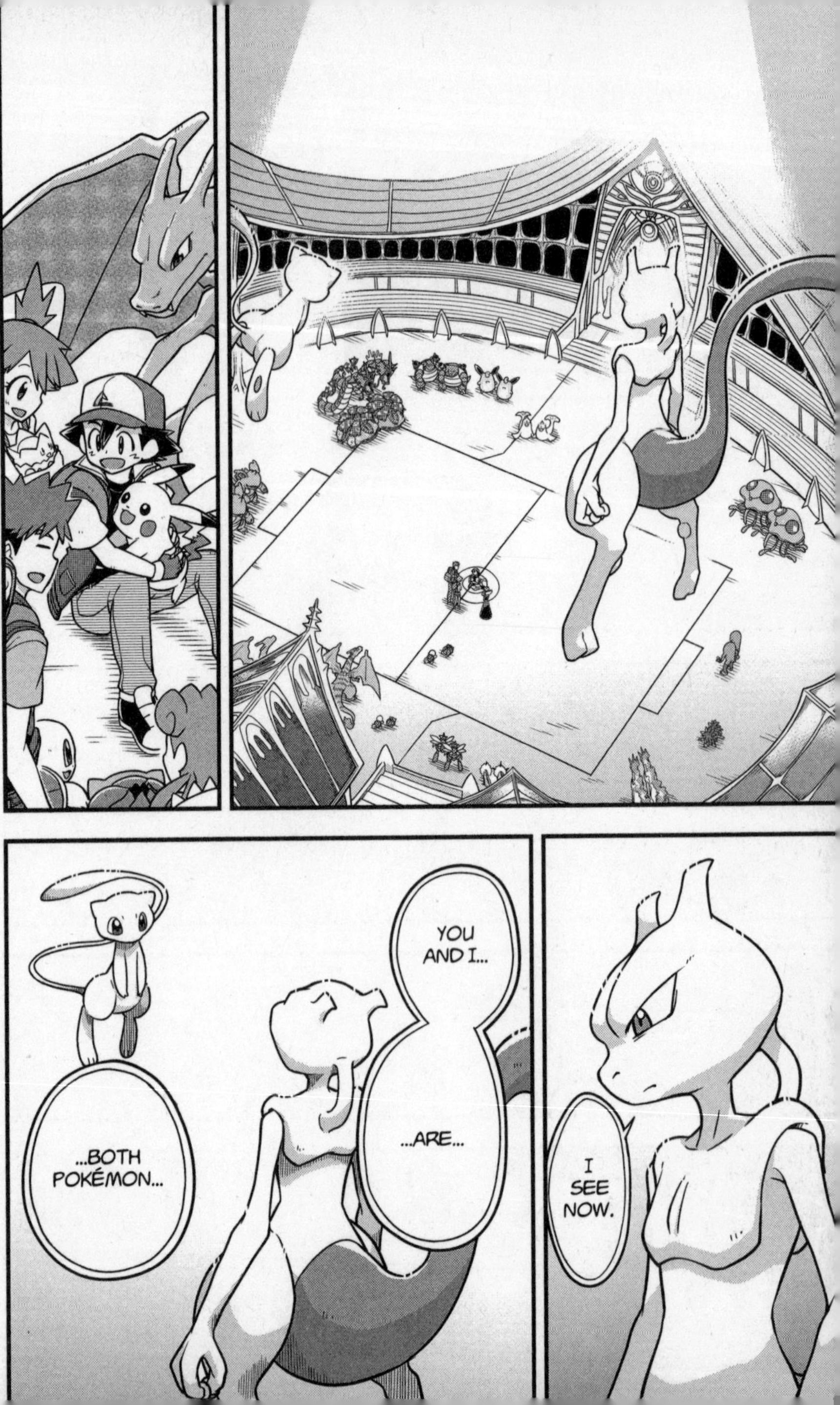
I SEE NOW.
YOU AND I...
...ARE...
...BOTH POKÉMON...

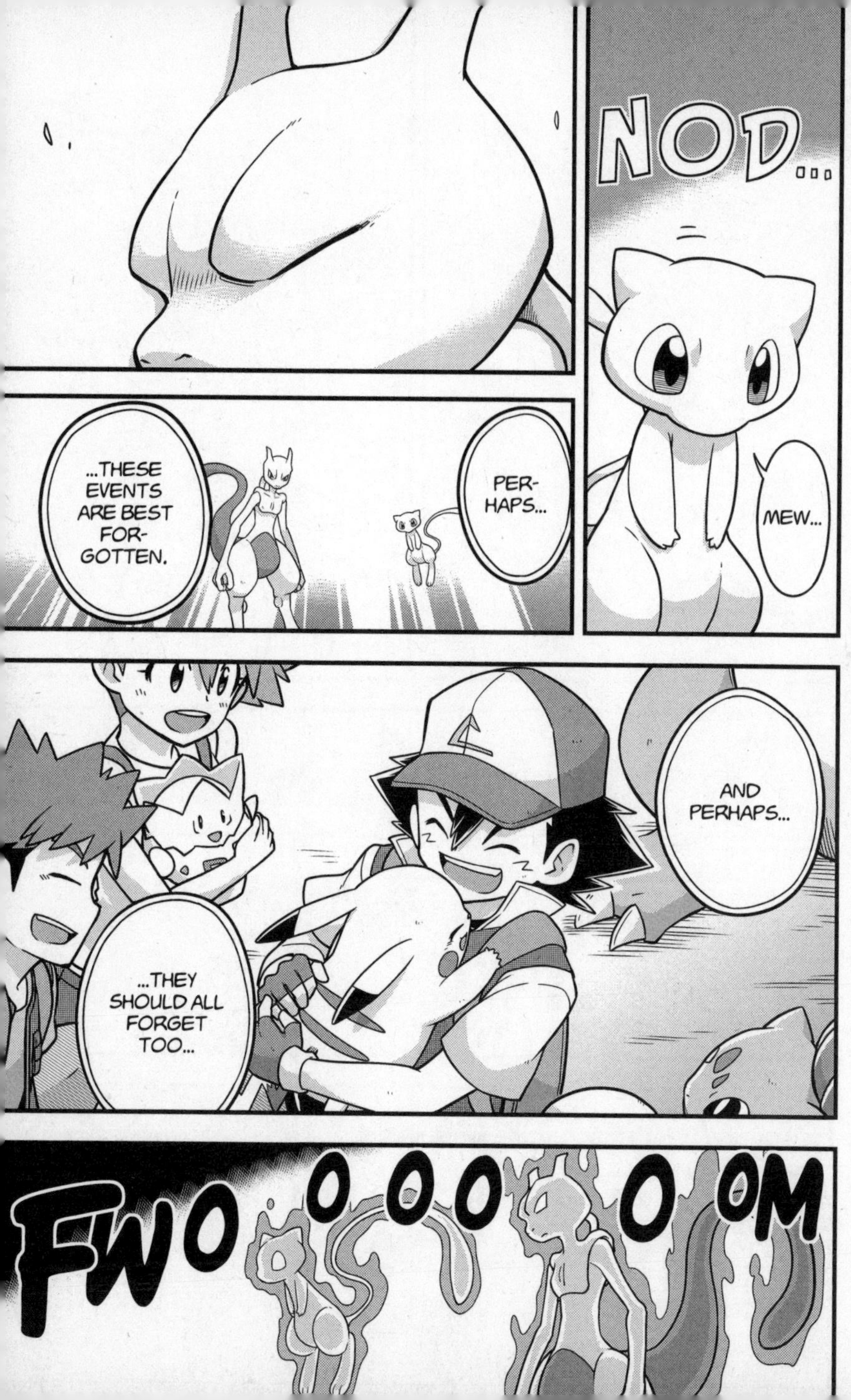
NOD...
MEW...
PERHAPS...
...THESE EVENTS ARE BEST FORGOTTEN.
AND PERHAPS...
...THEY SHOULD ALL FORGET TOO...
FWOOOOOOM

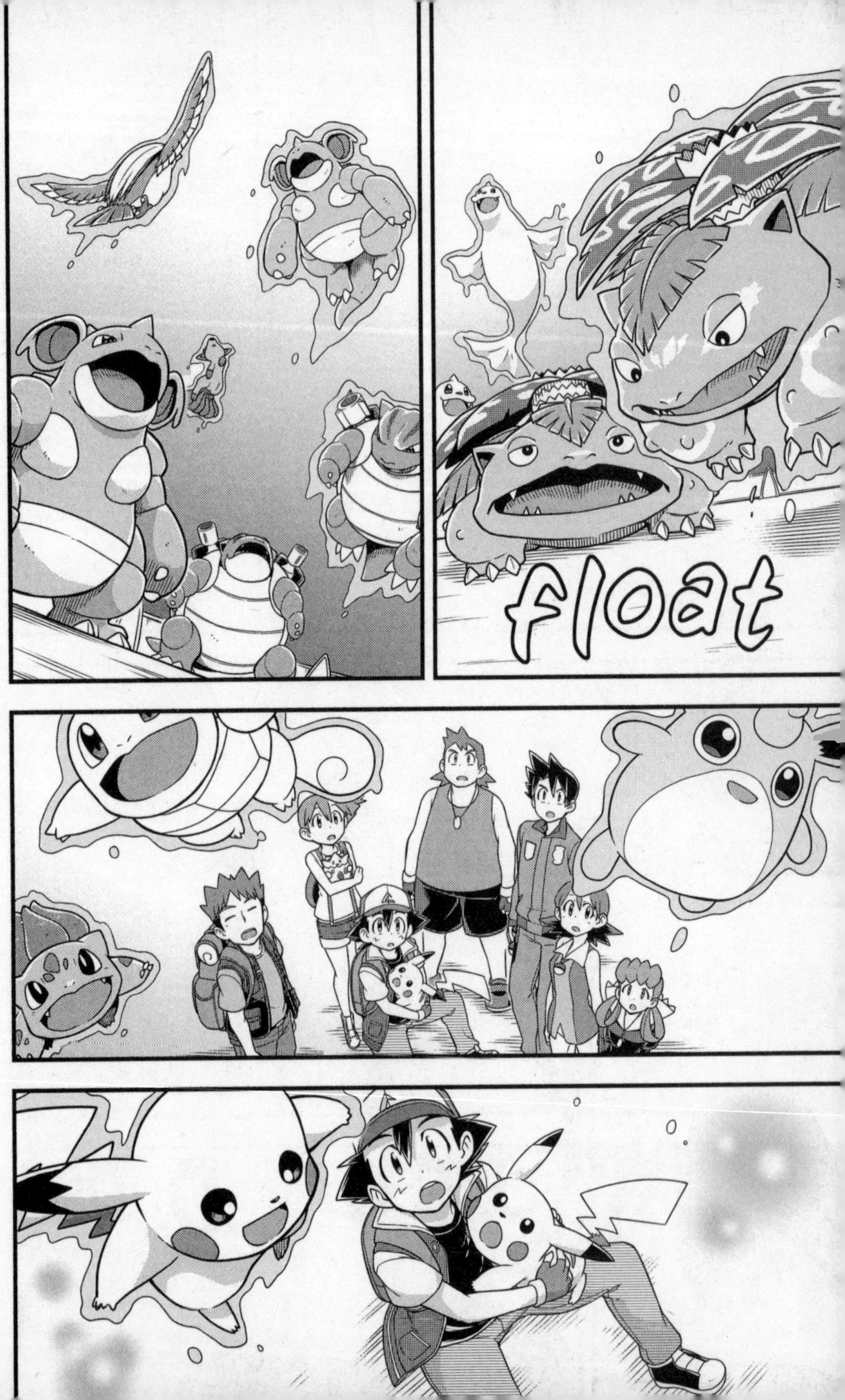
float

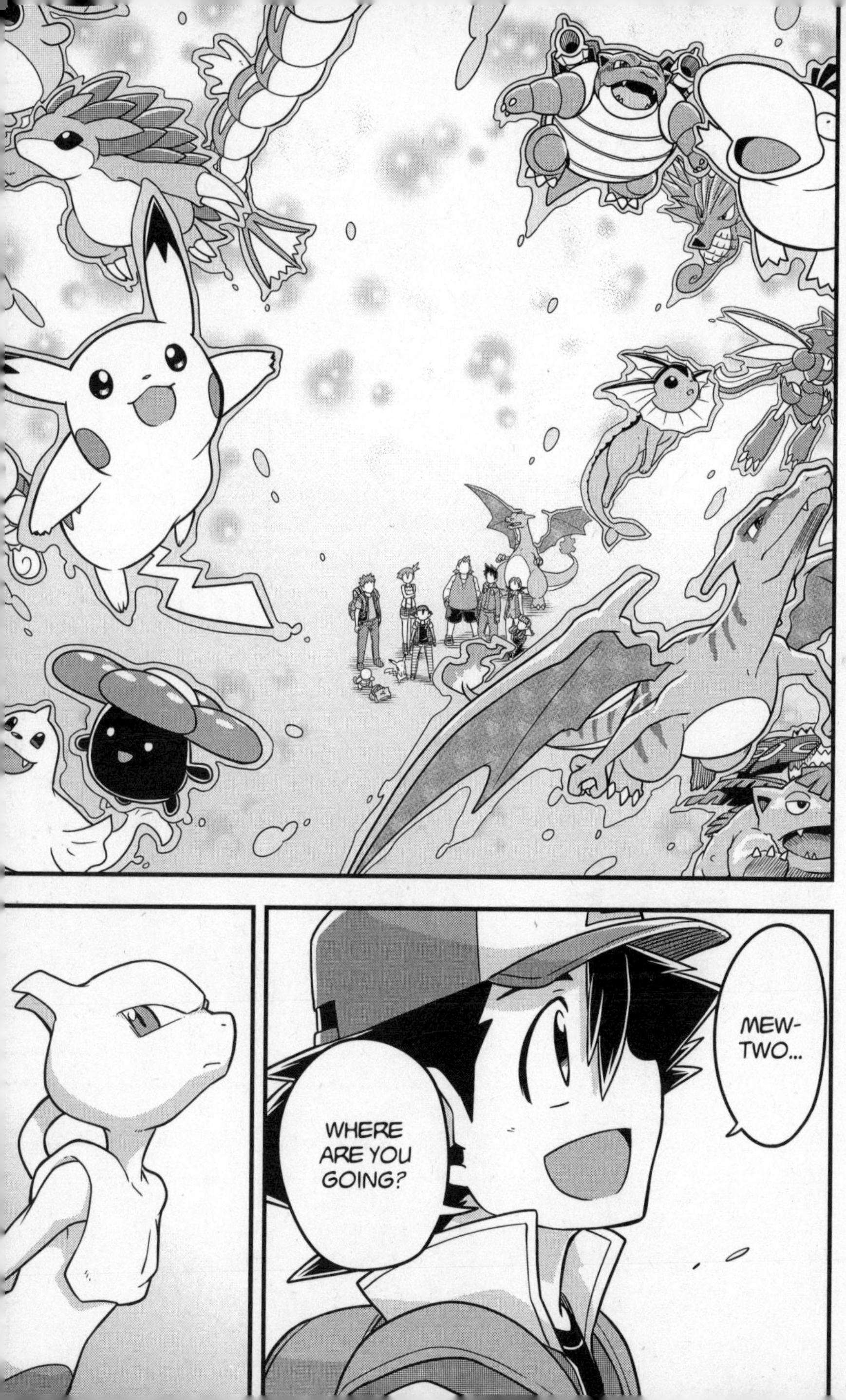
MEW-TWO...
WHERE ARE YOU GOING?

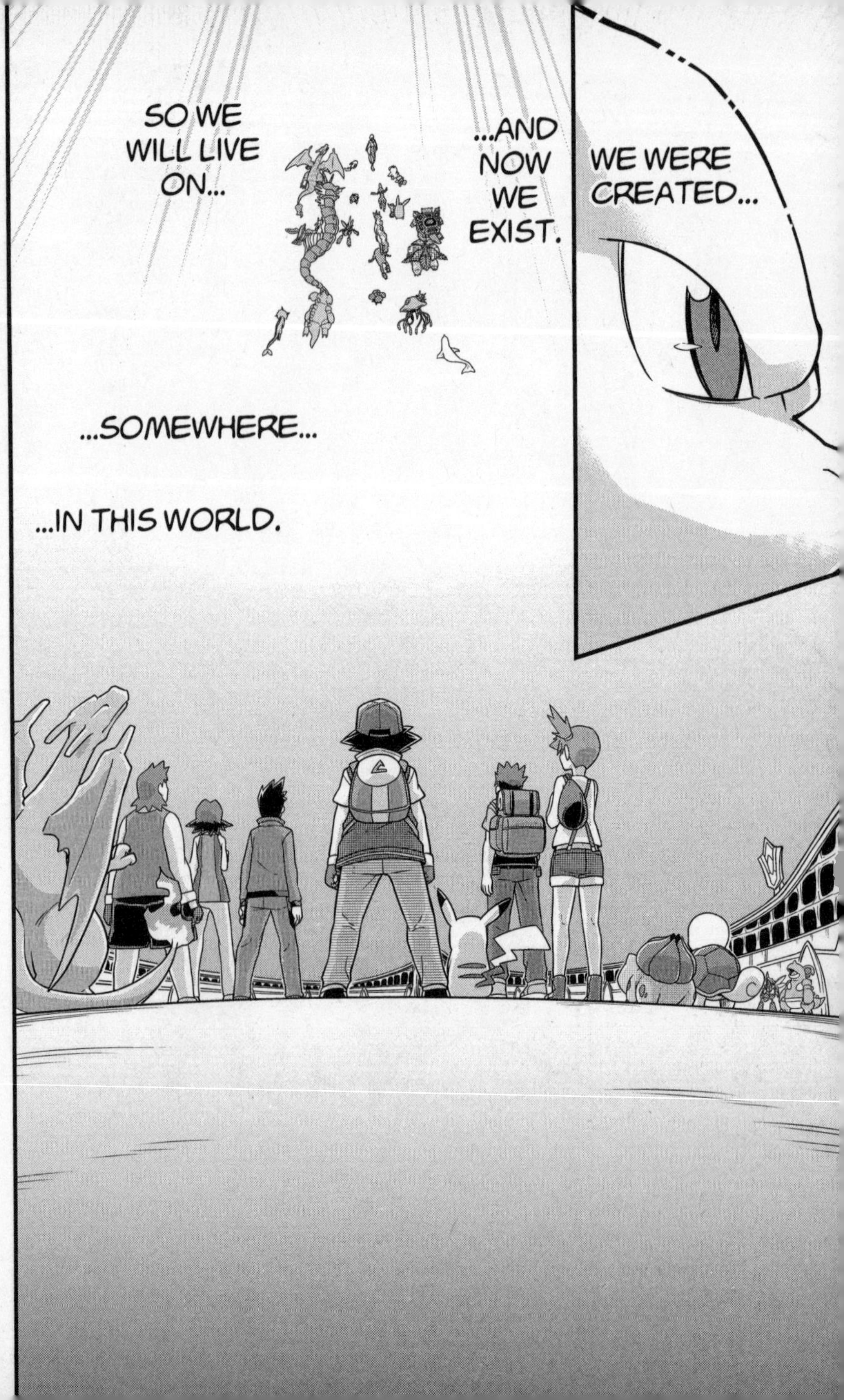
WE WERE CREATED...
...AND NOW WE EXIST.
SO WE WILL LIVE ON...
...SOMEWHERE...
...IN THIS WORLD.

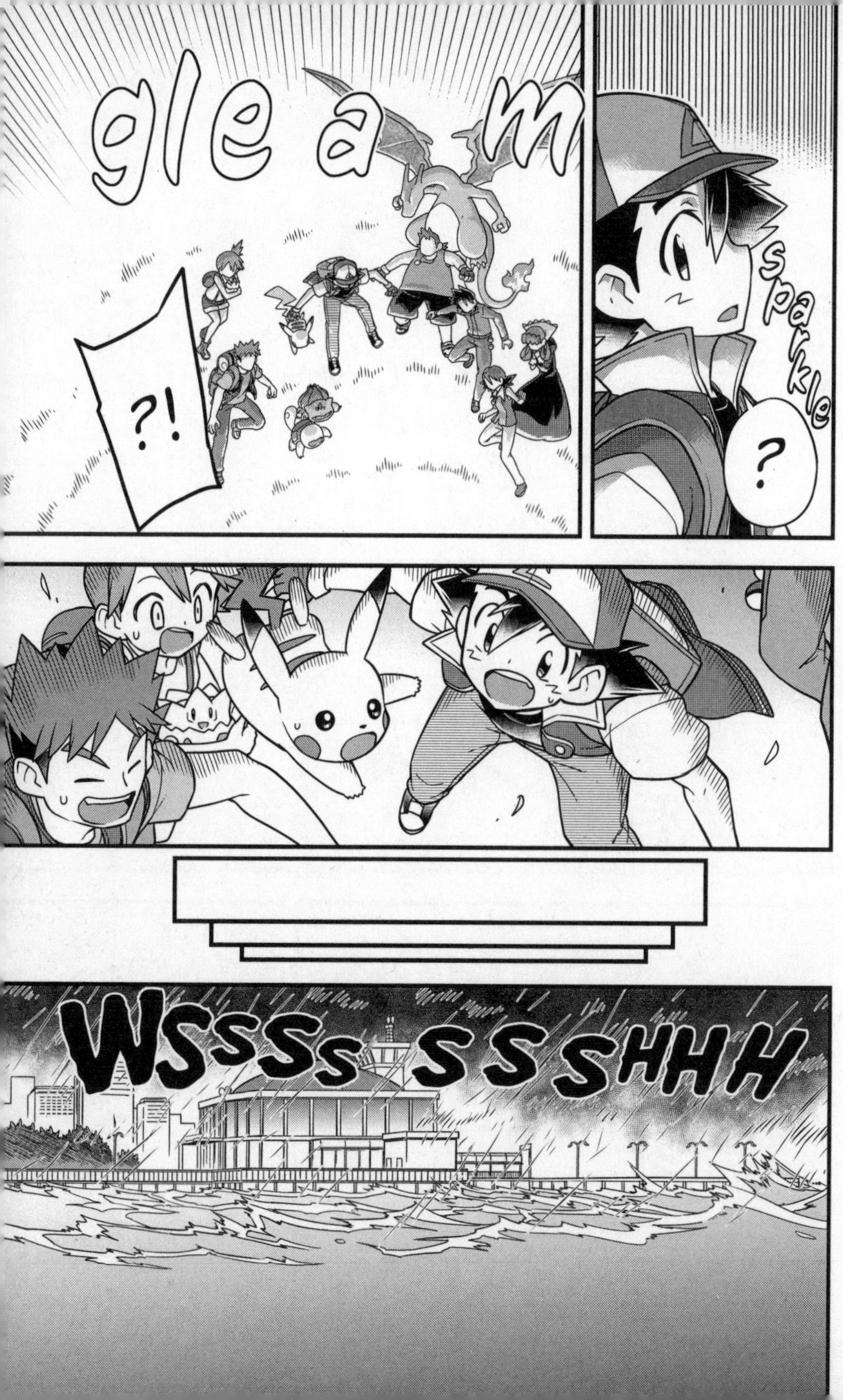
sparkle
?
gleam
?!
WSSSS SSSHHH

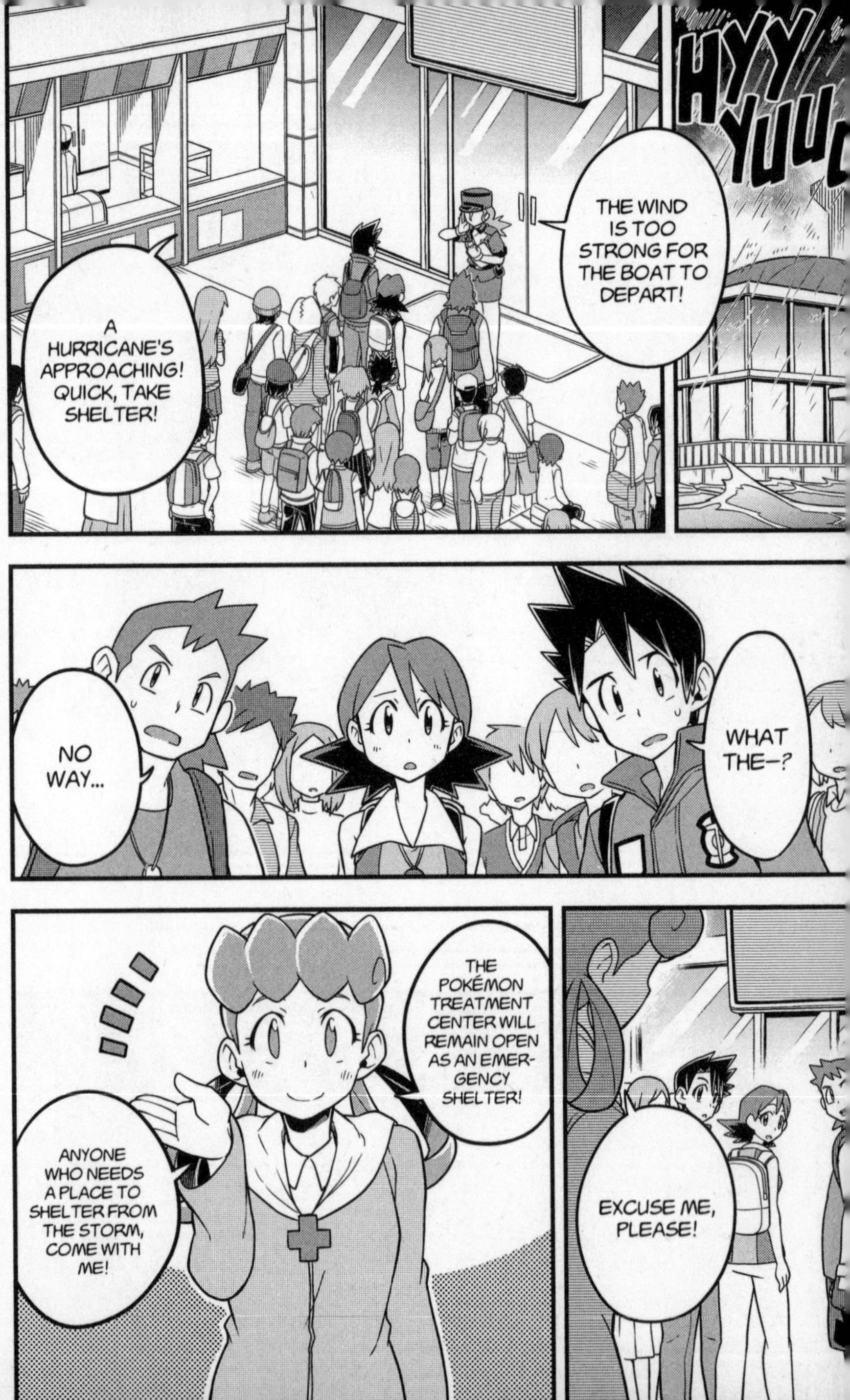
HYYYUUU
THE WIND IS TOO STRONG FOR THE BOAT TO DEPART!
A HURRICANE'S APPROACHING! QUICK, TAKE SHELTER!
WHAT THE–?
NO WAY...
EXCUSE ME, PLEASE!
THE POKÉMON TREATMENT CENTER WILL REMAIN OPEN AS AN EMER-GENCY SHELTER!
ANYONE WHO NEEDS A PLACE TO SHELTER FROM THE STORM, COME WITH ME!

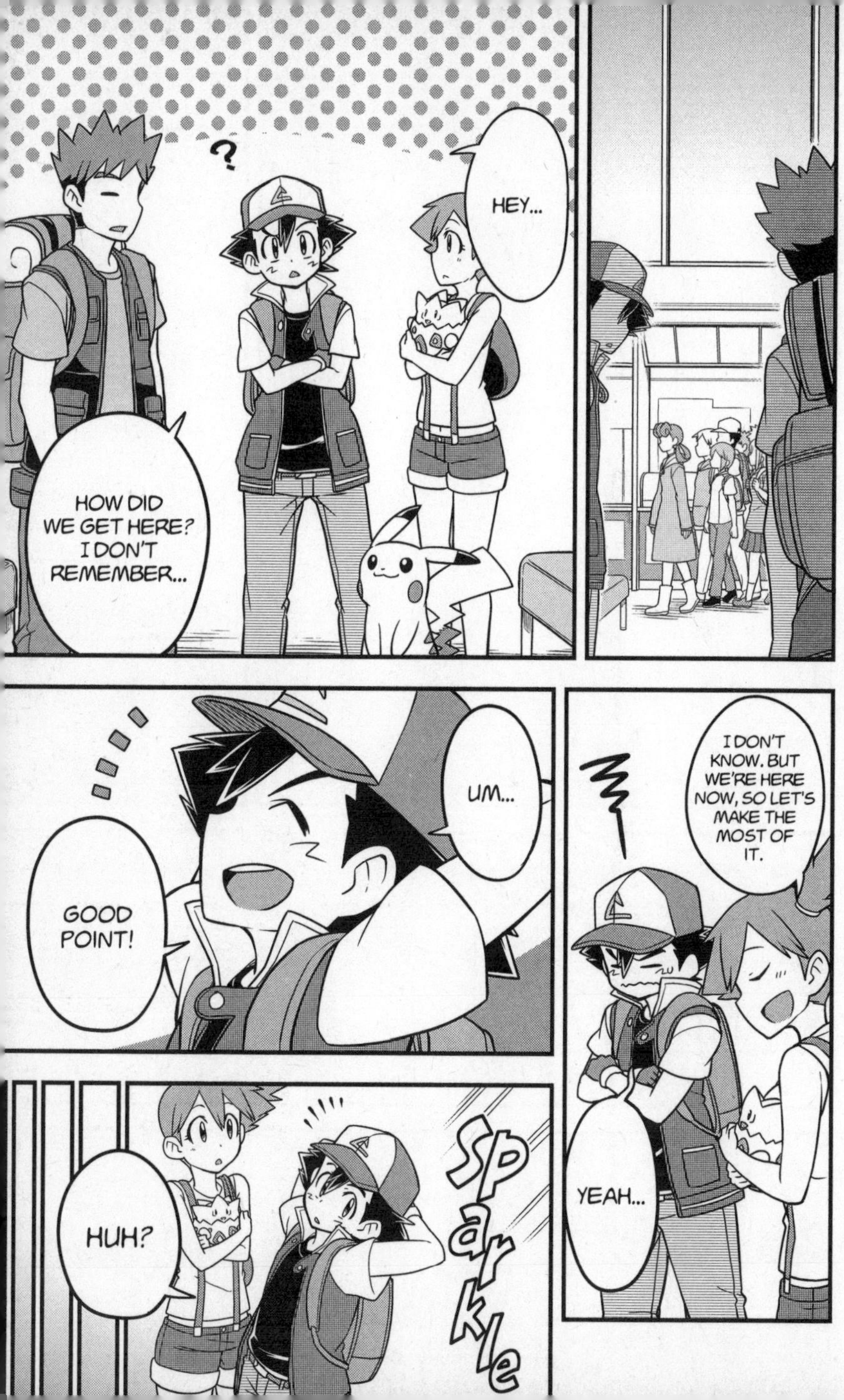
HEY...
HOW DID WE GET HERE? I DON'T REMEMBER...
I DON'T KNOW. BUT WE'RE HERE NOW, SO LET'S MAKE THE MOST OF IT.
YEAH...
UM...
GOOD POINT!
Sparkle
HUH?

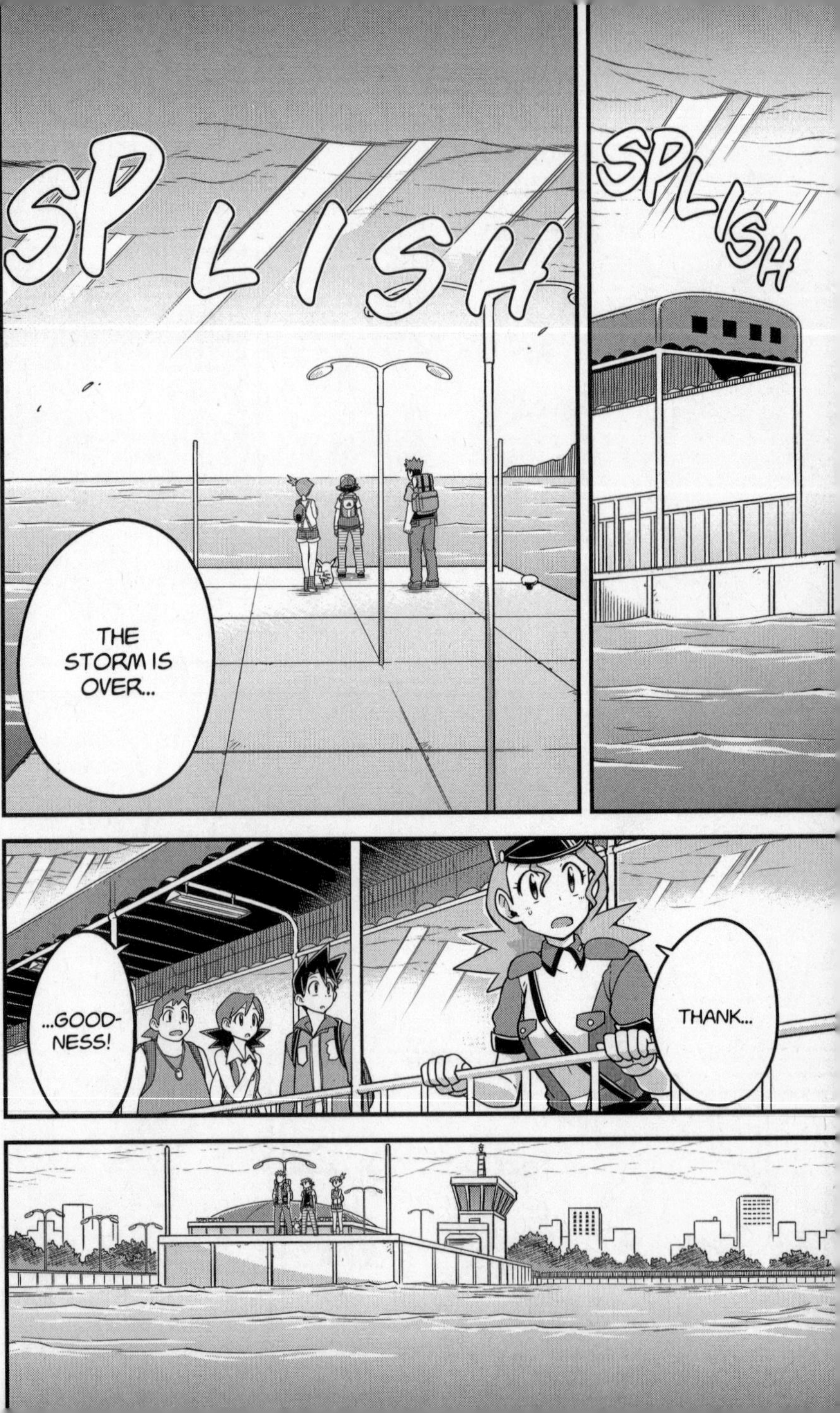
SPLISH
SPLISH
THE STORM IS OVER...
THANK...
...GOOD-NESS!

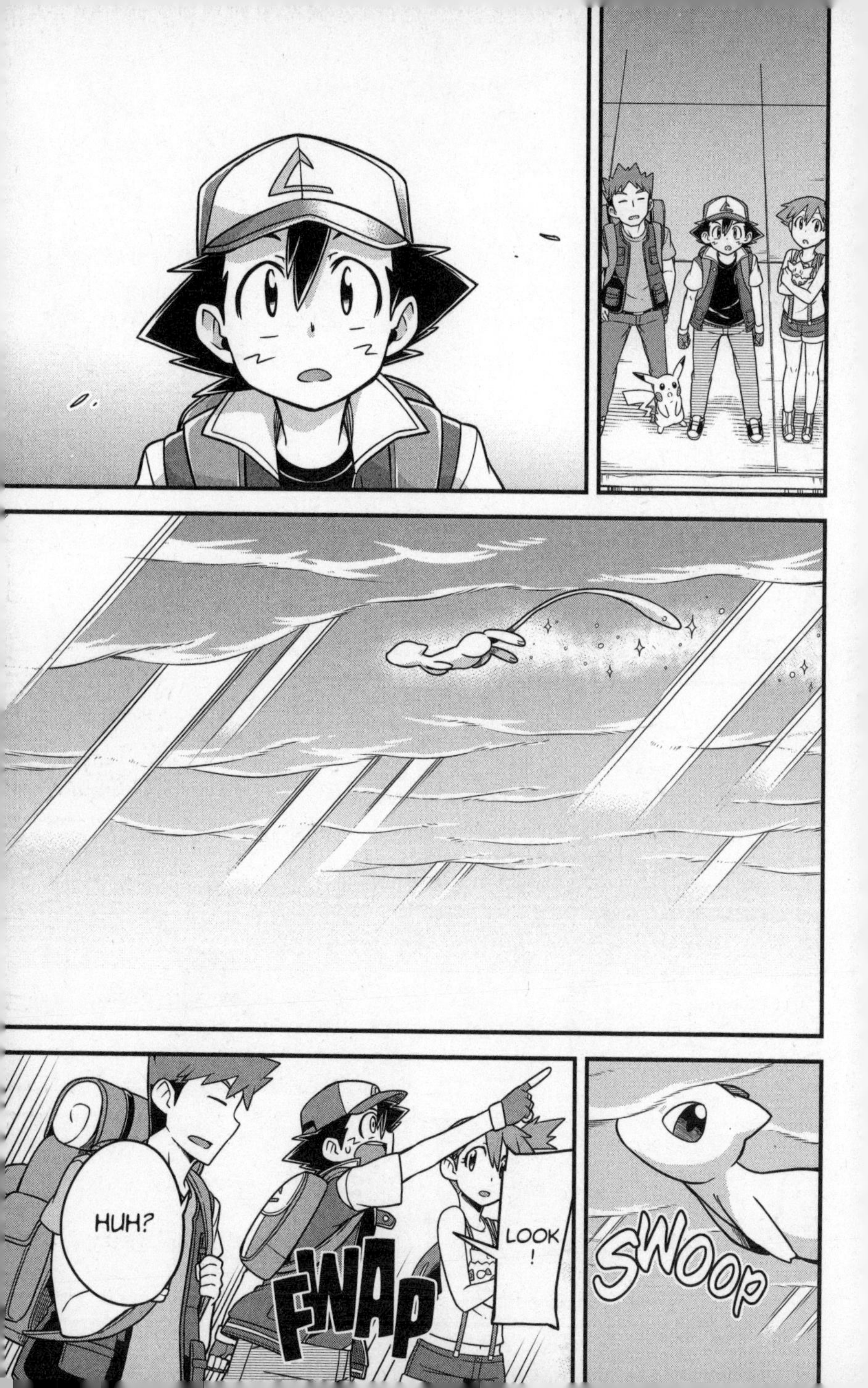
SWOOP
LOOK!
FWAP
HUH?

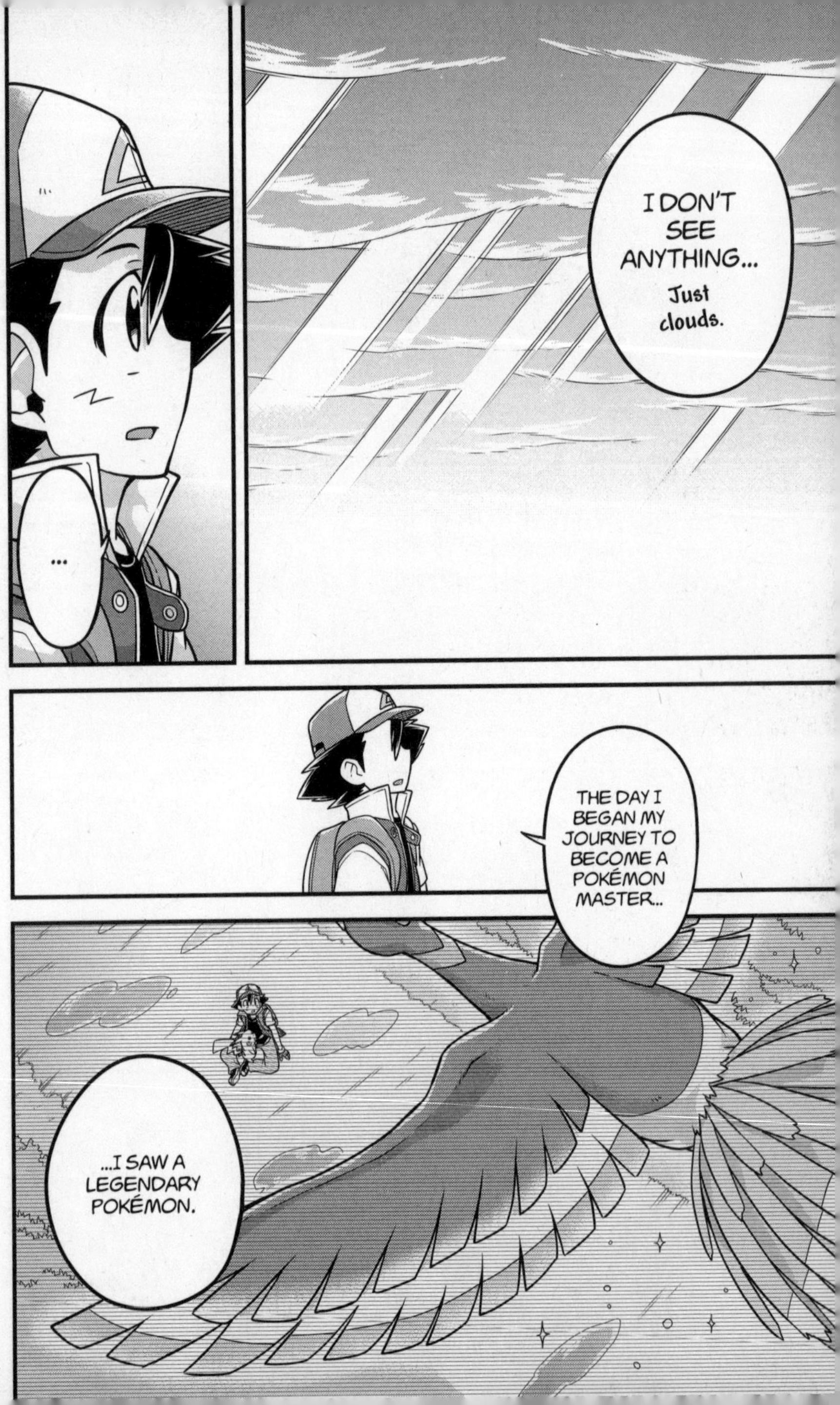
I DON'T SEE ANYTHING... Just clouds.
...
THE DAY I BEGAN MY JOURNEY TO BECOME A POKÉMON MASTER...
...I SAW A LEGENDARY POKÉMON.

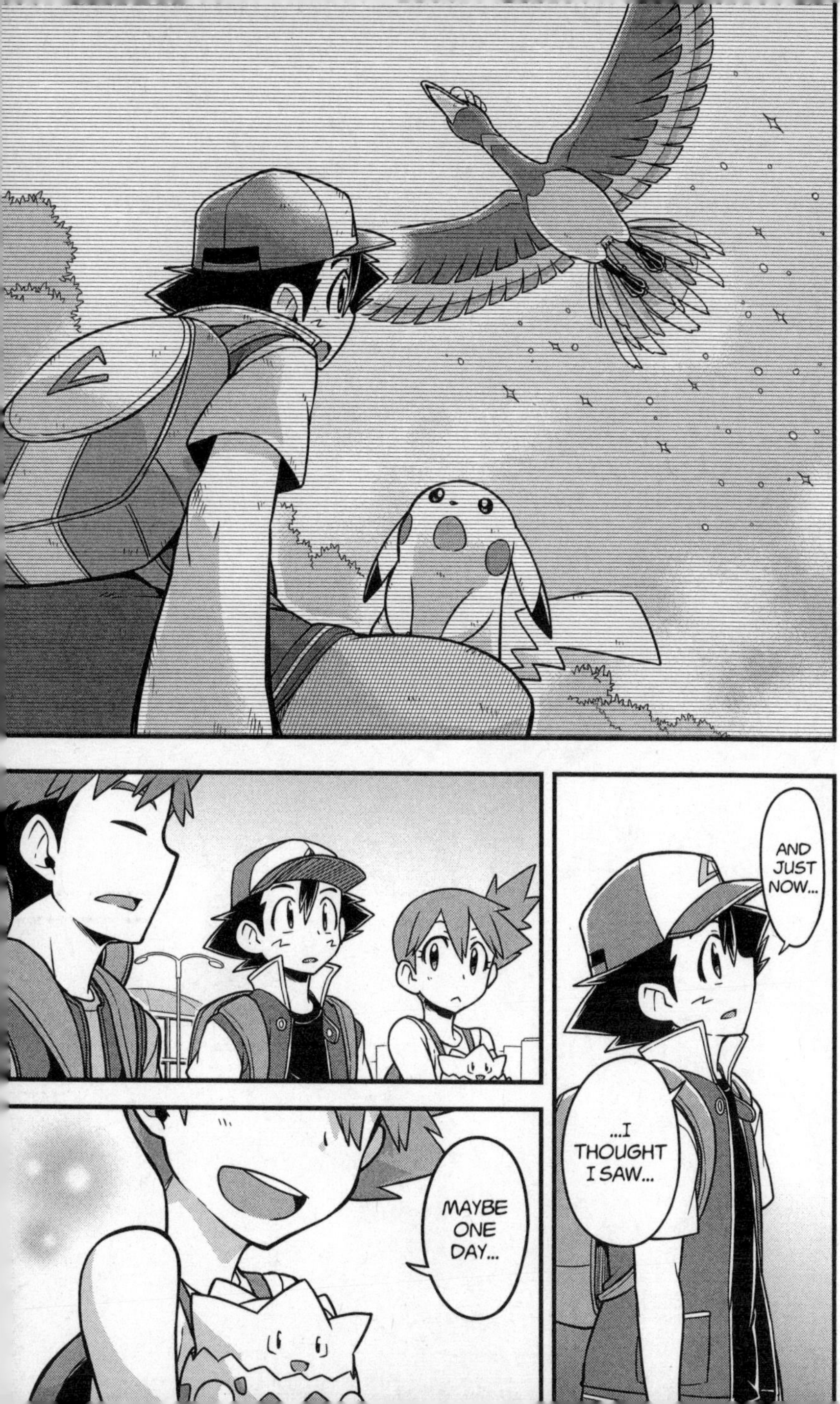
AND JUST NOW...
...I THOUGHT I SAW...
MAYBE ONE DAY...

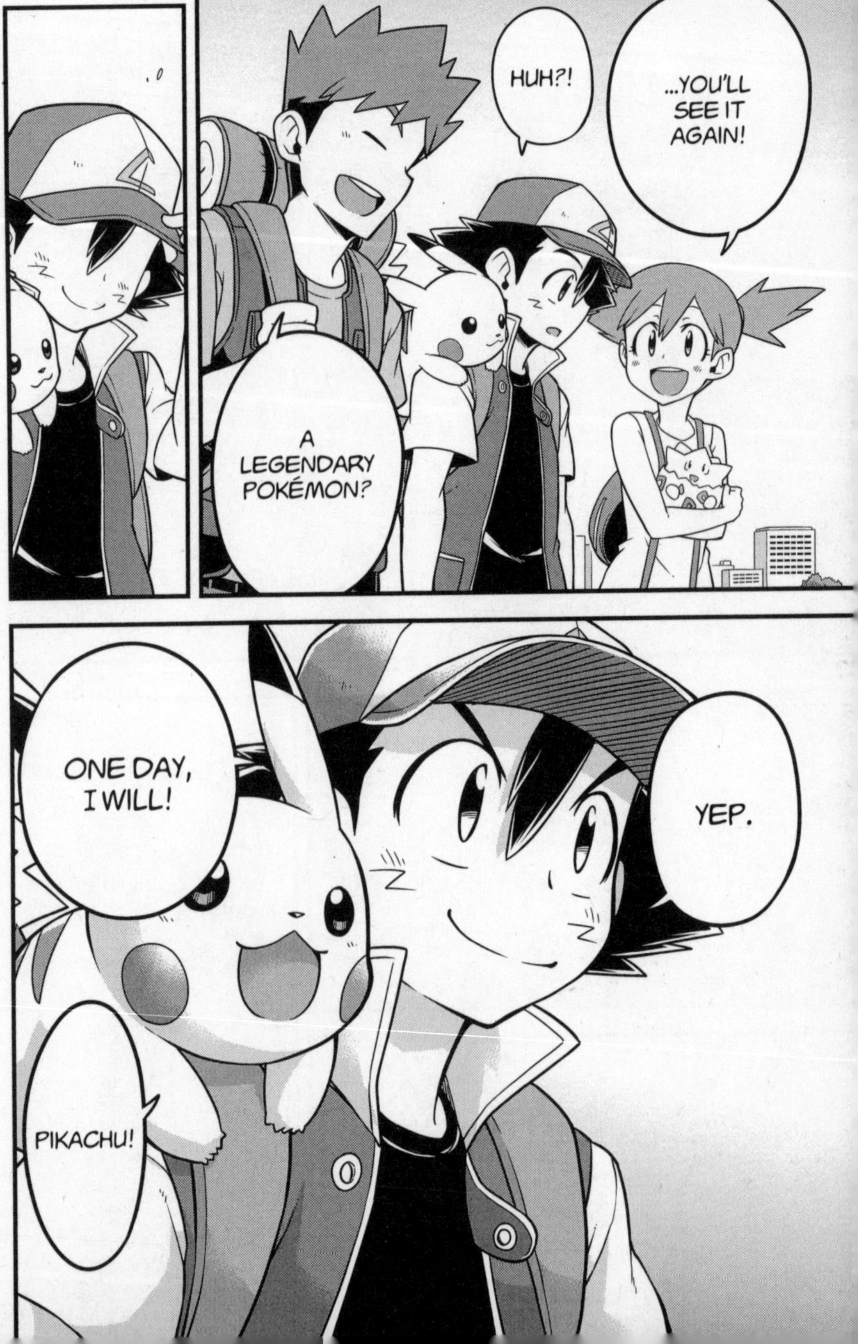
...YOU'LL SEE IT AGAIN!
HUH?!
A LEGENDARY POKÉMON?
YEP.
ONE DAY, I WILL!
PIKACHU!

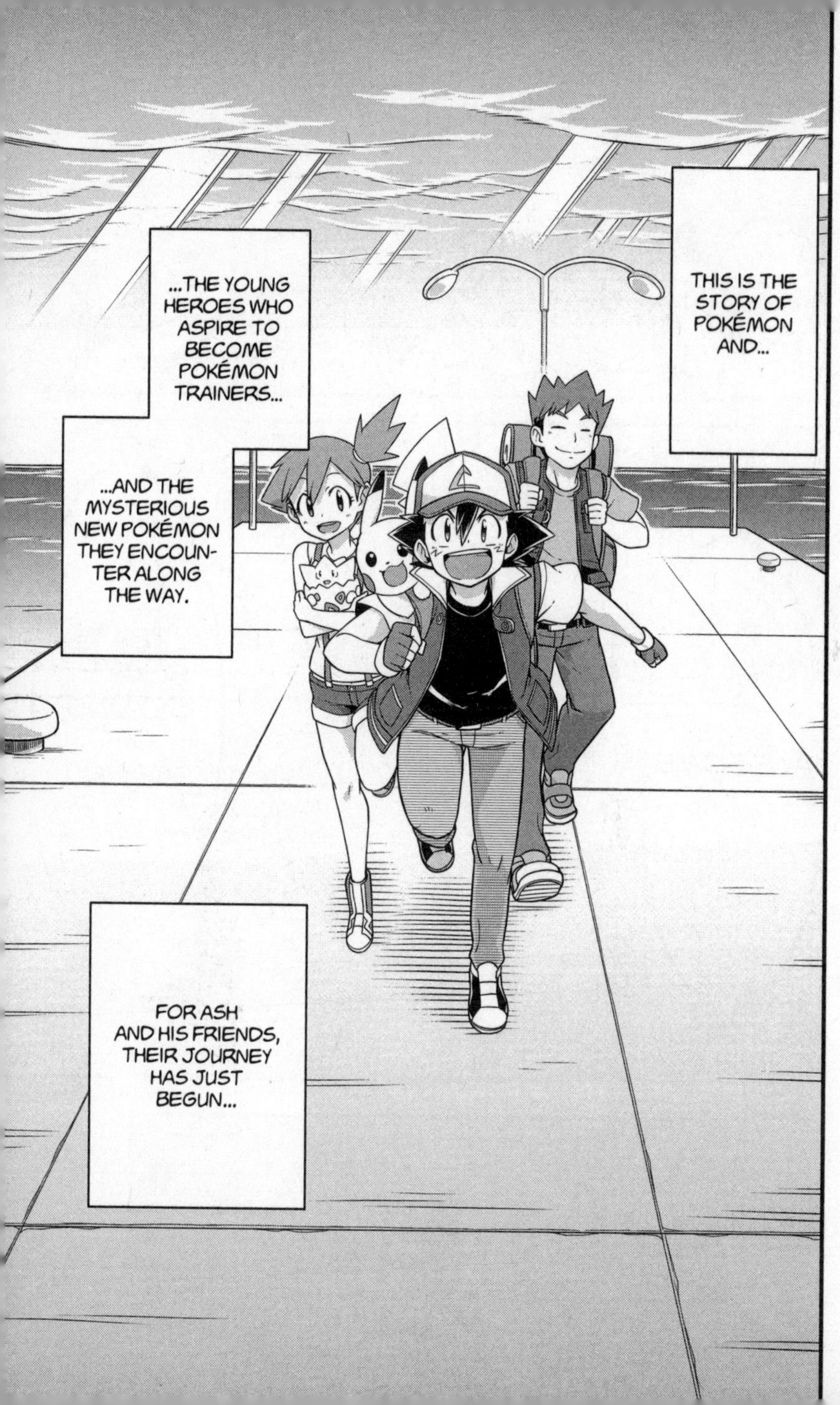
THIS IS THE STORY OF POKÉMON AND...
...THE YOUNG HEROES WHO ASPIRE TO BECOME POKÉMON TRAINERS...
...AND THE MYSTERIOUS NEW POKÉMON THEY ENCOUNTER ALONG THE WAY.
FOR ASH AND HIS FRIENDS, THEIR JOURNEY HAS JUST BEGUN...

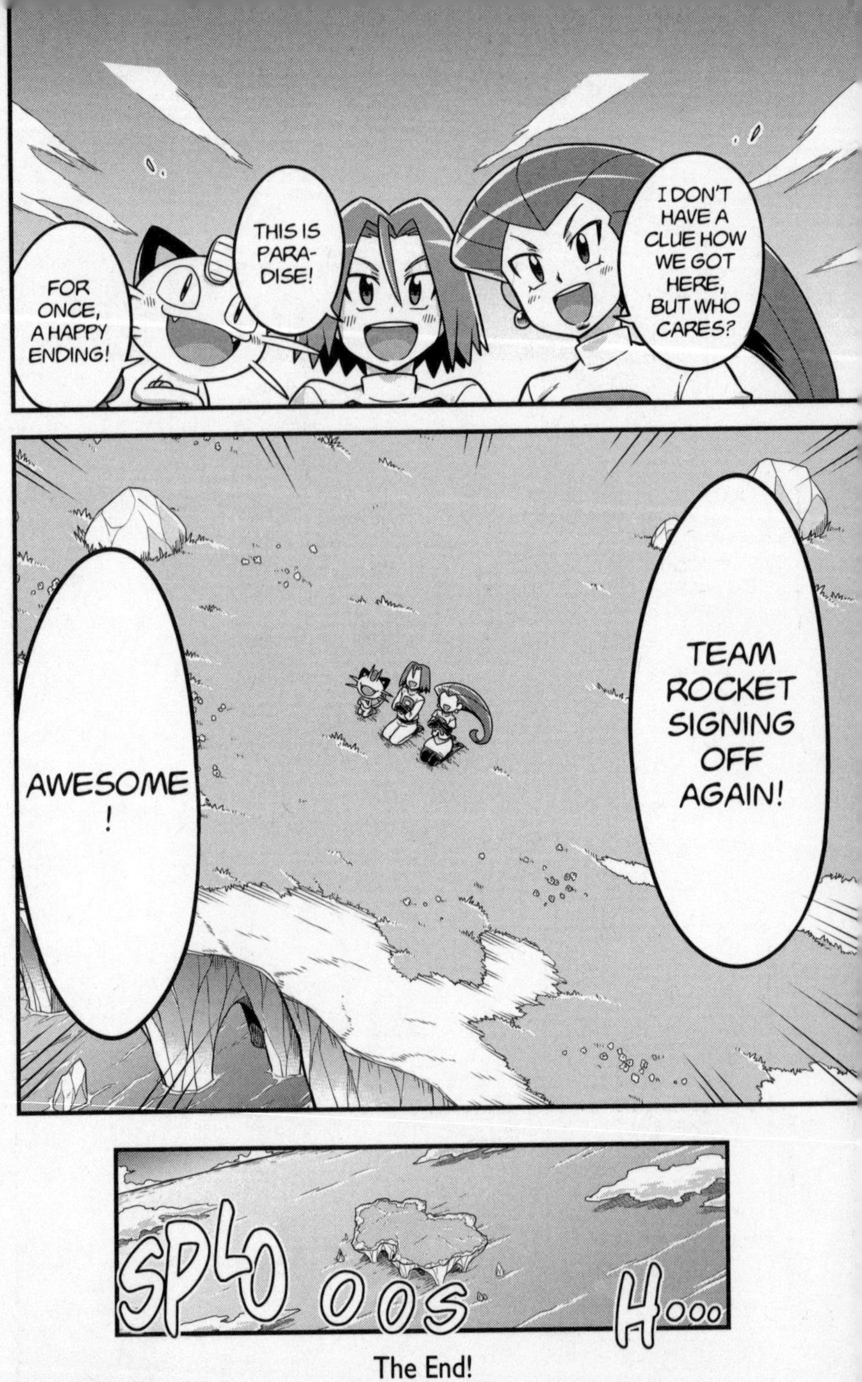
I DON'T HAVE A CLUE HOW WE GOT HERE, BUT WHO CARES?
THIS IS PARADISE!
FOR ONCE, A HAPPY ENDING!
TEAM ROCKET SIGNING OFF AGAIN!
AWESOME!
SPLOOOSHooo

The End!

Special Thanks

Masafumi Watanabe

Yoshihisa Teramoto

Yuki Katayama

Haruki Igarashi (Editor)

Thank you to all the people who
helped make this comic and to
all of the readers!

POKÉMON

MEWTWO STRIKES BACK

EVOLUTION

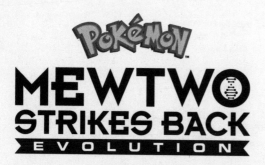

MEWTWO STRIKES BACK
EVOLUTION

VIZ MEDIA EDITION
STORY AND ART BY **Machito Gomi**

MEWTWO NO GYAKUSHU EVOLUTION
by Machito GOMI
©2019 Machito GOMI
All rights reserved.
Original Japanese edition published by SHOGAKUKAN.
English translation rights in the United States of America, Canada, the United Kingdom, Ireland,
Australia and New Zealand arranged with SHOGAKUKAN.

Original Cover Design/Plus One

Translation & Adaptation/Emi Louie-Nishikawa
Touch-Up & Lettering/Susan Daigle-Leach
Design/Julian [JR] Robinson
Editor/Annette Roman

Printed in the U.S.A.

Published by VIZ Media, LLC
P.O. Box 77010
San Francisco, CA 94107

10 9 8 7 6 5 4 3 2 1
First printing, August 2020

viz.com

PARENTAL ADVISORY
POKÉMON: MEWTWO
STRIKES BACK—EVOLUTION
is rated A and is suitable for
readers of all ages.

Begin your Pokémon Adventure here in the Kanto region!

POKÉMON™ ADVENTURES

RED & BLUE BOX SET

Story by HIDENORI KUSAKA   Art by MATO

POKÉMON
ADVENTURES
RED & BLUE BOX SET:
POKÉMON ADVENTURES VOLUMES 1-7

Includes POKÉMON ADVENTURES Vols. 1-7 and a collectible poster!

All your favorite Pokémon game characters jump out of the screen into the pages of this action-packed manga!

Red doesn't just want to train Pokémon, he wants to be their friend too. Bulbasaur and Poliwhirl seem game. But independent Pikachu won't be so easy to win over!

And watch out for Team Rocket, Red... They only want to be your enemy!

Start the adventure today!

RATED A ALL AGES ratings.viz.com

PERFECT SQUARE

VIZ media www.viz.com

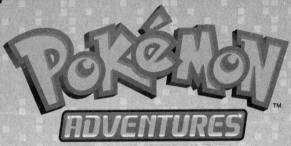

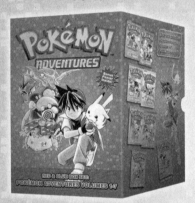

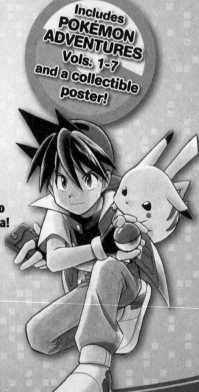

POKÉMON™
SEEK AND FIND

Find your favorite Pokémon in five different full-color activity books! Pick your adventure: will you search for the special Pokémon of Kanto, Johto, or Hoenn? Or will you seek fan favorites like Pikachu or Legendary Pokémon? Each book includes tons of Pokémon-packed seek-and-find illustrations as well as fun facts or creative quizzes about the Pokémon inside.

← READ THIS WAY!

1
2
3
4
1
2
5
6
7
8
3
4
9
5
142

Follow the action this way.

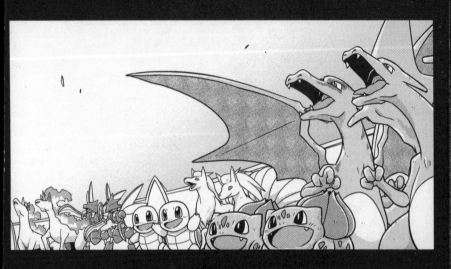

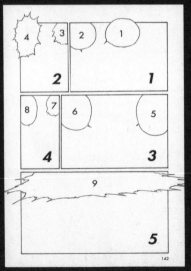

To properly enjoy this VIZ Media graphic novel, please turn it around and begin reading from right to left.

This book has been printed in the original Japanese format in order to keep the placement of the original artwork.

Have fun with it!